SHATTERED OBSESSION

HUDSON YARDS SERIES: BOOK ONE

TINA SPENCER

Editing: Erica Russikoff

Proofreading: Rachel's Top Edits

Cover Art: Cass at Opulent Designs

To those who suffer in silence, hiding behind masks and bearing the weight of feeling misplaced or unseen

And to all the women out there who crave a different type of thrill

"Tell me every terrible thing you ever did, and let me love you anyway."
— **Edgar Allan Poe**

CONTENT WARNINGS

Shattered Obsession is a **DARK** hockey romance. The contents are heavy at times and may be triggering for some readers. To avoid spoilers, I have put all the triggers warnings on my website (www.tinaspencerbooks.com) and some down below. I'm also active on socials if you have any questions or would like to discuss the triggers before you read the book. Your mental health matters, please take care of it.

If you're like me and want the shock factor then please skip the following trigger warnings. Otherwise, stay hydrated and enjoy the ride.

*

*

*

*

*

Graphic sexual content, which include kinks such as, voyeurism, exhibitionism, rough sex, choking, bondage, degradation, praise, adult toys, dual masturbation, orgasm control, orgasm denial, cum play, and more.

- BDSM (dom / sub interactions)
- Dub-con

CONTENT WARNINGS

- Consensual non-consent
- Stalking
- Primal play
- Mask kink
- Mention of parental abuse and childhood neglect
- Mention of past thoughts of abortion (not FMC)
- Mental illness (depression, anxiety and suicidal ideations)

SPOTIFY PLAYLIST

Animals - Maroon 5
I Don't Wanna Leave - Rufus du Sol
Empire State of Mind - JAY-Z, Alicia Keys
Remedy - Alesso
One of the Girls - The Weeknd, Jennie, Lily-Rose Depp
Cravin' - Stileto, Kendyle Paige
10:35 - Tiesto, Tate McRae
RUNRUNRUN - Dutch Melrose
Silence - Marshmello, Khalid
…Ready for it? - Taylor Swift
Buttons - The Pussycat Dolls
Daisy - Ashnikko
Found It With You - Piece Wise, Ali Bakgor, Lewyn
obsessed - zandros, Limi
Pieces (Hushed) - Andrew Belle

PROLOGUE
DOMINIK LEWIS

Isn't it funny how in a single moment, you can meet a stranger who was once just a speck in your universe, and suddenly they become your everything?

I never believed in that shit.

Not until I met *her*.

Not until she utterly transformed my entire existence.

An obsession so lethal that even I didn't stand a chance against it.

We all start out as strangers, and more often than not, we drift back into the same void, ending up as strangers once more. Promises and plans for the future wash away, becoming meaningless until they're forgotten.

Yet, when it comes to her, it has always been different.

It will always *be* different.

A type of connection that refuses to fade into darkness because she's in my fucking veins.

In the depths of my soul.

Our story isn't something I can ever erase, and I was foolish to think I was stronger than us. That we would ever be anything less than meaningful.

I was stupid to believe that I could forget about her.

There are moments in life that define us and reshape us in irreversible ways. Carving patterns into our souls while changing the course of our futures. Some of these moments appear inconspicuous, like rain tapping against glass on a cloudy day. While others overcome the confines of time itself. In those rare instances, it feels like someone pressed pause, allowing us to simply exist and enjoy a glimpse of total happiness. Other moments are harrowing, leaving a crack so deep that nothing can ever mend the initial impact. Those ones shatter through you, breaking down every barrier and wall you have worked to put up.

These moments have shaped my life. Likely, yours as well. They made me into the person I am today. The same man standing here, watching the girl I love with everything I am, slip away.

But nothing lasts forever. Isn't that what they say? The good, the bad, and the ugly…it all passes eventually.

Then how come this desire, pursuit—this need to claim her—has never passed?

This obsession with my best friend's little sister has consumed me for so long. It's made me do things I'm not proud of, hurt people I love, break promises I intended to keep. This spiraling obsession has turned me into an animal. Someone I hardly recognize.

And for what? To end up losing her all over again?

The damage is done.

I can't turn back time, or fix this mistake…or even attempt to say something that would erase the pure disgust and shock from her face.

I broke her because I couldn't walk away, consumed by an unyielding hunger. It all replays in my mind like a busted record player. Her frail figure hidden in my closet. My box of secrets open and exposed out on the floor. The mixture of shock and revulsion etched across her face as she stared down at the contents in her hands.

"How could you?" Her whisper was barely audible.

2

There is no coming back from this, is there? Because I've ruined everything again.

But that can't be how we end.

It won't be how we end.

She can despise me. Push me away, run from this...she can try to hide, but I won't allow it.

I will always chase after her.

If I can't escape this, then she can't escape me.

Have you ever wanted something with such a burning desire that it consumes your every waking moment? It's the type of affection that grips your soul, refusing to let go no matter how much time passes. This need doesn't diminish with time; it only intensifies. Growing stronger until the ache is unbearable.

I can't stop myself from wanting her.

Zoe belongs to me.

She has always been mine.

PART ONE: NOW
NEW BEGINNINGS

CHAPTER 1

ZOE JACKSON

I shouldn't have answered Greg's phone call tonight. Should have stuck to my original plan of wine and bingeing a new Netflix series. But no, my desperate, horny ass decided to accept his booty call and drive over to his house.

All for a terrible lay I'm not forcing myself to fake-moan through.

Biting the inside of my cheek, I try to save the self-hate talk for later when I'm alone and crying in the shower. That's normally when my anxiety likes to remind me what a disappointment I am. It's better to let the self-loathing marinate for now.

Glancing down, I cringe as Greg continues to aggressively press three fingers onto my clit as if he's a DJ playing his first live performance at Tomorrowland. He's not even hitting the right spot; it's actually starting to hurt at this point, and the urge to kick him is festering.

I try to shift away from him, but he nudges closer to me, his sweaty chest hair pressing against my skin. Greg adds a finger inside me while continuing his off-aim vibration rub, and I finally look up to see his eyes on me.

"You like that, baby?"

I close my eyes. "Mm."

Mother Nature, now would be a great time to step in and do something.

Maybe if I fake an orgasm.

"Why aren't you wet yet? I know how much you love it when I touch you like this."

I would be if you weren't so terrible at it, I inwardly groan. With the amount of tail this man gets, I assumed he would at least be good in bed. But no, he's mediocre at best, and sometimes, he's so rushed to get off, he misses the point of this entire thing altogether. My pleasure has never been about just me, no matter what Greg says.

When Greg and I first started sleeping together nearly two months ago, I told myself it would be just a small, casual fling. After scratching the itch, I would get out like I always do. Seems like our time is up. Too bad I'm the biggest idiot and decided to sleep with my boss this time around. I never actually thought about this moment—past me didn't consider future me, and the crap I'd need to do to get out of this awkward situation and still keep my job.

Fuck. I'm out here just collecting regrets and grudges like trophies.

Can I blame this shitty behavior on my mommy/daddy issues too, or have I used that excuse way too many times now? As I lie here rethinking my life decisions, drier than the Sahara Desert, I realize I desperately need a distraction.

And quickly.

The faster I get off, the sooner I can leave to go wash the stale smell of Greg off my skin and lie in my own bed...alone.

Closing my eyes and tapping into the fantasy bank, I picture Henry Cavill on top of me. Maybe Jensen Ackles. Ian Somerhalder...damn, that's a good one. Chris Hemsworth. Sebastian Stan. Jamie Dornan, God, that Irish accent always does it for me.

Maybe all of the above. Maybe we're in a cabin in the woods.

It's working...a little. Maybe? I don't know. This method usually works when I'm alone but not right now with a man who smells like stale potato chips and rotten apples hovering above me. Where is that smell even coming from?

Focus.

Okay, where was I? Ian Somerhalder. Thor. Charlie Hunnam. Oh, that man is fine.

Young Brad Pitt.

An image of a shirtless Dominik Lewis skating on ice.

What the hell?!

Did that name seriously just pop into my head?

Lunging forward, I sit up, and Greg instantly backs away. Running my hands through my hair, I focus all my energy on erasing that last thought from my mind. But the harder I try, the more I think about him.

"What's wrong?" Greg asks, pulling me from my disturbing thoughts.

"I don't know. I suddenly don't feel so good," I lie.

He smirks. "You just need some dick. Boss's orders."

I'd rather eat tuna, and I loathe tuna.

Reaching over to his bedside table, he pulls open the drawer to grab a condom. Greg is such a stupid shithead; instead of offering to make me feel better, he just wants to make sure he has the chance to come before I bail. I would feel like a total piece of trash if this was the first time this has happened to me, but sadly, it isn't. I sure know how to pick 'em.

Unfortunately for boss man here, I have exactly zero fucks to give and cannot be bothered to put up with a pity fuck session tonight.

Quickly slipping off the bed, I walk around the dim room in search of my discarded pieces of clothing. I left my bachelor apartment so quickly, I didn't even bother changing out of my sweatpants and Sum 41 T-shirt.

"What are you doing? I just grabbed a condom."

"I'm going to head home. I feel like I'm going to be sick." I've never gotten dressed so fast in my entire life. Now, where are my shoes?

"Seriously?" He sounds pissed, but too bad, I don't care.

"Rain check?" Finally spotting one shoe by the door, I nearly sprint out of his room. I don't even bother waiting for a response. My skin feels cold and my stomach churns with unease as I pad down the dark hallway.

I wasn't lying about feeling sick. Because I am sick of being this person. I'm twenty-five, and I have nothing to show for it. I haven't had a promotion at work in years, I'm single, barely make enough to support myself and pay for my dinky apartment, which isn't even close to my shitty office. My parents hate me and pretend I don't exist. None of my friends truly know the real me, because I'm too scared to get close to anyone. Why bother when they all eventually leave?

My brother is the only person in this world who actually loves me, and he lives in New York City, which is hundreds of miles away. And he would absolutely murder me if he knew I was having a sexual relationship with my boss who happens to be incredibly power hungry. Greg wouldn't even hesitate to bury me if the opportunity ever presented itself.

I knew all this before sleeping with him, and I did it anyway.

"You're seriously just going to leave? Do you want to stay for a bit? See if you start to feel better?" Greg's voice screeches from behind me.

Painting on my usual docile smile, I swallow down the large knot in my throat as I turn to face him. He's standing in front of me, butt naked and still holding the condom. Pursing my lips, I glance up at his face.

"I don't think so, unless you want me to puke all over your sheets. See you tomorrow."

"You better not call in sick," Greg mutters under his breath right as I turn to open the door.

Pretending I didn't hear him, I slip out, and the door clicks shut, the sound echoing down the concrete hallway.

Jackass.

Forcing the tension to roll off my shoulders, I don't bother waiting for the elevators. Instead, I climb down the stairway. Greg lives in a low-rise apartment, and I can use the cardio to sift through my thoughts. If there is one thing I'm great at, it's pretending like I don't give a shit, and I'll keep telling myself that until it's the only voice in my head.

Sometimes, I wonder what it would be like to slip away into nothingness. To vanish without a trace, leaving everything behind. The thought brings me comfort, and it's times like these when I wonder what is actually stopping me. Would anyone even miss me? How much time would pass before anyone realized I was gone? Sammy would notice and then maybe my brother?

These thoughts dissipate as swiftly as they emerge because, regardless of my readiness, tomorrow inevitably arrives. This feeling, as crappy as it is, will fade away too. Nothing ever remains permanent; everything eventually passes.

I'll be okay.

Tomorrow, I'll do the right thing and end it with Greg. Tell him we should go back to a professional relationship and never speak of this again. All will return to the way it was. I'll continue to do his job for him, securing clients and networking with people in the industry to get him more business, and he'll continue dicking around in his office like he always does.

Boston's frigid, January air smacks me right in the face, making me shudder all over as I pick up the pace toward my car. Slamming my door shut, I don't bother glancing up at Greg's window even though I want to. Not sure why; it's not like I care—I'm the one who ran out. The engine struggles to turn on for two terribly long seconds, but then the time flashes red, letting me know it's past three in the morning. Grunting audibly, I rest my forehead on the cold, plastic steering wheel, knowing tomorrow is going to be an extra-long day.

Bring on the shit storm.

I want to call Aaron, but he's probably asleep. Actually, knowing him, he might still be up working. It's no surprise he's managed to become a billionaire before thirty with the insane work ethic he has. As tempting as it might be to text him right now just to hear his voice, it would only worry him. He'd grill me, and there is no way in hell I could tell him about tonight. Aaron is weird about sex stuff. My brother is borderline psychotic when it comes to me. That's one of the main reasons I didn't pack up and follow him to New York so many years ago.

Now he lives in a penthouse suite with his two best friends, Dominik and Tristan, living nearby.

Dominik...

The big, fat elephant in my head tonight. What the hell was that? That man had no business popping into my mind in that situation. Not like I've seen the guy in ages. The last I heard from Aaron is that Dominik made captain of the New York Slashers hockey team. I would have reached out to congratulate him, but the man has disliked me since we first met in high school. He and Aaron, on the other hand, have been inseparable since then.

I haven't actually seen Dom since he graduated from Winchester High and left Boston. I've occasionally stalked his socials and checked his stats and speedy climb up the charts. I'm happy for him, even if he has something against me. And that's likely why his face popped up at the worst time tonight. The guy is incredibly good-looking, and that hasn't changed with age. If anything, he seems to have become hotter. But looks can only take you so far, and he's a douche canoe. Except for the first day we met when I helped him find his class. He was sweet and shy, looking at me as if he'd never seen a girl before. I shake the old memories away, reaching for my seat belt and putting the car into drive.

Those days seem like forever ago now. Most people hated their high school years, but I loved mine. They were filled with hope and new possibilities, where my future was unwritten. I could be whoever I wanted to be. The days when chasing dreams actually felt like a possibility.

TODAY SUCKS.

I barely got two hours of sleep. Last night was a disaster, and this morning, I opened up my work email to learn we lost a potential client since I forgot to add an important detail to Greg's presentation deck last week. Maybe he would have caught it if he looked it over, but why would he do that when it's easier to blame his assistant? I'm definitely going to get an earful about that one later.

I have no idea what I had in mind for my life, but I never thought I would find myself at twenty-five, confined to a junior position at a PR firm, completely unrelated to my true passion of architectural design.

Speak of the devil, an incoming email from Greg with the subject "Meeting" pops up in the corner of my screen.

Do you have a few minutes? I need to see you.

My stomach dips, wondering if he wants to see me because of the client fiasco or because of last night. We have a rule to not discuss our non-work-related activities during office hours, but people love to break rules when it's convenient for them.

Maybe he wants to check in on you because he's worried about you.

Unlikely. When has he ever done that? He didn't seem remotely concerned last night.

Logging off and grabbing my phone, I straighten my skirt and head out of my cubicle. I keep my eyes down on my phone and pretend like I'm messaging someone even though the screen is black. Doing this brings me comfort, knowing I won't catch a judgmental glare or a blank expression staring back at me. Maybe it's the fact that I enjoy being an antisocial introvert, or maybe it's because I don't actually like anyone in this office except for Sammy. And frankly, they don't like me either.

Greg's corner office comes into view. He's leaning back in his black leather chair, laughing and running a hand through his blond hair while talking on the phone. He's attractive, I guess. He's never had trouble getting the attention of the women here or anywhere else we go. They stare at him, and he stares back at them, sometimes winking, and he doesn't give a shit who's watching. He asked me once at a bar if it made me jealous, and I shook my head, telling him I couldn't care less, but that seemed to only piss him off. Why should I care if Greg wants to sleep with half the town? It's not like there is a future here.

Our eyes meet, and his easy smile instantly drops. He averts his gaze, murmuring something into the phone before gently placing it back on the receiver.

Here we fucking go.

I give a customary double knock before opening the door and stepping inside. In here, the dynamic is firmly professional.

"Thanks for coming so quickly, Zoe. Please have a seat."

I release a shaky breath, regaining composure as I shut the door. With a plastered smile, I stride toward the pristine, white leather seat opposite Greg's desk.

"Everything all right? Any new files for me to handle?"

Loosening his tie, Greg takes a labored breath. "Listen, I'm just going to cut to the chase because Betty from HR is going to be here in five minutes."

I hold my breath, my nails digging into my palms.

"You're being relocated to New York. Some rumors have started circulating around the office, and I really can't afford to have my reputation tainted right now. I'm up for a promotion in a few months, and it's too risky to have you here. They wanted me to manage the new events division in New York a few months ago, but I didn't want to move. A couple of weeks ago, they asked if we recommended anyone for an assistant position, and I put your name in. They sent an email yesterday saying they want you."

I blink at him in disbelief. "Yesterday?"

Greg's eyes are cast down as he plays with a mechanical pencil, ignoring me completely.

"Your files and existing clients will remain here, and I'll take over the correspondence from here on out. You'll be working in social media over there, so you won't need to touch base with any of the clients here."

"But they've been dealing with me from day one. A couple of them don't like working with anyone else."

Internally, I'm kicking and screaming at this news. At the way he's brushing me off like I don't matter. But outwardly, I remain as cold as ice. Not a single flinch in response to his words.

"That's fine. I've got it," he reassures me, finally looking up at me for a split second before glancing at something behind me.

"Wow. Okay."

"I'm doing you a favor, all right? I could have fired you."

I've been Greg's assistant for three years with no opportunities to move up in the company. It's not for lack of trying on my end; I applied for three internal positions in the last several months, but I never heard back, even after following up. Now, I'm being shipped off to a brand-new department in a different city. An interview isn't even required?

Fuck Greg, and fuck this place.

"You should just let me go," I finally say.

It would be the push I need to start looking for another job. Maybe at an architectural firm or at a design and consultation company. Something I'm actually passionate about. It's about time I go after something worthwhile.

Greg smirks. "That would cost more than you're worth. We would have to pay you a hefty severance package, and the company can't afford that."

Wow. That's nice.

I exhale softly, glancing at my clenched fists before releasing my grip and crossing my legs. I remind myself to maintain composure until later, to never reveal my pain or vulnerability on the outside. Emotion equals weakness.

"So my options are to go to New York or quit?"

He nods. "Betty can explain everything to you once she gets here."

Right on cue, as if the universe was just itching for the perfect moment, the door opens and Mrs. Wilson, also known as Betty from HR, walks in holding a binder and wearing the same navy pantsuit she always wears. She either loves this navy suit, or she has purchased multiples of the same outfit to take out the guessing game in the mornings. Betty looks frazzled and breathless as she walks to Greg's desk. There is a noticeable coffee stain on her blouse, and I can't stop staring at it.

"Sorry I'm late. It's been a crazy day."

"It's always crazy in HR. Thank you for making the time for us today, Betty."

"It's Mrs. Wilson."

"Apologies." I notice the small smirk before Greg erases it off his face. He did it on purpose, knowing it gets under her skin anytime someone calls her by her first name. Our Human Resources department is all about rules and regulations, and Betty probably knows every single one by heart.

She clears her throat, standing beside Greg, and casts her eyes down at me.

"Thanks for joining us, Ms. Jackson. I'm sure you're wondering what's going on, so I'll get to it. You're needed at the New York office. Your manager here has graciously offered up your services to them. This is a permanent move, and there are no other options available at this time. If you choose not to relocate, you will be dismissed effective immediately at your own discretion."

I don't speak, only continue to blink at her mindlessly, trying to imagine myself anywhere but here.

"Normally, we would cover moving expenses, but given the quick circumstances, you're to relocate at your own expense. If you choose to accept the job, I will email you all the details. You'll need to be in New York by Monday."

"It's Thursday," I force out.

"I'm aware."

"Can I get more time to decide?"

"I'm afraid not."

I force down the fiery anger building inside me, preventing it from clawing up my throat and suffocating me. I wish it fucking would, then I wouldn't have to sit here and deal with this bullshit.

"Of course, you can choose to decline the offer, but that is entirely up to you." Greg speaks.

"Understood."

"Are you accepting?"

"I don't really have a choice, do I?"

"You always have a choice, Ms. Jackson." Betty's voice perks up at the end.

Not really. Not when I have rent to pay and literally twenty-eight dollars sitting in my bank account because this job pays shit and I have never bothered to look for something in my actual field of work after I graduated with a degree in Architectural Design.

I straighten my spine, keeping my eyes fixed on Betty. "Thank you for your time. Will that be all?"

She glances at Greg who is so absorbed in his phone, clearly distracted by something on his screen, he isn't even tuned in to this conversation. Betty finally looks back at me and nods. I shoot up from my seat, needing to get the fuck out of this office before I do or say something foolish.

"Thank you, Mrs. Wilson. I'll look for your email."

She tips her chin down. "Also, today is your last day here. There will be a box on your desk when you get back."

Seriously?

I adjust my pencil skirt and approach the door, a tumult of emotions urging me to have the final say, to strike where it hurts and soil Greg's reputation or jeopardize his job. But petty revenge like this does nothing but feed my anger and turn me into a darker version of myself. I grip the door handle and blink back the tears welling in my eyes.

Not yet. Not here.

I'm pretty sure I just hit rock bottom.

CHAPTER 2
ZOE

Good riddance.

I start throwing stuff into the empty, white box perched on my desk, fuming over which one of these motherfuckers placed it here. Three years of continuous effort in a dead-end job, and this is how it ends. This is my humiliating achievement. I can practically feel the burn radiating off my cheeks from the intensity of nosy gazes around me.

I know they're all staring. Whispers ripple from all around me, but I keep my face down, focused on grabbing everything that belongs to me and getting the hell out of here. It's an effort to block out the chatter as I continue to throw more useless office shit into the box.

Stapler.

Scotch tape. Not mine.

Planner. Mine…in the box you go.

I grab the framed picture of Aaron and me taken in front of the Charging Bull in New York City. It was a special day for my big brother, as he had just made his first significant sale as a NYC realtor. I had been visiting him during spring break, staying in his cramped studio apartment with barely enough space for one person, let alone a guest. Yet, that week turned out to be one of the best of my life, and I felt fortunate to share a significant milestone with Aaron.

I'll forever remember the sheer excitement in his eyes when he burst into the apartment that day, sharing his good news. We celebrated by jumping and screaming, probably infuriating his neighbors downstairs, but neither one of us cared. In that moment, he was that much closer to everything he'd ever wanted.

Then he insisted I dress up so he could treat me to a fancy lunch. We ended up in Manhattan's financial district where he wanted a selfie with the Charging Bull. We both placed our palms on its bronze behind and beamed. After taking the photo, he told me he was going to live in a penthouse suite close to the bull one day, and I knew he would do it.

I never doubted him for one second.

Because unlike me, Aaron always gets whatever he sets his mind to. He never gives up, and that's why he's an incredibly successful billionaire. He's always been driven, dedicated, and passionate about his career. He's the crown jewel of the family, making up for the ocean bottom feeder (a.k.a. me). At least I'm good at being the worst.

Holding the title of our family's greatest disappointment at twenty-five, I'm single with zero prospects and have never experienced a long-term relationship. Commitment has always been something I avoided like the plague. I rent a small studio apartment near my job, which I've recently lost. My life seems to consist of nothing but a collection of underwhelming thoughts and memories. And now, I'm being forced to leave Boston, the few friends I have, and my meager excuse for a life to start anew in a city I can't even afford.

Wait until my parents hear about this one.

The one good thing about this pile of shit is that I'll be close to Aaron again.

What am I even going to tell him?

It doesn't matter; he won't judge me. He might be disappointed for all of about twenty seconds, but he'll jump right into problem-solving and try to help me find an "optimal" solution. Even though the only thing I'll be able to afford once I get there is a fancy cardboard box.

Aaron is the only person in this entire world who has never made me feel worthless. He's always loved me, even if I don't have the big achievements in life like everyone else. He has been there for all the highs and lows in my life. When my parents would talk down to me, my protective brother would comfort me and always have my back. If it weren't for him, I don't know where I would be. Probably more of a hot mess than I already am, if that is even possible.

Maybe I should quit and stay here, look for another job.

I refuse to be a burden to Aaron, no matter the circumstances. Maybe I can stay with him for a few months and search for a job in Boston before returning. Subletting my apartment seems like a viable option, but there's not enough time. I gently run my thumb across his smiling face in the picture before placing it carefully inside the box.

God, I miss him.

"What are you doing?" Sammy Laub, my work wife, struts over and hops on my desk, knocking over a fake potted plant as she pokes her head inside my box. "Are you moving to a new cubicle?" She smacks her gum with an audible pop.

"Yeah, in New York City," I mutter, placing some binders in the box.

"What?!" Sammy yells, and I shush her, snatching my planner out of her hands. She slaps my arm playfully. Sammy and I have been friends since the first day I started at Bloom Public Relations. We have lunch together almost every day and have a refreshingly straightforward relationship. No bullshit from the start. I suspect everyone at the office dislikes us, which is what drew us together in the first place.

"I'm being relocated. Karma is a bitch and loves to teach me hard lessons," I whisper, trying not to feed the hungry gossipers sharpening their ears.

"Did someone find out and tell HR?" she hisses, her brown eyes turning into saucers.

"No. I suspect Greg is just trying to cover his ass. Get ahead of it by getting rid of me. I should have known he would pull something like this."

Maybe I knew all along and didn't care. I love to self-sabotage; it's one of my strong suits.

"Oh my God...that motherfucker! I'm going to kill him."

"Shhh...I'm pretty sure the town over can hear you." I try to throw a bundle of pink sticky notes into my box, but she grabs them from my hand.

"Did you speak to HR? Tell them what's been happening?"

"No. Why would I?"

She hops off my desk, firmly grabbing my shoulders. "Zo...you can't do this. He's getting away with harassment if you don't speak up. You can't let him ship you off like this."

"It's not harassment if I wanted it too."

"That's bullshit, and you know it. He is your superior, and he took advantage. He should be the one getting fired."

Biting the inside of my cheek, I scan the desk for anything else that might be mine.

"It doesn't matter, Sam. It's done. I already accepted the job. Digging myself a bigger hole won't help me right now. Sometimes, it's easier to just walk away."

She frowns. "But you always walk away."

Moving aside, I continue packing my things into the box, but Sammy reaches her arm in, taking my stapler out.

"Hey...what the hell?"

"You're not leaving. Go to HR. This is absolutely ridiculous."

"Betty was in Greg's office. It's done. I'm not going back."

I sink into my chair, pressing the heels of my hands against my eyes. A headache is starting to throb at the back of my skull from this conversation.

"This place is the worst." Sammy rustles around, withdrawing more items from the box. Leaning back further in my chair, I open my eyes and notice her holding the picture of Aaron and me, closely examining it.

"I know it's awful timing, but it's my duty to remind you that your brother is a total smoke show. And that means a lot coming from a lesbian. I wouldn't kick him out of my bed, that's for sure."

I roll my eyes and let out a laugh. "Doesn't that mean you're not a true lesbian?"

"No. It just means I make special exceptions for super-hot older brothers."

"I'm sure he'd be thrilled to know even lesbians would fuck him."

"Didn't you say his friends are hot too?"

"Maybe. I don't know."

"I'll take that as a yes. Have you boned any of his friends?"

I quirk an eyebrow at Sammy. "Are you serious? My brother would murder them right in front of me and force me to watch the entire thing."

"Overprotective much?"

"You have no idea," I respond, standing up to grab the frame from her hand.

Sammy doesn't say anything else or fight me for my things anymore. She hovers quietly as I finish packing up my small cubicle. The minutes begin to weigh me down as I realize there is nothing left. It's time for me to go.

Looking up, I notice Sammy leaning against the small opening. Her arms are crossed and her chin is quivering.

Shit. I don't know how to say goodbye to her.

"I'm sorry, Zo. You deserve better."

I hate this. How am I supposed to walk away from her? From my apartment? My home? This city? I've never lived anywhere outside of Boston.

My eyes sting, and this time, I don't fight the tears. Not with Sammy. I want her to know how much she means to me. Closing the distance between us, I pull her in for a tight hug.

"I'll see you soon. This isn't goodbye."

"It better not be. You and I are connected, bitch," she whispers into my hair.

I lean back, forcing a smile as a lone tear slides down her cheek. "I know." My thumb brushes it away.

"I'll quit too. I'll come with you."

"Don't be ridiculous."

"Zo...I won't survive a day here without you. I hate everyone. They'll fire me for saying something supremely inappropriate or getting into a fist fight with Platinum Ashley."

"Promise me we'll call and text every day. We'll be one another's lifeline, okay?" Grasping her shoulders, I look into her big, golden eyes. "You've got this, and if you hate it that much here, you should find something else. Something that you love, and leave this all behind you."

She rolls her eyes, pinching my chin. "You're always great with the advice except when it comes to yourself. Why don't you do the same? New York is the city of opportunity. Don't go there just to be miserable somewhere else. Take this opportunity to create a better life. One you're proud of and happy with. Let someone love you, Zo."

"All right. That's enough." I laugh, pulling her in for one last hug.

Grabbing the final item off my desk—the fake ficus plant—and plopping it on top of the pile of crap I'll likely never use again, I lift the heavy box and take a deep breath.

My heart and chest feel heavy, filled with emotions I can't quite process or don't want to confront at this moment. Nevertheless, I muster a forced, sizable smile as I gaze up at Sammy.

"Guess this is it."

"No, it's not. I'll see you soon, bitch."

Repositioning the box on my hip, I lean in and plant a kiss on her cheek. Her face is wet as she wraps her arms around my neck.

"I love you," she exhales, and I realize she smells like Twizzlers. She always smells like candy.

"I love you too, Sammy Bear. Call me anytime."

My left heel wobbles, unstable like my life, as I place the tough girl mask back on my face.

I give Sammy a wink, step out of the cubicle, and walk with my head held high. I avoid making eye contact with anyone as I head toward the elevators. This is my final stroll through this hallway. Tomorrow, I won't be returning. It's that simple; it's over. All those years, the tears shed over deadlines, the meetings I endured—they all feel like it was for nothing.

I want to scream, to unravel in the middle of this crowded office in front of all these people who would love to see me fall apart. But I resist, putting on a smile, ensuring my posture remains upright as I stride out of here as though I've just won the lottery.

Standing before the elevator doors, I watch the numbers climb until the chime signals their opening to an empty box. I step inside, feeling numb as I lean against the gray and white wallpaper adorning the interior. I glance to my left and catch my reflection in the mirror. My golden hair flows in loose curls, impeccably styled as always, a result of the early morning routine I never skip. My physical appearance stands in stark contrast to the woman inside, which is why I take the time to do my makeup. It's the one aspect of my life I can control, even when everything around me is falling apart. My lips are never without my favorite pink nude lipstick, my soft smokey eyes and winged liner are perfect as always. But the green orbs gazing back at me feel hollow and lifeless.

I don't recognize the person standing in front of me.

If I could go back in time, would I have made different choices? Stayed away from Greg?

The sad thing is, I'm not sure I would have. Burning things to ash is my favorite pastime. I ruin everything before it has a chance to settle in my heart and grow roots.

Because when you love something, when you allow someone inside your soul, that's when they hold the power over you. That's when they can break your heart over and over again. And I've broken my own heart more times than I can count.

Hope and love are things I have no interest in obtaining.

Taking a deep breath and releasing the negative thoughts, I place the box between my feet and pull out my cellphone. I glare at Aaron's name on the screen for a long while before summoning the courage to tap the phone icon.

The elevator doors open right as he answers the phone.

"Zozo, everything okay?

"Hey, bro. Guess who's coming to see you in New York?"

CHAPTER 3
DOMINIK

Sweat drips down my back as I skate off the ice, stepping onto the plush floor and shuffling for the already-crowded dressing room. Pulling off my helmet, I run my other hand through my sweaty, disheveled hair. The black strands are longer than I like to keep them and my natural waves are starting to annoy me as they grow out. Many of us grow our hair longer close to playoffs; it's become a tradition, and our fans seem to enjoy it.

In more ways than one.

The familiar scent of sweat and stale ice wafts through the locker room alongside the laughter of some very happy hockey players. We've really been coming together as a team in the last couple of months, and I'm grateful to be leading the New York Slashers into the playoffs this year. First year as captain, and the team has never been stronger. I'm not saying it has to do with me, because hockey is all about teamwork, but I've never given up on these guys, and they know they can count on me.

Hockey has always been my top focus in life.

I've worked so hard to finally get here, and my journey is far from over. This is the time to prove to everyone that the title of captain belongs to me and that I'm worthy of it. There is no room for any type of distraction in my life right now.

I peel off my damp gear and toss it in front of my locker before plopping down onto the cushioned blue bench. Stealing a glance at my nameplate in bold letters, now sporting the newly added "C" for captain, still makes me smile. It's a small detail, but I love seeing it every time. It's a daily reminder of the hard work I've put in to get here. Everything I have today is the result of my efforts, not out of obligation, but because hockey is my life; it defines who I am.

It's everything I know. And I'm on cloud nine right now because I truly believe we have a genuine chance at winning the Cup this year.

"Great practice today, boys," Coach Bradley charges in, shouting cheerfully as he plants his feet in the middle of the dressing room. "With Lewis leading as our new captain, I'm confident we will bring the Cup home this year. No, scratch that. WE WILL BRING THE CUP HOME THIS YEAR!"

The room fills with screams and shouts, including my own. Coach glances at me, winks, and gives me a reassuring thumbs-up.

The boys begin chanting my nickname over and over.

DOMINATOR! DOMINATOR! DOMINATOR!

Out of all the nicknames they could have given me, this one has to be the best. And the most fitting since I've been dominating every game this year.

Fucking unstoppable.

Has it gotten to my head a bit? Sure. But it's because I never lose.

Axel Vines, my assistant captain, looks at me from across the room and smiles, reminding me that it's my turn to give a little speech. I love pumping the boys up, especially after a killer practice like today.

I rise to my feet, offering a playful bow and flipping my hair as the guys burst into laughter. I can be the joker when I want to be, but when we hit the ice, it's all business, and everyone understands that. The team has a deep respect for each other, and we genuinely care about one another, both on and off the ice. These guys are my family. That's what fuels us, and it's what's going to secure us the Cup this year.

"All right, assholes. Settle down." Chatter quiets down almost instantly as every eye lands on me. "You guys are putting in the work, and it's really starting to pay off. We've got this. Go in with that mindset every time you hit the ice. It doesn't matter if we're practicing or at a game, we need to go all in. Take a page out of my book and DOMINATE each game. We're all winners here. And don't forget, there is no stopping the Slashers until that trophy comes home with us."

The boys all nod in agreement, exchanging high fives and fist bumps. Liam walks over to me, wrapping his sweaty arm around my head. I throw a punch into his hard stomach, and he backs away, chuckling.

"You may be unstoppable on the ice, but your tongue needs work. You kind of suck at giving speeches, Dom," Josh remarks, walking backward to his locker. He's got a stupid grin on his face, but I know exactly how to wipe it off.

"That's not what your sister said to me last month. She thought my tongue was exceptional."

A few of the guys snicker, but none of them speak up. Josh's eyes shoot daggers, and his face turns crimson against his dark complexion. I bite my tongue, attempting to stifle my laughter.

"Fuck you, we agreed you wouldn't bring that up again."

I lift my hands in the air, pretending to surrender. "You were the one who told me it was okay to date her."

"I don't want to fucking hear about it," he spits out, hands balling up at his sides. "Especially since your second profession is being a manwhore."

A part of me really wants to tell him how much his older sister begged me to fuck her. How she basically clawed at my pants so she could suck my dick, but he's a friend and my teammate so I hold my tongue. He was okay with me dating her, mostly because she told him if he got involved, she would never speak to him again.

Even though I did warn her from the beginning that I don't date. I fuck once. It's a hard rule, and there are no exceptions for anyone.

Ever.

They scratch that itch, can tell everyone they slept with a hockey player, and I get to get off without using my hand. Win-win for everyone. I don't date because I don't have time and because there is no room in my life for attachments. Besides, I'm not interested. There is no challenge or real desire, just the need to have some fun. The women always approach me, and I set out my conditions up front. A lot of them actually don't even want to date me. Why would they? I have a reputation, and they don't want their hearts broken. Which works out perfectly for me.

Let them think what they want about me. I prefer that, actually. Even if it's not who I am; even if, deep down, I ache for something I'll never have again. I'd rather remove the emotion from the act entirely. I'm comfortable there even if it might sound horrible. I just don't have the desire or time for relationships.

Josh calling me a manwhore should sting, especially when his tone has a bite to it, but I don't give a shit. I want them to think that about me. Let them believe I'm the cold-hearted captain who gets shit done. The opinions other people have about me are none of my concern, especially when I'm standing at the top.

"Noted." I look Josh dead in the face as I walk past him, heading for the showers. Anger radiates off his body, but I pretend like it doesn't phase me.

And honestly, a part of me doesn't really give a shit what he thinks. We're all consenting adults, and if I want to fuck his sister and she wants to fuck me, then so be it. If he has a problem with it, he should take it up with her. The no-sister rule has only ever been a non-negotiable with one person in my life, and she belongs in the past now.

STEPPING INTO THE ELEVATOR, I enter the passcode for Aaron's penthouse suite. My gaze drops to the floor, reflecting my own image back at me. It's a four-by-four, floor-to-ceiling mirrored box, which currently frustrates me because at times, I can't stand the sight of my own face. I clench my teeth, fighting the urge to shatter the glass before me. Sometimes, I just want to escape from the judgments people pass when they see me and from the image I continue to project into everyone's minds: the NHL's all-star, the player with a stone heart, here for a good time but never a long time.

I've meticulously crafted the facade of a professional man known for his flings, indifferent to anyone but himself and hockey. Yet, despite the effort to build this reputation, why does it occasionally repel me? Especially when I'm alone and caged in, surrounded by mirrors reflecting my own image—mocking and challenging me. Reminding me how I don't quite belong.

Josh's words from today replay in my head, twisting and turning until there is nothing left. I shake my head, the damp curls brushing against my neck and cheek as I physically swat away the negative thoughts. I envision them as if on an Etch A Sketch, watching the letters gradually fade away.

They're just words.

They mean nothing.

Forcing my thoughts back to the present, I take in the smudge-free mirrors surrounding me and the pristine floor. How is the floor not even scratched after four years of constant use? It can't be glass, or the constant scuff from shoes and boots would have scratched the shit out of it.

Seventeen Hudson Yards is still one of the most sought-after apartment buildings in Manhattan. The entire building is known for its sweeping panoramic views high above the city. Depending on how deep your pockets go, you can see the Hudson River, the

Statue of Liberty, or the Empire State and Chrysler buildings all from here. Each side of the apartment building was designed so residents could enjoy whichever view they could afford. Aaron gets to see the entire city light up every single night because the penthouse is wrapped in floor-to-ceiling windows, offering an unparalleled panoramic view of the metropolis. He told me it gives him the sensation of being on top of the world, as if he owns it. And Aaron loves that feeling.

If anyone deserves the title of being king in this building, it's him. He works harder than anyone I know. Nothing was or has ever been handed to him. Even when his parents offered to buy him a car or pay for college, he worked to earn it. I have so much respect for my best friend. He inspires me to push harder every day and become better at my own game.

Tristan and I live three floors down from Aaron, facing the Hudson River. And my commute to Madison Square Garden—the world's most famous arena and home to the New York Slashers— is a nine-minute walk from this building. Hudson Yards is quickly becoming a premier, sought-after location. According to Aaron, it's currently the hottest spot in New York City.

Living near my two best friends is the icing on the cake. Aaron scored Tristan and me a fantastic deal at Seventeen Hudson when they began selling units, and it just made sense for all of us to live nearby, given how much we see one another and the business ventures we've started together. With the demanding schedules we maintain, free time is a rare commodity, so being neighbors has been a game-changer. Our proximity allows us to spend our time wisely, and we actually get to hang out once in a while too, like tonight.

Aaron might be a hot-shot realtor in the heart of New York City, but what I respect most about him is that he doesn't let it go to his head. He's consistently stayed grounded, and I doubt any sum of money could change that. Regardless of how ambitious we are or how successful we become, Aaron and I try to hold on to our humility and remain tethered to our roots. We will never forget where we came from and what it took to get here.

Leaning my six-five frame against the back of the elevator, I finally muster the courage to look up, straightening my sore back muscles. My eyes crawl upward, catching on my washed-out jeans and gray hoodie. I'm usually in hockey gear or suits for games, so any opportunity to dress comfortably is a welcome one. A hint of black ink adorns my neck, winding down my veiny forearms. I began with a few tattoos years ago, but the addiction has only grown. I only visit the shop when there's something truly worth inking onto my body, and I doubt the well of ideas will ever run dry.

My shaggy black hair is damp, the top curling over my forehead and occasionally brushing into my eyes. The first thing I'm doing after the playoffs is getting a damn haircut. One deep-blue eye and one pale-hazel eye stare back at me. My mismatched eyes often throw people off; one is dark, the other light. It tends to make people uncomfortable, and no one usually holds eye contact with me for too long. I don't take offense to it; I know it's an unusual trait. Even my own father couldn't stand to look me in the eyes, and he often wondered why I had heterochromia when no one else in our family did. He would accuse my mom of cheating, and as I grew older, those comments pissed me off more and more. He was always a fucking dick to her.

I love my mismatched eyes. They're the one thing I genuinely appreciate about myself. It's as if my own body couldn't make up its mind and decided to take one of each. This uniqueness sets me apart, and I've never had any interest in blending in.

Dark circles mar the skin under my eyes, evidence of sleepless nights and grueling hours at the rink, compounded by restless evenings with different women. It's beginning to take a toll on my body, and with playoffs fast approaching, I can't afford to let anything slow me down. I'll have to slow down on the partying, at least until hockey season is over.

Yeah, right. Let's see you stick to keeping your dick dry.

Repositioning the six-pack of beer in my arm, I'm thankful for a quiet night in with the guys tonight. No distractions, no women, just the three of us probably watching a movie and talking about our goals for the month. Tristan will probably tell us about his flavor of the week, how he's desperate to secure a woman before his time runs out. Something about his inheritance clause and the conditions his father and grandfather set in place for him. Unlike Aaron and me, Tristan comes from unfathomable money. But from the stories I've heard, they are scoundrels and have been nothing but monsters to Tris since he was a small child. One day, I'm going to make them pay for everything they've put him through. Tristan jokes about everything, but it's a front. Deep down he's dealing with some heavy shit, and I would bet good money he's buried a lot of things that should have been dealt with a long time ago.

The elevator chimes, and I push off the mirrored wall, stepping into Aaron's grand marble foyer. Every detail of this place exudes luxury, an interior designer's wet dream. When Aaron first took possession, he had a team of designers work on his home. He's so wealthy that he didn't have to lift a finger when he moved in. Everything was ordered and in its place before he walked through the door. Even his fucking silk boxers were meticulously folded and tucked into a drawer inside his massive walk-in closet. Closet might be the wrong word. The guy has so much money, he doesn't know what to do with it.

I stroll past the open-concept living area, now bathed in New York's skyline. I hear voices and laughter as I walk toward the kitchen. I thought it was supposed to be only us tonight. Just as my frustrations begin to bubble, a smooth, honeyed laughter cuts through the air, and the sound sizzles my skin, causing the hairs on my arms to stand.

I'd know that laughter anywhere.

My heart starts to race erratically in my chest as torturous recognition catches me off guard. I haven't heard that laugh in six years—six long years since a night I swore I'd take to my grave that turned everything upside down.

That voice belongs to the one girl I've always wanted and the only girl I can never have.

The cold, metal beer cans dig into my flesh as I tighten my grip on them.

No, it can't be her. She's in Boston. I know this for a fact.

My unsteady legs carry me inside Aaron's sleek kitchen boasted with top-of-the-line appliances and marble countertops. And before I have a chance to control my thoughts or slow down my racing heart, piercing green eyes lock on mine, releasing a flood of memories and thoughts from the past. Time seems to stand still as it all washes over me like a sudden chilling wave, pulling me under.

Those unforgettable green eyes. Just as bright as the first day I met her at Winchester High.

God, she is as beautiful as ever. So fucking unfair. I take a moment to drink her in, and instantly regret it. Gazing at her, feeling that same desire I'd felt all those years ago, does something to the inner workings of my heart. It pinches the breath out of my lungs, forcing me to tear my eyes away.

How does she still have this power over me?

"Dominik...hi," Zoe utters, a hesitant smile tugs at her lips.

She stands upright, her relaxed demeanor gone at the sight of me.

"Zoe," I hear myself mumbling as I glance away to place the beer on the kitchen counter.

I decide to give her the cold shoulder, pretending like she doesn't exist, just as I did back in high school—those torturous years when I was so near yet worlds apart. The last time I saw her was the night that changed everything, the night I've worked tirelessly to forget but can never truly erase, no matter how hard I try or how many other women I sleep with. There's no forgetting that one night in Boston with Zoe.

Nobody truly knows what happened that night but me. If she ever found out, she'd never forgive me.

A normal person would approach their best friend's younger

sister and give her a hug, but I can't bring myself to get close to her. Maintaining space and keeping my head down seems like the best course of action.

I can't afford to lose control, not now, not again.

What the fuck is she doing here? Why didn't Aaron say something? If I had known she was here tonight, I wouldn't have come.

"About fucking time, Dom. You good?" Tristan's voice yanks me out of my thoughts.

I tip my chin down, opening a can of beer and chugging half of it before taking a breath. I might need some hard liquor tonight.

"Nice of you to join us, Dominik. Remember my sister?" Aaron walks in the room, loosening his tie and giving me a relaxed smile. One of his signature I'm-reading-you looks.

My eyes drift to Zoe again.

How could I ever forget her? Her jade eyes lock onto mine, carrying a certain curiosity. I'll never forget the only girl my heart longed for but could never have. The girl I pushed away simply because I was too afraid to get close. She still haunts my dreams, and now, she's standing right here, so close, yet still so far from reach.

I can't lose control, for her sake and mine.

CHAPTER 4
ZOE

Dominik Lewis is staring at me as if he's seen a ghost. I suppose he has; we haven't seen each other since high school. And after graduation, he disappeared without even a goodbye. Not that I expected one.

By his reaction, I'd say my dear brother failed to inform his best friend I was coming to town. That's going to be awkward for them later.

"I hear you're a hockey superstar," I say, extending an olive branch as I reach for my glass of wine.

Dominik forces a smile and pulls out a stool tucked underneath the island countertop.

He doesn't respond or ask me how I'm doing. Eventually, the three guys break into easy conversation, and I allow my eyes to roam over him.

He's changed so much since high school. He's always been strikingly good-looking, even before he fully grew into his adult self, but this current version of him is on an entirely different level. His hockey pictures online do not do him justice. He's a thing of masculine beauty, even in casual clothing, the mop of damp hair sitting on his head, and his relaxed smile with a beer in his hand.

He exudes a powerful masculine energy and intense charm. It's hard not to be captivated by it, even for someone like me who wants nothing to do with him. His towering presence and imposing physique dominate the room, they always have. He sure is dominating my attention right now because I'm ogling like an idiot. I would bet money other people stare at him like this though. How can they not? I've heard the rumors about him, and he isn't discreet about his extracurricular activities with all types of women.

The man gets around.

A sensation resembling jealousy pools in the pit of my stomach, but deep down, I recognize it for what it is. It's simply my urge to explore him for myself, to peel back the layers and find out if he's truly as impressive as they claim.

I doubt it. I bet he wouldn't be able to satiate my impossible tastes.

Stop it.

I know, I know—look, but never touch. My brother would have my head, and Dom made it abundantly clear over the years that he never viewed me in that light. I'm well aware that he's completely out of my league.

Not like my traitorous eyes give a shit as they scan his athletic physique, which is proudly showcased despite the hoodie that conceals most of it. I catch glimpses of the intricate ink covering his forearms. A tantalizing trail extends up his neck, piquing my curiosity more and more. I just want to strip him naked and see where his tattoos end. I've always had a thing for tattooed men, and all that ink wasn't there when I knew Dominik. We were too young.

His jet-black hair is curled and long enough to brush against the nape of his neck. It's the perfect length to run my fingers through while being…

That's enough of that.

Freckles line his high cheekbones and dark brows, and his full, plump lips look as though someone was just sucking on them. I bite the inside of my cheek, wondering what it would feel like to kiss him. What his hands would feel like fisting my hair. Seriously, when did he get so hot? Is it all the training and hours spent at the gym?

I need to meet more hockey players, Jesus Christ.

You're drooling.

I tip my glass up, my eyes still fixed on him, savoring him as easily as the wine gliding down my throat. Suddenly, his gaze shifts to mine, a deep fusion of hazel and blue. One eye reminds me of the warm sun at dusk, while the other makes me think of the ocean at night. A perfect blend of light and dark. His eyes pull me in like a magnetic force, and in this moment, everything fades as I stare into his eyes, feeling an enigma squeezing my lungs tight.

We remain frozen like that for what feels like an eternity before his brows bunch in confusion and he glances away. I could swear his breathing is labored as he looks back at my brother.

Well, that was fucking obvious and awkward as hell. Way to go, weirdo. Now he's going to think you're a complete nut job.

I turn around, taking a moment to catch my breath. I try to focus on Aaron's espresso machine, sitting on the counter right against the exquisitely expensive-looking marble backsplash that runs down his long and spacious kitchen. While I haven't had a full tour of his penthouse yet, it's clear that not a single detail went unnoticed during the design process. I feel a hint of disappointment that he didn't involve me in the process, but I was just a junior in college at the time. Everything I knew was pulled from Pinterest boards.

"You seem off tonight. Is everything okay?" Aaron's voice piques my attention as I begin sifting through cabinets, looking for his glasses. How much stuff does one single person need that would require this amount of kitchen space? A lot of these cabinets are empty.

"I'm fine," Dominik answers. His voice is low and deep as it brushes against me from across the room.

I either need to stop drinking or leave this room before I say something stupid.

"No, you're being weird. Was practice shit?"

Pause. "No. It was great, as usual."

"Did you look at the portfolio I sent you today?" Aaron finally asks, seeming to drop the conversation. A sliver of disappointment weighs me down. For some reason, I feel like I'm the reason for Dom's sour mood tonight. I saw the way he looked at me, and I can't help but place the blame on myself. Perhaps that's me over-thinking things per usual, but I'm with Aaron on this one. He's acting weird.

I open another cupboard, finding rows of crystal glasses in all shapes and sizes. Some are stacked so high up that I'm not sure anyone in this room would be able to reach it. Although, Dominik is crazy tall, so maybe he would be able to—

"So, Zoe...how are you liking New York?" Turning my head, I see Tristan leaning against the edge of the island, grabbing a handful of chips from the porcelain bowl and studying me carefully.

Tristan is a different type of beautiful, a captivating blend of model-like charisma mixed with the confident aura of a billionaire. He looks like he just stepped out of an Armani photoshoot. I assume the suit he's wearing is worth more than any condo I could ever afford. He gives off an air of pure control while remaining entirely approachable.

He's got a great smile, big and inviting against his rich, golden skin. Dark-auburn hair, which is so unique in color that it high-lights all his other features in a perfect way. And let's not forget those piercing, blue eyes that are currently scanning me, causing a rush of desire to trickle down my spine. I bite my lip and his smile stretches wide, making my attraction to him that much harder to resist.

Is he flirting with me?

"I mean, I just got here a couple of hours ago, but so far, so good."

"Sounds like you need a tour guide. I know the city like the back of my hand."

Tristan raises a chip to his mouth, and I trace the movement, the way his tongue brushes his bottom lip.

I swallow hard.

What the fuck was in that wine?

"What a generous offer. I'd love that," I finally breathe out, forcing a smile while trying to hide my burning cheeks behind my nearly empty glass of wine.

"What's a generous offer?" Dom appears out of thin air, towering beside us.

I nearly jump out of my skin, but Tristan just smiles, squeezing Dom's shoulder with a shit-disturber expression on his face.

"I was just offering Zoe a tour of New York City since she's going to be staying here for a long time."

"What?" Dom asks.

"Didn't Aaron fill you in? Zoe's moved to New York City. She got transferred from her Boston office, and no one knows why yet. But I think she probably got a promotion and she just doesn't want to seem like she's bragging." Tristan winks at me.

Definitely not the case, but I don't plan on sharing that piece of disappointing news anytime soon. My eyes ping-pong between Dominik and Tristan as they share some weird look between one another, seeming to communicate effectively in bro language without needing words. Not sure when I got jammed into this awkward man sandwich but it's probably time for me to exit stage left.

As I turn, Dom suddenly moves, and I accidentally smack his arm, causing the beer in his hand to spill and create a pool on Aaron's floor. Panic grips me, and I quickly reach for the roll of paper towels on the counter. Kneeling down, I start cleaning up the mess.

Fuck, I can't help but feel like an imposition. I look around as if Dad is going to materialize out of thin air, berating me and reiterating what a colossal screw-up I am.

Dominik crouches down beside me and tries to grab the ball of paper towels from my hand. "Let me. It was my fault."

I don't look up at him, keeping my eyes on the floor. "It's fine. Don't even worry about it."

His inked hand gently rests on top of mine, and the warmth from his touch sends tiny shocks of electricity racing up my arm.

"This isn't your parents' house. You don't have to do that," he whispers, low enough for only me to hear.

Lurching upright as if I've been stung, I look over my shoulder to see Tristan and Aaron watching me. Tristan with a cool, carefree look, and my brother with an expression of familiar concern. Aaron is a closed book with most people, but when you grow up with someone, it's hard to hide most of yourself from them. And I recognize that look. It's the same one he wore whenever he witnessed my parents tearing me down.

Avoiding everyone, I walk to the sink to wash my hands and wet some more paper towels to clean up the sticky gunk the beer spill left on the floor. I feel my brother approaching, but he stands there for a few minutes, not saying a word. Simply existing beside me.

"Thank you," I finally address him.

He nods, reaching for the bottle of wine and topping off my glass.

"Zoe, are you going to tell us what type of promotion brought you here?" Tristan finally breaks the uncomfortable silence settling in the room.

Answering this question might be easier than enduring the last five minutes all over again.

"Do I have to?"

"Yes," Tristan and Aaron say at the same time.

"Give her some space." Wow, Dominik is standing up for me for once in his life? I'm equally shocked and impressed.

"Relax, Dom. I'm just curious. Need to figure out what type of long-term plans I can make with Aaron's little sister," Tristan teases, laughing, but Aaron and Dominik look as if they're going to murder him and hang his body upside down to bleed dry.

"My sister is off-limits, Tristan. Don't even fucking think about it. You can have any woman in New York but not her," my brother grits out as if I'm not standing right here. I'm a grown-ass woman fully capable of making my own goddamn decisions.

Anger burns my lungs, and the all too familiar knot tightens in my chest. "And who are you to say who I can and cannot fuck?"

All three heads turn in my direction. Dominik looks shocked, like I've just uttered an obscenity in the middle of a church service. Tristan, on the other hand, is smiling cheek to cheek as he crosses his arms across his broad chest. Aaron looks to be turning red—or more hulk green, actually.

"Watch it, Zoe," he warns.

"No, you watch it. I'm twenty-five, and if I'm going to live here in this house with you, then you're going to have to get used to the idea of me dating. If you have a problem with that, I am happy to leave right this second."

"Dating is one thing—"

I turn to face Tristan, ignoring whatever my brother is about to say. "I got sent here because I was screwing my boss… and when he got bored of me, he booted me here. There were some rumors circulating, so this was a good excuse to get rid of me. So here I am."

Tristan smirks, turning to face my brother without a care in the world about the wrath he might face. "I like her. She's feisty."

"You were having a relationship with your boss?" Aaron asks, ignoring Tristan.

I glance down at my nails. "I wouldn't call it a relationship per se, more like a fuck buddy."

"Jesus Christ." Tristan chuckles under his breath, and I watch my brother's patience grow thin.

Aaron's nostrils flare as he keeps his fiery gaze on me. I match his stare, two seconds away from screaming at him for thinking he can tell me what to do. I don't need his protection.

Maybe once upon a time I did. But I grew up and learned how to defend myself.

He was the sole person who watched out for me in a house

where no one seemed to care. He was the one who truly loved me, and sometimes, it felt like an overwhelming flood, as if he was compensating for everything my parents failed to provide, for everything they couldn't see. Aaron was always there, holding my hand, wiping away my tears, until one day, I made a decision to strip away my parents' power. I wasn't going to let their toxicity and my pain define me any longer. I wouldn't let them shatter me anymore.

"That fucker needs to pay for using you like that and then kicking you to the curb. What's his name?"

Aaron and I both come to a halt. Dominik's voice distracts us from entering a potential shouting match that could have ignited in just a matter of seconds. Although, I'm uncertain whether my brother would ever raise his voice at me. I've always been the one with a quick temper—the storm—while he remains the calming presence.

"It's fine. It's done," I say, grabbing the bottle of wine.

"It's not fine. We'll take care of it," Tristan pipes up.

"No, you won't." I glare at him, welcoming the tart burn from the red wine as I tip the bottle back.

"You're going to get drunk," Aaron says, reaching for the bottle.

"That's kind of the idea."

"I think you need to sleep it off. A lot has happened, and you're probably still processing everything. I can take you out around New York and Hudson Yards, show you everything and hopefully get you excited for a fresh start." Aaron actually smiles. His kind offer is genuine, which makes it so hard to stay mad at him.

I don't want to fight with him after just getting here. Especially not in front of his friends.

I nod. "You're right. I'm sorry."

"Do you want some food?"

I shake my head.

"Enjoy guys' night," I say to the room as I turn around and head for the hallway toward my room.

42

Rounding the corner and turning for the bedrooms in the back of the condo, I glance over my shoulder to find a pair of dual-colored eyes on me. Has he been watching me the entire time? A painful expression flashes on Dominik's face, but he doesn't turn away from me, and for a second, I slow down, not wanting to break his gaze. Butterflies stir in my stomach uncomfortably before I remind them that Dominik is not someone I can ever touch.

He doesn't want me.

Never has, never will.

CHAPTER 5
ZOE

Aaron's tiniest guest room dwarfs my entire one-bedroom apartment in Boston. That's not saying much considering my measly salary, but it's mind-boggling to realize how well-off my brother is, and he's just two years older than me. Maybe my parents were onto something from the beginning.

Maybe they were right, that I would never amount to anything.

"You're a worthless piece of garbage, Zoe. When are you going to fix your shit?"

They're just words from the past. They don't mean anything.

Then how come I can't forget them no matter how much time passes or how hard I try?

Chugging wine straight from the bottle, I take in the giant walk-in closet and the most luxurious en suite I've ever seen in real life. Honestly, I would be content living out the rest of my days in this bathroom alone. The walls are covered in warm stone, giving off a feeling of endless relaxation, as if I've just stepped inside a luxurious spa. It even smells like one with the fresh bundle of eucalyptus hanging from the rain shower head.

Turning on the gold faucet, I watch the crystal-clear water pool in the large sink bowl. There isn't a single speck of dust or mark of water anywhere. I'm not even sure if this bathroom has been used once since Aaron took possession. It still has that new home smell even though it's been a few years.

Glaring at my reflection in the mirror, I feel nothing. Alcohol is amazing for numbing your senses until the next day when shame settles in. My hair is dull, my eyes are cold and lifeless, nothing about me feels good right now.

Has it ever?

Once.

That night close to Christmas years ago, when I embraced a different side of me. Indulging in some of my darkest thoughts and fantasies. I met someone who changed my world. Who met my fire with the same intensity. Showed me what it felt like to taste freedom, to not think or second-guess everything I do. He made me forget who I am. And since then, I've dabbled here and there when I had a chance. But that first time was unlike anything else. I think a part of me will always chase that first high with my mystery masked lover, knowing I'll never be able to replicate it.

Draining the last of the wine, I place the bottle on the counter, wiping my mouth with the back of my hand.

Turning on my heels, I stumble toward the back of the room, hypnotized by the twinkling New York City skyline stretching out into the night and beyond. It looks like it goes on forever. The vibrant energy of the city pulses in the distance, a symphony of lights painting a picturesque backdrop against the darkened canvas.

The Hudson River ripples in the night, the water shining bright like small diamonds twirling around one another in the moonlit sky. I can picture myself in bed on a rainy day, reading and occasionally staring out at the city. Being a part of it but from a comfortable distance. I'll never even come close to owning a home like this, but standing here now, I get the allure of it all.

Who says money can't buy happiness?

This is the definition of happiness. Emotions, love, having people to hold close, all those things leave you raw and exposed.

Open for copious amounts of pain. This though, this right here is perfection. A type of happiness you can depend on.

I jump at the sound of a knock on the door.

Should have slowed down on the wine chugging.

"Come in."

"Are you okay? Drunk yet? Do you need a bucket? Maybe more wine to drown your sorrows?"

I roll my eyes at my brother, turning to face him. "I'm fine. And sorry about...earlier."

"No, I overstepped. I'm sorry. I just don't like thinking about you..." Aaron says, struggling to finish his sentence.

"With men? Well, I'm sorry to have to be the one to inform you, but that ship sailed a long time ago."

He makes a face, practically turning green like he's about to hurl, and it makes me laugh a little. He's so weird with sex, I wonder what his problem is.

"Stop."

"What's you deal with sex anyway? Or is it the fact that you don't want to picture your little sister with dudes?" I tease, watching as Aaron grows more uncomfortable with every word.

"Let's just forget about it," he says. "Please."

"Fine."

He lets out a loud sigh, clearly relieved by my willingness to shove this under the rug and never speak of it again. "Do you want a tour before I'm six shots deep with the guys?"

I narrow my eyes at him. "A tour? Right now? I get it, you're rich, bro... I think I'll take a tour during daylight hours, thanks."

He laughs, shaking his head. "Fine, enjoy the bright sun in the morning."

Oh shit...the windows.

"Wait."

"That's what I thought." He steps inside, flashing me his signature cocky grin before partially closing the door and turning to face a tablet-sized monitor on the wall.

Seriously? I didn't even see that thing.

"Is that an iPad glued to your wall?"

"Do you think you can sober up for two minutes and remember all of this?"

I shake my head. "Probably not, but go ahead."

"This is how you access the blinds. They are on a schedule to rise at seven, but if you want to change the time, you can do it by going into the settings. I can show you in case you'd like to sleep in."

The wine must be hitting me straight over the head because I bend over laughing.

"Fuck, Zoe...will you just pay attention for a minute?"

"Stop. This is ridiculous. You've made it...like really made it, Aaron. Do you remember when we used to dream about all this? You did it." I inch closer, looking at the interface. The man has Apple products embedded inside his walls.

"Is this technology in every room?" I ask, poking the flat screen.

"Of course," Aaron says flatly.

I straighten up, trying not to laugh again but fail miserably. "I'm sorry, do you hear yourself? If we weren't related, you wouldn't pay me any mind."

"You're right. Now, blinds." He rattles on, and I do my best to focus, but my brain is fuzzy, and the last thing I care about right now are the blinds. That seems like future Zoe's problem, and currently, I just want to get more wine, put on my headphones, and dance in the dark.

Nodding along, I pray my brother finishes his speech and leaves the room as soon as possible. I'm also thinking about the soaker tub in the bathroom and how wonderful it would feel to take a bath right now. After a full day of travel, it's exactly what my body needs. Maybe some buzz action to take the edge off from earlier. I might be the right amount of drunk to let my mind fantasize about whomever. Maybe a dark-haired...

"Got it?" Aaron's voice interrupts my inappropriate thoughts at the perfect time.

"Got it."

"You didn't retain any of that. And you're turning red. You definitely drank too much." He runs a hand down his face, defeated.

"No, I got it. Settings, blinds, up and down. Now go be with your friends. Forget I'm even here." I place my hand on his back, ushering him out the door.

His tall frame retreats for a split second before he turns, his expression changing. "If you need anything, help yourself. Also, Zo..." he says, looking down awkwardly.

"Yes?"

"Dom and Tristan are my best friends. They are here all the time, so you're going to see a lot of them. No funny business, okay?"

"Define 'funny business.'" I blink at him, closing and opening my mouth several times but decide I'm going to torture him with this a little bit longer.

"You know what I mean."

"I really don't. You might have to spell it out."

He grunts, rubbing the back of his neck. "No...forget it. Just, they're family, all right? Brothers to me. So they're brothers to you too."

"Hmm, sure. Okay, whatever you say. I won't touch your friends. Good night."

"Good night, Zoe bear."

"Don't call me that," I utter before closing the door and locking it.

I lean against the wood, unable to stop myself from running a mental list of the recent events in my life.

Let's face it, things could be a lot worse than they are right now.

At least I am safe and situated with my brother. I still have a job to go to—a shitty one, but it's better than nothing. Maybe I'll change my career once I'm settled. I can focus on a new goal while residing in The City of Dreams, as they call it. This might be my chance at a fresh start. It's the perfect time to let everything roll off my shoulders and pray to whatever god there is that I don't repeat the same mistakes twice.

This is just another lesson learned.

Maybe moving here will finally be the push I need to get my life in order and pursue dreams I haven't dared to think about. Just maybe... Or maybe this will be another disappointment.

Knock. Knock. Knock.

The loud banging and someone fiddling with the doorknob startles me awake, making my heart leap into my throat.

What the actual hell?

Glancing over at the digital clock on my nightstand, I blink several times to make sure I'm seeing the time correctly. Two forty-five in the morning.

Knock. Knock.

Thud.

I hear a deep sigh outside my door before annoyance propels me out of the cozy warmth of my covers.

Day one and I already have to deal with my brother's drunk friends. Fantastic.

Being woken up in the middle of the night is a surefire way to get on my shit list, so someone better be bleeding or tending to broken bones out there.

Just as I'm about to reach the door, another series of knocks, this time gentler, force me to pause.

"Zoe," a deep whisper.

Channeling all my frustrations into my wrist, I unlock and swing the door open, but before I can even organize my thoughts, a towering body moves toward me, falling to the ground. I tried to move out of the way, but not fast enough, as a hard shoulder comes down onto my toes.

"Motherfucker!" I curse, clutching my foot while hopping on the other leg.

Dominik lies on the ground with his eyes closed, his back flat against the hardwood floor as if he's just taking a midnight nap.

He better be fucking dead.

"What the actual fuck, Dom?!"

He groans, eyes fluttering as he inhales before further melting into the floor. The scent of hard liquor fills the air.

"How much did you drink?"

It must take a lot of booze for a guy his size to go down like a log. I wonder why he even decided to show up at my room tonight.

Then again, maybe this is his usual crash pad. But you know what? At this point, it doesn't really matter. He can't sleep on my floor.

Didn't he call my name a second ago?

A loose wave of onyx drapes across his forehead. His dark lashes kiss the edge of his high cheekbones, and I can't help but notice how peaceful he looks in this moment. Completely unaware of his surroundings. For a split second, the thought of capturing a photo of the hotshot hockey star sprawled out on my bedroom floor in a drunken stupor flashes through my mind. It could be useful later or even make me go viral online. After all, I could use some shopping money.

Ugh, it's too bad I would never do something like that. Especially to Dom.

I skip over to my door, sticking my head out and hoping Aaron or Tristan is awake to help me get this giant out of my room. I don't hear anything, though; the place is too quiet.

The other idiots are likely also passed out from excessive alcohol. Funny how Aaron was giving me shit earlier for drinking too much wine. I can't imagine Aaron letting himself get out of control like this. He sticks to a very strict routine. Consisting of waking up early every day for a workout, followed by self-guided meditation, and a nutritious breakfast—all before seven in the morning. He is always two steps ahead.

Forever on his game—sharp, alert, and in control.

Maybe tonight he decided to let loose with his friends. God, I hope so. The man is a straight up robot sometimes.

Looking behind my shoulder, I see that Dominik hasn't moved a muscle. His chest rises and falls softly as he continues to sleep soundlessly.

I'm so glad he woke me up just so he could crash on my floor. Frustrated and exhausted, I decide to call out to Aaron but am met with more silence.

"Dammit," I groan, running my hand through my still-damp hair.

Squatting down, I wrap my hands around Dom's ankles and straighten my back, preparing to pull his gigantic, six-five body out of my bedroom. I almost feel bad, praying this doesn't wake him up since I'm in no mood for a confrontation right now.

Sweat begins to break out on my lower back as I yank on Dom's legs, making headway close to my doorframe. I'm moving slower than a snail, but it's better than being at a standstill. How much protein does this guy eat to be this heavy?

"Aaron is totally going to hear about this in the morning. Fucking ridiculous that I have to deal with his friends in the middle of the night. Grown-ass men!" I mumble to myself.

Dominik grunts. "Zoe?"

Oh shit. He's awake and staring at me.

"Zoe...what are you doing?"

I drop his legs. "What am I doing? What are you doing?! You came knocking on my door and decided to pass out on my floor. You almost took me out on your way down."

"What?" His voice is hoarse and groggy, maybe even a little slurred.

"Can you stand up? I'd like to get back to sleep."

He brings himself to a sitting position ever so slowly, glancing up at me. His dual eyes cause my pulse to change.

51

"This is my room. What are you doing here?" he slurs.

For fuck's sake.

"You're drunk. Go home, Dom."

"I am not."

Leaning on his palm, he makes a feeble attempt to rise. Before I know it, I find myself stepping closer, reaching out to steady his leaning Tower of Pisa-like posture.

"Easy. You're going to hurt yourself."

A hint of a smile brushes his lips. "Aw, is Zo Zo concerned about me?"

"Don't call me that," I spit out.

"Forgot you don't like that."

"You didn't forget. You're just being a prick," I say, hoisting his arm over my shoulder.

"So brazen. I like it. You've always been such a brat."

"Excuse me? You woke me up, asshole."

He's still staring down at me, his smile widening across his beautiful face.

"It's so good to see you, Zoe," he whispers, his face so close, I can feel his warm breath on my cheek.

"All right, big guy, that's enough from you. Let's get you back to the couch so you can join the rest of your crew."

He's still smiling at me when he speaks. "But my bed is overhhh there...back there." He hitches his thumb behind him, swaying with the movement and nearly knocking me into the door.

I grunt. "No, that's my bed."

A heartbeat later. "Could be ours. Used to be mine. You just had to show up, didn't you? I was doing fine until you showed up."

Gee, thanks. "Sorry to be such a burden, Dom."

He stumbles, pulling out of my grasp. "That's not what I meant. You... I wish you knew."

"Knew what?"

"Nothing," he breathes out, dropping his head.

I shake the thought away, trying to reach for him, but he takes another step back.

"It's okay. Come on," I say.

"No."

"No?"

"I'm glad you're here," he whispers.

"That's not what you said a second ago."

"You surprised me. There is so much you don't know."

I blink at him, not knowing what to do with all of that in the middle of the night.

"Come on, Dom. I'll take you to the other bedroom, and then we can both get some sleep." I reach out my hand, and he stares down at my palm for a few seconds before he nods.

"Okay." His droopy eyes roam down my exposed skin as he walks toward me.

I cross my arms over my chest, feeling myself flush under his gaze. He takes a step closer to me but veers right at the last second, as if trying to put more space between us.

There is the Dominik I know. The alcohol is starting to wear off, and he now remembers his strong distaste toward me. As we make our way down the hall, he stumbles and collides with the wall. I manage to grab his waist at the eleventh hour, preventing a permanent Dom-sized hole in the drywall.

"Jesus, Dom, how much did you drink?"

I'm slightly concerned he might projectile vomit on me before I have a chance to show him to his bed. Wasn't he drinking beer at the start of the night? Now he reeks of tequila and vodka. I can't imagine the war waging in his stomach right now.

He tips his head down, his face close to my head, and I swear he's smelling me.

"Did you just smell me?"

Dominik shakes his head, chuckling.

"You smell good. You always have. I missed you."

His laughter makes my skin tingle...oh my God...it should be illegal how good it sounds. How did I not remember the deep gravel in his laugh that seems to reverberate off every inch of my body?

I'm at a loss for words.

Thankfully, both of us stay quiet as we near a closed door at the end of the long hallway. I go to reach for the handle, but Dom pulls back, leaning his shoulder against the doorframe. He fixes his eyes on me. I'm not exactly short, standing at five-six, but with Dominik so close, his towering presence makes me feel like a small animal staring up at the clouds.

"You seem sad," he says, his eyes fixed on my lips.

"I'm not. You're just drunk."

He huffs, offended by my words. "I'm not *that* drunk. And stop changing the subject."

This is turning out to be the longest night of my life.

"I'm not. I promise. Now, can you please go to bed?"

Opening the door, I step inside another bedroom similar to mine.

"You're always trying to get rid of me. Always running. Leaving before things get hard," he mumbles from behind me.

What the hell is that supposed to mean? It's late. I'm tired, and it doesn't matter what Dominik decides to throw my way while intoxicated off his ass. I'm on a mission, and I plan on getting back to my own bed as soon as possible.

Also, that statement made no sense.

Dominik has always been reserved around me. I saw how he was with other kids at school and around my brother. Outgoing, extroverted, and full of zest. It was addicting to watch him, even from a distance. But he's never been that way around me. He has always acted...uncomfortable. On edge, as if he's trying to hold back.

I hear Dom shuffling behind me, and I turn just as his body sways into mine, pushing me backward, my hands gripping his solid forearms for support.

"Jesus Christ."

"Hi." He smirks down at me right before he lays his forehead against mine.

I pull away instantly, irritated by the sudden closeness of our bodies. "Okay, Casanova, that's enough. Let's get you to bed."

He exhales deeply, and I feel his warm breath scatter across my scalp. A tingling sensation trickles down my spine and settles deep in my core. Grabbing his arm, I nudge him down onto the bed, and he flops onto the mattress, staring up at me through half-hooded, alcohol-soaked eyelids.

His shoulders sag. "I'm sorry...for everything. It's my fault."

"What?"

"You hate me," he sighs, his words almost inaudible in the quiet night. "And I don't blame you. I've been trying to get you to hate me for so long."

"What are you talking about? Do you think I'm someone else?"

He shakes his head, his face drooping like a wilted flower.

I crouch down, bringing myself to eye level with him, a sense of uncertainty washing over me as I offer him comfort. Maybe it's the sorrow in his eyes that's stopping me from leaving his room this way.

"I don't hate you, Dominik."

You're the one who hates me, remember?

Some inexplicable impulse drives me to reach out and brush a loose wave of hair away from his eyes. I regret the decision as soon as my fingertips graze his skin. His eyes close, and his body tenses up as it has so many times before. My touch acts like a sobering jolt, reminding him that it's me he's talking to, causing him to raise his guard...or whatever that was. I quickly withdraw my hand, recalling the strange, nonexistent nature of our relationship and recognizing that I have no business touching Dominik Lewis.

My hand is still midair when his fingers wrap around my wrist. Searing heat radiates from him, digging into my flesh and marking the spot like the sting from a tattoo gun. There is something familiar about his touch, something comforting I can't put into words. It somehow feels like an echo from a distant memory.

I should move. Leave and go back to my room.

I should do a lot of things...

Instead, I gaze down at him, finding his multicolored eyes already glued to my face as he studies me, as though he's allowing himself to fully drink me in for the first time. Too scared to move, I stare back at him, getting lost in the heat of the moment as his eyes start to travel down my body. It feels like he's undressing me, taking his time as he soaks in every inch of my bare skin.

I lean in, and his reaction is swift, dropping my arm as though he's holding on to something scorching.

God, I'm such an idiot. What the hell was I thinking? I clearly read this entire situation wrong.

I let the rejection roll right off me.

"Do you need anything? A bucket? Water? Toast?"

His eyes fall to the ground as he shakes his head.

"All right, good night."

"I'm sorry," he says.

And I pretend like I don't hear him as I turn, quickly making my way out the door without looking back.

CHAPTER 6
DOMINIK

Everything hurts.

When did the sun get so goddamn bright?

My blistering, blinding headache is all I can think about as I stagger out of one of Aaron's guest rooms. Stagger isn't quite the right word; it's more like I'm dragging my aching body, trying to fend off the urge to vomit all over the floor.

I need coffee and an aspirin. Might as well throw in a time machine so I can go back and punch myself in the face for drinking so much fucking alcohol. I rarely ever drink this much, and it's been years since I blacked out. I hate how it wreaks havoc on my body and leaves me feeling like utter death for days afterward. The closer I get to thirty, the more I realize I can't recover from long nights as quickly as I used to. Plus, it messes with my on-ice performance, making me feel sluggish and mentally foggy.

What the hell was I thinking?

It was supposed to be a laid-back night with the guys, but then Zoe appeared out of thin air, like a ghost from my dreams, in the middle of Aaron's kitchen last night. The whole encounter threw me for a loop.

Zoe.

The woman I've been unsuccessful at erasing from my

thoughts for years is all of a sudden here, in the heart of New York City. An echo from a past that's been haunting me from the very first moment I laid eyes on her. She'll be living just a few floors above me, sharing the penthouse with her brother, who also happens to be my best friend. Reinforcing her untouchable status, much like before, as she remains the object of my desire but one I'll never attain. The universe is playing a sick joke on me.

You can't have her, not then, not now, not ever…remember that.

After high school, I felt as though I could breathe freely again. Like the metal rod buried deep in my chest was removed. Leaving Boston marked a fresh start, and even though I missed Zoe, I was no longer in physical pain knowing I couldn't have her. Wanting her in that way is something I can't let myself feel ever again. It's too much. Even I can't contain it.

I never thought she'd leave Boston. Zoe always stayed somewhat close to her family, even after Aaron left and they kicked her out. She felt the need to remain nearby when they couldn't give a shit about her. Was she hoping at some point they would change their minds? If they ever did, why would she take them back?

Just thinking about the way Zoe's parents have always treated her infuriates me, more than a heated brawl on the ice ever could. They didn't ever bother to hide their terrible behavior, and I caught it all from a distance since I basically lived at their house. It's unfathomable that anyone would treat their own child that way, a child who only craved love and affection from the very people whose only job was to love them without conditions. My own father abandoned me, but even I know he still loved me in some way.

Zoe's parents are monsters. They should have never been parents at all. The way they treat Aaron versus Zoe should be illegal. And the fact that they don't see it or refuse to do something about it still gnaws at me. It killed me to see her wilt away at their hands every day. There is this animalistic need in me to make them pay, to force them to their knees and have them beg for her forgiveness while kissing her feet. I wanted to protect her, to shield her from the harm they inflicted, but the harsh reality cared little for what was right and wrong. It wasn't my place; I wasn't meant to show that I care.

And now she's here, bringing back all those memories and emotions I worked hard to store away. The moment I laid eyes on her last night, my heart twisted just like it used to, and I realized I am not over it. Maybe I'll never truly be over it. You don't just move on from someone like Zoe.

But I don't know her anymore, and she never really knew me. I've changed, and so has she. We're different people now, and those feelings belong in the past. That's where they'll remain.

That night in Boston never happened. No one can find out about that.

The same reasons from before are still there. She's my best friend's little sister. And Aaron is a protective asshole who wouldn't hesitate to kill me if I touched her. He even said so once right to my face. I may not agree with it and, hell, may even be a little hurt that he doesn't trust me with his sister, but I respect him for it. And our friendship means more to me than anything else. I won't be the one to break my promise and bring down the empire we've worked so hard to build together.

Aaron has been there for me from the beginning. When I had no one and nothing, Aaron took me in, invested in me, and believed in me like we were brothers. We *are* brothers, and I will never do anything to hurt him.

Walking past Zoe's room, my heart picks up the pace, thrashing in my chest. Her door is ajar, and I can't help glancing over at her perfectly made bed, sighing in relief to see she's not sprawled out on top of it. I notice the empty suitcases tucked into the corner of her room as well as three sealed boxes labeled BOOKS.

Maybe she's keeping everything out and accessible since she's planning on finding her own place soon. Preferably somewhere far from here.

A fresh wave of pain smacks against my skull, karma

reminding me how much of a piece of shit I am for wishing her away already.

Gripping the side of my head, I vow to never drink this much again.

How did I even get to the bed last night? I don't remember much after we decided to open the second bottle of Patron. Tristan was worse off than me; he passed out early with his mouth wide open. Or was that Aaron? No, Aaron went up before Tristan passed out and didn't drink like the two of us. He is always in control. I've only ever seen him let loose maybe twice.

The remainder of the night is a hazy blur. I must have stumbled my way to the couch before opting to crash in the guest room. I made a point to avoid passing out beside Tristan, given that the last time it happened, I woke up with his arm wrapped around my chest and him drooling on my shirt.

I run my hand through my hair, groaning as my stomach twists and turns. My mouth feels drier than a sand box. I need some water…and aspirin, then I'm headed straight to the elevator. I need to get out of here before I run into Zoe this morning.

I can't believe my first day off in a long time is going to be marred by a hangover. Once I stop feeling like death warmed over, maybe I'll hit the ice. That's the one place I can rely on to help me feel like myself, where I can shut down my racing thoughts and fully exist in the present. The moment my blades hit the cold ice, everything else fades away.

It's just me and the ice, locked in laser-focused harmony.

The smell of coffee and the blinding sun greet me before I step past the tall archway leading to the open-concept living room. I squint, raising my arm to cover my face from the scorching sun. My head pounds harder, and I groan, cursing myself for the hundredth time. An entire condo of glass is not ideal for the type of morning I'm having.

Goddammit.

Aaron is sitting at the island, typing furiously, perched behind his laptop. He has his reading glasses on and wearing what he considers house clothes. Which, for most people, would be fancy dinner-date attire. He doesn't look up at me as I make my way over to his butler's pantry, which is the equivalent of a small coffee shop.

"About damn time you decided to join the world of the living," Aaron remarks in a monotone voice, and I stick my middle finger in the air without turning to face him. He chuckles, but when I turn, he's not even looking at me. His fingers are moving swiftly across his silent keyboard. The man looks like he got his full eight hours of sleep. I would bet my left nut that he even went for a workout this morning.

"How are you not hungover? I feel like a zombie this morning."

"It's almost noon."

Shit, I slept all morning?

"This is all your fault." Pressing the button on Aaron's fancy coffee maker, I lean my back against the counter and bury my face in my hands.

"Sure. Blame me. I wasn't the one who drank tequila like it was water." Aaron stands and makes his way over to a cupboard. He pulls out a bottle of extra-strength aspirin. He fills up a glass with water and approaches me.

"You're an asshole, but I love you," I mutter, grabbing his offerings and popping the pills in my mouth as I down the entire glass in one go.

"What crawled up your ass last night?"

"Nothing."

"Is it work?"

"No."

"A girl?"

"Yeah, right," I say and we both chuckle.

"Yeah...heaven forbid you actually let someone in. If I didn't know you any better, I'd say you swing for the other team."

"Shut up. You know I don't do relationships." I press my thumbs to my temples, praying to God this conversation will end soon. If it wasn't for the coffee, I would have walked out already.

"And why is that? I've known you forever, and no one has ever broken your heart. Not like you have PTSD from previous relationships. Why are you so scared of commitment?"

If only he knew.

"Can't break a heart when I don't have one."

Aaron snorts. "We both know that's not it. Is it because of your acquired tastes?"

"Stop trying to read me."

Aaron rolls his eyes, not giving me the time of day as he walks back to his laptop.

"It's no use anyway. You're a fucking vault."

"There is nothing in my brain, remember? I'm just a stupid jock," I say, hiding my lips behind the mug as I sip my fresh coffee.

"Dominik...will you cut it out? It's me. Don't try that bullshit with me. I've known you forever."

Aaron has always been quiet and calculated. He works in silence, perfectly content existing inside his head. The complete opposite of me. I would kill to peek inside his brain for even five minutes. Learn the ways he collects his thoughts and how he manages to keep his mouth shut at all times. He's silent but extremely observant. Nothing gets past him.

Over the years I've managed to get him to open up a couple of times, but our relationship doesn't work like that. We don't talk about our feelings. We're always there for one another, will always have each other's backs, but emotions are never involved. Maybe it's the way we were both raised. Who knows, but I'm thankful for that because I can never tell him the one secret I've been holding on to for years.

The one thing that still haunts my dreams at night. It's not regret or shame that troubles me from that night. It's the exact opposite. The realization that it was everything I had ever hoped it would be and more. I don't regret a single minute of it, and if I had a chance to go back, knowing everything I know now, I'd do it over and over again.

Sipping my coffee, I scald the tip of my tongue and let out a muted curse. Every fiber in me urges me to down this drink, retreat to my apartment, and seek solace in a frigid shower until this headache subsides. Meanwhile, Aaron's piercing glare persists, signaling his expectation for a response. I'm aware he won't let this go until I offer him some kind of reply.

"I had a rough day at practice yesterday with one of the guys, and I needed to let loose. I guess I got carried away."

"Performance problems on ice?" he asks seriously.

I sniff, arching a brow at him. "Seriously?"

He shakes his head, laughing. "Sorry, forgot you are perfect and never make mistakes."

"They don't call me 'Dominator' for no reason."

"You're so full of yourself."

Blowing into the mug, I take a careful sip and don't even care if it burns my tongue anymore. No one has better coffee than Aaron, not even Starbucks.

"Fuck, that's good. This is why I crash here. This right here." I take another long sip, closing my eyes and thanking the universe for small pleasures in life.

My stomach grumbles loudly. "You got any breakfast food here?"

"Check the pantry. I had my housekeeper do a grocery run before Zoe arrived."

Of course, he did because Aaron doesn't eat breakfast. He does intermittent fasting since he claims it helps his mind stay sharp. Walking into his pantry, I take notice of the colorful boxes of cereal. There are three boxes of Captain Crunch...Zoe's favorite. I hate that I still remember things like that.

I hate that I know so many things about her, but what I hate even more is how pieces of the past blend into the now. I don't want to think about that and how I remember watching her sitting at the dusty kitchen table in their old suburban house in Boston with her head down, looking distantly into her bowl of cereal with puffy eyes. I watched her cry that night. Alone in her bed, and it killed me not to go to her. It killed me how alone she was and how she never asked for anything.

And so it begins.

Nope. We're not doing this. Not now, not tomorrow. Not ever.

Grabbing the unopened box of Honey Nut Cheerios, I walk out of the pantry.

"Hitting the ice later?"

I nod, pulling out the carton of milk, a large bowl, and a spoon.

"I thought today was your day off."

I blink at him. "Says the guy who doesn't know the meaning of those words."

"I'm not an athlete who requires rest days."

"You don't get as good as I am by taking days off. Besides, the ice clears my head."

Aaron sighs exasperatedly. "You're impossible, even with a headache."

I smile as I pour the milk, satisfied with myself for winning this round. Grabbing my coffee, I take a seat at the other end of the kitchen island.

Stealing glances down the hallway, I secretly hope to catch any sign of Zoe still being here—the sound of the shower running, quiet footsteps. But the place is eerily quiet, save for the silent clicking of Aaron's keyboard.

Eventually, the typing comes to a halt, and I can sense that Aaron is about to break the silence. I quicken my pace, gobbling up my breakfast even though my appetite has vanished. Alcohol and processed breakfast foods don't mix well.

"Dom, I need to say something."

There it is.

Glancing over at him, I shove a spoonful of cereal in my mouth, shooting daggers at his face. "Do you have to?"

He ignores me. "It's about Zoe."

Nervous energy courses through me, setting my skin ablaze

with a surge of tension. I keep my composure in front of Aaron, casually dipping my spoon back into my bowl.

"What about Zoe?"

I have no reason to be this nervous.

Aaron hesitates, carefully watching me, trying to pick up on something my body might offer. But I'm a pro at turning everything off. I learned at a young age how to shut off my emotions, and unfortunately for me, I became too fucking good at it.

"I don't know what happened between you two in the past; maybe you guys had a falling out. I never bothered to get involved because you're my brother and she's my sister, so I left it alone when we were younger even though it was uncomfortable to be around the two of you at times. I appreciate you staying away from her when I asked you to." He takes a deep breath, glancing down at his computer screen for a split second.

"But she's going to be staying here for awhile. You and Tristan practically live here, and I don't want that dynamic to change, but I want Zoe to be comfortable too. Our schedules are jam-packed and with our joint business ventures, I can't afford for you to ghost me."

"I won't."

He narrows his eyes at me from across the room before he stands and walks over to me. "Good. My door is always open, but she's also my sister, and I don't know what is going on with her right now except that she's hit rock bottom or is close to it. She's in a rough spot in life, and I want to make sure we're all supporting her. She has no one else, Dominik."

Hearing Aaron's confession rips through my chest. I noticed the way Zoe appeared absent last night, unusually quiet and contemplative, her gaze fixed on the window as she stared out at the skyline. It was the same familiar sadness that had consumed her when she sat hunched over at the kitchen table all those years ago, appearing utterly defeated and lost.

I swallow hard, focusing back on Aaron. "Of course, man. She's family."

Aaron visibly relaxes, a lazy smile appearing on his lips.

"Thank you. I'm going to try to cut back on work so I can make her feel at ease, but I may need you and Tristan to step in. I trust you more than Tris since he will try to get in her pants at some point."

The way Tristan was staring at Zoe last night sent my blood boiling. Seeing the expression on his face, as though he was mapping out their future, made me want to tear his head off clean.

"I'll take care of Tristan."

Another smile, followed by a deep sigh before Aaron turns around to get back to his laptop. I think he was expecting an awkward conversation or maybe a fight, but the truth is, I'll do whatever I can to help Zoe out.

Aaron pauses, looking at me as if something else is bothering him.

"What?" I say, picking up my spoon.

"Just, thank you. I really appreciate it. She's like your little sister too, you know. We all have so much history."

I suppress the cringe threatening to escape, my eyes falling down to the half-empty bowl of soggy cereal. He wouldn't dare utter those words if he had any inkling of the thoughts I've harbored about Zoe over the years, or if he knew what transpired six years ago in Boston.

My sweet butterfly.

PART TWO: THEN

BOSTON, SIX YEARS AGO

CHAPTER 7

DOMINIK

I'm back in the place I called home for many years. It's where I finally achieved my dream of becoming an NHL hockey player, the place I found my brother, and where I first met her.

But Boston isn't home anymore. It never really was to begin with. It was just another stop to me, filled with ghosts from my past and a life that could have been had Zoe and I been given an opportunity to write our own ending.

Boston also happens to harbor a lot of negative memories from a shit time in my life. I witnessed my mother fall apart when Dad decided to abandon our family and choose his own happiness. He ended up getting remarried two years after Mom and I moved to Boston, and he started a new life with someone else. As if we never existed at all. That broke her into unrecognizable pieces. She hasn't been the same since, no matter how many lies she tells herself. Do you ever really recover from a loss like that?

Total abandonment from the one person who promised to love you.

And in a way, I left her too, spent all my free time at Aaron's house, and when I wasn't there, I was at the rink, playing hockey. Anything to numb the pain and forget about my life.

Forget about how I wasn't good enough for him. I would replay his words in my head every day. He thought my mother was foolish for moving around the country, chasing my dreams when he thought I didn't have what it took to become a professional hockey player. I used his venomous words to fuel my obsession. To become better than the previous day.

To beat myself at my own game, over and over again.

I pray that whenever he sees my face on his TV screen, he's reminded of the bullshit he used to say to me and how utterly wrong he was about everything. I hope he regrets ruining our family when life got too hard. I hope one day he chokes on his regrets and dies a slow, painful death.

He still calls from time to time, but I don't pick up the phone. Part of me hopes, one day, the calls stop completely, but another part of me is relieved when I see his name flash on the screen. Even though I have zero interest in talking to him, it's nice to know I cross his mind from time to time.

What shit is that? Some sort of child psychology bullshit I can't seem to shake.

It's all in the past now. Time has a funny way of forcing you to keep moving, to forge ahead and transform into someone else, even in the midst of chaos. And one day, you realize that the memories no longer hurt. You'll never forget them, but they just turn into a fleeting thought. That is comforting to me. I won't be thinking about my father this Christmas. I'm here to see my mom, have a nice holiday, and then head straight back to Pittsburgh.

Dragging my suitcase behind me, I wave to a vacant taxi, and the driver hurries out, stomping through the wet sludge to open my door.

"Good evening."

"Evening," I say to the driver as he pops open the trunk, allowing me to throw in my carry-on luggage.

"Did you have a nice flight?"

Offering the man a half smile, I nod. "It wasn't too bad."

Grabbing the edge of my pea coat, I bend my large frame

down, slipping inside the tight cabin. The stench of stale cigarettes engulfs me, and I'm tempted to roll down my window, but it's late and cold, and I don't want to piss anyone off tonight.

"Where to?" the taxi driver asks, resetting the taximeter.

"34 Highland Avenue in Winchester, please."

"Sure thing," he says, his eyes pinned on me in the rearview mirror.

Pulling out my phone from my coat pocket, I turn off airplane mode and wait for all the notifications to pour in.

Emails, texts, missed call alerts. Fuck me...I really don't have the energy to go through everything. But I need to know if Aaron is going to be in town. We haven't connected in a few weeks, and it would be nice to catch up without the distractions from our daily grind.

Aaron and I were inseparable in high school, and before I left for Pittsburgh, we promised we'd stay in touch and try to regroup somewhere we both love. He's trying to make it in New York as a realtor while I continue to break hockey records.

I've received two Hart Trophies, and last year, I was part of the championship team. Making me one of the youngest players to achieve this status, alongside two of the greatest. And I'm just getting started at twenty-one.

Skimming the various text messages from girls I've already forgotten about, I don't bother opening a single one. Been there, done that. A very small part of me feels bad for ignoring them, but I always make my conditions clear before hooking up with anyone. I never want to cause guilt or shame, but if they think they're the exception to the rule, then that's on them, not me.

My dating rule is as straightforward as it gets: I don't date; it doesn't exist in my world. I fuck their brains out, and then we say goodbye. That's the way I frame it when we discuss how the evening will unfold. The rules are always crystal clear, and if they decide to go along with it, whether we end up at their place or a hotel, after one incredible night, we go our separate ways.

I take my time while we're together but once our time runs out, they drift away from my mind. Fading into the past, nothing more, nothing less.

Sometimes, the terms are hard to accept, so begins the phase of blocking and ignoring. Most of the women I meet can't even scratch the itch inside me. They don't know about the things I desire the most. The primal need to chase and hunt, to control and punish. Tame the beast and the brat, take what I want in the way I know it's desired. This need is unique, and not everyone understands it or feels the desire to experience it, which is absolutely fine, but it also dulls every vanilla interaction I continue to have. I'm just not interested anymore.

Maybe I can visit the club while I'm in town. They usually have events during holiday time.

It's the place where I started to explore my kinks and didn't feel ashamed for the things that bring me pleasure. Once I had a taste of that life, I knew I'd forever crave more. You can't scratch an itch this profound and not become addicted to the sensation, the animalistic urge to pursue and possess. But I've become used to suppressing my urges, burying them away and paying them no mind. Occupying the void with hockey and a relentless commitment for self-improvement. That's my sole focus right now.

ME

Are you home for the holidays?

AARON

Not this year, man. Zoe and I are spending Christmas in New York. She's coming up in a couple of days.

My heart drops at the mention of her name.

ME

Everything okay?

AARON

Yeah, just some shit with my parents, and I don't want Zo to be alone. Let's catch up soon. I want to come out to one of your games.

My chest twists at the mention of their family dynamic. It must be bad if Zoe is leaving Boston to go stay with Aaron.

ME

Of course. Let me know when. I'll get you VIP seats.

AARON

Thanks, man. Have a good break.

ME

You too. Merry Christmas.

AARON

I'm calling you on Christmas. Save that shit for later.

Shaking my head, I chuckle and begin clearing my notifications when a new one pops up on my screen.

Reminder: Dark Fantasy Christmas Ball is fast approaching, confirm your attendance.

Speak of the devil. Must be a sign since I was just thinking about the club.

Clicking on the email, I skim the information quickly as a dormant zing uncoils in my stomach. One night of discreet fun hosted by a well-established BDSM club in Boston.

A masquerade ball.

Total anonymity.

A night in a place where I won't be Dominik Lewis. A chance to become someone else, slip into my dominant side and hide behind a mask. A few hours where I can cast aside the burden of being the all-star hockey player. There will be no need to be on my best behavior or fret about projecting an image that might impact my career.

A carefree night of fun for me to take control and own someone's mind and body. These parties are for people who understand the risk, people who crave to hunt or be hunted. Everyone is properly vetted and has gone through extensive questionnaires to ensure they want to be there. There are rules set in place for anyone who wishes to participate.

It doesn't take me long to make up my mind. I click on the link in the email and confirm my attendance.

This is exactly what I need to take the edge off. To be myself for one evening, free of responsibility and obligation.

Free to roam and hunt and take and fuck.

"IT'S SO good to see you, baby. You've gotten so much bigger! What are they feeding you over there?" my mother says, standing on her tiptoes and squeezing my cheeks as if I'm five again.

"Hey, Ma."

"Let me take your coat," she says, tugging on my pea coat as I shrug out of it.

"It's good to see you. Everything good here?"

When she turns to face me, her smile doesn't reach her eyes. "Yeah, baby. Everything is great."

I don't buy that. "What's wrong?"

"Nothing. Look at your hair! It's gotten so long. Do you want me to cut it for you?" Mom grabs my shoulders and pulls me down to inspect my hair. She runs her hands through my tangled mop, and I realize I haven't had a proper haircut in months. My hair is out of control, but I don't want her working while I'm here. I just want to spend time with her.

"It's fine. Why are you avoiding my question?"

She frowns, brushing me off. "I'm not. Everything is great. Let me fix you up some food."

"I'm good. Ate on the plane," I lie.

"Nonsense. You hate airplane food. I made your favorite: garlic roasted chicken with all the fixings," Mom scoffs, immediately calling me out.

She walks over, attempting to grab my suitcase before I snatch it from the floor. She always does more than is necessary, or maybe it's her way of keeping herself busy. Ignoring the painful conversations and topics like a professional.

She turns for the kitchen without glancing back at me. "Don't forget to wash up!"

"When are you going to move to Pittsburgh?" I say to her back as I open the door to the outdated powder room.

The house hasn't been renovated since I lived here. Frozen in time like the first day we walked through the doors. I remember how excited Mom pretended to be about the whole thing. She kept saying it was our fresh start, the place we would finally settle. We had to come here for my hockey career, and Dad was supposed to retire from the army and join us, but he never did.

Over the years, I've made several offers to renovate the place for Mom. I've even offered to buy her a new house in Boston or move her closer to me in Pittsburgh. But she refuses to leave.

I don't get why she doesn't want a fresh start.

The hardwood is weathered and graying, even though it was once likely a rich brown. The paint is out of style and peeling in the top corners of the ceiling. The doors have a yellow tinge to them now, and it's not because they're dirty, it's because the place is outdated. Likely harboring unwanted memories from previous owners, my own included in the mix.

The kitchen and two bathrooms mimic a 1970s style. Clunky mirrors are fused with pale pink walls as my hazy reflection stares back at me. And looking down is no better; matching the walls are small pink tiles forming the countertop. If she won't move, I'm paying to renovate this house for my mother. She's not living in these conditions anymore; it's not up for discussion.

Washing my hands, I shoot a hostile look at my reflection in the mirror, recognizing the dark circles beneath my eyes and my unkempt, ebony hair. I briefly contemplate letting my mother cut it but remember why I don't normally cut it short. Because of something I overheard Zoe say once when she thought she was home alone. She didn't realize I was nearby. I always tried to grab a few extra moments with her when Aaron wasn't around. Even if she wasn't aware I was there, in true stalker fashion.

I think that's when my obsession to watch her first began.

She was talking to her friend on the phone, likely telling her I had stayed the night again because I basically lived at the Jackson residence. She said I was a jerk, and then she laughed. I think I miss the sound of her laughter the most. It's been three years since I've seen her, but the ache deep in my chest is just as painful as the first day I left.

"No, I don't think he's hot."

Another intoxicating laugh.

"He really does have great hair though, doesn't he? I need to get the name of his stylist because the way his curls fall over his forehead just make his eyes pop, or maybe it's because his hair is black and his eyes are so bright."

A grunt. "Shut up, they are unique. His hair is beautiful too. Too bad he has no manners. Oh my God, Em...you better not tell anyone I said that or I'll kill you."

I still smirk whenever I recall that day. After slipping back into Aaron's room, I lay on the floor, gazing at the ceiling for hours and grinning like a complete idiot, knowing her bratty attitude was merely a façade. If she noticed the little things, it meant she was contemplating the bigger ones too. That was around the time my needs began to surface. I couldn't help but imagine pressing her against the wall with my imposing frame, trapping her with my hand gently encircling her throat, watching her eyes widen as I bit down on her lip.

And that was just the beginning. My cravings have only intensified with time. The more I indulge myself, the more voracious the beast inside me becomes. But he longs for the one person who's forever out of reach. I consistently choose women who share her features, hoping one will finally satisfy me, but it's never enough. They only make me want her more.

Miss her more.

I wish there was a way to kill this desire for Zoe. Why can't I let it go? Why can't I fight off my urges? I should be able to control myself, but it was never possible when it came to her. It's still not possible. I haven't seen her in years, and I still want her just as intensely as the first day.

"YOU GOT MORE ink since the last time I saw you," my mother observes, sitting across from me, cradling her tea while she watches me try to scarf down her homemade meal close to midnight. I thought I wasn't hungry until the smell of rosemary chicken wafted through the kitchen and hit me square in the face.

"This is really good, Mom. Thank you."

"Anything for my baby," she says, yawning and trying to cover it up with her teacup.

"Go to bed," I say before shoveling another forkful of crispy potatoes into my mouth.

"I will when you're done eating." She looks down, tracing the new ink on the back of my hand, trying not to grimace.

"They're just tattoos."

"But on your hand? Everyone can see."

I shrug. "So what? It's my body. I like it."

Mom bites her lip, looking away and trying her hardest to not say anything hurtful. I appreciate the effort even though it's obvious she hates the way I'm marking my skin.

"It's okay. You can say it, Mom."

She exhales, placing down her cup of chamomile tea.

"Do girls really like that?" Her lips twist, and I can't help but laugh at her subtle distaste in the ink that adorns my body. I have around twenty or so tattoos, but I will probably get more. Sometimes, I know what I want, other times, I let the artist use my body as a blank canvas.

"They do. Girls like the badass look."

Her brows furrow and she stares off, as if she remembers something. "But nice girls like Zoe don't like bad boys. They don't need bad boys. They need good guys that will take care of them."

The food gets stuck in my throat. "That was random. Is everything okay with the Jacksons?"

She shrugs, picking up her tea and sipping on it without making eye contact. "Have you spoken to her?"

"No...why would I?" I school my features.

"Has Aaron said anything?"

I'm trying really hard to remain calm and look disinterested, but my stomach is flipping in on itself.

"Mom...what's going on?"

Her blue eyes finally meet mine as she hesitates to speak. I rest my elbows on the table, feeling it shift beneath my weight, my patience wearing thinner by the second.

"Things have been a bit difficult for that poor girl lately. I saw her crying in the grocery store parking lot a few months ago. I asked her to go to coffee, and she refused, poor thing was so spooked and didn't want anyone to see her. She finally agreed to come for tea after I told her I wasn't leaving, and we talked for a long time. Right where you're sitting, actually." Mom shakes her head, her expression changing. "Her parents are awful human beings. They should be put away for the way they've been treating that sweet girl." Mom's eyes bulge and she smacks her hand over her mouth.

Fresh anger wells up deep within my chest. No, they shouldn't just be put away; they need to be addressed and permanently removed from Zoe's life. They should be dealt with properly.

"Those assholes deserve way worse than to be put away. What did they do this time?"

"Dominik!" Mom gasps, shocked by my blunt words. As if she's not thinking the same thing about Bob and Elaine, Zoe and Aaron's parents. I've always put my head down and stayed out of it out of respect for Aaron. And because it was none of my business, but every time I hear more shit has gone down in that household, it makes me want to interfere and take care of them myself, even scare them a little.

After an extended pause, she levels me with a firm look. "They kicked her out when they found out she was dating a guy who had tattoos. Well...kicked her out is not the correct term, actually. She was apparently paying rent while living with them, and they put a lock on the outside of her door. A nineteen-year-old woman, can you believe it? Just because she was dating someone they didn't approve of. Something about her tainting their image."

I'm not sure I heard her correctly.

"When I caught Zoe crying at the grocery store parking lot, she was living in her car. She had bags of stuff in her back seat. She told me she was trapped in her room for days with no food. They took her phone so she couldn't call anyone. She was so shaken up. I forced her to come stay here with me for a couple of weeks. She left as soon as she found a place. She was so broken, Dominik."

I'm going to fucking commit murder; hockey career be damned.

They were always looking for a reason to punish Zoe for simply existing. Sick fucks.

"Jesus fuck...Mom, that's incredibly sweet of you to take her in. Thank you. I can't believe she didn't tell Aaron. It's not like her to hide shit like that from him."

Mom shakes her head, looking as defeated as I feel right now. "No, and she begged me not to either. She said she didn't want to worry him or cause a fight between him and their parents. She was worried that would have set him off."

"You're damn right it would have! He would have wanted to know," I growl, gripping the edge of the wooden table with my hands.

"I know. But it's not our place, sweetheart. No matter how sad it might be."

Of course Zoe would take Aaron's feelings into consideration before her own, even though she quite literally had no place to go. I drop my head, focusing on the dents and grooves in the table, trying to sort through the hurricane in my own head and figure out a way I can make this problem go away for Zoe permanently.

I glance up to find my mother looking over my features, picking out the clear concern in my face.

"One more thing... I found out last week that she's back at home with them. She was all smiles, acting like none of it had happened. When I tried to bring it up, she just walked off." Mom frowns.

Fucking Christ.

"That's why you wanted to stay here for Christmas? For her? In case something happened?"

She nods slowly, frowning down at her tea.

Chewing the inside of my mouth, I force myself to stay in my seat and not lunge at my mother to give her a big hug. She has always had a heart of gold, not being able to give up on anyone or anything, and expecting nothing in return.

"Everyone left her here. You all moved on, but she's stuck in this hell hole with parents who constantly abuse her, and I don't understand why. Why would she choose to stay? She can go anywhere. She can go live with Aaron in New York."

Because she doesn't know any different. How can you want something better when you've never seen it, felt it in the palm of your hands, felt the flutter of its beating heart? When all you've done is love everyone but never received it in return. She's only known pain and heartbreak, or maybe she's never allowed herself to want things she believes she doesn't deserve.

Because who would love you when your own flesh and blood can't?

"Zoe doesn't think she deserves love." And when you've lived with that type of loneliness your entire life, you become frightened to even hope for the alternative.

CHAPTER 8
DOMINIK

I should be exhausted after hours of travel and talking to Mom until way past her bedtime, but sleep is the last thing on my mind. I keep tossing and turning, unable to shut my brain off, especially after everything we talked about tonight.

Everything Zoe has been battling all on her own. Alone and likely feeling completely lost in a dark world she can't escape. I want to drag her away and save her from all of this. Save her from herself, because she would rather hide in darkness than seek the light.

The need to see her is overpowering. I know it's wrong. That I have no business showing up to check in on her, but I need to make sure she's okay. Because after everything life has thrown at her, she still gets up every morning and moves forward. I can only imagine the disarray inside her head, but she's become so good at hiding it all. She thought no one saw the sadness she carried on her shoulders, but I felt the weight of it just by looking at her.

She is one of the strongest women I know. It takes a different kind of strength to tuck your tail between your legs and move back home after your parents kept you prisoner in your own room. She could have reported them, but she didn't…fuck, I can't imagine what that must have felt like.

I find myself wondering if Zoe still laughs wholeheartedly, allowing herself a moment of stillness amongst the chaos in her life. I miss her in all the ways.

I miss the little things she did and the way her hair whipped in the wind. The tiny dimple that appeared beside her lip whenever she was concentrating on something, or the way her right brow twitched when she was angry. I miss her like the flowers miss the sun at night. Like a book missing its favorite chapter, longing to finish a story untold. I'm a puzzle, missing my final piece, incomplete and in utter yearning for something I've obsessed about for years.

My need for her is an echo in an empty canyon, searching endlessly for my cadence.

If the guys were to find out I'm secretly into poetry and classical literature, they would never let me live it down. Athletes aren't supposed to like reading, right?

Maybe I want Zoe because she's always been unattainable to me.

Maybe just a taste would liberate me from her haunting grasp.

Getting out of bed, I take note of the time. It's after two in the morning, and she's likely asleep, but that's never stopped me before. Throwing on my black jeans, oversized hoodie, and hat, I head for the door.

Zoe and Aaron's childhood home sits just a block away from Mom's house. It made our high school hangouts effortless, especially when I faced strict curfews, but staying over at Aaron's place was always allowed for some reason. His parents were fond of me, seeing me as a positive influence on Aaron, but truthfully, I think it was the other way around.

The guy is more competitive than an entire Olympic team

combined. He challenges himself every day, striving to be better than he was from the day before. I'm a driven person, and naturally, that kept the fire growing in Aaron as well. We competed in everything. Grades, sports, likability....and even getting girls. As soon as Aaron and I started hanging out, our grades went up and my performance skyrocketed on the ice.

So it wasn't a surprise when I found out our sexual preferences were aligned as well. Although, Aaron is a true dominant, in the sense that he has to have control in every aspect, inside and outside the bedroom. He is a master and seeks a true submissive. He's very secretive about his relationships though, so I've had to piece things together over the years.

And when he found out about my certain tastes in the bedroom, he forbade me from ever going anywhere near his sister. Not that I had expressed interest in Zoe to him, but suddenly, being a dominant mask player with primal urges made her off-limits. Though, I believe Aaron hates the idea of Zoe dating altogether. He's protective and doesn't want her to experience any more pain, especially considering everything she's gone through. So, I promised to maintain my distance because I cared about our friendship, and deep down, I was relieved, knowing Zoe could never have her heart broken by my hands. That I could play a role in guarding the one truly precious thing in this world.

I've lingered on the sidelines, observing... seizing moments and stealing glances whenever the opportunities arose because that's the extent of what this could ever become. They were stolen moments within an invisible realm I'd constructed.

A fantasy forever stuck in a dream state.

The cold December wind cuts through the deserted streets of Boston suburbia as snowflakes dance in the air, transforming the dark street into a glistening wonderland. The sound of my footsteps crunching on the cold pavement linger in the night, reminding me that half the world is asleep. Amidst the stillness, I push forward, my pulse quickening the closer I get to her. It's as if my body can sense her presence drawing near. The excitement growing stronger, louder with every step.

I secure the black, disposable mask I found in my drawer from a couple years ago. The stale scent of dust permeates through the cloth, reminding me of how much time has passed since I've last seen Zoe. It's been years. I barely look the same.

With measured steps, I quicken my pace, my heart beating anxiously in my chest, counting down the seconds until I set my sights on her while remaining hidden in the shadows.

The familiar Jackson brick home is nestled in a quiet corner of a dead-end street, shrouded in tall trees and shadows. I shove my body behind some trees in the back, seeking out one particular window in the corner of the home, hoping Zoe is home.

Anticipation courses through my skin, setting every nerve on edge.

This was a mistake. Being here only amplifies my desire for her. Time did little to diminish my longing for Zoe, it's never been a factor for me.

You have to stay away. That's the only way.

Ignoring the voice in my head, I focus my eyes on her room which is shrouded in darkness. No light or movements. Pulling out my phone, I notice it's close to three in the morning. She's either out or passed out already. But I have a feeling she's not home. Zoe always used to sleep with some sort of night-light. And if she's not asleep in her bed with her light on, then where the fuck is she?

My thoughts scatter at the sight of headlights rounding the corner, halting in front of her house. A couple of minutes later, Zoe steps out of the car. She turns, waving to the driver, and it's as if the world takes a pause. My breath catches in my throat as I take in the sight of her. Golden tendrils of hair cascade around her in flawless curls, framing her face like a halo, even in the darkness of the night. From where I'm standing, I can see the faint, rosy hue on her cheeks and her full, crimson lips.

Zoe was always a thing of beauty, but this version of her reeks of pure sophistication, heightened by the form-fitting black dress she's wearing. Her black coat is draped over her shoulders, its buttons abandoned as if she was in a hurry to leave.

I wonder where she was tonight. Who she was with. I wonder if I got close enough to her, if she would smell like another man. Why does the thought of another man touching her make me want to hurt someone? Break fingers? Zoe is not mine to keep or control. I have no right to feel this way, but I can't help this possessiveness toward her.

She belongs to me. She's always belonged to me.

I watch as her delicate fingers fumble in her handbag, searching for her keys. The flickering streetlight kisses her cheeks as shadows dance around her. She's still such an enigma to me, and with every movement, she commands my thoughts and attention. She is a siren who calls to me, and no matter where I am, I will always come for her.

She can never hide from me.

Resting against a chilled tree, I watch her vanish into the house, only to reemerge a few minutes later in her bedroom. As she shuts the door behind her, the soft glow of the lamp on her bedside table flickers to life. My heart aches with a type of longing I don't understand. I wish I could be inside that room with her, holding her, touching her, kissing her. I want her in more ways than one, but instead of experiencing any of that, I stand here like a fucking psychopath, watching her. Guarding her and wishing I could protect her from the world. But we have always been fated for nothing more than this—stolen moments in the shadows, where she's oblivious to my very existence and how I feel about her.

Does she even think of me still? Do I ever cross her mind?

With each passing moment, the chill of the winter night seeps deeper into my bones. But the cold doesn't bother me, not against the fire raging in my soul. I carry the weight of a million unspoken words, never having the courage to obtain the one thing I truly want. I'm a coward who's afraid of getting too close, and it's in these moments that I regret the choices of my past. Fearful of losing the only people who've made me feel a sense of belonging, I choose to observe her from afar rather than risk losing them both. I made peace with this choice long ago, and I have to stay on course.

I'll do what I've always done, remaining far away, a solitary guardian of her happiness.

CHAPTER 9
ZOE

The car slows down as we approach the iron gates. Two cameras point directly at the vehicle as the gates creak open, revealing a long, winding driveway lined with towering trees. My heart drums in my chest as I quickly glance down at my phone for the millionth time, trying to decide if I should order the driver to turn around. My anxiety over all of this is killing me tonight.

I want to be here. I've been wanting to do this for so long. This wasn't a spur-of-the-moment decision, so why am I having cold feet now? I'm overthinking it.

Tonight, I'm free to do whatever my heart desires. As long as I can find a compatible and willing partner, someone trustworthy and willing to play along, I want to dip my toes properly into the BDSM world. Find out if reality is just as good as fantasy.

Once I enter this place, I will no longer be Zoe Jackson, the girl who is struggling to hold it together. I don't feel shame for my kinks or the deep-rooted desires I crave. I'm choosing to hide behind an elegant dress and a mask, taking on a new identity, a stronger woman who takes pleasure in exploring her wild side. There is no shame in that, only beauty.

Freedom to give in to temptation and every dark fantasy.

The car continues forward as I tilt my head, looking up at the full moon glowing in the dark sky, knowing the night is just beginning. I can't wait to find out what's waiting for me inside the mansion we're approaching.

The fact that I went through an extensive vetting process and received an exclusive invitation for tonight makes me feel more at ease about showing up here alone. This masquerade ball has been months in the making, and I'm lucky to be here.

Looking behind me, I watch as the outside world fades into darkness, as though I'm entering a different realm altogether. Taking in the meticulously manicured gardens on either side of the long driveway, I note all the lighting spread across the estate. There is a red flag in the distance, close to what appears to be a tall, green maze. Could that be where the chase happens? Primal play was outlined clearly as one of the activities for tonight.

My stomach churns with equal excitement and fear, knowing the main reason I opted for tonight's event was so I could take part in the outdoor chase. I spoke to the event coordinator several times, and she assured me I am free to watch if that's all I want to do, or if the mood strikes me, I can join in on the fun. The fact that I have control over tonight brings a certain level of comfort. Considering I'm a woman with zero experience, driven by fantasy alone, it's important to keep my safety and the safety of those around me at the forefront of my mind. Safety coordinators will also be there tonight, making sure everyone remains unharmed and consent is exchanged between all players involved.

I've been reminding myself of these facts for the last three days. Saying I am nervous and filled with anxiety is an understatement, but I'll take this distraction any day. I have this need to have someone force my mind to quiet, to shut down and remove all the weight from pulling me under.

I want to feel alive. To forget who I am and where I come from. To forget that no one has ever loved me, chosen me, stayed with me…to forget that if I were to disappear tomorrow, no one would even care. No matter what happens, life will rearrange itself to fill my absence, and that thought alone is terribly sad. I'm tired of being sad and angry all the time. I want to feel desired, pleasure, excitement...I want to feel truly wanted, even if it's for one night.

The massive manor finally comes into sight, stealing my breath as I stand in awe of the towering Gothic Revival architecture. Having studied buildings like this for years, the wannabe architect inside me can't help but drool. I wouldn't mind spending the entire night exploring every intricate detail of this remarkable structure.

"Wow," the driver whispers, his voice startling me.

"I know."

The car stops, and the driver turns, waiting for me to exit the car.

"What do I owe you?"

He shakes his head. "Nothing. It's all covered. Have a good night."

Grinning, I feel a flush creeping across my face as I give one final glance over my deep-red, skintight dress. The slit, starting at the top of my thigh, descends gracefully down to my black heels. I briefly check to ensure everything's in place, adjusting my dress. Picking up the black-and-red masquerade mask adorned with delicate crystals from the seat beside me, I secure it firmly to my face.

"Thank you." With a shaky hand, I pull on the handle.

Grabbing my clutch and stepping out of the vehicle, I'm distracted by the majestic mansion, taking in its tall spires which appear to be kissing the sky. A true, fairy-tale castle come to life; as though I've been transported back in time to the 1800s and am about to attend one of the many lavish balls from The *Vampire Diaries*.

With unstable legs, I pinch the side of my dress and walk up the marble staircase leading to the most beautiful wooden doors I've ever seen. The swirls and carvings are so acutely elaborate, they could only have been carved by an artist. The doors are triple my size, and at each end, stands a man, both dressed in all black suits with simple, matte black masks.

I pull out my discreet, black invitation card, as one of the doormen approaches me with a small device. He scans the seemingly empty black card, and before I finish that thought, a light shines down, highlighting a holographic barcode. The man looks up at me and gives me an expressionless nod. The other man opens the door for me, and I take one last look over my shoulder, watching the taillights of the car disappear down the empty driveway.

Here we go.

DOMINIK

THIS FEELS SURREAL, like a hallucination.

Not a single drop of liquor has passed my lips, so I can't blame it on alcohol.

But it can't possibly be her, can it?

I recognized her figure from afar, the unique way she moves, the gleam of her hair... It must be her.

What the fuck is she doing here? Is she lost? Did someone invite her here under false pretenses?

There would be one dead giveaway to know for sure it's Zoe—a small, purple butterfly tattoo on the inside of her left wrist—but she's too far away for me to spot it.

My eyes track her around the dark room as she reluctantly hands her invitation card and her cellphone to the blonde sitting behind the propped-up desk in the front foyer. The club owners rented this estate forty minutes outside of the city limits, knowing the players would want to let loose tonight. Special events like this don't happen often, and no one would be able to get in without being vetted prior to the event or personally invited by someone. I need to know which one of these assholes let in a nineteen-year-old, vanilla woman. And after that, I need to corner Zoe to find out why the hell she would think it's a good idea to attend a BDSM party alone.

She can't know you're here.

Goddammit.

If it's Zoe and she's here alone…

No…this can't happen. She won't identify me in this guise—these brown contacts I wear to obscure my distinctive eyes and the mask that conceals half my face. I'm doubly disguised tonight, feeling the need to cover my tracks more thoroughly, aware that I could be easily recognized here. I even allowed Mom to cut my hair, opting for a style that would make it harder for people to spot me. She trimmed the sides short, leaving the top slightly longer.

I thought I was being a bit too paranoid, but as luck would have it, my best friend's little sister just walked through the doors.

Fucking hell.

She's still off-limits to you.

What if she came here on her own? Does she desire to be used? Forced to submit like a good toy? Does she ache to be cherished and fucked by two men at the same time? Does she want to be hunted and chased by a primal beast? I want to climb inside her head and discover all her dirty kinks.

It doesn't appear she's here with anyone. She's walking around, not bothering to search for anyone. Which would mean she's here to find someone to play with.

It doesn't matter. No one is going to touch her tonight, and that includes me.

I made a promise to Aaron that I would keep his sister safe, and that is exactly what I plan to do. Before I do anything irrational, I need to make sure it's really her. I was really hoping to blow off some steam tonight, but I guess any plans of that happening just went down the shitter.

I'll need some drinks if I'm going to be on babysitting duty all night.

The atmosphere inside this lush estate is similar to the club this group owns in downtown Boston. Dark, marble floors line the open-concept space, with thick, red curtains covering the windows, providing ample privacy for everyone who plans to indulge in all the various types of activities tonight. Everyone is here to let the darkest parts of themselves out. It doesn't matter who we are or what awaits us tomorrow; we left all of that behind as soon as we walked through those double doors. Coming here with clear purpose and intent. It's been too long since I've let my primal out, and now that Zoe is here, there is no way in hell I'm touching anyone else. The mere thought of it makes my skin crawl.

Goddammit.

I shift further back against the dimly lit hallway, blending in perfectly with the shadows as I watch groups of people dressed in elegant, colorful gowns and sharp, classy suits trickle through. As my mystery woman turns to face the grand staircase, she's bathed in the warm, golden light of the crystal chandeliers hanging above her, casting her in a glowing aura which has me captivated. I take in her widened eyes and the small dimple that appears in the corner of her mouth. She turns toward me, biting down on those ruby lips, confirming what I knew all along.

It's definitely Zoe.

I don't even need to see her tattoo to know it's her. I have never seen such bright green eyes in my life. So vibrant and breathtaking. She's the embodiment of elegance and allure, and I can't get enough of her.

She's wearing a tight, deep-red gown, highlighting the contours of her body perfectly as it clings to every curve with an intimacy that makes my cock twitch. The silky fabric flows like water as she slowly moves toward the oak stairs, her eyes constantly bouncing from one thing to the next.

Another telltale sign this is Zoe: she's fascinated by interior design and architecture. I've been meaning to ask Aaron if that's what she's studying in school, but there hasn't been a good time to randomly bring up his sister. And I don't ever want to make Aaron suspicious.

She's drawn to the expensive art plastered along the white walls. The magnificence of the place draws her further into the depths of the mansion. My eyes stick on her, watching as she takes her time exploring the artwork. These walls will never witness anything more beautiful than Zoe Jackson.

She is the most priceless piece of art there is.

Her golden waves tumble gracefully over her bare shoulders and back. Wisps of hair frame her enchanting mask, which only draws more attention to her eyes and the most kissable, red lips. I soak up the way her body moves, tracing the slit down the side of her dress as it opens up to reveal her bare, toned legs. My dick hardens against my pants as my eyes continue to travel up her thighs, thinking of all the ways I want to touch her, explore her with my tongue, taste her sweetness. Wondering what my cock would feel like buried deep inside her tight pussy.

She looks like my last fucking meal, and I'm beyond tempted to collect.

CHAPTER 10
ZOE

This place is my idea of heaven. Seriously, forget all the BDSM activities; I'm happy to be here for the soaring ceilings and the adorning murals. Entering the grand ballroom, I'm absolutely floored by the entire setup for tonight.

Christ...I wasn't sure what tonight would entail, but this is something straight out of the movies. The grand ballroom has been transformed into a black-and-red fantasy playroom. With blood-red suede furniture and leather tarps hanging from the walls, the room displays an assortment of toys, whips, chains, ropes, and handcuffs. I can't believe how much stuff is here.

There is an entire table full of dildos and vibrators in the corner of the room—all sealed and in their original packaging. My cheeks heat, and I have to remind myself that there is no room for shame within these walls. I'm in good company tonight.

There are four tall, metal apparatuses set up in the middle of the room, similar to gym equipment, but these are special. They can support a person while they're being hung or tied up for an extended period of time.

No one is playing yet. Instead, groups of people stand together, drinks in hand as they engage in easy conversation. I notice a couple sets of eyes on me as a masked waiter approaches, holding a tray of champagne flutes. I graciously grab a glass and thank the man before he wanders off.

Raising the flute to my lips, I focus on the house music playing in the background as I walk along the wall, sipping on champagne and praying it starts settling my nerves.

Turning around, I nearly choke on my drink as I take in the massive wall of masks. So many torturously delicious masks in various shapes, sizes, and colors. They serve to remind me of the one dark and twisted fantasy that I've never been able to get out of my head. The thought of being hunted and chased through the woods by a man shrouded in darkness, his face hidden under a veil.

Maybe even more than one man.

My eyes zero in on a Halloween purge mask with neon-red lights. The mask is eerily grinning back at me, molded in an unsettling combination of red and ebony. Two Xs mark the spot where the eyes should be, and the sadistic grin on the mask sends arousing shivers down my spine.

It's devious but so alluring that I can't help but to reach out, tracing the light with my fingertip.

"I don't think I've seen so many masks in one place."

I practically leap out of my skin at the intrusion of the rich, husky voice coming from behind me. My entire body ignites as soon as I take him in. A tall, broad-shouldered man stands just a foot away, dressed in an all-black suit that molds to his muscles perfectly. He appears to be just as taken by the rows of masks as I was a second ago until I got distracted. His black hair cropped short on the sides yet left longer on top, artfully tousled and draping down slightly over the edge of his stunning, matte black mask. The mask veils half his face, while the other side elegantly covers down past his cheek. My attention is stolen by his sharp jaw and full lips. From what I can tell, his eyes are a dark brown, and even in this dim, red lighting, he's striking.

Definitely my type.

Turning around to face the display of masks, I take a deliberate breath, urging my racing heart to calm the fuck down before I finally speak.

"They're remarkable, aren't they?"

"Do you know what they're used for?" His deep voice makes me tingle in all the right places.

Sipping on more liquid courage, I take a second and think of how to answer his question without sounding like a complete thirsty idiot.

"I think I have an idea. One that doesn't involve trick-or-treating."

Stepping closer, his arm brushes my shoulder as I take in the heady scent of his cologne.

He chuckles. "You don't strike me as the type of woman who would know what those activities might include."

A little judgmental of him to assume I'm green. He's not wrong, though.

"And how would you know that?"

His eyes lock directly onto mine, almost causing me to lose my balance. They're a different shade of brown, one I've never seen before. But then again, maybe it's the red lighting in the room.

Fuck, he's hot. Too hot.

There is something about him that's giving me déjà vu. Have I met this man before? It's possible but unlikely. I don't know anyone who is adventurous enough for this lifestyle.

He quirks a brow at me, a soft smile dancing on his lips. "You reek of innocence. Do you know what primal play entails?"

Raising my glass to my lips, I finish the last of my drink and swallow hard. This guy thinks he knows me, and I'm about to prove him wrong.

"Primal play is a form of consensual role-playing that explores our primitive instincts, our raw and unfiltered needs. It forces willing participants to tap into their animalistic side. Sometimes, it might involve a chase in the woods, slipping into the roles of predator and prey. There might be biting, wrestling, clawing, growling, and other forms of physical contact to help tap into that untouched side. It can be intense and often requires a lot of trust, since we're going based off of our inhibitions and acting on instinct."

He looks surprised, but that also wins me a smirk. "Impressive. You've done your research."

I narrow my eyes at him. "What makes you think I'm not speaking based on experience?"

He leans in close to my ear, his lips barely grazing my skin. "Because if you had any, you wouldn't have traced the mask with your fingertips like that as goose bumps broke out all over your bare skin, biting your lip like you were imagining what it would feel like for someone to rip that pretty dress in half."

Holy shit, I'm on fire.

I stare at him with my mouth open, catching the slow crawl of his eyes as they land on my lips. Deliberately, I lick my bottom lip and watch his gaze harden before he withdraws, his body straightening as if he's forcing himself to create some distance between us.

Interesting reaction.

I extend my hand out to him. "I'm Parv...short for Parvaneh."

It took me some time to come up with the perfect fake name for tonight. Every article I researched suggested having one when you attend your first BDSM event, especially if you decide to be in disguise. Parvaneh is a girl's name, which originates from Persia and directly translates to butterfly in English. And since I've been obsessed with butterflies since I can remember, it was a no-brainer.

Mr. Tall, Dark, and Handsome stares down at my hand for a second too long before finally shaking it.

"What a beautiful name."

"Thank you."

"What does it mean?" His thumb starts lazily moving on the back of my hand, sending curls of fresh desire up my arm.

"Your name first," I croak.

A dark chuckle slips past his lips as he releases my hand and reaches for his phone. His mask is briefly bathed in the glow from his screen. He is likely looking up the meaning behind my fake name. Not that it matters.

Something shifts in his expression as he returns his phone to his pocket and directs his attention back to me. His eyes follow the path down my arm, and before I can figure out what he's thinking, he pries the empty champagne glass from my fingers and rotates my hand, exposing the purple and black butterfly tattoo on the inside of my wrist.

"Butterfly. So special. Is that your real name?"

"That's not how name exchanges work around here. And you're not supposed to ask me that," I snap back, unable to hold my tongue for a second longer.

His lips curl into a cunning smile. "I'm suspecting a bit of a brat in you. Name is Runi."

"Should I pull out Google as well? Oh, wait, I can't since they took my phone at the door, but I guess you got to keep yours. Special privileges?"

"Definitely a brat," he confirms, pleased with himself as his smile grows wider. "It helps when you're not a newbie. Also, you don't need Google. I'll tell you whatever you'd like to know. It's Old Norse, meaning secret lore or secret knowledge."

"Do you enjoy keeping secrets? Is that why you're here, Runi?" I tease hoping to get another smile out of him, but he glances away, staring at the wall of masks glaring back at him.

"There are things I can't share openly. Places I can't be my true self. Desires I hold close to my chest. I don't enjoy it, but sometimes we don't get to keep the things we want. After all, aren't we all hiding parts of ourselves we don't want others to see?"

His words resonate with me on such a deep level, I have to look away and pretend like I'm taking inventory of the room. But the truth is, I'm replaying his words in my head over and over again, counting the rapid beats of my frantic heart as though there is a speaker close to my ears.

Aren't we all hiding parts of ourselves we don't want others to see?

I'm tired of hiding. Tired of the shame, the guilt, the feeling of never being good enough. I'm tired of wishing I could wake up tomorrow and be someone else, anyone else but the person staring back at me in the mirror. Sometimes, I wish I wouldn't wake up at all, remain forever trapped in a beautiful dream.

But not tonight; tonight, I don't want to hide. I want to let it all go and feel alive.

Turning my attention to the wall of masks, I keep my eyes locked on the two vivid, crimson Xs as I take in a deep breath.

"I'm not hiding tonight."

Feeling his lingering eyes on me, I know with every fiber of my being that I want to play tonight. And I think I just found my partner.

CHAPTER 11
DOMINIK

Like a wildfire, she blazes through me, destroying every ounce of willpower I have remaining.

I wish I could find a different way to describe what it's like to watch Zoe as she takes in everything around her—every moment, every gesture, each subtle touch and glance. But nothing quite captures it like the relentless intensity of fire.

Her warmth draws me in, much like a moth drawn helplessly to a flame. I'm completely under her spell, and there's no escaping it.

At least not for tonight.

And I'd be lying if I said I didn't want to play with her. Because right now, I want nothing more than to taste her, pull her close against my body in the secluded corners of this place.

Next to hockey, I don't believe I've ever wanted something as intensely as this. To experience the sensation of touching her, kissing her, embracing her in my arms, gazing into her eyes as I kneel before her. My tongue exploring her most sensitive parts as I bring her to the edge of euphoria over and over again.

I crave to make her mine in a way that no other man could ever dare to. I know it might not be fair, but I couldn't care less. I'm going to brand her tonight.

When she thinks of me six months from now, while she's alone in bed or washing her hair in the shower, I want her to get wet remembering the way my cock felt buried deep inside her. I want her to touch herself and imagine it is my tongue on her clit.

This might be my one and only chance to get close enough to Zoe to finally touch her, watch her...be with her in the way I have only ever allowed myself to dream about.

It's wrong. She doesn't know it's you.

That's true. I'd be deceiving her and breaking the promise I made to Aaron. Yet, if she entices me to join the game, I'm uncertain if I'll be able to resist. Witnessing her favor someone else might stir an undeniable urge within me to assert my claim over her.

She will never find out. I'll make sure of it.

Tonight, we're not Zoe and Dominik. Tonight, we're Parv and Runi.

Walking to the end of a darkened hallway, I watch Zoe turn to face a dimly lit room. The door appears to be wide open as she takes one hesitant step forward. Her chest rises, nerves bubbling inside her as her gaze widens. She appears captivated by whatever is happening inside that room.

Half her body is veiled in darkness as she continues to watch, not taking her eyes off for even a second.

My girl likes to watch. Definitely high on the voyeurism scale by the looks of things.

I wonder if she would rank high on exhibitionism as well.

Voyeurs feel pleasure from simply observing others engage in sexual activities while an exhibitionist finds it arousing to be watched as they engage in sexual activities, either on their own or with a partner.

There is a way to find out which one Zoe prefers.

Pushing away from the wall, I straighten my suit and begin to slowly approach her. The glow of ambient lights casts down, my pulse quickening as I draw close to her, careful not to overcrowd her. Zoe is in a trance, and I'm nearly vibrating with pure curiosity to find out exactly what has her hooked. Her nipples, like pebbles, protrude through the delicate fabric of her dress. A wave of goosebumps ripples across her exposed flesh as her breaths become increasingly shallow. I zero in on the way Zoe delicately bites down on her lip, feeling the pressure as her tongue glides along.

She looks so incredibly alluring.

It takes everything in me not to reach for her.

She steals a glance in my direction, her gaze heavy with desire as she appraises me, tilting her chin down once. A silent acknowledgment or maybe even an offering.

Fucking hell.

Zoe looks back at the open doorway just as I walk behind her, leaving a few inches between us. She trails her fingers up her stomach to her chest and along her neck, stopping at her throat. She massages the hollow of her neck, hoping to find some sort of contact.

There is a group inside the room, one woman and three men. The woman is naked and tied to the large bed. Her wrists are bunched together, held by rope above her head, and her ankles are spread apart, restrained to a post on either side of the metal frame. The woman is blindfolded as the men take their time, slowly edging and teasing her with various toys and tools. She's squirming, moaning, and whimpering with need, but not one of them is bringing her remotely close to orgasm. She might be tortured like this all night.

She tries to close her legs, and the chains rattle. One of the men growls before taking her leg and spanking the inside of her thigh as punishment. She lets out a mangled cry of pleasure and pain.

Zoe takes a sharp breath, and I glance down, watching as she shifts uncomfortably, trying to put pressure in between her legs. I know if I reached down and ran my fingers along her slit, she would be soaked.

Just the thought is enough to drive me wild.

My lips ghost behind her ear. "Do you like watching them play, little butterfly?"

Zoe exhales slowly, nodding her head.

"Show me how much you like it."

"What?" She sounds surprised.

My palm curls around her neck as I press her back against my chest. The feel of her delicate skin under my hand is intoxicating, but I'm careful not to put too much pressure there. And to my absolute surprise, she leans into it...taking pleasure from being commanded in this way.

She smells amazing, and I need to take a second to remind myself that she is not mine to touch. She's off-limits to me. Forbidden. I've never done drugs, but I imagine this is what they mean when they're describing getting hit with your first high.

"Runi..." Zoe whispers.

"Yes?"

I feel her pulse double in speed, and she waits for a long time before she speaks. "I want you to touch me."

This is better than I could have ever imagined. I'm not man enough to turn away from her, not when she's asking me like this.

"Are you certain that's what you want?"

Another nod.

Inching even closer, my lips brush the back of Zoe's ear, and I feel her shiver. "Just so you know, once you say yes...once we start, there is no going back. You're mine for the night."

As she tilts her head upward, meeting my gaze, it feels as though my heart is on the verge of bursting through my chest.

"Yes."

"Yes what? I need to hear you say it."

"I want you, Runi. I want you to bring all my fantasies to life." She whimpers and my cock hardens instantly.

Fuckkk...that is my undoing.

I want you.

Those three words will never sound sweeter. And with that, I don't hesitate.

I groan, biting the inside of my cheek. "Reach down in between your legs and touch yourself."

TINA SPENCER

I expect her to react negatively, tell me no, maybe put up a fight, but her body relaxes against me, and her hand curls behind the slit in her dress. She lets out a soft moan, her eyes fluttering closed. I'm mesmerized watching Zoe's hand slowly move as she begins to pleasure herself.

I can barely take it, her squirming against me like this, touching herself and whimpering.

"Eyes on them," I command, and she listens, opening her eyes slowly and focusing on the four naked bodies in front of us.

I could die and go to heaven right now.

My hand tightens ever so slightly around her neck, which she seems to really enjoy. Her hips begin to slowly grind against her hand, and her moans grow louder...and it's the best sound I've ever heard.

"That's enough. Pull those soaked fingers out, and show them to me."

"No," she protests.

"Yes, little brat. Do as I say," I growl into her ear.

She stops then, pulling out her hand and holding up her two soaked fingers in front of my face. Grabbing her wrist, I bring her fingers close to my lips.

Just then, one of the guys looks over at us and smiles, half his face hidden behind a mask. He gets on the bed, crawling toward the restrained woman sprawled wide open in the center of the bed. He grabs her thighs, keeping his eyes on Zoe right as he buries his head in between her legs. He laps her up, feasting on her, and her cries of ecstasy echo in the room.

"Oh, fuck," Zoe whispers.

Keeping my eyes only on her, I lean down, our lips centimeters apart as I bring her still-drenched fingers close to her face.

"Suck yourself clean."

Her eyes shift to her two fingers as she swallows audibly. She's going to say no.

But then she surprises me by leaning in, tongue darting out as she licks up her fingers while keeping her eyes trained on me. She plunges her fingers deep inside her mouth, licking and sucking hard, bringing my fantasy of her warm mouth wrapped around my cock to life. I've thought about it for years, having her like this in front of me. I've waited too long to be here, and it takes every last morsel of control I have to not grip her head and guide her down to my cock.

I don't think I can walk away anymore. It's too late for that.

"That's a good fucking girl."

Her hand quivers slightly before it falls to her side, her eyes effortlessly revealing raw vulnerability and desire. With no second thoughts, I tenderly cradle her neck, guiding my thumb beneath her chin and pulling her face toward me. The atmosphere seems to sizzle and vibrate around us as our eyes remain interlocked. The world suddenly comes to a halt as I finally accept that I'm going to give in to this overwhelming temptation.

In the very next heartbeat, her lips meet mine, and my entire world fragments into countless shards. Pieces of me explode and hang suspended in the air as if defying the laws of gravity. The taste of her breath mingles with mine, causing an intense wave of forbidden desire to crash into me, and I surrender to it all.

She kisses me back, and the softness from the initial kiss fades into something more electrifying. Her hands wrap around my neck as she pulls me closer. I want to fuse our souls together until whatever rhythms our hearts beat to sound the same. Until she only calls out my name. I want to be the only one who knows the rhythm of her beating heart and what she feels like when she surrenders herself to me. There is nothing and no one else.

A torrent of emotions overwhelms me as I finally kiss the one woman who has eternally occupied my heart and soul. This kiss with Zoe encapsulates years of unspoken words and suppressed emotions that linger despite my countless attempts to let go. It's been more than mere desire for me, and this kiss right here cements it. It feels as though our souls have surpassed the limitations of time and space, reuniting after all this time, persistent to bring us back together.

The feeling of her lips against mine will forever be etched into my heart.

⟶

"WHY ARE WE IN THIS ROOM?" Zoe asks as she sits down on the bed in one of the basement chambers. I take the chair at the round table ten feet away from her, not trusting myself to not jump her bones this instant.

"Because we need to talk before anything else happens."

Her shoulders sag. "I'm sorry."

"For what?"

"For the kiss."

For the love of God, she thinks I don't want to sit beside her because I regret the kiss. That couldn't be further from the truth.

"It's not what you think at all. It's that I need to know what you want from tonight, from me, before I touch you again. This is a delicate game, and your safety is my number one priority."

I have an unfair advantage here, knowing her true identity when she thinks she's talking to a complete stranger, but it has to be this way. This is the only way I'll be able to fully give myself to her tonight.

With nothing left to trace.

One night is all we get.

It's better than nothing, and if I had to choose, I would pick her a thousand times over. I should have picked her from the beginning...

I can see her visibly shutting down, retreating into the depths of shame, doubt, and whatever other emotions cloud that beautiful mind of hers.

Walking over to the bed, I crouch in front of her, willing her to stare into my eyes. I wrap my hands around her ankles, trying to anchor her to the present. Anchor her to me, to us and this journey we're about to experience together. Whatever tonight might look like for her, I'll be right here, holding her hand throughout it all and granting her whatever she wants.

"I've got you," I promise.

Her hand softly brushes the hairs away from the corner of my face.

"Okay, Runi. I'm with you." She smiles and it lights up my world.

As simple as that.

Sitting back up on the bed, I take her soft hands in mine.

"What are your kinks and limitations?"

A nervous laugh falls from her lips. "Getting right to it, I see. All right, well, this is my first real-life encounter. Before, I had only ever explored it online."

"Online?"

"Yes, through role play by talking to different guys."

A pang of unjustified jealousy hits me out of nowhere, and I try to brush it aside. "And what did you enjoy during all those conversations?"

Her eyes fall to our joined hands, and she moves her fingers as they start a slow dance on my skin. "Rough play, being dominated, outdoor primal chase. I would be open to experimenting with a lot of different kinks, but I do have some hard limits. Like no severe pain, scat, watersports, and no heavy degradation."

"We're going to take it easy tonight since it is your first time."

She looks a bit shocked. "What about the outdoor stuff? With the masks we saw downstairs."

My smile grows at her eagerness. "Don't worry, little butterfly. I will gladly chase you around that maze until you're breathless and spent, ready to beg me to stop while screaming my name. Because when I catch you, there is no way in hell I'm letting you go."

I'm going to devour every inch of her.

She holds her breath, and I hope she's imagining all the ways I'm going to have her. Because God knows I've thought about this exact scenario a million times over. I just never imagined it would actually come true.

"And don't worry, the masks will stay on when I'm around you."

Her brows furrow. "All night?"

I nod, leaning forward and softly biting her shoulder.

"Are you famous or something?"

The corner of my lip tips up against her skin. "Something like that."

I can feel her eyes on me, and maybe she's trying to figure out if she knows me from somewhere, but I took the time to carefully conceal myself for tonight. There is no way anyone will recognize me. Besides, the Dominik who Zoe remembers is vastly different from the one sitting in front of her.

"Okay," she finally utters. She hesitates for a long time before finally nodding. "What are you into?"

Interlacing our fingers together, I look up at her. "You. And whatever fantasies you have."

The perfect shade of pink blotches her cheeks, bringing my attention to her freckles that I adore so much. "But don't you want more? You came here for a reason."

I kiss her knuckles. "I'm a dominant predator, and I think I found the perfect prey to chase around for the night. I'm very content."

Zoe bites her bottom lip, a smile spreading across her lips.

"You'll need a safe word."

She chews on the corner of her lip. "Red."

"And you want all of this? All of me? Unfiltered?"

She leans in close, our faces inches apart. "Yes, Runi. I want all of you. Unhinged. Show me this part of your world, and make me forget who I am."

My heart pinches uncomfortably at her last admission, her need to forget who she is and become someone else entirely. To forget for even a short amount of time. It all makes sense now, why she's drawn to BDSM and this desire to let go. And if I can give that to her, if I can set her free and make her feel alive for just one night, to be the first to help her discover hidden parts of herself, then I will gladly do it. Not just the first, but the only one to give her exactly what she craves.

My eyes fall to her lips as I inch closer.

"I'll make you forget everything and everyone. Are you ready to play?"

She smiles, tipping her chin down.

"Better show me then."

Before the words leave my mouth, she's kissing me with fervor, as if she can't wait another second for me to claim her.

And I'm going to do just that.

I'm going to ruin Zoe Jackson for everyone else.

CHAPTER 12
DOMINIK

I turn around, lean against the now-locked door, and cross my arms, squarely facing Zoe.

"What are you doing?" Her brows pinch with curiosity while she sits on the bed, one leg crossed over the other, her bare skin on full display.

I can't take my eyes off her.

She's utterly intoxicating.

This is my last chance to walk away before doing something I might come to regret. Am I going to turn around and leave like a gentleman would?

No chance in hell.

Not while I'm standing here and she's looking at me like she wants to rip my clothes off piece by piece.

"We're going to stay here for a bit, get to know one another."

"I thought we just did that."

I smirk down at the ground, loving her eagerness already.

"This time, with much less talking."

Slowly, I make my way toward the oak table at the back of the room, unbuttoning my jacket and carefully peeling it off my body. I hang my coat over the back of a chair, settle into the seat, and fix my gaze on Zoe. I consciously absorb every detail of this moment, realizing it will be all I have of her later—just a handful of memories to treasure.

As if she were actually here. Sitting in front of me, ready to open herself up and trust me with her mind and body.

But it's not me she's giving herself to. It's Runi.

Would she still be a willing participant if she knew I was her brother's best friend hiding behind this mask? About to completely use her body, worship her, deny her pleasure until I'm fully satisfied? Have her begging for me to stop while simultaneously needing more?

A part of me hopes Zoe would still want me if she knew my true identity. Even though it's unlikely, considering I spent years under the same roof as her, actively trying to not pay her any attention. Making it seem like I wasn't interested on purpose. Pretending like I didn't care in hopes that I would eventually forget about how much I wanted her. Leaving her alone was for her own good. It would have gotten messy, and I didn't want to lose both Zoe and Aaron. But no amount of time or lying to myself ever worked.

It's better to remain hidden. We can be different people tonight, without all the past weighing us down.

This will forever be my secret to guard. No one can ever find out.

"And how exactly are you planning on doing that, Runi? Are you going to make love to me?" Zoe gives me a shy grin, leaning back on her palms as she presses her thighs together.

I've been wanting to tame that mouth of hers for far too long. We're going to have so much fun together.

Smiling to myself, I remove my cuff links and unhurriedly roll up my sleeves.

"I don't make love, little brat. I fuck, hard and fast. I'll take what I want until I'm satisfied. You'll be screaming, pleading, and begging for me to stop."

I look up in time to see Zoe reposition herself, squeezing her thighs tighter together, her mouth popping open in shock.

"If you want someone to make love with, you're not going to get it from me. Now, uncross your legs and spread them open. I want to see how wet you are."

She takes a deep breath, her eyes narrowing with lust as she locks her gaze onto me, erasing any trace of the confident smile she wore earlier.

The Gothic, dungeon-style room matches the other ones spread across the basement of the mansion. From what I've been told, all the rooms are soundproofed, but you'd never suspect it with how timely the stone walls appear and the flickering candlelight dancing on the wooden floors, creating a haunting glow. Dominating one side of the chamber is an old, gray, stone fireplace, its massive hearth covered in ornate carvings that appear to hold years of history. Above the mantle hangs a tapestry of a dark, moonlit forest with two shadow figures in the distance, but the details aren't important right now.

What is important is the woman sitting on the edge of the large, red bed in the heart of the chamber. Waiting for me eagerly as I approach her. She still appears to be a little shell-shocked by my crude tongue but not enough to take her eyes off me as I stalk toward her.

Standing above her, I lift her chin up, forcing her to look up at me. Her outstretched neck is inviting as I get a perfect view of her perky breasts.

"Do you still want this?"

"Yes," she breathes out instantly.

"Remember that when you think you can't take anymore. When I'm telling you to give me more."

Bending down, I kiss her, not getting over the way her lips seem to fit mine perfectly. As if she were made for me. Sliding one hand down her neck, I wrap my other arm around her back. She deepens our kiss, dragging her nails across my shoulders and down my chest. Shivers rush down my body, and Zoe tugs at the buttons on my shirt.

"I need you."

"So impatient," I growl against her lips, gently biting the corner of her mouth as she lets out a soft whimper.

She has no idea what I have in store for her.

"Can I take off your mask?" I say, and she nods, gripping the front of the plastic as she pulls it off her face. I've looked at her a million times, but it never gets old. Her beauty never ceases to take my breath away. This magnetic pull I've constantly felt for her is getting stronger, and I know tonight is going to forever bind me to her. I said I would ruin her for any man who touches her, but I have a feeling she's going to ruin me just as much. Maybe even more. The thought of the aftermath makes my heart tremble, as tonight will forever be etched onto my soul like a tattoo.

This realization should make me turn around, walk out that door, but a stronger urge forces me to stay. My need for her is unwavering, and there is no way in hell I'm leaving her tonight. Nothing can stop this from happening.

I need to feel her body, to own her mind, and to make her mine.

"God, you're so beautiful," I barely manage to get out. "Stand up."

Zoe turns crimson, and her gaze falls, embarrassed by my words. I wish she could see herself through my eyes, see how utterly special she is and always has been.

"Look at me."

Her jade-green eyes crawl up to mine as my fingers play with the loose curls dangling around her face.

"You're going to relinquish all control over to me. I'll need you to let go, move into everything your body wants to feel and enjoy without question. You think you can do that for me?"

She bites the corner of her lip. "Yes, but you might need to take it from me. I've never been able to turn my brain off before. But I want you to do it, take it all."

"That's a good girl," I growl, bending down to bite the edge of her jaw while tugging down the tiny strap of her dress. My lips explore her neck as she swallows nervously. Admiring her from this angle, I realize that I've never been this close to her before. I'm getting carried away already, but when it comes to Zoe, I don't have any defenses.

My eyes ping-pong between her lips and her eyes, which are growing heavier by the second with desire. She waits for me to lean in, to make a move, but I'm in no rush. This right here is what tonight is going to be all about. Claiming her lazily, with precision, as I drive her close to oblivion just to pull her back down. I'm not going to waste a single second of the time I have with her.

Zoe leans in close, and I run my nose along hers, watching her eyes shut as she breathes us in. Not being able to wait another second, I finally claim her lips, and she moans. Her fingers find the back of my hair, and she tugs at the strands as we become a storm of lust, with tongues and teeth clashing like angry waves at sea.

Her body rocks against mine, her movements hungry, but I take my time. I run my fingers down the back of her body, feeling goosebumps form as I pinch her hard nipple beneath her dress. She whimpers impatiently, and I lap up her sounds, getting so turned on by every whimper and moan that comes out of her.

I haven't even had her yet, and already, I can't get enough.

Pulling away, I take a step back and turn her body around, gently working down the seamless zipper tucked in the back of her dress. The material parts, exposing Zoe's tanned skin, a few freckles peppered throughout.

I'm about to see Zoe Jackson naked.

My secret high school crush.

My best friend's little sister.

I wait for the guilt to come, but it never does.

Undoing my black tie, I whip it off my neck, smoothing out the material as I extend it out in front of her face.

"I'm going to blindfold you and then remove my mask. No peeking, okay?"

"Yes, sir."

Jesus, I didn't even have to tell her to say that.

As I gently secure the tie over her eyes, a soft whimper escapes her lips. I feel the smooth, silk fabric gliding through my fingers as I trace a path down her back, slowly peeling off her dress. The dress, like liquid silk, cascades around her ankles, creating a delicate pool at her feet. With a gentle tap on her ankle, I signal for her to lift it, allowing me to remove the dress.

Looking up at her body from this angle, I take in her peaked nipples, her toned stomach, and the way she's pressing her thighs together, already glistening.

Letting out a breath, I control my own urges as I pull off my mask. Running my hand through my hair, I slowly rise, kissing up Zoe's leg, my fingertips circling close to her inner thighs. Taking her hand, I guide her toward the edge of the bed. She sits, biting her lips impatiently. Kneeling down in front of her, I continue to kiss her bare legs, removing her black heels one at a time.

"Runi," Zoe breathes.

"Yes?"

She doesn't answer me. Forcing me to slide my hand up her torso, find her perky breast between my fingers, and twist.

"Fuck," she moans.

"Use your words. Tell me what you want."

A long silence. "Touch me."

I slowly guide her to lie on her back as I crawl on top of her, taking her pink nipple in my mouth. Sucking and tugging on her perfect flesh as her soft moans begin to fill the room. Zoe's back arches up to me as I tug and pull on her other nipple with my fingers before switching sides.

Zoe writhes, grinding her needy little pussy against my leg.

Grasping her outstretched throat firmly, I delicately trace my tongue along the indentation between her breasts, gradually ascending toward her neck and jawline. Pausing at her tender, swollen lips.

"Such an impatient little pet."

She cradles my cheek as her fingers explore my face. Grabbing the back of her neck, I shove her body up close to the headboard.

Spreading her out, I grab her arm and wrap the dangling rope around her small wrist, ensuring it's not too tight.

"Does that feel okay, or is it too tight?"

"No, it's perfect."

Swinging my leg over, I tighten the rope around her other wrist, restraining her upper body to the bed. I decide to leave her ankles unbound, knowing I'm going to enjoy watching her twitch and squirm, rubbing her thighs together in hopes of finding some sort of relief but having no such luck.

I trace my knuckles down her stomach, moving atop the thin material of her panties, smiling when I feel them already ruined. Zoe moves to close her legs, but I grab her thigh.

"I will command your orgasms tonight. You won't come until I tell you to, and when your needy pussy can't take any more, you can beg me for release."

"I don't beg," she rasps.

Chuckling, I hover overtop her, feeling her nipple brush against my shirt, taking in the state of her perfect body, bound and blindfolded for me like an offering.

"You're soon going to regret saying that," I whisper against her nipple, just before biting down with enough pressure to make it pleasurable. Zoe jerks her arms, making the bed protest loudly.

"Fuck," she screams.

I drag my tongue down her stomach, sucking and biting on the sensitive flesh close to her navel. She squirms underneath me, chewing on her lips as she tries to hold back her moans.

"I wish you could see yourself right now. So fucking perfect lying here, your body already searching for release. But we haven't even started yet."

Dragging my tongue farther down, I trace her perfect pussy with the tip. Licking down her core with enough pressure to cause her to tremble.

Zoe's moans echo in the room as I drink her up. "You're soaked."

"Oh my God," she moans loudly, the sound going straight to my dick.

This woman will be the death of me.

"That's right, baby, I'm your god tonight. And you'll only call out to me, little butterfly. Because I'm the only one who can give you what you want." I collect the wetness crawling down her inner thighs on my two fingers, moving up overtop her as I coat her lips in her juice, as if I were applying lipstick.

"Lick your lips, baby. See how good you taste."

She does as I say, her tongue darting out to get a taste of her own juice on her lips.

Tightening my grip around her thighs, I pull them wide apart as I dive in, feasting on her like a starved man. Licking and sucking on her clit, tantalizing it into my mouth as I drive my tongue inside her.

"Oh...my...fucking...God."

As the rope tightens, I hear the faint creaking, a symphony of anticipation. The animal within me stirs, yearning to break free. But I rein it in, reminding myself of the endless night ahead. My gaze remains fixated on Zoe, absorbing her every reaction, longing for her delicate fingers to become entangled in my hair. My desire for her burns in a way unlike any other. In this space, it has always been about play and pleasure, nothing more, nothing less. Yet, with Zoe, it's always been different. The intensity of our connection somehow reaches far beyond the physical. How does it feel this way with her and no one else? Why did I ever believe that sex would tame my desire for her? If anything, it seems to have the opposite effect.

Taking my fingers, I press them at her entrance, toying with her while my tongue continues to play with her. Her chest is heaving, toes curling as she whimpers, refusing to beg me for it.

That's when I remove my fingers entirely, drawing one last final lick up her before sitting back on my ankles.

"Don't stop, please," she mewls pleadingly.

"We're just getting started."

CHAPTER 13
ZOE

The air is thick with the scent of desire and anticipation. Runi has been teasing me for what feels like an eternity. He uses his tongue, his fingers, an array of tools to make my skin so sensitive that I think I'm going to go mad any second. I'm a sweaty mess, and I couldn't care less about anything else right now.

I need to come badly.

"I can't get enough of the noises you make, but if you want something right now, you're going to need to use your words."

"I can't," I whisper for the eighth time. I can't bring myself to say the words he wants me to say because there is a blockage in my brain preventing me from doing it.

"You need to let go. Stop hiding from me."

Lips brush the inside of my quivering thighs before his tongue gently crawls up my swollen clit. I breathe out, my body on extreme edge, so fucking sensitive, I can't take it anymore. My arms are numb from being restrained, but I'll stay like this for the rest of the night if I have to. I don't beg for things, and I sure as shit don't ask for them.

"Have you ever had a proper orgasm?" he says, planting a soft kiss onto my sensitive skin.

"Yes."

"Internally?"

"No, sir," I groan.

He softly moans. "I love the way you say my name when you're so desperate to come. Just say those two words, and I'll gladly make you come over and over again until you beg me to stop."

Fuck my life. I'll take a half-assed orgasm at this point. Anything. Please, God...how is this man so good at self-control? I need to take lessons after this night if I plan on visiting one of these establishments ever again.

"I can't."

Runi's laugh bounces against my stomach, sending a thousand bolts of electricity up my body. "You will beg."

Something soft and cold grazes up my chest, coming in contact with my nipples as the sound of a vibrator switches on.

"Oh, fuck," I breathe out, knowing exactly what kind of torture is in store for me. I'm not going anywhere or getting what I want until this man is satisfied. He's a dominant force of nature, and he gets off on taming stubborn women like me.

"Maybe this will teach you how to be a good girl and use your words."

My body ignites the second the vibrator touches my core. My back arches forward, and my legs begin shaking. His fingers tease my entrance as his lips trail kisses up my neck. The vibrator is on a low setting, placed right on my clit, and it's driving me absolutely insane.

"Sir..."

A groan rumbles from Runi's lips. "Yes?"

"I need more."

The vibrator increases in speed as Runi pushes one finger inside me, curling his finger and massaging my G-spot.

"Need more what?"

Whimpering, I bite my lip, choosing not to answer him. His fingers, as well as the vibrator, move up in speed as Runi circles my clit with the toy, hitting my bundle of nerves in the best way possible.

"Yes, yes. God, yes."

I feel my climax rising like a symphony, my senses heightened as my eyes remain in darkness. But right as my orgasm is about to claim me, a sharp coldness hits my clit, and all sources of pleasure are stripped away. I just want to scream from the utter emptiness. I'm mentally struggling to stay in this moment, the last bit of control slipping away.

"Are you ready to beg now, little butterfly?"

I shudder at the commanding tone of his voice but refuse to answer.

Suddenly, my back is twisted as I feel the air hit my bare ass.

"Use your words," he growls against my ear right as I feel the first sting of his palm on my ass. His fingers drag over my aching pussy with terrible softness. All the senses at once—the pain, the deep ache inside me, the loss of sight—have a powerful shiver shooting down my spine, sending a wave of goosebumps across my skin.

I can't think.

Another sharp sting jolts through me as his open palm hits the exact same spot as before. The impact sends a heady shock wave down my legs, settling in between them as I feel myself leaking.

Fuck, this is turning me on more than I care to admit.

His voice carries a smile, evident in its soft breathiness as it reaches my ear. "Are you enjoying the punishment?"

"No," I whisper, instantly regretting it the second the word leaves my mouth. Because another sharp slap smacks against my backside, and a soft moan spills from me.

Goddamn.

Runi presses a finger deep inside me, sending a jolt of pleasure through my body, while simultaneously tugging sharply on my nipple. He works me meticulously, drawing out whimpers and sounds I don't even recognize as my own.

"You're not enjoying this then? Because your pussy and that mouth of yours are definitely saying something else."

I can't help but grind against his hand as he slips another finger deep inside me. I revel in the feel of it, his fingers curling and making my eyes roll to the back of my head.

"Oh, God."

And just like that, he stops. Leaving me breathless and empty once more.

"You will submit to me. I will own every inch of this body by the end of the night before I claim you. It will be my name you are screaming, not God's."

He sure can try, but I don't belong to anyone. I never have. Why would I ever want to give someone that type of power? But he's not talking about any of that. He's just playing the part of a dominant trying to subdue a brat, and I need to slip into that role too. I need to play along and give him what he wants. That was the promise for tonight.

Runi taps my lips with his fingers, the same ones that were just inside me.

"Suck your juices off my fingers, and then tell me you don't enjoy being punished."

I willingly part my lips, and Runi guides his soaked fingers into my mouth. I begin to suck eagerly, tasting myself on him again and pretending like it's his dick I'm lapping up. There is a hint of berries, but that could be because of all the smoothies I drink. They say fruit changes your PH levels and can impact the way you taste.

Are you seriously thinking about PH levels right now?

Runi groans, snapping my attention. "That's a good girl."

His tongue sweeps my bottom lip, as if he's trying to lick up whatever juices of me he left behind. With a strong hold on the back of my head, he intertwines his fingers with my hair, igniting a passionate kiss that leaves me gasping for air. A smoldering heat brews between us, something I haven't experienced with anyone else. The exploration of our lips and tongues seems endless, leaving me wanting more and moaning in anticipation.

"I'm going to untie you, but you're going to keep that blindfold on. Understood?"

"Yes, sir."

"Good girl," he praises.

Those two simple words coming out of his mouth have me feeling all sorts of ways. I don't understand the sheer power behind it, but I do know, right now, I'm going to go feral on him as soon as he unties me. Robbed of his body heat, the bed dips as Runi moves to untie the ropes, securing my wrists in place.

"It's going to feel a little tight and sore, but I'll make sure you forget about it in a few minutes, Flutter."

"Flutter?"

"Shorter than little butterfly and Parvaneh. Can I call you that?"

"You can call me whatever you like."

"You're perfect," he hums.

Taking his time untying the knots, he cradles my wrist and places a soft kiss on the angry skin. It's sore but nothing too distracting or painful. Nothing that would deter me from loving every second of being restrained. Giving up control to someone else, someone I shouldn't trust in this way, is thrilling. It only makes me want him more, to give more to him than I've been willing to with anyone else.

He repeats the same steps on my other arm, kissing my wrist and carefully placing my hand down on the cool, silk sheet. The blindfold remains firmly in place over my eyes, but I'm still naked, exposed, and buzzing with nervous energy to find out what Runi plans on doing to me next. Now that I'm unbound, is he going to finally fuck me?

The room is strangely quiet. If I focus, I can hear the slightest shuffling, maybe a bit of scratching, but the hum from a fan and some noises from outside in the hallway prevent me from concentrating on what Runi might be up to.

"R—Sir?" I feel the bed dip, and his fingers brush my cheek.

"I'm going to pick you up and place you on your knees."

"Okay."

Feeling his strong hands on my waist, he picks me up and flips me as though I weigh nothing, seamless and without discomfort, propping me up on my hands and knees. I don't know what I'm facing or what I even look like in this position. Every fiber of my being is telling me to get up and run, to hyperfocus on the discomfort.

"You look so good, so fucking inviting."

Runi's hands grip my thighs, inching them apart as he opens me up.

"Reach out and hold on to the headboard," he commands, and I do as he says, gripping on to the cold metal. My heart is skipping at a thousand beats a minute, my skin burning hot and cold at the same time, pins and needles digging into my flesh as I patiently wait for my next order.

A kiss grazes my right thigh, and I feel the short stubble on his chin as his face settles in between my thighs.

My body goes stiff, and my face drops. Even though I can't see him, I know he's there.

"What are you doing?" I utter right as Runi pulls my legs further apart.

"You're going to sit on my face."

Is he shitting me? There is absolutely no way in hell.

"No."

Suddenly, a sharp bite pierces the skin on the side of my thigh. I jolt and struggle to break free, but his iron grip keeps me from escaping.

"It wasn't a request. You are going to ride my tongue like the good fucking girl you are, and I'll let you come all over my face."

His words set me on fire. No one has ever talked to me like this; no one has ever wanted me like this. I've absolutely never sat on anyone's face before, and the fact that this complete stranger wants to do this to me is beyond terrifying.

My sweaty palms tighten around the bed frame while my body shudders as I attempt to hold myself up and as far away from Runi's face as possible, knowing he probably has a close-up picture of my vag.

"I...I can't. I don't like the compromising position I'm in right now, hovering above your face."

In a matter of seconds, he's sitting up, grabbing me by the waist, and turning me so that I'm straddling his lap. I grip his shirt, just realizing now that he's still fully clothed.

I anticipate his words, yet they never come. Instead, he extends his hand, tenderly brushing my cheek and delicately tucking a stray strand of hair behind my ear. His touch guides my chin upwards.

Even though I can't actually see him, it's easy for me to picture how he looks. His brown eyes are on me, inspecting the mess I must be right now, wondering what thoughts must be going through my head and how he can get me to break. I'm sure that's what he craves most, to get women to break and bend for him.

The silence drags on forever, spiking my ever-growing insecurities with each passing second. If he doesn't say something soon, I'm going to remove this blindfold.

"Do you have any idea how utterly beautiful you are? I noticed you the second you walked inside this mansion. I was leaning against the back wall, completely entranced by you. Everyone was staring at you. And if you really don't want to do this, we don't have to. Just use your safe word, and I'll help you get dressed."

"No," I get out quickly.

"Just know that I've been dreaming of doing this...you have no idea how long I've wanted to fucking worship this body."

Couldn't have been that long considering we met just a couple of hours ago, but there is something so charming about those words. I want this man more than anything, and somewhere deep inside me, I want to please him. To give him the ownership he seeks from me tonight.

I'll never see him again, so why am I worried about how I'm

going to appear riding his face? I need to trust this man, even if I don't know who he is, because we only have tonight to make it count.

"That's a very bold admission considering we just met."

I feel him smile against my lips. "It feels like I've been searching for you for a long time."

Those words. They brush past my heart and make me feel things I don't want to feel.

Maybe this is a bad idea. What if he finds me after tonight?

No. He won't.

He wants to remain anonymous. We made a deal.

His fingers brush down my arm, sparking fresh tingles in their wake. Grabbing his neck, I drag him in for a kiss, and all that desire comes rushing through me at once. My body begins grinding against Runi of its own accord, and I feel him grow hard.

Oh. My. Fucking. God. That has to be his arm. I'm blindfolded, so my judgment cannot be trusted right now in my current state of mind. Because if that is what I think it is, I'm not sure it'll fit anywhere.

It's okay, don't panic.

No...but I want him to chase me down in the woods and fuck me until I'm raw. I doubt it'll last long with the behemoth STILL growing in between his legs.

RIP, pussy.

"Mm, little butterfly, you're making a mess on my pants," he groans, the lust in his voice sending me into a frenzy.

I run my hand down his chest, but before I reach his belt, his fingers wrap around my wrist.

"You're going to use your safe word now or fuck my face until my tongue goes numb. You don't get to touch my cock yet. Do you understand?"

"Yes," I pant, needing to find release and throwing my insecurities out the window.

He manhandles me with little to no effort, placing me back in position with his face in between my legs and my fingers tightly holding on to the metal headboard.

"Now, sit," he commands.

I lower myself an inch, but Runi grips my thighs and pulls me down until I feel his lips brush along my pussy. He begins to kiss me softly all over, taking his time to torture me with the slow movement of his tongue. Then he starts to lick hungrily, devouring me as his tongue moves in and out of me.

I cry out, gripping the headboard and trying to hold still but failing. Runi pulls me down harder until I'm seated on his face. It feels like I'm about to suffocate him, but the second I let go, he lets out a deep groan.

"Fuck, you taste incredible. I could do this every day and never get tired of it."

His words escape me; everything evaporates in this state. All I can focus on is his masterful tongue on me, pushing me closer to orgasm as I begin to ride his face. My body grinds against his mouth as he sucks furiously, inching me closer and closer to the edge.

"Harder, pet. Fuck my face harder," Runi commands, and I start riding his face as if I were grinding on his dick. The vibrations from his mouth have my toes curling, along with the intense pleasure coursing through me.

"Fuck. Oh, fuck…yes." My legs start to shake, and my moans grow louder. I lose control of myself, releasing the bed frame and gripping his hair tightly.

Runi lets out a deep grunt as he squeezes my thighs tighter, clearly enjoying the way I'm leaning into all of this. I feel my thoughts slipping away one by one just as a finger thrusts inside me.

I quake, crying out his name. "Runi…I need to…fuck, I need to come."

"Beg for it," he says as he pushes another finger inside me, filling me in the perfect way while his mouth continues to work my clit.

I can't hold on any longer, and I know he's going to punish me for this later, but frankly, I don't give a shit about any of that right now because I let go...chasing my orgasm without permission. This release is unlike anything else I've ever felt. An out-of-body experience.

I expect Runi to pull away, but he continues to work me like an animal. Drinking me in as though he's dying of thirst.

Eventually, my orgasm fades, and I start to come down, attempting to pull away only for his grip to tighten around my legs.

And it only takes seconds for the sensation to become too much.

"Stop. That's enough." But he just sucks harder.

Runi doesn't stop. Not even close.

He pushes a third finger inside me, switching his tongue placement and forcing another fierce orgasm out of me in a matter of seconds. I'm covered in sweat and buzzing from the aftermath of my second orgasm. But he's still not done.

"Sir...please," I finally beg, but it's for him to stop punishing my clit.

"One more, give me one more," Runi utters right before he sucks on my sensitive core, pumping in and out of me with ease as I lose myself, pain and pleasure fighting as another orgasm rushes through me.

My screams and pleads fill the air, and that's when he finally releases me. My entire body slumps against the bed frame, breathless and spent as I try to will my body to stop shaking.

Moments later, I sense his imposing figure behind me as his fingers wind around to the front of my neck. He draws me back against his chest, and I feel the rapid thud of my pulse against his grip. It's not an overly tight hold, just enough to command attention.

His lips brush my ear. "You came without my permission. I own you tonight, remember? You're going to be punished for what you just did."

I know that's supposed to scare me or make me feel bad for going against his wishes, but at the same time, there is a twisted part of me that is insanely turned on by whatever awaits. I want him to punish me. To make it hurt. I want to look at myself in the mirror tomorrow and see marks all over my body from him.

But I don't say that. Biting my tongue, I say the one thing I don't mean. "I'm sorry."

Runi groans disapprovingly, his grip loosening around my neck before he disappears altogether and I collapse back against the bed.

CHAPTER 14
ZOE

After two more intense orgasms, Runi picks me up and carries me to the bathroom. He stays quiet, not giving me any praise or attempting to fill the silence with words, which is really nice. I sit on the bathroom counter as he removes my blindfold, his intricate, black Victorian mask back in place, covering half his beautiful face as he slowly caresses me, wiping my body with a warm towel.

I'm not used to engaging in any sensual or emotional activity after sex. My go-to move is to get dressed as quickly as possible and leave. But I'm fully aware that aftercare is sometimes just as important as the act itself, so I remain perfectly still and watch Runi work.

He applies cream to the angry, red scratches on my wrists before retreating into the room again. Glancing at my hands, a smile forms on my face as I observe the assortment of marks on my body. They aren't solely from the rope; there are clamps, teeth imprints, and hickeys too. He truly didn't leave any part of me untouched.

I have the sudden desire to face the mirror and take a look at myself, but fear claws at my insides, preventing me from confronting the person staring back. I dread hearing my mother's disapproving tone as I gaze at my lips, or seeing my father's disdain reflected back at me. I won't let them shame me. Not when this feels so right.

Nothing has ever felt this good.

Runi walks in, holding a pile of black clothes in his hand. He sets them aside and steps in between my legs, inspecting my face.

"Those are for you. After I get you cleaned up."

He grabs a fresh wet cloth and begins dabbing my cheek.

"Does it look bad?"

Avoiding eye contact, a subtle twitch marks the corner of his lips, as if he's trying to hold back a smile. He chooses to ignore my question, leaving a disquieting knot of unease in the depths of my stomach. It makes me want to get as far away as possible. Put as much distance between him and myself. Forget everything and everyone. That's where I thrive; in the aftermath surrounded by loneliness.

After what seems like an eternity of silence, I can no longer help myself. "Is this it, then? Can we wrap it up?"

His eyes find mine, sharp and demanding. He's so incredibly beautiful that it's hard not to get lost in him.

"Why would we do that?"

"You don't have to do any of this."

He shakes his head, a loose curl falling in front of one eye. "I want to. Does my silence bother you, little butterfly? I'm just trying to figure you out."

"There is nothing to figure out." I shift from his touch, and he quirks a brow at me.

"You have more brat in you than I thought."

I cross my arms across my naked chest, feeling very exposed all of a sudden. "You thought I would be a perfect little sub for you? Sorry to disappoint, sir."

If he's giving me the silent treatment because of those orgasms, well, there was no way I could stop them. Not after hours of teasing and edging mixed with intense denial. My release crashed into me like a fucking angry storm, unstoppable and utterly mind numbing as I surrendered to it. Besides, I wanted to come. Plain and simple.

He chuckles, and the sound of his laugh takes my breath away. It's deep, but there is something familiar about it, as if I heard it a thousand times in another lifetime. It's a strange sort of familiarity.

"No, Flutter. I never expected you to be the perfect sub." Runi cups my cheek in his hand, gently lifting my face toward his. As he draws nearer, intruding into my personal space, all the air is robbed from my lungs.

"I want you to be exactly as you are. Nothing less, nothing more. You're perfect just like this."

His words are potent, and I don't know what to say.

"You don't know me."

Runi sets the cloth aside and retrieves a hairbrush, offering a casual shrug, appearing entirely in control. At peace and in no rush.

"I know you better than you think." He pauses, staring at me. "Can I brush your hair?"

"Is that necessary?"

"No, but you gave me something back there. Trusted me even though you didn't want to or need to, so I want to take care of you. This is part of aftercare. And I want you to continue to trust me because what we're going to do outside is going to be a completely different experience. Something that might terrify you, and I'm going to need you to know that, no matter what, I won't hurt you."

I grab the brush from his hand and place it on the counter.

"I know you won't, Runi...or whatever your real name might be. I know we don't know one another, but for some reason, we're linked in a way. And it might be stupid of me, but I trust you. I know you're going to take care of me out there. But we still don't really know one another, so you don't have to pretend to care about me or my hair, or the marks you left on my body. I like them."

131

His jaw clenches, and then he grips the back of my neck, drawing me toward his lips.

"None of that matters. It's always going to be me. I will always be in the back of your mind. A fracture in time and space that will only belong to you and me. You'll have me there, always."

Jesus Christ.

Am I even breathing? I can't be certain.

His lips meet mine, engulfing me like a flame. Our fires intertwine and rage on. And we burn hot, pulling and kneading until I'm left breathless, my core tightening with need. But when my hands reach for his belt, he stops me and puts space in between us.

"Get dressed. I want to get you fed before we head outside."

He turns swiftly, heading for the door as one hand rakes through his hair.

I want to break him like he's attempting to break me. But I'm not sure one night will be enough time for that.

Dominik

IT'S EERILY QUIET TONIGHT, the perfect setting for a chilling game of pursuit. There is a damp weight to the air, which means it's going to snow soon. I waited for the maze to empty out, the remaining players dispersing after the group activities concluded hours ago. I don't want to share this experience with anyone else but her.

There isn't a single soul outside, and near the tall, hedged maze lies an open forest for us to run through. If my butterfly manages to make it that far. Maybe I'll go easy on her since it is her first time.

But then again, maybe not...since the need to have her is driving me insane.

I want to watch her flee, lose her footing as she lunges forward. Anticipation and fear creeping in as she wonders where I am or how far I am behind her. I want her mind to play tricks on her, giving her mixed signals when she hears the smallest sound in the wind or a snapping of a branch.

It feels surreal to stand here, looking at the empty, green maze covered in a light blanket of white, knowing I'm about to have the wildest chase of my life with the woman of my dreams.

Never in a million years did I think Zoe would be into this, let alone that I would be the first one to help her explore her kinks. What an absolute gift. An addiction I don't ever want to quit.

Tasting her nearly sent me to my grave earlier, but this...this might actually be my undoing.

I was obsessed with her before; now, I'm captured forevermore.

It doesn't even feel real. I'm worried I'll wake up any moment from the most perfect dream.

Snap out of it.

As I close my eyes and inhale the chilly, December air, I invite the slumbering animal within me to awaken and reveal itself.

The soft crunching behind me causes my shoulders to tense. I can still smell her, taste her lingering on my lips. I'm the predator, yet somehow she has burrowed herself deeper inside me, her jaws clamped tightly around my heart.

"Wow...you look... Fucking hell," Zoe whispers as I turn to face her, desire dripping from her voice.

I changed into something more comfortable before coming outside. I'm covered in black from head to toe, the perfect attire to blend into darkness. Black shirt, hoodie, and black jeans. And of course I had to pick up the mask Zoe had her eye on earlier. The purge mask with the red LED lights. I personally love this mask since the crimson glow casts an eerie gleam in the night, creating the perfect fear response. Securing the mask on my face, I pulled my hoodie over my head and headed outside to the maze's entrance, where I waited for Zoe to join me.

Soon, this is going to turn into a hunt, but I need to make sure one last time that she's sure about this. She can revoke consent at any point by using the safe word, but I still need to know she wants this. That she wants me.

"Are you still sure about this?"

She doesn't hesitate. "Yes. Are you?"

My heart thumps in my chest. "You have no fucking idea how ready I am."

She looks so incredibly good, I'm tempted to ditch the chase and take her right here.

Zoe's eyes light up with curiosity, catching me completely off guard. I was expecting her to bail long before now, but she continues to surprise me.

"Are you ready?"

She gives me a nod, wrapping her hair around her fingers a few times before tucking it into her sweater.

I tilt my head to the side, leaning close to her face.

"I'm going to give you a forty-five second head start. Fly as fast as you can, little butterfly, and just for fun, try to hide from me. Because when I capture you, there is absolutely no chance in hell you'll escape."

I'm going to fucking destroy her.

My beast unfurls his claws, stretching as he rouses from a long sleep.

"Forty-five seconds?" Zoe confirms.

"That's right. Are you scared?"

"No," she whispers, sounding unsure.

I bring my face near hers, hovering by her ear, ensuring she can hear my next words as I growl through the mask.

"You should be. Now...run."

Zoe doesn't hesitate, swiftly turning into a fleeting whisper of movement ahead. I click the button on the side of my watch, initiating the forty-five-second countdown. My legs vibrate with the urge to chase after her, akin to a bear watching its prey attempt to escape.

I'm ravenous, not knowing what I'm going to do with her first once I get my hands on her. Do I ease her into it, knowing this is her first time, or do I let her have all of me?

Watching Zoe disappear around a tall hedge, I notice she doesn't even bother looking behind her. Rookie mistake. She won't get far like that, and it's not like there are many places to hide. I'm fucking fast and eager right now. Nothing is going to stop me from claiming what's mine.

She's fucking mine.

But only for tonight.

And then I'll have to forget all about this. Go back to the same dynamic as before. Pretend like I didn't just betray my closest friend to get my dick wet. Pretend like I don't know what Zoe's lips felt like against mine. How her moans echoed in an empty room or how her cunt squeezed my fingers so tightly, I almost came in my pants.

But it's not even about that. Zoe is so much more than sex. This night is so much more for both of us, even if she doesn't know who is lurking behind this mask.

The halfway countdown is signified by the clicking of my watch. I find myself itching all over, unable to control the persistent tickle, while my pulse thumps loudly in my ears. The anticipation within me becomes unbearable as I get ready to sprint directly toward her.

I can smell her presence in the air, and it brings back memories of my past and the countless sleepovers at Aaron's house. It's frustrating how much I know about her, and how we remain connected no matter how much time goes by or what happens between us. Everything around me serves as a reminder of her, and that's what I hate the most.

That's a lie. What I despise the most is the fact that I can't truly have her.

I can't keep her.

I hate how much I want her, need her in a way that feels criminal. It doesn't make sense, and as I stand here, counting down the seconds, I'm not sure if I'll ever rip her from underneath my skin.

Beep. Beep. Beep.

All those memories evaporate into the cold night. I twist my neck, feeling the bones crack as I lunge forward.

Ready or not, baby, here I come.

My breath is measured, silent as I start the chase. I'm hungry but focused and charging with intent, knowing exactly where she's going. She'll likely go around the main course several times before her fear response kicks in and she ventures out to the forest. The maze feels like a warm hug, pushing me closer to her. I can already taste her. Feel her naked body beneath mine. Her knees on the ground, eyes staring through the mask and into my soul.

My needy little slut, she'll get what's coming to her.

CHAPTER 15
ZOE

My breaths are ragged gasps, revealing my struggle to stay ahead. No matter how many times I glance over my shoulder, expecting him to be right there, all I see is darkness and towering green hedges.

Right now, I'm completely lost in this maze. Everything is becoming indistinguishable, and I might just be going around in circles without realizing it. Any corner I turn could lead me straight into the clutches of my predator. I had my doubts about this feeling genuine or authentic, but the sweat trickling down my back tells a different story.

I'm completely aroused by all of this. If Runi caught me right now and stuck his hand down my pants, he'd find my panties ruined. This entire experience is exceeding my expectations already, and he hasn't even touched me.

I want him to catch me and do unspeakable things to me.

A few years back, I started experiencing a recurring dream where I was being dominated. It was quite exhilarating. I started exploring more literature on the subject, and before I knew it, this fantasy became an obsession that consumed me. The idea of someone desiring me with such intensity that they couldn't resist pursuing me, possessing me, and taking what they wanted, whenever they wanted. The deeply ingrained need is what gets me high.

Call me a masochist, I don't care. We like what we like.

Up until now, nobody has been able to fulfill the secret desire that has always been within me.

From the moment I looked into his dark eyes, I recognized something uncanny in him. Something dangerous and inviting called out to me. For one night, I can be a savage and not feel bad about it. I've finally found a man who is into the same twisted shit as me, who gets off on it just as much as I do, and someone who is showing me how intoxicatingly freeing it feels to just *be*.

Rounding the fiftieth corner, I decide to take my chances, leaning against the rough grass as I grip my knees, holding myself up while gasping for air.

I forgot about the cold as soon as I started running, but after minutes of nonstop chase, it feels like a layer of ice has attached itself to the inside of my chest, making every breath feel as if I'm swallowing shards of glass. I look around feverishly, waiting to hear boots or rustling or something...but it's dead quiet.

Too quiet.

Maybe he lost me. This maze is a fucking disaster, and I sure as shit wouldn't be able to find anyone. If I can find my way out of the maze and stop going in circles, maybe I'll find a good hiding spot.

A branch breaks in the distance, causing me to whip my head toward the sound. Suddenly, the soft lighting around the perimeters of the garden shuts off, casting me in complete twilight.

What the fuck...the outdoor garden lights have been on this entire time.

Does Runi have that much pull?

What if he owns this entire mansion? Didn't he say he was rich or famous or whatever?

Crunch.

This time, I don't wait to see anything. I stand up straight and start running for the bend at the end. A cold shiver runs down my body as fear and exhilaration intermingle within me. My ankle rolls as I round the corner, and I glance behind me just before the hedge comes into view. I spot a dark figure standing right where I was leaning seconds ago.

His mask is glowing red.

My steps become a mix of grace and urgency as I focus my efforts, trying to find an escape in this confusing, dark mess. That's when I see a small gap in the hedge.

I can squeeze through there.

This is probably a really bad idea, but I'll have more visibility running out there in the forest.

Dashing ahead with an urgency that suggests my very existence hangs in the balance, fear courses through my veins, transforming into an exhilarating intoxication. It all feels fucking incredible. I push myself to run even faster, fully immersing myself in the unfiltered intensity of the present moment, acknowledging that this may be a once-in-a-lifetime experience.

Finally reaching a clearing bathed in silver moonlight, I glance around, my breaths a whisper in the wind. I turn, wondering how far away Runi is and how he'll attack first. As I walk farther into the open clearing, the ground covered in a light dusting of snow, I take a moment to appreciate the utter silence. I know all of this will be over too soon, and I want to soak it all in.

Closing my eyes, I sense his presence before the sound of his boots reaches my ears. With a gradual turn, I find Runi standing just ten feet away. Nightfall envelops him, allowing him to seamlessly merge with his surroundings. His mask emits a brilliant glow, accentuating his towering figure as he tilts his head, facing me head-on.

I consider staying, but in the moment, my body decides for me. Twisting around, I make a run for it, but only manage to get a few feet before a firm arm wraps around me, yanking me back.

"You're mine now, little butterfly."

CHAPTER 16
DOMINIK

I find myself out of breath, but it has nothing to do with the chase. No, my breathlessness is solely caused by the fact that Zoe is in my embrace amidst a desolate clearing in the forest where her screams will go unheard.

A deep growl rumbles out of me, and I feel her shudder. Her measly attempts to squirm away are futile, causing me to hold her tighter against my chest.

"Still trying to get away? Is that what you really want?"

"Yes," she answers quickly, and I peer down at her through the slits in my mask.

"Such a beautiful liar."

"I'm not lying. Let me go," she hisses, putting effort into twisting her body.

My left hand crawls up her chest as her breathing quickens. I wrap my hand around her throat, lifting her neck up as my other hand snakes down. My cold fingers linger close to the seam of her tight leggings as I play with my food. Zoe goes perfectly still when my hand slides down her pants, finding her panties absolutely drenched. She's been getting off on the chase and standing here, pretending like she's not loving every second of it.

Is it the anticipation that turns her on, or the fear? I hope it's both.

Circling her entrance, I slide two fingers inside her torturously slowly. She lets out a deep moan, her insides tightening around my fingers already. Goddammit, this is the hottest thing I've ever experienced, and I haven't even been inside her yet.

Curling my fingers, I withdraw my soaked hand, lifting my fingers to her face to show her the evidence of her arousal.

"Doesn't seem like you want to run that far. Lift the bottom of my mask."

Zoe cranes her neck, her hooded eyes on me as I keep my grip on her throat. She reaches up and slowly reveals the bottom half of my face.

The neon-red light illuminates her beautiful face, casting her in an ethereal, red hue—a perfect representation of everything this night has given us. Lifting my hand to my mouth, I slide my fingers past my lips, wanting to taste her as I lick them clean.

"Fuck...Runi," she breathes, her eyes glued to my mouth as I drop my hand and lick my lips.

Such a stubborn, delicious fucking pet.

Bending down, I swiftly seize her legs and hoist her over my shoulder. Her piercing shrieks fill the air as I sprint toward the forsaken cabin nestled behind the line of trees at the clearing's far end. The wind seems to be working against me, ever-changing and unpredictable.

"Put me down."

I slap her ass hard, and she yelps, her body flinching.

"You're not going anywhere. You're all mine for the night, but I appreciate the fight you're pretending to put up."

"I'm serious."

"Use your safe word then."

Silence. Yeah, that's what I thought. After she's satiated and completely spent from all the times I'm going to make her come on my cock, I plan on digging into that beautiful mind to learn how many times she's fantasized about this particular scene and if I lived up to her expectations.

Amidst the towering trees, tucked in the back of the property, there's a small cabin—weathered and forgotten. The forest has both embraced and shrouded the cabin over the years. Its overgrown branches and creeping ivy seem to be nature's way of attempting to reclaim what has been abandoned.

I looked into this place before showing up tonight, knowing full well not many people know about this little treasure tucked away in the woods.

Lucky for Zoe, I won't be fucking her in the middle of the forest on a cold, snowy night.

I feel her twist in my arms, as if testing my grip, a silent challenge to see if she can break free and make a run for it.

No way in hell I'd let that happen.

Walking up the flimsy, wooden steps, I kick the door open, causing it to crash against the wall. The air inside is stale, carrying the scent of dust and dirt. In the corner of the small, square cabin stands a threadbare armchair covered in a thick layer of dust.

"What the..." Zoe whispers, her breaths coming in quickly against my back. But before she can finish her sentence, I charge over to the chair and throw her onto it.

A cloud of dust douses the air, making her cough. She swipes her hands to clear the air. Her eyes are wild as she finally glares up at me. She can't see me, but I can see right through her. The way she's nervously anticipating my next move and how she's trying to hold back from rubbing her thighs together to bring relief to that need growing deep inside her. To that sweet pussy I'll claim tonight, filling her with so much cum, it'll be dripping out of her for a day. If I'm going to hell for betraying my best friend, I might as well enjoy the ride.

"Undo my belt," I utter, and Zoe's mouth parts as she takes in a sharp breath.

Her fingers tremble as she undoes my buckle with slight reservation. I brush her hands away, gripping the metal clasp, and whip the entire piece off in one motion, relishing the sound of leather slapping the air sharply. It ignites something animalistic and hungry within me as I take a step closer to Zoe, towering above her, as if she's a little lost bunny trapped inside an inescapable prison.

I unzip my pants and pull them down, stroking my cock a couple of times over my boxers before I yank myself free. Zoe's eyes grow into saucers as she takes in the sight of me.

My cock might be a bit bigger than what she's used to working with, but she'll worship it all the same.

"Jesus fucking Christ, Runi…what the hell is that?"

Grabbing a fistful of her hair, I tilt her face up to meet the hollowed gaze of my mask, my other hand stroking my hard cock.

"It's your last meal. Now be a good fucking girl. Open up wide, and choke on my dick."

Guiding my cock to her lips, I wait for her to pull back, show any sign of restraint. I wouldn't normally hesitate in a primal play situation like this when everyone has agreed to the rules, but I can't help being more protective with her.

However, she opens up eagerly and wraps her hand around my thick shaft, pumping me while my cock disappears inside her beautifully sinful mouth.

She bobs her head eagerly, keeping her eyes on me the entire time.

"Fuck, you feel so good. Your lips wrapped around my cock like that, such a beautiful fucking sight."

I have to remind myself not to call her by her first name. But the feel of her warm, wet mouth sucking on my dick is so intoxicating, I'm worried her name will slip out.

I need more of this, more of her.

"Tap my leg if this becomes too much."

She nods, tears starting to prick the corners of her eyes, and I commit it to memory, wanting to bend down and lick every droplet. Fisting her hair tighter, I start to fuck her face, moving faster and deeper. Feeling my cock hit the back of her throat as she starts to gag. The reflex feels so intense, making her jaw lock up and her lips tighten around my dick. She grips my thighs, and her nails digging into the back of my legs feels too good.

"You're taking me so well, baby. Doing such a good job."

She closes her eyes and begins rocking her hips against the chair, desperate to find some sort of friction. This is turning her on, Jesus Christ....this is fucking turning her on and making her needy. Me owning her body like this, taking control of her.

I need to be inside her, and soon, before I waste my load down her perfect little throat. Stroking her cheek, I collect the drool sliding down her chin and smear it into her hair. Thrusting into her mouth at a steady pace, I smudge the tears running down her face, coating her temple and watching the black ink from her mascara trail across her skin.

The sound of my groans and her gags echo in the small, empty cabin, and it's music to my fucking ears.

Shit, I can't take it anymore.

I need to be inside her more than my next breath.

Pulling out of her mouth, Zoe gasps instantly, taking in mouthfuls of air as she looks at me with nothing but confusion.

Leaving my pants undone, I grab the bottom of Zoe's sweater and yank it off. I watch as her hair pools around her shoulders, illuminated by the dancing shadows of the cabin. Sitting there like a regal queen on a throne, her makeup is smeared, giving her rosy cheeks and neck a captivating allure. Clad only in a black tank, she is truly sensational.

With a firm grip on her chin, I gently lift her up and raise my mask slightly, revealing my lips.

"Close your eyes." I bring my lips to hers as if it's the last time I'll kiss her. "You're so perfect, you know that?"

She does as she's told but cringes, as if my words made her feel…well, just that…made her feel something.

"Are you going to give me praise, or punish me?"

Avoidance as usual—typical Zoe.

She wants punishment? That's fine.

Placing my hand behind her, I kick out her legs from underneath her and she falls back. I catch the brunt of her impact, making sure she doesn't hurt herself.

"Fucking asshole," she whispers.

"What was that, pet?"

Pulling out the switchblade from my back pocket, I flick it open and get right up in her face, grabbing the bottom of her tank and slicing it in half. Her breasts spring free, nipples peaked and hard as I move down to her pants, yanking them off her body. I flip her over, pressing her chest into the cold, hard floor as I bring her ass up. She tries to squirm out of my reach, and I administer a hard slap to her ass.

"Palms glued to the floor. Every time you move, I smack this perfect ass. You got it?"

"Yes."

Smack.

"Fuck," she hisses. "Yes…sir."

I drop my pants and boxers down to my ankles, bending over Zoe to keep her face pressed to the floor. Circling her wet entrance with the head of my cock, I hear her let out a needy moan as I nudge the tip inside ever so slowly. Her tightness hugs me instantly, forcing my eyes to roll into the back of my head.

"Are you safe? Do you want me to use a condom?"

"I'm on birth control, and we're both clean." She's right, we had to submit a recent health test before being admitted tonight.

I take my time, pushing inside her inch by inch, allowing her to adjust to my size before I bury myself inside her.

"Oh, God, Ru… Sir, it's too much. I can't."

"You can, and you will. You can take me, little butterfly."

She whimpers, and I press in another inch, feeling her relax slightly as she tilts her ass further into me. She's so goddamn tight, I'm worried I'll blow my load within a few minutes of being fully inside her.

"Runi," she moans, and I push deeper until I'm fully seated

inside her. We're both panting for air, lost to the feeling of one another.

I grip her hips and thrust in and out of her, deep and slow, once...twice. Zoe screams, and it takes every bit of self-control I have left to not come inside her at that moment.

This...this right here is what heaven must feel like.

She tries to reach for me, but I grab her arms, pinning them behind her back as I start grinding into her.

"Oh...God," she moans.

She arches her back, trying to deepen our connection as I pick up speed, feeling the way she responds to me as she begins to come undone.

What I'm about to do might kill me, but I need her to beg. I need her to submit to me. I need her to break. That's when I'll own this pussy, her body, and a part of her mind.

I stop, pulling out of her completely.

"No...don't stop."

"Beg me for it like the good little slut I know you are."

Silence and no movement.

Nudging my cock to her entrance, I circle the tip against her clit, and she nearly loses her mind.

Zoe squeals. "Okay, okay...please, sir."

"Please sir, what?"

"Fuck me," she whispers.

I start to slowly thrust inside her once more, but not in the way she needs me. Her soft whimpers tickle my ears as I wait for her to open up more.

"Please," she repeats.

Reaching over, I pinch her nipple tightly as the deep, primal need in me takes over. I begin thrusting inside her, hard and fast, as my balls slap against her clit. Palming the side of her head, I press her cheek to the floor as we fuck with a type of hunger I've only ever dreamt about. A new desire takes hold of me, seeing Zoe like this, submitting to me and loving every second of it.

Taking exactly what I want, in the way I want it. In the way I know she's loving.

Over and over again.

Marking her.

Making her mine *forever*.

PART THREE: NEW YORK CITY

PRESENT DAY

CHAPTER 17

ZOE

The elevator doors ding open, and I plaster on a fake smile while my anxiety has me wanting to press the ground button and turn back around.

What must they think of me? Have the rumors spread here too? What if the assholes in Boston told everyone I'm the new whore... discarded and sent here out of pity?

What am I doing here?

I don't know. You should just go back to bed. This is going to end terribly for you. You're going to be humiliated. Your new boss will know you're a scumbag; she'll think you're only here because you opened your legs. No one will like you.

Shut up. Shut up. Shut up.

I shut my eyes tightly, squeezing out any remaining space for tears. Today, I refuse to cry. There's no way in hell. It's just my anxiety, always whispering the worst possible outcomes and painting dreadful pictures in my mind, urging me to flee. But I won't succumb to its tricks. The scenarios that haunt me are never as terrible as they seem, and often, I come out of them feeling alright. Yet, without fail, the anxious thoughts persist, sometimes louder than others. At least my mental illness is consistent, always there for me.

What a joke.

Taking a deep breath through my mouth, I muster the forced smile back onto my face.

On the outside, I exude confidence, sporting a sharp outfit that screams *everything you may have heard about me is wrong.* My black pencil skirt hugs my curves perfectly. I paired it with a beautiful, deep-plum, sleeveless top and a matching blazer, ironing out everything twice this morning. There isn't a single line or speck of lint on my entire outfit. I appear completely different from what I truly feel inside. However, that's exactly what I aim for. Today, I must make a lasting impression on every individual in this office and eliminate any negativity that may be associated with my name.

I run my hand through my perfectly curled locks.

You can do this.

Fake it till you make it, am I right?

By the end of the day, everyone is going to forget about Greg and whatever venom he may or may not have spread after I left Boston. Karma always has a funny way of coming back and giving people exactly what they deserve.

Exiting the elevator, I walk with confidence toward the expansive glass doors at the end of the hallway. Each click of my heels resonates in perfect union, a rhythm that I fixate on as I twist my butterfly necklace between my fingers, seeking comfort in the cool touch of the metal as I attempt to steady my racing pulse.

Above the doors, a massive, neon-orange sign proudly declares "Bloom Management New York." Its glowing light overwhelms me. I'm not going to blend in here either, am I?

Have you ever blended in anywhere?

Will you just shut the hell up?

I stand motionless, fixated on my outstretched hand hovering above the metal door handle.

Every fiber of my being feels immobilized, as if time itself has come to a halt. It's a familiar sensation, another instance where I know I'll mess things up. What's the use? I have lived up to my parents' expectations, accomplishing nothing but disappointment and failure. It doesn't even matter anymore. It never has. I am destined to ruin this as well.

Forcing myself to press the invisible "unpause" button, I charge through the impending wave of emotions and swing open the heavy, glass door. This office dwarfs the one in Boston, boasting luxury in every aspect. White marble and granite adorn the entire space, along with vibrant bursts of color and carefully positioned greenery. The minimalist design appears effortlessly executed, designed to attract high-end clientele.

The place is dead. No one behind the massive, stone reception desk yet. Glancing up at the oversized clock, confusion creeps in. It's well past eight thirty, and I expected more activity by this time. Perhaps they follow a different schedule here—starting late and working even later? Double-checking Tracy's welcome email, I don't find anything out of the norm nor any mention of irregular working hours. Despite her instruction for a nine a.m. start, I showed up slightly early because I believe in strong first impressions and like to get a lay of the land.

One positive thing I've learned while working for a PR company is the necessity of being ever-ready. Ready is the wrong word—more like standing there, feet apart, arms outstretched while bracing for the multiple fireballs heading your way. Serving and thriving in this industry require the type of preparedness I've mastered. Besides, I never half-ass anything.

"Hello?" I call out into the silence.

Peeking around the corner, my eyes catch on a colossal wall covered with floor-to-ceiling, lush greenery. Intrigued, I reach out, feeling the soft leaves beneath my fingertips. My gaze continues past the wall, revealing a vast, industrial brick chamber lined with desks and white laptops. Everything seems perfectly in order, with the computers gleaming in pristine white, undisturbed. It's almost like this place is haunted by tidy ghosts. How on earth do they

151

maintain this level of neatness? Clearly, this office has a different culture and work ethic than the one back in Boston. And maybe that's a good thing.

My attention is drawn by the clicking of shoes behind me. I turn to see a tall woman walking directly toward me. She is engrossed in her phone, her perfectly straight, platinum-blonde hair partially obscuring her face. Thick, black-framed glasses adorn her features, and as she approaches, I notice a sprinkle of freckles on her cheeks. She giggles to herself, her fingers dancing rapidly on the glass screen of her phone. Finally, she looks up, revealing big, round, hazel eyes that meet mine, causing her face to light up with a wide grin.

"Hi! You must be Zoe." She closes the distance between us and wraps me in a tight hug, squeezing me half to death with her strong grip. She pulls back, grimacing and adjusting her glasses up the bridge of her nose. "I hope you're a hugger, and if not, I'm so sorry for just throwing myself at you like that."

I chuckle nervously. "It's fine. Nice to meet you. Yes, I'm Zoe. Are you Tracy?"

"Oh, God, no. I'm Olivia, but everyone calls me Via. I'm Tracy's assistant."

"That's a great name."

She shrugs, smiling again, and I notice a dimple in the bottom of her right cheek. Her bubbly personality reminds me of a Christmas elf, and she's just as nice too.

"Thank you. Come," Via says, grabbing my hand. "I'll show you around before Tracy gets in. She usually doesn't get here until around ten."

"Great. Thank you," I say, trotting behind her.

"I'm so happy you're here. You're going to love Tracy; she's a badass."

I release the nervous energy that was tormenting me earlier, telling my anxiety that she is an absolute asshole and needs to take a hike.

WE'VE BEEN WALKING for what feels like twelve straight hours. This place is huge, and I didn't need to see every nook and cranny on day one. But try telling Via that. She is strong-willed and on a mission this morning. I've behaved like the perfect employee— staying quiet, taking notes, answering questions only when spoken to. Aaron would be proud.

But a transfer shouldn't be this intensive. I'm getting hangry and hurting from these stupid heels.

"And here we are, home sweet home," Via says, pointing to a large, rectangular desk with two computers on either side. Behind the desk sits a massive office with more glass doors. Apparently, no one likes privacy here. Won't be catching Tracy picking her nose —God, I hope not anyway.

"I'm on the right, and you're on the left. Don't worry, I'll try to keep the clutter on my side."

That might be the messiest desk I've ever seen. The cleaning ghosts apparently haven't bothered with Via's stuff, because she has papers and all sorts of colorful pens scattered around her desk. And as if there is an invisible line right down the middle of the table, my side is completely empty and clean.

A little mess never hurt anyone though.

"Don't worry about it. It's nice to see a little mess here." I smile, trying to make her feel less self-conscious about the whole thing.

"Thank you! Finally, someone gets it. Everyone here is too clean and organized. I can't stand it."

I nod, pulling out my office chair. "It is a bit unsettling how clean all the desk areas are. Is that a mandate here?"

Via plops into her chair and turns on her computer. "The CEO prefers we keep a clean space because they're going for a mini- malist look, but there is nothing minimalist about me. I am chaos and disarray down to my bones. Thankfully, I am a wonderful assistant, so Tracy just puts up with my shit."

"And if you're her assistant...what will I be doing?"

Via pushes aside a stack of papers, tugging on a turquoise notebook trapped underneath some books.

"You'll be covering events, but Tracy will go over all of that with you once she gets in." Via grunts, struggling to set the notebook free.

Taking a quick look around our spacious office, I can't help but notice the various miniature fake pots and tiny cereal boxes scattered across Via's already-cluttered desk. It seems like she is a big fan of trinkets, and I wonder if she collects them herself or if someone has a penchant for buying them for her. It seems foreign to me, that some people have loved ones in their lives who care about them so much that they would think of them when passing by a small, fake cactus plant, prompting them to step into a shop and purchase it just to see them smile.

Aaron has done something similar for me a couple of times. However, it was my parents who used to do that for him constantly. They were always concerned with making him happy or lifting him out of his sad moods. Whatever Aaron desired, he would receive, even things he didn't particularly want. It became clear to me early on that my parents loved him more. In fact, my father had no problem telling me that I was a complete mistake and my mother had been on the verge of aborting me. They had actually been sitting at the abortion clinic when she'd had a change of heart, and they'd walked out without looking back.

He told me that on a rainy day after he finished yelling at me over getting a detention slip. I'll never forget how those words changed me. How they made me not want to exist.

"My grandmother painted me that. She was such a talented artist." Via's voice snaps me into reality, and I realize I was zoned out, staring at a small, purple butterfly painting propped up on a metal easel close to her computer screen.

Of course, of all the things, it's a butterfly.

"It is beautiful, Via. I love butterflies so much. I'm sorry for your loss."

Via's brows raise up in surprise. Either she's pissed or surprised I caught the *was* in her sentence. She glances down at her keyboard before looking up at me with glassy eyes.

"Thank you. I miss her every day."

I nod, wanting to get out of my seat and give her a hug, but as always, I second-guess myself and stay pinned to my chair.

"It's okay. You don't need to look so sad. I love talking about her. Keeps her spirit alive. She lived an amazing, full, and successful life. A life many of us could only dream of."

Smiling, I nod, truly feeling happy for a woman I've never even met. But there is something to be said about someone who achieves it all in their lifetime. Isn't that what everyone hopes to have? Aren't we all just praying we make it to the other side of this thing we call life unscathed and in one piece? I'm happy Via's grandmother got to experience it all. The good with some bad.

"That's a great way to look at it."

"I know. You're going to find out real soon that I'm kind of amazing. You're going to want to keep me around."

A laugh bursts from my mouth, and Via looks at me with surprise, her eyes lighting up.

"Oh my God! You do laugh. I was seriously worried you were AI or just the most depressed person on the planet."

Not sure why, but that sends me into an even bigger fit of laughter. Maybe it's her candor or the fact that she's unapologetically herself, but there is a certain comfort knowing Via is likely not putting on a fake front just so she can turn around and talk shit behind my back.

Once the laughing dies down, Via tips her chin at the butterfly painting on her desk.

"So, why butterflies?"

I let out a soft breath. "They've always fascinated me. I love how they start out as one thing and completely transform into something entirely new. No one remembers the old version of them, probably not even themselves. Once they burst out of their cocoon, they are completely reborn. No reminders of their past life as a caterpillar. They go from slithering to flying. How beautiful is that? They just get to begin again with wings, out of all the things. A glorious second chance."

"Wow. That was deep as fuck."

"It's wasn't, I just like butterflies," I scoff.

"Why? Because you want to transform into something else?"

Feeling my face flush under the new attention and the direction this conversation is taking, I distract myself by pretending to rummage through my very empty drawers.

"Do you need some supplies? I can take you down to the supply room. They have everything down there."

"Sure," I say over my shoulder as I close the bottom drawer.

"Where is all your stuff?"

"I decided not to bring much for my first day."

She narrows her eyes at me, studying me carefully. "Are you planning on staying?"

I hesitate, trying to figure out where she's going with this. "Um...yes. Unless I get fired on the first day."

Via pushes her glasses up her nose, looking away as her shoulders tense ever so slightly. Her unspoken words sit heavily on my chest.

"Go ahead. Say it."

Her eyes shift to mine. "Say what?"

"Whatever it is you heard about me."

She crosses her arms, looking completely offended. "Nope. I don't do office gossip or drama. Especially when it comes from the mouths of two-faced bitches who have nothing better to do with their time than discuss Greg's love life. Gross."

I smile, hoping to hell I just made a new friend. "I like you."

"Good, because I like you too."

Her confession takes me by surprise, and I glance over my shoulder at Via, watching her grab a piece of paper as she scribbles something down. It's nice to have a potential friend on day one. Some might call this hope, but I tend to label it delayed disappointment.

I'm going to count this as a win for now.

CHAPTER 18

ZOE

"So, what's your story, Zoe?"

Via bites into her burger as a giant piece of tomato falls onto the foil wrapping in front of her.

"No story."

She rolls her eyes at me, chewing and shaking her head. It seems that my two-word answer didn't satisfy her. In an attempt to give myself more time to think, I take a bite of my burger. Via's eyes widen, signaling her impatience for my response, but I just laugh and take a sip of my soda.

"Should have taken a smaller bite."

We're sitting in a crowded cafeteria in the building next to Bloom, which happens to be close to the Rubin Museum of Art. Via claimed the food here is much better than Bloom's, so we walked over for lunch.

Outside, in the midst of January, snow softly falls while busy New Yorkers stride briskly, unaffected by the cold, or anything else, for that matter. In this city, everyone is always on a mission, and the city itself never seems to rest. It appears that leisurely pursuits are not the norm here, or maybe they are and I simply haven't experienced them yet. Aaron mentioned that he plans to take a day off soon to show me around Hudson Yards and give me a tour of New York City.

"Earth to Zoe. Dish, girl," Via says before stuffing a handful of fries into her mouth.

I shrug. "Honestly, not much to tell."

"I don't buy your bullshit. Sorry."

I take another bite out of my burger, even though first-day work jitters have robbed my appetite today. I don't bother stopping the groan as the smoky goodness and fresh flavors of the burger burst in my mouth. Via was right; this might be the best burger I've ever had.

"I know, right? But I don't care if your mouth is full of meat. Let's hear it, boo-boo."

Nearly choking on my food, I reach for my soda, glaring at her while punching my chest with my other hand.

You know what? Screw it. What do I have to lose?

"Zoe Jackson. I'm twenty-five, born and raised in Boston in a cute little suburb outside of downtown. I interned at Bloom in Boston when I was in college and then got hired as an assistant. It was supposed to be temporary while I looked for jobs in my actual field, but I guess somewhere along the way, I decided to stick around."

"Decided to stick around, or just gave up on your dreams?"

Via's style seems to be a mix between blunt and straight up gut punch.

"You don't hold back, do you?"

"No. It's a waste of time for both of us."

She's right, can't argue with that one. "I didn't give up. I think I just got too comfortable where I was."

"And what is your dream job?"

"I don't know."

She leans back in her chair, eyeing me with the same look as before. "You don't know? What did you study in school?"

"Architecture and design."

Via's jaw snaps open. "And you're working at a PR and event management company? How? Why?"

My shoulders tilt up, and I feel the onslaught of shame rising deep within my chest.

"It was one of the few internships available at the time. They didn't have any positions in my field."

"Good lord, that sucks. I'm sorry."

"Don't be. Shit happens, right?"

"Right, but it's never too late, you know."

I laugh, reaching for a fry and trying not to let her words mean more than they sound. "Thank you."

"I mean it. You're in New York now; you can do whatever you want. Start over, go after your dreams."

"Trying to get rid of me?"

She rolls her eyes at me. "Don't be ridiculous."

Via sips on her drink, looking like she's on a mission. "Single?"

"Yes."

"Newly?"

Yep, she's definitely onto something.

"No."

Via's brows raise for a split second before she schools her features. "Oh."

"What?"

"Nothing."

Here is the dreaded moment I've been hoping to avoid all day.

"Go on. Say it," I sigh, staring down at my wicker basket full of fries.

"Don't let the rumors from Boston get to you. I don't believe them, and I won't start to. Anyone who takes anything Asshat Greg says seriously is just a fucking idiot."

I glance up and quickly assess Via's genuineness, but I can't detect even a hint of dishonesty on her face.

"Thanks. But just tell me—I'd rather know what I'm walking into."

"All right. I told you I don't do gossip, which means I did not take part in these conversations, but I have heard people running their mouths. The usual suspects."

I nod, bracing myself for the worst and begging my heart to settle down. I'm not there anymore. I don't have to run into him or deal with this problem directly. These are just meaningless rumors. I know the actual truth. That's all that matters, right?

My anxiety only lives in the past and future, and I need to focus on the present.

None of these words help calm my nerves, no matter how true they might be.

"The word is you were sleeping with half the office back in Boston and Greg had to let you go, but you threatened to end your life, so he felt bad and relocated you."

"WHAT?!" Lurching up, I nearly knock over my drink as I gape down at Via in complete shock.

Via flinches, and the pity in her eyes reels me back in.

Looking over both shoulders carefully to ensure no one witnessed my sudden outburst, I try to think of something to say to Via.

"I'm sorry, Zo. I know I don't know you yet, but this sucks."

"None of it is true."

"I know."

I slowly sit back down. "I hope so, because that's not what happened. Greg and I were casually spending time together here and there. Just to scratch an itch, and he wasn't any good at it, by the way. Not for me anyway. I didn't tell anyone; we were discreet. I never asked for anything more, and before I got let go, I actually wanted to end it. I don't understand why he would come after me like this."

Via reaches across the table and places her hand on top of mine. "He's an asshole, that's why. He likes control and power, and when he felt like you were getting the upper hand, he decided to do this. Let it go, babe. You don't need to waste any more energy on him."

Tears sting the backs of my eyes, but I blink them away.

"I always do this to myself. Making choices that come back to bite me hard in the ass."

As Via's brows furrow, I contemplate telling her to stop feeling sorry for me. But, before I can even respond, her face suddenly brightens, as though a metaphorical light bulb has just lit up in her mind.

"I know how you can forget about him!"

"What?"

Via pushes aside her food and leans her elbows on the table.

"There is a site, completely anonymous, where people post whatever they want. I've used it to get all sorts of things off my chest before. Others can comment or react, you can ask for advice, look for someone to talk to... There are literally threads for everything and anything you can think of. And I mean, anything." She winks at me, and I'm not sure where she's going with this.

"You want me to post about Greg on an anonymous site?"

"Sure, if you want to. You can change his name. You can even connect with other people in the area. You can creep around and read people's confessions. It's like the dark corner of the web for free therapy, and you never have to worry about anyone finding out your true identity. You can write a hate letter to Greg, and even though he may never read it, other people will, and it might make you feel better."

I'm not sure how it would help.

"Thanks. I'll check it out," I lie, knowing I don't have the energy to write a message that will go out into the web for a bunch of strangers to read and comment on. What purpose will that serve other than to continuously remind me?

"It's also a great place for newcomers to any city. You can find out where the hot spots are, or if you are in need of something... there are always recommendations."

I nod absentmindedly, biting off a piece of cold fry. "What's it called?"

"Rabbit Hole." Via pulls out her phone and flips it around to show me what the app looks like.

"Thanks."

"Also, if you ever actually want to go anywhere and need some company, I'm happy to show you around the city."

"Yeah, I'd really like that." I smile, hoping the offer is genuine, but not sure I'll ever take her up on it. Making the first move to hang out with anyone is always scary.

It's not that I don't want to be friends with Via. I just don't know if New York will become my home. I can't afford anything here with my current salary.

Disappointment is not something I seek regularly, so if I can avoid relationships and interactions, I do. Because when they end, and they always end...it is easier to sever the tie. Besides, the fear of rejection is crippling.

"Now that all my dirty laundry has been aired out, tell me about you."

"Not much to say. I've been at Bloom for years and will probably never leave. I'd love to get into more of the event management side of the business, but we'll see if Tracy will ever let me go. I'm sort of her right hand." She shakes her head, smiling as if this is something they joke about often.

"Does she pay you well at least?" Grimacing, I quickly correct myself. "Sorry. You totally don't have to answer that."

"It's fine, girl. Yes, I told her if she wanted me to stay, she had to pay me way more than an assistant's salary, and she somehow pulled it off. She's a magician, that one."

"Good. I'm happy you did that."

"Of course. I don't take bullshit from anyone. It's every person for themselves out there, and you have to always remember that."

"Always," I say. "Okay, my turn. You grilled me earlier, now give me your resume."

Via bursts out laughing, but she doesn't shy away. "Okay, okay. I'm from New Jersey, born and raised. I'm twenty-four and currently single. I love relationships but loathe dating. Trying to find epic love in hook-up culture is next to impossible." Her face scrunches up, as if she's trying to remember anything else she might have forgotten to mention. "Oh, and one fun fact about me is I love smut."

"Smut?" I question, having never heard the word before. I'm hoping it's some sort of New York lingo and I don't look like a total idiot.

Via's jaw drops to the table. "Excuse me? Did you just ask me what smut is?"

Instantly regretting asking the question, I mouth sorry, pulling into myself. Why couldn't I have Googled it later like a normal person?

"Girl, we're going to the bookstore so I can introduce you to smut. Or actually, just take my books. Do you have a Kindle?"

I nod, and she lets out a sigh of relief. "Good. So you do read… What is your genre of choice?"

"Horror. Mystery. Psychological thrillers."

"That's fine….but you're going to love smut."

"You haven't told me what it is yet." Still confused, I resist the urge to pull out my phone.

"Look it up." She smirks, sipping on her soda and watching me intently as I pull out my phone and type the word into the Google search bar.

A small flake of soot or other dirt.

Nope, that can't be it.

I click on Urban Dictionary next.

Erotic writing that contains explicit, sexual content.

I laugh, looking up to see Via's eyes beaming as she nods her approval.

"So, erotica?"

"Oh, sweetie, it's so much more than that."

"I don't know. I'm more of a murder-in-the-alley kind of gal."

"Just work through my list, and if it's still not your thing by the end of it, I won't harass you again. But I'm dying to have a real-life, spicy book friend, so I'm hoping to rope you in."

Laughing, I glance at my watch and start clearing our table. "You like porn, just admit it."

"It's not porn. It's romantic and addicting. Once you read your first smutty novel, you'll never go back."

***

"THANK YOU, GEORGE." Glancing up at the smiling doorman, I pull my hair away from my face, but the cold, January wind is relentless, forcing it back over my eyes.

George, the doorman at Seventeen Hudson Yards, has the most gentle and compassionate eyes I have ever seen. He exudes an aura of safety and security, instantly putting me at ease. I don't know, he seems like the kind of person one would willingly confide in, as if his wisdom could potentially solve all of life's dilemmas. Although I have yet to put this theory to the test, George just gives off a certain energy that suggests he has this remarkable quality.

With a beaming smile, he graciously holds the door open for me.

"You're very welcome, Ms. Jackson."

"Please call me Zoe."

He bows his head, still smiling. "Certainly, Ms. Jackson."

I can't help but laugh, knowing George will probably never call me by my first name. But I will keep trying because I want us to become the best of friends. Maybe, one night, I'll come down here with a pint of ice cream and just tell him about my day. People don't do that anymore. They don't just talk about their days or make real connections.

Sometimes it feels like I just don't belong here, because the things I crave aren't what everyone else wants or seeks out.

"I'm going to get you to cave eventually." I turn, walking backwards, and my voice echoes in the tall, enormous lobby.

The whole place is like a futuristic dream with its sleek combination of glass and marble. It's so cutting edge, yet it all blends together seamlessly. Other than the chic leather couches and some statement plants, it's all about the spacious minimalist vibe. Suspended high above, there's a floating rainbow glass installation that adds sophistication and a bit of enchantment to the building. When the sun hits those tiny glass pieces, they scatter, fanning across the lobby as the light moves. I haven't been lucky enough to capture it at sunrise or sunset yet, but I'm sure it brings the space to life. It's almost like they wanted to inject a bit of New York right into the heart of this building. Being on the design team for this spot? That's a gig I would've killed for.

"Oh, Ms. Jackson? Mr. Jackson has a package. Do you mind if I walk up with you to deliver it to him?"

Seems a little unnecessary since I'm heading up there myself.

"I can take it up. I'm heading there."

"Oh, I couldn't possibly burden you with it."

George has to be in his seventies. He is short, around five foot seven, and he's always dressed in pristine, black suits. A uniform provided by the building management, I'm sure. He has thinning, silver hair and the kindest, faded-brown eyes. He is exactly how I envision grandparents to be. I never got to meet mine from either side, unfortunately, but I have a feeling I would have been close to at least one set of grandparents. I can't help but feel that my paternal grandmother would have genuinely cared for me, particularly considering the difficult circumstance of being the neglected child. Given my father's intense dislike toward me, it would undoubtedly irk him if his own mother developed a fondness for me.

Too bad karma never got to play that hand. It might have been fun, and maybe I would have had a taste of what real love is like. Or, maybe she would have hated me too.

Slowly making my way to George, I watch him retrieve a small, brown box and place it onto the empty counter.

"You were going to go all the way up for this? You're silly. And for the record, I would have even come down to grab this from you if you had called."

He looks shocked, as if I just blurted out a string of foul words. "Oh, I would never."

"You're ridiculous. I'm happy to help. Although, I don't think this counts as helping since I am on my way up." I reach for the box, but George pulls it away from me.

Arching my brow, I hold out my hand. "I would like to take this up myself."

He knows exactly what I'm doing, so he chuckles softly as he places the box in the palm of my hand.

"You are too kind, Ms. Jackson. Thank you, and have a great night. Please send my regards to your brother."

"Will do. And it's Zoe," I say one last time, turning to head for the elevators.

CHAPTER 19

DOMINIK

This party fucking blows.

If I had my way, I'd be at home, sitting on my couch, playing a round of online hockey or diving into a good book. Surprisingly, not many people are aware of how much I truly enjoy reading. Often, people perceive me solely as a sports-focused individual, with hockey and women occupying my every thought... and while that may not be entirely untrue, I also have other interests, such as reading. However, my appearance wouldn't give any indication of this, and I am okay with that.

Showing up tonight was somewhat mandatory since it's Liam's birthday. I had to make an appearance even just for a couple of hours before I crash for the night. No one will notice if I duck out early; they're all past drunk, and it's close to midnight. Not that I blame the team—we had a difficult game. I wish I could get shit-faced too after that disastrous performance, but I decided to skip it. Considering I've met my quota for hangover regrets for the year.

My mind has been off since running into Zoe at Aaron's house. Seeing her brought back all those old memories from Boston. Especially the ones from that night in the woods. God, just seeing her out of the blue and knowing she's going to be around, so close to my personal space, is messing with my head more than I care to admit.

The last place I want to be right now is at this party.

I'm not usually like this. Most of the time, I leave these parties with one or two women draped on my arms. Navigating the dating scene used to be a breeze before the spotlight found me, but now it's almost too effortless. I don't need to say a word, and they come flocking. Some might see it as the dream, but truth be told, it's anything but. Beyond the fleeting pleasures, there's an undeniable emptiness. I'm not remotely interested anymore.

It's not what I crave anymore. I'm not sure I ever did. I think I might have just been trying to forget by drowning in others, but even that proved to be ineffective.

Glancing around, I notice the girl who lives in this open-concept Chelsea penthouse suite. She's had a crush on Liam for months and hasn't given up her pursuit. She's a vibrant redhead who has shown up to every game, sporting Liam's number proudly on her back, hoping to catch his attention, and it seems like it's finally paid off. Liam is loving the attention from her tonight. He wraps his arm around her bare shoulders, his smile so big and genuine as they stare at one another.

Oh, young love. It'll be over before it even begins.

Then again, what do I know? I've never been in love...not in the way love is meant to be shared.

What about her?

Admiring someone from afar doesn't count. That's just an obsession I haven't learned how to escape yet.

The rest of the guys are standing next to a giant, marble fireplace that stretches twenty-five feet up as they talk to a group of fresh puck bunnies.

The thought of turning around and leaving the busy apartment crosses my mind, but just before I seriously consider it, Liam glances up. Our eyes lock, and a broad smile stretches across his face. With an inviting wave, he motions for me to join the group.

Too late now.

Bailing right as I arrive would be a pretty lousy move, especially considering it's Liam's twenty-first birthday and he can finally partake in the drinking at these parties. Typically, he plays the role of our sober buddy, ensuring none of us goes off the rails and winds up with a cringe-worthy social media post. Coach is all about maintaining a certain team image. He couldn't care less about what we do behind closed doors as long as it stays hidden from the public eye.

That's another reason hitting up a party tonight has my nerves on edge. I screwed up big time last week, and I'm just relieved that nothing surfaced in the aftermath of that threesome. I have a hard rule of keeping phones out of the room or turning them off completely. All my non-negotiable rules are laid out before anyone even thinks about getting naked. I need understanding and agreement from everyone involved, and it's normally not a problem.

Rule number 1: no phones.

Rule number 2: no seconds, ever.

If a woman agrees to spend time with me, it's just that. One night. We can have as much fun as she likes during that night, but in the morning, we go our separate ways.

Rule number 3: no kissing on the lips.

Last week, I got a bit too drunk and forgot about the cellphone rule, and I'm pretty sure one of the girls was documenting bits of our fling. The realization hit me the next day, and I immediately reached out to Noa and Oliver—the only ones on the team I trust with this kind of slip-up. Together, we combed through every social media platform, but didn't find anything from the girls. It took days for me to finally exhale and resume my routine.

Striding past the large, black kitchen island, I grab a shot from a round tray and down the tequila before making my way over to the guys. Just one shot to help me get through the next couple of hours. It might also help get my mind off Zoe for a bit.

Yeah, right.

Even the thought alone sounds ridiculous. I haven't been able to purge myself of that woman fully since the day I met her, so what are the chances I will now that she's living a few floors above me?

I spotted her in a conversation with George, our building attendant, the other night as I returned home from practice. I don't know how long I stood outside just watching her talk to George as her face lit up, reminiscent of the carefree expression she used to wear when we were in high school. She seemed at ease, unguarded and carefree. The usual mask she hides under wasn't in place. I couldn't stop looking at her, and I found myself grinning just watching her smile.

It's no surprise that George is the one capable of bringing that kind of light to her face. The man has a magnetic presence that draws everyone in; even I've found myself opening up to him on rare occasions. He's a sealed vault, and seeing her warm up to him was a welcome sight. With Aaron so busy with work, I worry that she might be spending too much time alone in that condo. But it's not my place to intervene. Zoe is a strong woman, and if she needs anything, I'm sure she'll reach out to her brother. She's been navigating life on her own for as long as I've known her. She thinks people don't see the way she hides, and maybe she's right, maybe people don't notice, but I do.

I've always noticed.

God, that night, I longed to be near her. I wanted to stand just inches away from her in the elevator, but I restrained myself, clenching my fists tightly to keep myself in check. She's the only person who has ever possessed such power over me, and it frustrates me. I refuse to let my emotions dictate my actions. I am always in control.

Why is it that I can't rid myself of this one thing? This one person?

It's maddening, and it only makes me want her that much more.

Jesus fucking Christ, get a hold of yourself.

"DOMINATOR! About time, man."

"Happy birthday, little Liam. This party is on fire. Enjoying your newfound freedom?" Smirking down at Liam, I ruffle his hair and he smacks my hand away instantly.

"Oh, this is more of a casual get-together for Liam's birthday. It won't get too busy tonight if you want to make some mistakes," says the redhead draped across Liam's chest as she gives me a coy smile.

My initial reaction is to say something snarky, but I bite my tongue, giving her a sideways glance as I grab Liam's beer and take a large swig.

"Happy birthday, Liam," I say again.

Liam gives me a smile filled with apprehension, his expression guarded, something I've grown too familiar with. He expects me to mistreat his girlfriend, but I'm not that cruel. Especially not on his birthday. Among the guys, I'm known as a wild card, someone who speaks and acts without thinking twice. But in reality, it's quite the opposite. I've carefully constructed a facade, meticulously selecting my words and actions to portray the image I want others to see. The true art lies in controlling the narrative, presenting a version of myself that aligns with people's expectations. I want to be seen as the jerk who goes after women as if it is a game.

A wave of hollering and shouting erupts from behind me before the guys crowd Liam, holding a tray of shots as Noa cradles what appears to be endless bottles of beer. I laugh as I quickly rush over to assist him, preventing any chance of him toppling over and injuring himself with the shattered glass. I'm sure Red over here wouldn't want her parents' expensive furniture ruined.

Noa leans into me a little too eagerly as I grab a few bottles and place them on the glass table behind me.

"Thanks, man. I think I saw my life flash before my eyes."

"You know you can make more than one trip, right?"

He snorts. "Yeah, yeah...I was being a lazy asshole. You can force me to do extra wind sprints if you want."

"Well...since you're volunteering."

That gains me a sideways smile, and I help him place the rest of the bottles on the table. Noa is twenty-five and has been with the

Slashers even before I joined the team. He is originally from Finland, and he's one of the best defensemen I've had the pleasure of playing with. He keeps to himself for the most part and likes to keep his private life close to his chest, which I respect. I've had to learn over the years how to keep my extracurriculars tightly knit and only show the media what I want them to see. I don't care if my image or reputation is tainted, but I know some of the guys like Noa want nothing to do with that part of our career. Being professional hockey players means we have to give up privacy, but that is something we all come to accept pretty early on.

"Shots?" Liam asks excitedly, jutting out a small glass against my chest as the liquid sloshes on my shirt. I stare at the droplets for a few seconds before grabbing the shot glass and downing it in one go. My plan to stay sober tonight is quickly going sideways.

"Yeaaaaa, Dom!" Liam screams, following close behind me.

"I think you should take it easy, big guy," Noa comments to Liam.

"Aw, come on. Let him be, Noa." Ben, my left defenseman slurs his words as he downs his own shot of liquor.

Right at that second, Liam turns and spews vomit all over one of Red's friends. An array of curse words and yelps fill the air as I realize these assholes have been feeding the twenty-one-year-old way too much booze.

Looks like I'm on babysitting duty for the night.

"Where's Axel?" I inquire, hoping that one of the inebriated fools will provide an answer. Scanning the room, my eyes search for his distinctive mop of curly, blond hair, but he's nowhere to be found. Axel stands at an impressive six foot four, making him hard to overlook. With his broad and muscular frame, he's easily recognizable.

"Somewhere around here."

Great. Thanks. That's super helpful.

"Watch Liam. I'm going to go find some water and get this mess cleaned up." I turn, but a hand grips my shoulder.

"Hey, Dom...actually, more like Pussy Dominator with that

thing in your pants. What's it like to be God's favorite man?" Oliver practically spits the words in my face, his boisterous voice carrying over the music.

Ben erupts into laughter, bending over as if Oliver just delivered the punchline of the century at a comedy show. I lean in close to Oliver's face, and though he stumbles back a bit, I maintain a tight grip on his shoulder.

"Did your mother not teach you it's rude to stare, Ollie? And if you want to know the answer to your question, why don't you ask your girlfriend? Those lips felt fucking amazing wrapped around my cock."

That sobers Oliver up real quick.

"Oh, fuck," Ben says from behind me.

"You did not. Stace wouldn't do that."

I sigh, feeling a little bad for messing with him but not bad enough to let him off this easy. I didn't fuck his girlfriend, but watching his world crumble in front of me is a little fun.

"Dom, knock it off," Noa growls from behind me.

I finally release Oliver's shoulder. "Relax, asshole. I didn't sleep with your girlfriend, nor did she suck my cock."

"You're such a dick," Oliver spits.

Yep, heard it before, but it still makes me laugh.

"It's not funny," Ben says, coming to Oliver's aid.

"Why? Because I'm such a fucking whore?" They all avert their gaze at that, looking anywhere but at me.

Not waiting around for another comment or snide remark, I make my way through the crowd, going to get some water for Liam like I promised. Only getting stopped six times by people wanting to congratulate me on making captain or asking me questions about the season. I have to remind myself four times that I'm a hockey player and being patient with people is part of the job.

Finally, I spot Axel in the kitchen talking to a tall brunette with sparkling brown eyes. Her gaze jumps to mine as soon as she sees me approaching, but I glance away, not interested in pissing off another one of my teammates tonight.

"Dom," Axel utters, not bothering to look my way.

"Liam is drunk out of his—"

"Dominik Lewis? I'm a huge fan," Axel's friend interrupts me mid-sentence. Her voice is as sweet as the rest of her, and I push back the urge to smile.

"Thank you."

"You're an amazing hockey player. Truly magical."

Glancing at her cherry lips, I can't help but trace the rest of her with my eyes. She's a delicious little thing up close.

"Does Liam need something, Dominik?" Axel's clipped voice lifts the sex fog from my mind as I turn toward him.

"He's a bit drunk. You may want to go check on him, since the party was your idea," I say, arching a brow at him.

"Shit," he groans.

"Yeah. Have fun."

Axel turns to the brunette, offering an apology and assuring her he'll return soon. Shooting me a cautionary look, he swiftly grabs four bottles of water and dashes off. As I pivot, the brunette's attention isn't on Axel's departure. Her eyes are raking down my frame as if she's mentally undressing me. Maintaining a sly smirk, I let her gaze ascend to meet mine, catching the precise moment she realizes she's been caught in the act. Her cheeks flush the perfect shade of pink, and if it was any other night, I would have found an empty room and had some fun with her.

But not tonight.

Not since *she* arrived, reminding me of everything I've told myself I don't miss. The memories of that night in Boston I can't rid myself of. That night that was meant to get her out of my system for good but ended up having the opposite effect.

I wonder if she's taken part in that type of fun since her first time... Fuck, why does the thought make me want to rage so hard? Why does it even matter? She doesn't belong to me.

Never has, never will.

"Enjoy your night," I utter to the brunette, offering her a tight smile before turning.

A gentle hand reaches out, clutching my forearm, and I find myself staring at her long, delicate fingers before lifting my gaze to meet her eyes.

"Leaving already?"

"Afraid so."

She bites her bottom lip, dragging the edge out in between her teeth. "Can I do anything to change your mind?"

A blow job?

But I don't say that, because if I do, this girl will blow me in the bathroom and Axel will find out. Then he won't speak to me for a week, and I'll likely get shoved into the barricades two hundred times during practice. And that would just be annoying.

Not to mention the fact that I don't really care to see anyone's lips wrapped around my cock unless it's Zoe kneeling down in front of me.

I wish I could just fucking stop wanting her.

I need to get her out of my mind, even if it's for a short time.

Making a last-minute decision and ignoring the knots in my chest, I turn to face the pretty brunette.

"What did you have in mind?"

With a smile, she intertwines her fingers with mine and gently guides me away from the bustling room.

CHAPTER 20

DOMINIK

I f I could go back in time, there is one decision I would definitely change. Right now, there is no one who despises me more than I despise myself.

A sudden gust of wind smacks the back of my head, almost as if the universe is echoing my thoughts. It feels like a force pushing me forward. Looking back, I realize I should have followed my initial instinct of leaving the party early.

I feel nauseous.

Numbing my emotions by burying myself in another woman was a terrible idea. I thought I would feel better from a temporary escape, but the entire time, I was picturing Zoe. The way her soft skin felt on mine, the taste of peppermint on her lips, the way her body fit perfectly against mine, as if she were made for me. The taste of her and the intense pleasure my primal beast got from leaving bite marks all over her sweet skin.

And the more I tried not to think about her tonight, the worse it got. Images blurred into one another until I got lost in the frenzy of it all, forgetting who was beneath me. What pulled me out was the woman screaming out "Dominator" as she came.

It nearly shoved me out of my skin. As soon as she finished, I didn't bother getting off as I yanked on my pants and ran out of there.

I need to forget about Zoe, that night, and everything it awoke inside me.

Maybe Coach was onto something. Perhaps I do need a substantial break from women for a while. Both my body and mind could use the reprieve, and it would offer me the opportunity to channel all my energy into hockey.

Tonight was a stark reminder that the women I have been pleasing aren't the one I truly desire. Despite pushing through, I found myself envisioning Zoe—her golden hair almost sparkling as it catches the light just right. Her jade eyes, piercingly intense, as if capable of revealing every hidden secret in my mind. I pictured her smiling up at me, that small dimple forming in the corner of her mouth when she laughs.

That's enough.

Is it though? Because it's never been enough, not with Zoe, and now she's in NYC. Living right under my nose. In my space. Our space.

Easily accessible for me to watch her.

She's Aaron's little sister. Off-limits to you.

He expects me to assist her in acclimating to life in New York City. I'll be there, a silent spectator, as she introduces a new guy to her brother. I'll witness her making choices that don't involve me, possibly getting married and starting a family. The mere idea of someone else standing beside her, sharing a life that should be mine, fractures everything inside me.

It was always supposed to be me at her side, holding her hand, walking alongside her.

Because I am the one who truly sees her. Embracing every hidden part of her mind, every dark corner. That's what draws me to her, even though she believes those aspects should be kept in the shadows of shame. I yearn to hold her hand as she peels away all the masks she wears, revealing her authentic self, and gains the confidence she truly deserves, even on her most challenging days.

She's fucking magnificent, and it feels like it should be me walking alongside her throughout life.

But we won't even get a beginning.

After all these years, I still can't fathom why Aaron has such a strong grip on her. Why wouldn't he want his best friend to whole-heartedly take care of her? Does he fear I'll abandon her just like their parents have her entire life? Because the truth is, I'd sooner cut out my own heart and toss it onto the ice in front of a packed stadium than ever consider doing that to Zoe. She means way too much to me.

It might be better for everyone if Zoe returned home. I could finally move forward with my life without constantly anticipating her around every corner, waiting for her to step out of the elevator. Maybe I can get a hold of her old boss and get him to apologize, offer her her job back.

That might not be a terrible idea.

For the time being though, I'll need to acclimate to this situation and pretend like Zoe isn't here. Keep my focus on the game, on work, and the playoff season. The trade deadline looms in two months, immediately followed by the playoffs the month after. Our team must stay unified and laser focused to claim the Cup this year. Competing with my former self has always been a top priority, and I need to secure my position for the coming seasons.

Approaching the building door, I nearly run into George all bundled up in his black pea coat, leather gloves, and gray scarf. I gifted him that scarf for Christmas two years ago. He said it was the most expensive piece of clothing he's ever owned, and something about that memory always warms my heart and makes me sad at the same time.

"George, I didn't know you were doing the night shift again." Pausing at the open door, I rest my hand on his shoulder.

His ears are red, his skin sensitive to the sharp January wind.

"I like to mix it up here and there. Besides, I haven't been sleeping well lately, so I figured I could cover a few nights for Robbie."

Robbie is one of the full-time doormen who works here.

"Hmm, sure. And it has nothing to do with Robbie's new baby?"

George's full brows curve up as he tries to hide his smile. "Do you always have to be a smart-ass, boy?"

A laugh bursts from me as I nudge George inside the building. George is very proud and will not budge, not even for me. Even after all our chats and gift exchanges over the years, he forces a level of professionalism to remain between us.

"With you? Always."

"Robbie is young; he needs to recover and look after his family. It's more important for him to be there for his wife."

"You're a good man, George."

"I know. You should take some notes from me. Find yourself a nice woman." He beams, rubbing his red, cracked hands together to warm them up.

"That doesn't sound too fun."

"Another exciting night?" George says, ignoring me.

I grunt, rolling my eyes as I lean my back against the marble desk.

"Not exciting then?"

"Not at all. Wish I had stayed home."

The beeper goes off at George's desk, and he whips around to see who's approaching. I look down at my watch, noting it's well past three a.m. Normally, it's pretty quiet around here between three and five, but it is New York. There is always movement, and I'm not sure anyone actually sleeps here. We're all a bunch of workaholics.

The door swings open, and Zoe strides in. My heart lurches in my chest, and I divert my attention to George's feet as he makes his way toward her, already apologizing for not holding the door open for her.

"George, stop! It's fine. I am totally capable of opening a door."

Even the sound of her voice drives me wild.

She's dressed in matching bright-yellow mittens and a fluffy hat, looking adorable despite the apparent lack of warmth in her attire. There's no makeup on her face, and her curls are flowing wildly around her shoulders and back. She's clad in comfortable sweats, as if her decision to leave the house was a spontaneous, last-minute choice. Clutching a green grocery bag, the tip of her nose is crimson.

I want to kiss her nose and wrap my arms around her.

She must have walked to the store farther down High Line Street. Does she not realize there is a Whole Foods right beside the Vessel, not even ten feet away?

Jade eyes lock on mine, rooting me to the cold, stone ground.

"Hey," she whispers.

Just leave.

But I don't leave.

"Everything okay? It's late."

Zoe straightens her shoulders, pulling the plastic bag further up her arm.

"Yeah, all good. I was craving ice cream, and Aaron apparently doesn't keep it in the house. When we were kids, he would polish off a tub before I even had a chance to have a bite. Now, I'm not allowed to have any because temptation is forbidden." Zoe rolls her eyes.

That's Aaron. He loves to be in control and gets rid of anything that might steer him away from his perfectly structured routine. He wasn't always this anal retentive, but he's gotten worse over the years.

"Come on, I'll take you up," I offer, holding out my arm, but Zoe doesn't take it. Her eyes simply fall down to my outstretched hand.

"I think I'll be able to find my way," she says without looking up at me. Instead, she turns on her heel to throw George the biggest smile ever.

"Good night, George!"

"Good night, Ms. Jackson. Sorry once again."

"Stop it! And it's Zoe."

181

Winking at George, I offer him a half wave and take two full strides, closing the distance between Zoe and me.

Her body tenses slightly as she feels me walking alongside her. I look down at her from the corner of my eye, but her gaze is fixed on the metal elevator doors.

We pause a couple of feet away, the air thick with wordless tension as we wait for the elevator to arrive. She has her own penthouse elevator access, but I don't point it out, wanting to steal a few more moments of silence standing next to her, trying to ignore her intoxicating scent. She's buzzing to speak, to break the silence, but she's too stubborn to say anything, and I'm enjoying her discomfort right now.

"You walked too far for that."

She looks up at me, and I nod down at her bag.

"What do you mean?"

"There is a Whole Foods right by the Vessel." The elevator doors slide open, and I step inside, biting my cheek to hold back my smile. I keep my eyes on her face while she avoids looking at me. Her scowl is growing by the second, and I want to reach out, cup her cheek, and kiss in between her brows. I fist my hands, looking away and trying to focus on the tower of buttons in front of me. Anything but the need to get close to Zoe.

"The Vessel?" she finally asks.

"Yeah. Has Aaron not taken you out yet?"

A long pause before her voice fills the small space. "No. He's been busy with work, but he's planning on taking some time off to show me around soon."

It's hard not to see her in the box of mirrors all around us—the way her eyes drop and the evident disappointment flashing on her face right before she schools her features, pretending like she doesn't care that she still feels like a complete stranger in this city.

"The Vessel is the giant honeycomb staircase structure outside our building."

"Right. That thing is amazing. Maybe I'll take a walk around Hudson Yards on the weekend and get lost around here, explore."

Aaron's words from last week cloud my vision. *She's in a rough spot in life, and I want to make sure we're all supporting her. She has no one else.*

I should have been there for her. We all need to do better and show up for Zoe. Change is hard for anyone, but it's especially difficult when you feel like you have no one, and Zoe has felt like that her entire life. I promised Aaron I'd do better, but instead of sticking to my word, I've been avoiding her. And for what? Because I can't get a grip on my feelings?

Fuck that.

"What are you doing tomorrow? Actually, today."

A stray curl drops in front of her eyes, and I practically have to restrain my hand from reaching out to tuck it away.

"Nothing. Why?"

"I'm taking you out."

"No. That's all right."

I face the mirror straight on, pretending like I don't hear my heart thundering in my ears.

"It wasn't up for discussion, Zo. Tomorrow morning, we're going on a little NYC tour. You and me."

"No." Her voice echoes through the room, resolute and piercing like the blade of a knife.

"Why?" As my eyes meet hers in the mirror, I'm slightly taken aback when I realize she's staring back at me. However, her gaze quickly shifts to my neck, and that's when I notice the massive hickey.

"You don't like me, and you don't need to start now because you feel sorry for me."

She is entitled to her own thoughts, even though they couldn't be further from the truth. I turn my body toward her and look down, but she deliberately avoids making eye contact. It is at that precise moment, mustering all of my bravery, that I extend my hand and delicately place my finger under her chin, directing her gaze toward mine.

Her breath hitches, but she doesn't pull away.

"I'm not offering because I feel sorry for you or because I feel the need to."

I lean down, eye level with her. She stares between my two irises, not knowing which one she wants to settle on.

"I'm doing it because I want to. I want to be the one to show you around New York City, to welcome you home." Her lips part and her eyes dilate. The way her body reacts to me drives me to oblivion, as if some part of her recognizes me. The connection we have always fought but share so deeply.

I can't help but stare down at her full, red lips, wanting to feel them in between my own, remembering how soft they feel.

As the elevator dings, seconds stretch into what feels like hours, compelling me to instinctively retreat a step while the doors gradually slide open.

"Hot date?" she breathes, staring at my neck once again before she starts to walk out.

"What?"

"Never mind. Good night!"

Glancing at the floor number, I bite the inside of my cheek to stifle a laugh.

"Hey, Zo," I call after her, and she turns ever so slowly.

"Hmm?"

Extending my arm against the closing elevator door, I hold it open, expecting her to catch on, but she simply remains motionless, arms crossed, staring back at me.

Am I sensing a bit of jealousy?

"This isn't your floor; it's mine."

She glances around and mutters a curse under her breath before hastily returning inside the elevator. Choosing the farthest corner away from me, she seems to avoid any contact. Maybe she doesn't hate me as much as she wants to.

"Enjoy your ice cream. And I'll be seeing you soon," I utter, walking backward and keeping my eyes glued on her. She finally looks up, her cheeks red and eyes filled with something that looks very similar to desire, just as the elevator doors close shut.

CHAPTER 21
ZOE

Strong hands grip my hair tightly as they force me down, turning me onto my back. Staring up at the tall, dark figure, I lie there panting for breath, feeling his cum dripping down my thighs. My clit is deliciously swollen, and the beads are still inside me as my body continues to tingle, remembering the way he gripped me while stretching me from behind.

I don't even remember what round we're on.

"Such a beautiful sight. You're wet and covered in my cum, yet still so needy for me."

I'm trembling, sore, and satiated, but I can't deny that I want more of him. I can't get enough. Desiring to delve into so much of who he is, to understand his mind and influence him in a way he'll never forget. To memorize every touch, bite, and kiss I have with him.

My mystery man crouches down, leaning his forearms against his knees as he stares at me through his crimson purge mask.

"You're devastatingly perfect." Reaching out, he smears the cum off my cheeks with his thumb. It was from our session earlier, when I was kneeling down in front of him and asked him to cover my face. He went crazy for that and nearly emptied himself instantly at the sound of my plea.

When he's finished tracing his thumb across my cheek, I grab his hand and bring his thumb to my lips, sucking the remnants of his cum off his flesh and groaning as I taste him again. My abused pussy already throbbing to feel him inside me again.

Beep. Beep. Beep.

Not another dream about that cold night with Runi.

Shutting my eyes, I turn and pull my pillow close to my chest, hoping to step back through the shimmering curtain of my dream world and find my way back to him.

Back to that night when everything changed for me.

And the last night I had a full orgasm.

Unlike most women, climaxing doesn't come easy for me. My thoughts are too loud; my anxiety is relentless, even during sex. And since Runi, I haven't met anyone who has been able to take that all away from me. He brought me back to life, made me feel things I never thought were possible in less than twelve hours. I felt whole, different...renewed. And I know I'll never find that again. Every man since him has only been a distraction.

But I'm in New York City now, which is full of opportunity and people walking around with kinks. I found the Boston BDSM group on an anonymous website, and after the masquerade ball, I deleted my account and never looked back. I needed time to process everything that had happened, all the blossoming changes within me.

After some time, I decided to go to a few events in the area, secretly hoping to run into him again, but he was never there. It's as if he was a ghost, determined to haunt my dreams and thoughts and ruin sex for me forever.

Realizing sleep is definitely out of the question now, I open my eyes, letting out an exasperated breath as I stare up at my new ceiling. Correction, Aaron's ceiling.

Glancing at the clock, I nearly jump out of my skin when I note the time.

Dominik...ugh!

I have exactly twenty minutes to get ready.

"Shit."

Bolting for the bathroom, I quickly shower and brush my teeth. I throw on a pair of skinny jeans frayed at the knee caps and an oversized blue sweater. I adjust the neckline, hoping the one side doesn't keep sliding off my left shoulder.

I should just cancel, knowing Dominik is only doing this as a favor to my brother. But even knowing how close they are, I was still surprised when he offered to take me around town last night. I always thought he couldn't stand to be around me, and that's probably still true, but maybe he owes Aaron. Or maybe he feels sorry for me.

Whatever. I'll put on my normal, good-girl routine, walk around and nod, counting down the seconds until I can head back home.

Living life with zero expectations feels better. I made a conscious decision to switch off that part of myself a long time ago. It's a defense mechanism, really. When you come to the real-ization that the two individuals who were supposed to love you unconditionally couldn't, you learn to detach yourself emotionally. By not allowing anyone to get too close, you set realistic bound-aries and avoid the disappointment that inevitably comes when they eventually walk away. Because, in the end, everyone always leaves.

I choose to live my life without any expectations, avoiding any attachments to people or things. Emotions are for the weak anyway.

After scrunching hair mousse through my damp hair, I put on some concealer, bronzer, mascara, and a nude-pink lip. Somehow, I managed to get ready in ten minutes, which is a record for me.

Realizing I could use a cup of coffee before Mr. Grump shows up, I head for the kitchen.

No sign of Aaron, per usual. I'm not even sure the man is human at this point. Seriously, when does he sleep? I don't even think he came home last night. He wasn't home when I left to get ice cream, and he didn't come back while I was pigging out, bent over the kitchen island like a total weirdo. If my mom had seen me, she would have had a total fit.

You're disgusting. Grab a bowl. Who eats ice cream out of the container? Uneducated, ill-mannered women...that's who.

I haven't spoken to her in months, and honestly, I'm grateful for the much-needed silence for the first time in my life. I'm sure my parents feel the same way about me. Actually, I think they would be delighted if they were to get a call one day saying they needed to come identify my body.

Don't be dramatic.

Funny, that's something my mother would say.

I grab my coffee and get comfortable on the couch, looking out at the beautiful New York morning. The sun has just risen, the apartment is utterly quiet, and I'm going to enjoy this moment of peace. Pulling the soft, fuzzy blanket over my legs, I flip open my book and get comfortable.

There is nothing like silence and great literature. My entire world could be in utter shambles, but when I open the pages of a book, I get completely lost within the story. Transported to another universe. It's an amazing escape from reality and something I need to help me get by.

I don't even get through two pages when the penthouse elevator dings, signifying someone's arrival. My heart speeds up, urging me to sit up straight and get off my ass, but I ignore it. Maybe if I pretend like he's not here, Dominik will turn around and leave. Not bothering with me or deciding to waste his Sunday after all.

I read the same sentence four times before finally giving up on my book and turning around.

Dominik looks like a fucking god walking through Aaron's kitchen, shrouded in sunlight as if he's parting the clouds. My mouth goes dry at the sight of him. He's wearing black pants and a white dress shirt with a few buttons at the top left open to reveal hints of intricate black ink. My fingers tingle, wanting to trace the art underneath his shirt and explore all that's hidden.

His face is smooth, free of stubble, and his hair remains damp, starting to curl around his cheeks and the tops of his ears. His eyes glisten mischievously, and a carefully crafted smile tugs at the corner of his mouth. He stands tall above me, his blue and gold irises peering at me through dark lashes, and I'm certain I'm on the verge of melting.

This is unnecessary and unwanted.

He's also my brother's best friend. And he has absolutely no interest in me.

"Hi," he says, his morning voice deliciously hoarse with traces of sleep.

Finally regaining my composure, I tilt my head down, picking up my book.

"Didn't think you'd show."

Why do I sound so flustered all of a sudden?

Dominik casually walks over and takes a seat on the coffee table, positioning himself to face me. His strong legs stretch out, almost grazing against mine, as he leans forward and rests his elbows on his thighs. The intoxicating scent of Irish Spring and cedar quickly fills my nostrils, causing a stir within me despite my less-than-ideal situation.

"What made you think today was a suggestion? I thought I was clear."

There is nothing sexier than a man who takes control. But this isn't any man—this is Dominik, and these thoughts and flutters need to disappear immediately.

"And who says I have to listen to you?"

He arches his brows up in challenge. "Do you want me to make you, Zoe?"

Good lord.

Yes. I mean, no.

"Did Aaron put you up to this?"

When he doesn't answer, I glance back down at my book, praying he can't hear my thundering heart in this quiet room.

Men are easy. They provide surface value when I need it. Most of the time, it's shit, but I enjoy the company for a few hours. That's why I took an interest in Greg. He was nice to look at, but unfortunately, that's where it ended for him. Attractive men are not necessarily good in bed. Actually, more often than not, they are utterly selfish in bed.

Dominik's large hand comes into view abruptly as he snatches my book away, hurling it across the room.

"What the fuck, Dominik!"

"I don't take well to being ignored, little brat."

The nickname triggers a flurry of fluttering butterflies deep in my belly. It's a name I've been called before.

"Don't call me that."

"Why not? You're being a brat, ignoring me when I got up early to take you out and show you around the city."

Throwing my legs over, I look him dead in the eyes. "That's very nice of you, but I didn't ask you to do that."

Dominik's gaze has always been both intimidating and intriguing. It ignites a fiery sensation within me, gently licking at the corners as his intense stare threatens to fuel the growing flame.

"That's too bad. You can either enjoy yourself today or you can be in a sour mood. The decision is entirely up to you, but we're going to go regardless. I'm not leaving."

Those three little words tug at my heart, squeezing so tightly that it takes my breath away. I drop my head, playing with the edge of the blanket as I try to figure out a way to get out of today with Dominik. There must have been something in that ice cream last night that's making my emotions so volatile.

"Don't waste your time. New York is probably going to kick me out soon too."

"No amount of time with you would be a waste, Zoe. Now come on, we have an entire city to see."

Dom's voice softens as he takes my hand in his, standing up and gently pulling me off the couch. I don't dare to look up, questioning if I misheard him. Then, I feel his fingers toying with the ends of my hair.

"Is this for me?" he whispers, his gaze fixed on my hair as his fingers twist the ends.

The side of his palm brushes my chest, instantly causing my nipples to harden.

"Don't be ridiculous." Stepping away, I take in a strained breath and try to clear my thoughts.

"Whatever you say, Butterfly."

One word is all it takes to stop me in my tracks.

Butterfly.

Before I can process another thought, he strides past me and out of the room. I'm left standing there, frozen like a stone, watching his retreating back.

What just happened?

"Let's go, Jackson! There is a food truck close by that sells the best breakfast burritos. That's our first stop."

CHAPTER 22

ZOE

What are you doing? You've been MIA. Also, I'm seriously considering moving to New York. I hate it here without you.

I smile, staring down at my phone as a new text from Sammy pops up. I've missed her more than I realized. It's crazy how you get used to seeing someone every day and it feels like a part of you is missing when it all stops. She's the only person I've ever had a healthy, long-term, detached-but-attached relationship with. It's weird and wonderful all at the same time.

ME

I miss you. Please come. You can stay at my brother's place. I don't even care if he says no. I'll sneak you in.

SAMMY

I am packing. Are you loving NY? Have you been touring around? Is your brother being a good host? Stop forcing me to ask so many questions!

ME

Sorry, it's been busy. Currently out with Dominik on a NYC grumpy tour. He's getting on all my nerves.

SAMMY

Shittttt...I'm going to need a recap later. Expect a call after work. I'm going to leave you to your date.

My eyes bulge, and I glance up to see Dominik still standing at the breakfast food truck, waiting for his order.

ME

It's not a date, you psycho! I love you, talk later.

A date. Yeah, right. My ass.

Everything within me is screaming to throw Dominik Lewis in front of fast-moving traffic, or at least it was until today. It's maddening how badly I want to despise him, but the events of today have made that incredibly challenging. I can't help but wonder if Dominik has always been this eccentric and detail-oriented, or if his successful hockey career has transformed him into this person. I distinctly remember him not being this way when we were teenagers, but then again, I've changed too. I'm so much different than the person I was back then.

I expected him to be moody today and was pissed he had ruined my relaxing Sunday plans, but he has somehow crafted the perfect day with little effort. I'm convinced he could easily charm a rock if he wanted to. He's definitely leveled up over the years, and it's noticeable enough for me to want to ask him to teach me and help me improve, to become a better version of myself. But at this point, self-sabotage and I are in a committed, established relationship.

Hooray for me.

I've always believed Dominik harbored a deep dislike for my mere existence, perceiving me as an obstacle when all he truly cared about was getting closer to Aaron. I'd often drawn parallels between him and my parents, assuming they shared that sentiment.

But today, I don't know what to feel or think. He has been anything but selfish and uncaring.

We spend the rest of the morning walking around Hudson Yards. Dominik points out some of the must-see places and shops, including luxury stores like Chanel and Louis Vuitton, which I'll never step foot inside because I can't even afford a fingernail in there. He tells me all the places to eat and where I can find necessities late at night. He shows me shortcuts to take that are safe when I want to get home from work and which ways to absolutely avoid. He puts his number in my phone by force and tells me to call him immediately if I ever find myself in a rough area of the city. My safety is apparently a top priority for him all of a sudden.

News to me.

Aaron probably said something to him. He's always trying to protect me, as if I'm a wilted flower he's desperate to smooth out to its original state.

But that's impossible.

Aaron and Dominik clicked from the very beginning. An instant bond of brotherhood I never understood but admired more than I wanted to. Nothing has ever come between them, and I know nothing ever will. I'm happy my brother has such supportive people bonded to him by choice. I just never understood why Dominik disliked me so much. But then again, does anyone need a reason to hate someone? My parents have always hated me for simply existing. I wish my mother had had the balls to abort me when she'd had the chance.

Observing Dominik, I watch his movements as he beams while sharing the story of the time he scored three goals at one of his first NHL games. I believe he called it a hat trick. I remember Aaron talking about this game and telling me how proud he was to know Dominik. But, I keep this information to myself, simply watching as Dominik narrates the events as if he is reliving them in this very moment. I pay close attention to the subtle movements of his lips, the intensified gleam in his eyes, and the flawless curling of his dark hair. He really is beautiful.

The wind has been surprisingly calm today and the sun bright, perched high up in the clouds. It feels like the beginning of spring even though we still have all of February to get through.

We walk to Madison Square Garden where the New York Slashers play. A picture of Dom's face is hanging from the side of the building, along with all the other players. His blue and hazel eyes are large and commanding as they look down at the entirety of the stadium parking lot.

His eyes have always reminded me of the moon and the sun. Both intensely captivating.

I notice him watching me as I pretend to inspect the pictures, feigning interest in the other players. I just hope my poker face was on point while I was sneakily admiring him.

We walk around the streets of Hudson Yards and New York City like two tourists, and I can't help but blush knowing I am being shown around by a famous hockey player. I hadn't really looked at him that way until I saw his entire team lined up on the outside of a massive hockey stadium. Life is so different now than when we were both a couple of kids living in Boston.

There is an ease about the guys in Aaron's circle. Although they are all successful and wealthy, they don't flaunt it or treat anyone differently. They have managed to stay humble. I don't know Tristan that well, but I know Aaron, and he hates fake people just as much as I do.

"Surely you've been to Central Park? When you were here visiting Aaron last time?" Dom says before he takes another bite out of his hot dog. We ate lunch an hour ago, but he needed to stop at a hot dog stand for a snack. The guy never stops eating; it's remarkable. How does he manage all those muscles? I imagine he's just full of hard curves under all those clothes.

Let's not picture Dominik's naked body full of muscles, please and thank you.

"Yes, of course. Give me some credit."

He smiles, and I nearly trip over my feet.

"Aaron's old apartment was close to here, and I would come for runs in the park at night."

Dom stops chewing and glares at me. "Do you still run at night?"

"Sometimes."

"You shouldn't. It's fucking dangerous."

I love running in the dark. It's so peaceful being the only one out when most of the city is indoors or asleep. It's like I can step out freely, no masks...no hiding or pretending to be someone I'm not. It also reminds me of that night in the woods with Runi, which is always a welcome memory to pull up.

"What was that?"

I shake off the memories from six years ago. "What?"

"Where did you just go?"

My heart rattles in my chest. "Nowhere."

His gaze sharpens on me. "Don't lie. You just went down memory lane for a second. Anything in particular?"

He's good, or maybe I'm just that pathetic.

I shake my head. "Is our neighborhood safe for nighttime runs?"

Dominik chews carefully, deciding to let me drop the former conversation.

"No. Use the building's gym if you want to workout at night. It's safe and open 24/7."

"It's not the same as running outside."

"No. Because it's safe."

I shrug. "What's the fun in that?"

He pops the last bite into his mouth, crumpling up the foil and throwing it into a nearby trash bin.

A runner whizzes by me just then, stealing my attention toward the grassy park. A toddler is chasing a dog, his contagious laugh filling the air around us. I can't help but smile. The sound of a baby laughing instantly brings me joy. Maybe it's the innocence in their voice or the unfiltered happiness on their face. Life hasn't had a chance to dim their light yet, and something about that just brings me hope. Knowing they have more time.

"Do you enjoy being frightened?" he whispers, sending a chill down my back.

"What?"

His hand grasps my elbow, stopping me from taking another step. Dom stares at me with a pinched expression.

"Promise me you won't go running late at night in New York. It's a different city; there are more people, and a lot more crime. Let someone know if you want to go for a night run."

I shouldn't have said anything. "Okay, sure."

"I mean it."

"Okay."

He sighs out his relief, really looking the part of giving-a-shit. "Thank you, Zoe."

I roll my eyes, unable to stop myself. "Not sure why you've decided you care all of a sudden. You've been great at avoiding me all my life."

My words cause him to flinch, and he drops my elbow, taking a step back. Anger is quickly replaced by dejection, as if I dropped a bucket of ice-cold water all over him. My heart sinks, and I open my mouth to apologize, but he speaks before I have a chance to.

"Just because I wasn't there, it doesn't mean I didn't care, Zo. I've always cared about you. More than I should have," he utters almost too softly. The words strike me with such force, each one stronger than the next, as they land directly in the middle of my chest.

More than he should have? Meaning what, exactly?

We're interrupted by the sound of Dom's phone as he quickly fishes it out of his pocket, cursing to himself before remembering I'm standing in front of him.

"I'm sorry. I have to take this."

He places the phone up to his ear. "Hey, Coach."

Dominik walks away, and I replay his words in my mind a thousand times. Yet, with each repetition, I'm left more confused than before. I don't understand why I allow people's words to gnaw at me, why I obsess over them when they don't hold as much weight for others. Words linger for hours, days, weeks...even years.

I'm cursed with feeling too intensely and overanalyze every aspect of life. Even in moments of numbness, I experience it with my whole being, allowing it to engulf me completely until there is only emptiness remaining.

⟶

THE CAB RIDE back home is quiet. It's only quarter past four, but we have to head back since Dom's coach wants to see him immediately. I don't ask questions, and he doesn't fill me in. It must be some sort of hockey emergency if he has to go in right away. I'm staring out the window, watching people hurriedly walk down the sidewalks. Others are stepping out, trying to hail cabs. Purpose, drive, and motivation guide these people. And I'm over here with nowhere to go and no one to see. No purpose. No direction. Just here passing time.

"I'm sorry we had to leave," Dominik says, cracking his knuckles as nervous energy fills the quiet cab.

"It's okay. I understand. It's work."

His eyes lock onto mine.

Every time he looks at me, he takes my breath away. Both eyes are so vivid, so beautiful. Each tells a different story. Stories I have never been able to read and likely never will. Dom and I coexist, both tolerating one another for the sake of Aaron.

"I wouldn't be leaving, but apparently whatever it is can't wait."

"It's fine. You don't owe me an explanation."

"I intended to spend the entire day with you."

I extend my hand, gently placing it on the back of his. The moment our skin touches, a familiar sensation surges through me, one that I can't quite pinpoint. It feels as though his touch is encompassing my entire being all at once. Dom's gaze falls upon my hand, his eyes widening in surprise. His jaw clenches, revealing a flash of anger before he swiftly withdraws his hand. I instantly regret my attempt to connect with him, feeling like a complete fool. I'd hoped we had moved past all the unresolved issues and unspoken resentment he has toward me, but apparently I misread the entire day.

I won't be touching him ever again.

I won't be spending any more time with him, actually. The man has some serious issues, and I don't have the patience to get tangled up in his nasty web.

He is Aaron's problem, not mine.

When the cab pulls up at our apartment building, I slip out quickly, not looking back as I beeline for the tall, glass doors. Unable to hold back any longer, I allow a single tear to skate down my cheek. It disappears down my neck by the time George appears outside.

CHAPTER 23

DOMINIK

"**D**o you care to explain to me what the fuck this is, Lewis?"

Coach Bradley forcefully places his iPad on the table in front of me, capturing my attention. With unwavering eye contact, I lean in and swiftly glance at a substantial online forum thread. To my surprise, my name is prominently displayed in bold letters at the very top.

I scroll through hundreds, maybe thousands of posts directed at me, filled with spiteful words and labeling me as a despicable person. According to these posts, I've been deemed the ultimate NHL fuckboy, a notorious player who exploits women solely for my own fun. There's not a single mention of the number of times I've been begged to take a woman to bed or the number of orgasms I've handed out. They fucking wanted me.

All the posts are anonymous, allowing users to post openly.

His one-night rule is bullshit, and it's only there to get him off the hook.

Dominik Lewis is a prick and hates women.

Verbal consent can be removed, and I wanted to remove it after the fact, when he didn't even cast me a sideways glance before handing me my dress and telling me to have a good night.

Are you kidding me?

I tried contacting him, but he wouldn't answer me, and then the fucker blocked me!

He's a fuckboy, and the worst part is he doesn't give a shit who he hurts. Also, what the hell is up with the no-kissing rule? It's the biggest bullshit I have ever heard.

The man has no heart.

I lean back in my chair, crossing my arms across my chest. "What's the problem?"

As soon as the words are out of my mouth, I want to swallow them and punch myself in the face. The vein in Coach's forehead triples in size as he pins me with a terrifying look. I'm tempted to turn around and call for backup, but I keep my composure, knowing weakness is exactly what he's looking for right now and I can't show my cards until I know exactly what's going on. This isn't good, but I'm not the first guy to have a bad reputation as a player.

Coach Bradley is the best coach the Slashers have had in a long time. He is known in the industry for being an amazing tactician on the rink, skilled in every way to bring a team together and have them working as one smooth machine. He has never failed, and he isn't about to start now. He believes this sport can change lives and shape the future of so many people outside of the team. He was an unstoppable player in his time, until an unexpected injury cut his professional hockey career short. But he didn't let that setback stop him. He used it as fuel to become the best coach around, and we were lucky enough to have him join our team last year.

"Keep reading," Bradley bites out, dragging out every word.

I bring the iPad onto my lap and keep scrolling through the comments, determined to brush off all the insults being hurled my way. My sole concern at the moment is avoiding further aggravating Coach, as he has no issue benching problematic players.

One comment in particular stands out to me, and it has the most likes and replies.

Dominik used my sister and me at the same time, made us feel safe, but then as soon as he had his fun, he discarded us like trash.

"What the fuck?!"

Coach stands beside his desk, brows furrowed, arms crossed tightly, as if he's repressing the urge to lash out at me right here and now.

"This isn't true. I've never made anyone feel unsafe. I'm very adamant about consent and making sure everyone is willing and comfortable before anything happens."

"Does it fucking matter? It looks bad, and it's getting unnecessary negative attention."

There are tons of photos and videos of me with various women. In clubs, at parties, a dark photo of me licking a girl's neck in the back of a cab. Screenshots of the two girls messaging me. A video of one of them speaking out about me. The caption reading, "Dominik Lewis is a prick and hates women."

I shoot up and out of my chair. "Listen, Coach, I swear none of this is true. I don't hate women."

He whips his ball cap off, throwing it on top of the desk as he runs his hand over his bald head. His wrinkles crack in the corners of his eyes as he shoots daggers at me. The man is ready to murder me right here. I've never seen him this worked up, not even when we're losing a game. Coach is usually the definition of calm. Even if there is a war breaking out inside him, he's great at hiding it.

"It's all right there, Dominik. You can't fight it. Even I can't fight it. I've notified our PR team to try to take it down, but it's spreading like wildfire. They've advised me to just let it sizzle out, but we need to do something to cover our asses. This doesn't look good for the team. Especially before playoffs."

Shit, shit, shit.

I have worked too hard to get here just to lose it all over something like this.

"What can I do?"

"You can start by keeping your dick firmly in your pants."

Pressing my chin to my chest, I feel nothing but shame to be where I'm sitting, holding the position of captain on the team and getting reamed out for sleeping around like a careless asshole. So many guys sleep around. It's easy to get women when you are an athlete with deep pockets, but I guess most people cover their tracks and stay within the lines. I got clumsy.

"I'm sorry, Coach. This is embarrassing. It's always been—"

Coach cuts me off, his voice bellowing in the small office. "I don't give a shit about any of that, Lewis! You're my best player, and I can't have you pulling this kinda crap. If I have to trade you or bench you, it's going to cost us the Cup. Fix your fucking shit!"

He's right. This is unacceptable.

"I will, promise."

He approaches me. His anger seems to be ramping up, despite my promise to rectify the situation. Coach isn't exactly short; he stands around six feet, maybe six one. However, with my six-five stature and build, I usually tower over most people. I'm aware Coach despises this, so I keep my focus fixed on the wall. He thrusts a finger into the center of my chest.

"You fucking better, because the trade deadline is fast approaching, and I'm not losing my best player because he likes to get his dick wet by an endless lineup of women. I don't care what you have to do, Lewis. Fix it and fix it now."

I nod while desperately trying to hide my smirk.

"The fuck are you smiling at?"

Tilting my face away, I turn and grab my coat from the back of the chair. He wasn't meant to see that, but maybe I can lighten the mood a bit.

"Sorry, Coach, but I have to take a win where I can. You said I'm your best player." Turning around, I hope to see him crack a smile, but the man is unimpressed. Instead, he closes his eyes and pinches the bridge of his nose.

Read the damn room, Dominik.

"Get the fuck out, and don't make me drag you back into this office ever again."

Don't have to tell me twice.

Storming down the empty hallway, I wrack my brain, pulling up every night and random memory, trying to figure out where I went wrong. Who I pissed off so badly that it warranted an entire online thread which has bled over to other social media platforms. I'm not the first hockey player, nor will I be the last, to fuck for sport. We all get a lot of attention, and there is nothing wrong with that. Women love us, and we love them. So why am I getting blamed for something that has always been consensual? I take my time laying out the rules, making sure the women are always comfortable, and by the time we're done talking, they're basically begging me to fuck them.

Another hard rule I never break is the no-kissing rule. I haven't kissed any other woman on the lips since Zoe at the masquerade ball six years ago. It just never felt right, and after Zoe, it made sense to leave it out when it came to sex. It also establishes a clear boundary with the women I choose to share my bed with, or so I thought. Turns out my efforts were futile.

I have a thing for quiet, submissive women, and maybe that's where I went wrong. Because a lot of the time, they want more, and that's not something I'm interested in.

This is completely my fault. I should have been more careful and calculated in the women I chose, and I should've spaced out my rendezvous. It doesn't even matter at this point. There is no way to go back, and the only thing left to do right now is learn from this and figure out a way to shut down the rumors.

But how the hell do I do that? No one is going to listen to me.

There are too many comments, too many women who hate my guts right now. Most of the guys on the team have girlfriends or wives. The single ones keep things very secretive and for good reason. Why did I think this wouldn't happen to me?

And then it hits me.

Tristan will know what to do.

He works for one of the top Wall Street banks as a hedge fund manager. His guys are always getting into trouble at gentleman's clubs or after-hours events. Their problems always involve money and women, and the things he's shared with us, in very little detail — were way worse than this. Child's play, he would call it. Tristan should be able to sort this out in a matter of hours. Some of the assholes at the firm have done questionable shit, which Tristan has never disclosed but handled effectively. Aaron and I never asked because, frankly, we don't want to know. All I know is Tristan doesn't hurt anyone innocent, and he keeps his firm protected. These people never make the same mistake twice. The fuckers learn their lessons, even if they have to serve some time or get a good beating in a back alley. Although I don't know any names, I know no one dares mess with Tristan anymore. Everyone is scared of him, which sometimes makes me wonder what kind of dealings he manages if he's that intimidating.

I pull out my phone, opening the group chat between the three of us.

> ME
>
> Emergency meeting. My place in twenty.

> AARON
>
> How bad?

> ME
>
> Bad.

> TRISTAN
>
> Fuck, Dom... I think I know what this is about. I'll be there in thirty. Just finalizing a deal.

> AARON
>
> Both of you come to my place. I have better alcohol.

I quicken my pace as I head home, repeating to myself that it's not over until it's over.

I can turn this around. This is just a small hiccup. I will fix this, no matter what it takes.

Crossing the street, long, golden hair catches my attention, and the nail in my chest twists painfully. Feeling guilty for the way I left things with Zoe earlier.

Today is definitely not my day.

CHAPTER 24
DOMINIK

"This couldn't have happened at a worse time." Aaron throws my phone back at me as he continues to pace. He loosens his tie, pulling it off and carefully folding it before laying it on the back of his chair.

I came straight to Aaron's after speaking with Coach, knowing he and Tristan are the only ones who will be able to help me find a solution before this gets too far out of hand. I can't trust myself with making the right decisions now; I don't even know exactly how I ended up in this mess in the first place.

Watching Aaron pace is giving me a fucking headache.

"Cut it out and sit down."

Aaron glares at me. "Did you fuck every single one of them?"

"Are you going to judge me?...Right now?...Seriously?"

"I'm not judging."

"Yes, you are. I know that look."

Aaron sighs, dragging his hand down his face. "I'm not judging you for having sex with multiple women. There is nothing wrong with that. I'm concerned your"—he pauses, choosing his next words carefully—"other activities are going to pop up next, and if they do, I'm not sure how you will come back from that."

Gritting my teeth, I hold my tongue. "Care to expand on that?"

I expect Aaron to meet me with a similar wrath, but he doesn't. He never loses his cool. He leans his hands on the back of the sofa and stares at me dead in the face.

"You know exactly what I'm referring to, Dominik. And I hope you never took it too far."

"For fuck's sake, Aaron. You know I would never do that. Especially not with women I meet at parties. That type of shit requires commitment and trust."

"I know. And I'm sorry for bringing it up, but I just needed to be sure."

"I haven't done anything like that in a long time."

He nods, and I drop my head, needing to tamp down my anger over all of this.

Sex hasn't meant much to me in a long time. And the more I think about it, the more I realize that lately, it's only made me feel more alone. It's always the same exchange, just with a different face. How could I find meaning in random hookups after that night in Boston?

And now, I'm sitting here, dealing with this problem that I created only to try to forget her. Erase the feel of her from my body, as if that's even possible.

"None of these women even care about me. They just want the experience and the trophy to tell their friends about later."

Aaron is carefully watching me, deciphering my words as if they are coded in Egyptian hieroglyphics. He's always analyzing, calculating body language and hidden meaning behind words.

"I'm sure they have wanted to break down your walls, but you won't let them. You and your twenty rules. Have you ever considered going on a date for once in your life?"

I groan, running my hand through my hair and wishing Tristan would arrive already so we can resolve this and I can get the hell out of here.

"I don't want to go on dates. I'm not interested."

"And why not?" Aaron fires back.

"Why don't you go on any fucking dates, Aaron? Get off my case."

He raises his hands in the air to surrender, and I finally take a deep breath.

"Our careers are screwing us in the ass."

The ding of the elevator has me standing, facing the long entryway as Tristan finally comes to the rescue.

"About damn time," Aaron retorts, heading for the kitchen. "Drink?" he asks me, and I shake my head. "I'll get you one. You're going to need it."

Exasperated, I sit back and cradle my head in my hands. Praying to a God I don't believe in to help me get rid of this problem.

"I've got to hand it to you, man. Out of everyone, I really didn't think you'd find yourself in a PR mess like this. 'Dominik Lewis: Dominator and fuckboy' just doesn't mesh well," Tristan announces, laughing like this is a joke.

Maybe asking for their help was a bad idea. "If neither one of you plans on actually helping me, you can both fuck right off."

Something soft hits my face, and I flinch, catching the throw pillow before it falls onto the floor.

"Don't be a dick. We both left work early to come here for you, and I have an idea, but I need a drink first," Tristan says.

I watch as Aaron and Tristan exchange a few words, smiling casually as they make drinks. I wish I could be as calm as them, but then again, it's not their careers and lives on the line. It's mine, and I have every reason to want to panic right now. Hockey is the only thing I care about, and if Coach pulls me off…

I can't let that happen.

Tristan is in a gray suit today. His auburn hair is slicked back, perfectly in place like always. Even New York's strong winter winds don't seem to stand a chance. Both Aaron and Tristan take great pride in looking their best at all hours of the day. Maybe it has something to do with their professional careers, or maybe they just have sticks up their asses. Meanwhile, I'm the sloppy athlete with the mop on my head and tattoos all over my body. They fit together, and I don't. Maybe if I hadn't met Aaron in high school, I wouldn't be sitting here.

Tristan has always been an enigma to me. The guy has so much money, he doesn't even know what to do with it, yet he's frugal as hell and annoyingly down-to-earth. He is smart but plays dumb, purposely walking in the shadows. He is the only one who thrives, and even seems to outshine, in complete darkness. He loves to move in silence, and I admire him so much for it. He's like Batman. He keeps to himself, loves to play video games, and he makes smart financial decisions. He is level-headed and never shows his cards. I don't know how he does it. Sometimes it feels like he's Artificial Intelligence and we're just part of his experiment. Even though Aaron and I are his closest friends, there are so many things he hides from us. I just wish the guy would let down his guard once in a while. Maybe he only does with Aaron. Who knows?

I'm overthinking every aspect of my life right now. Usually, I'm not this self-conscious, but this entire ordeal is messing with my head. These guys are like my family, and no matter our circumstances, we always show up for one another.

Drinks in hand, Aaron makes his way over to me, handing me a whiskey before he takes a seat on the chair across the room. Tristan unbuttons his suit jacket, leaning against the kitchen countertop.

"I had a chance to look through all the social media threads on the car ride over. I know how to fix this, but I'm just not sure if we can find the right person for the job."

The right person for what?

"This is my mess. I don't want to hire someone to fix it for me. I need to fix this myself. Coach was very clear on that."

Tristan laughs, raising his crystal glass to his lips. "Sometimes, it's necessary to ask for outside help, and the way I see it, you only have one option here, Dominator."

I find my focus shifting toward the giant, floor-to-ceiling fireplace, distracted by the dancing flames. They flicker with hues of blue and red, gracefully engulfing the artificial logs behind the glass. I'm desperate to slow down time because I know I'm going to loathe whatever is about to come out of Tristan's mouth.

"Are you ready to hear my thoughts?"

I sit up straight, shifting closer to the edge of the couch. "No, but let's hear it anyway."

He takes a sip of his whiskey, his eyes fixed on the New York skyline. "You need a girlfriend."

I bark out a laugh. My friends look at me, their expressions somewhere between shock and confusion. Neither one of them even cracks a smile.

"Wait...you're serious? You can't be serious."

"I am. You need a girlfriend, or you need to make it appear like you have a girlfriend. People need to see that you don't actually hate women or the idea of commitment. And that the only reason you were jumping from woman to woman is because none of those girls were it for you. You hadn't found the one who changed everything. But now, you have."

This might be the funniest shit I've heard in a long time. "Oh, and just like that...I have found The One?"

Tristan shrugs.

"This is ridiculous. What else you got?"

I wait for Tristan to speak, to tell me he was joking, but when he continues to stare at me, I turn my focus on Aaron. He glances down inside his glass of amber, swirling it around as if it holds all the answers to my problems.

"I'm with Tristan, but I think I know how we can justify your behavior."

I stand and begin to pace, fighting the urge to pull out my hair and tell these two to go fuck themselves.

"Are you both hearing yourselves right now? I don't need a goddamn girlfriend. I need to fix this PR nightmare that's going around right now. Can we please get back on track? Me engaging with women is the reason I'm in this mess in the first place. Are you trying to get me traded?"

Unlike my best friends, I lack the ability to effectively manage my temper or emotions. The words effortlessly spill from my lips, my voice gradually escalating, and my fingers trembling with an overwhelming sense of frustration.

"I can find you someone trustworthy. Someone from my office who will be compensated generously," Tristan mutters, as if it's that simple.

I scoff, throwing my hands up in the air. "No fucking way. I can't believe that's the best you can come up with."

Tristan downs his drink, calmly placing his glass on the table behind him. Unlike me, he is utterly unfazed and sporting a borderline smile on that smug face of his. All it's missing is my fist.

"Dom's right. We can't pay someone at your work. It's too risky. He's a successful hockey player, and there is too much at risk with everything circulating. Someone could try to take advantage of him," Aaron finally chimes in.

"Thank you!" I extend my hand, grateful common sense is finally joining us.

"Like I said, I think I might have the solution." Aaron stands up and grabs Tristan's empty glass, walking over to the liquor cart to refill his drink. He walks back a minute later, and I might as well be watching a movie on pause, dying a little on the inside while I wait for these assholes to say something helpful.

"And that is?"

He quirks a brow at me, staying silent.

"Cut out the manipulative, quiet bullshit tactic, will you? It's just us."

They both remain quiet as Tristan grabs the whiskey from Aaron's outstretched hand, nodding his thanks to him. Feeling the weight of the world on my shoulders, I make my way over to the windows. Leaning my shoulder against the frame, I watch the sun lower into the Hudson River.

"Maybe I should just make a statement and apologize," I whisper.

"What are you going to apologize for? For not taking each woman you fucked on a date?"

I don't answer.

"Why don't you kiss any of them on the lips?" Tristan asks.

When I don't answer, he repeats the question.

"It forms an attachment."

"Not that the rule has helped any; they all still want you."

I wouldn't have wanted to kiss them anyway.

"But why is that a rule you've enforced?" Tristan presses further.

I turn to face him. "Does it matter?"

His right shoulder tips up. "Just curious."

Aaron takes a deep breath.

"It doesn't matter what he did or didn't do in the past. What matters is how he moves forward and does damage control from this moment on. You need to bury these posts with something new and exciting. Imagine posting a photo with a woman on Instagram. Everyone will flock. And then, you can maybe message the girls to apologize for hurting them and explain how it wasn't personal and your heart was never in it. How it always belonged to someone else."

I blink at him, not sure what he's getting at, but decide I don't care to find out.

"Please tell me you have something else, Tristan. Something actually good?"

The abrupt slam of a door followed by the shuffle of feet on the hardwood floor interrupts our conversation. All of us pivot our attention toward the noise.

Zoe, with her hair in a messy bun and wearing noise-canceling headphones, enters through the archway, singing at the top of her lungs. Her eyes are closed, and she's swaying her hips to the rhythm of The Pussycat Dolls' "Buttons" as she makes her way toward the kitchen. She's wearing nothing but tight black leggings and a blue sports bra, looking fucking mouth watering.

"Lord have mercy," Tristan breathes, his eyes fixed on Zoe.

She continues to sing and dance like she's the only one in the room. Shaking her ass and popping out her chest, highlighting her perfect, perky tits. Completely unaware that she has an audience standing a few feet away.

Oh, baby, I'll fucking loosen your buttons.

Tristan is basically drooling, and I want to strangle him for staring at her like that. I would do it if I wasn't distracted by the show. I'm worried that if I move an inch, she'll stop.

Her back is facing us as she drops to the floor, her ass sticking out in those deliciously tight pants as she starts to slowly make her way up. Her back arched and bent, she moves her lower body to the music. The sight of her grinding the air has my dick pushing against the seam of my jeans.

"I choose her. Fuck this friendship," Tristan utters, practically drooling on himself.

Aaron's hand flies out, shoving the side of Tristan's face as he goes down into the couch. But Aaron doesn't stop there; he delivers a vicious punch to Tristan's stomach, causing a guttural groan to fly out of Tristan.

Ouch, that didn't look too fun.

Aaron launches off the couch and grabs Zoe's elbow. She screams in shock as he drags her the rest of the way into the kitchen, both of them disappearing inside the walk-in pantry. I quickly adjust myself, but it's not enough. Nothing is going to cover up my fucking erection at this point. I get a flashback of her perfect ass pressing into my cock and feel myself grow even harder. Walking back to the chair, I sit down, grab a throw pillow, and press it into my crotch.

Goddammit, Zoe.

"Fuckkkk that fucking hurt, *bastard*!" Tristan sits up, one hand cradling his side while the other reaches for his whiskey. He downs the drink, smacking the glass down a bit too harshly before his eyes settle on me. Needing to occupy myself, I pull out my phone and scroll mindlessly...completely distracted by the mini-show that just took place in Aaron's living room.

When I look up, Tristan is smirking, eyes on the cream pillow that's currently resting on my crotch.

"I think I just found the solution to your problem."

CHAPTER 25
ZOE

I'm mortified.

I can't even express how embarrassed I am right now. My cheeks feel like they're on fire. There's absolutely no chance in hell I'm going back out there with those two hooligans lounging on the couch.

"A little heads up would have been nice!"

"I wasn't aware you would be performing a striptease while twerking over to the kitchen. What the fuck, Zo?"

My brother leans in, towering above me, somehow more pissed than I am.

The audacity of this guy.

"You're never here, and I had my headphones on. I've been cleaning and listening to music for hours in my room. How was I supposed to know tonight would be the night you'd actually be home?"

Aaron's brows furrow before he takes a deep breath and steps back.

"You're right. I've been too focused on work."

I can see the guilt written all over his face, and all I want to do is reach out, give him a hug, and reassure him that everything is all right. I understand that his career is his top priority, and I truly respect that. But it does feel like he's been avoiding me lately. I haven't brought it up because I don't want to come across as needy or make him feel guilty about it. It's not his fault that I lost my job and had to move to New York, basically crashing into his life, his home, and his daily routine.

Dropping my head, I glance at the perfect display of snacks in glass jars and containers sitting in his utterly neat walk-in pantry. This room is bigger than my entire bedroom in my shitty apartment back in Boston.

"This is your home, and I should have been more cautious. Sorry, Aaron."

His hands land softly on my shoulders. "Hey, this is your home too. Don't talk like that. I just don't—" His pause has me looking up, noting the hesitation on his face. "I don't like the guys seeing you like that."

"Like what?"

He glances down at my body, cringing.

"Not this again, Aaron."

"Not up for discussion, Zo. Now grab what you need and go back to your room. Put some clothes on."

Wow.

I shove past him, deciding to leave before I blurt out something entirely too harsh after I just apologized to him.

"I'm sorry. We're just dealing with something sensitive out there."

"Whatever."

A small, crunchy bag is shoved against my hand just as I'm walking out the pantry.

"Here, these are just like chips."

Glancing down at the bag, the word Kale stands out immediately. I'm two seconds away from strangling my brother.

"What a shitty peace offering."

He looks genuinely confused.

217

"They're good."

"You may have the palate of a sheep, but there is no way in hell I'm eating those." I shove back the bag and walk out, ignoring the nosy lurkers in the other room.

"Zoe, darling…can you please join us for just a second?" Tristan calls out from behind me.

I stop but don't turn around.

"Tristan, I swear, I'll kill you right here, right now," Dominik snarls.

"I'm trying to help you, jackass."

"No."

"I just want to propose this to Aaron and Zoe. If they hate the idea, then I'll drop it, I promise."

I slowly turn to face the guys, and my attention is drawn to Dom, who is standing behind Tristan with such a flushed face that it appears steam could erupt from his ears at any second. It looks like Tristan is one word away from Dominik spilling his blood all over Aaron's white couch.

"What's going on?" Aaron makes his way over to his leather armchair, grabbing his drink off the coaster.

"Nothing," Dom sneers, his nostrils flaring.

All right, I need to hear this now. There is definitely something juicy going on.

"You've got my attention," I chime in, smirking at Tristan, who turns toward me with a mischievous smile on his face, ushering me to take a seat beside him on the couch.

Crossing my arms, I shake my head. "I'm good right here."

"Suit yourself."

Tristan directs his attention at my brother, who is looking down at his Rolex, seemingly bored with this conversation already. A complete contrast to the other two men in the room. One is bursting with excitement while the other looks like he's about to shit his pants.

"Zoe should be Dom's fake girlfriend."

Come again?

I think I misheard whatever the hell just came out of Tristan's mouth because Aaron doesn't say anything. He simply continues sipping on his liquor as if he's enjoying a live jazz band at a fancy bar. Aaron should be reacting. Maybe spitting, yelling, throwing something. So I definitely misheard if Aaron is acting as cool as a fucking cucumber.

"I'm not listening to this," Dom bites out as he begins charging out of the room.

"Stop throwing a temper tantrum and get back here. Tristan might be onto something," my brother finally pipes up and nearly knocks the air out of my lungs with his words.

"What?!" I screech at the same time as Dominik speaks.

"We're not going to date," he growls.

I catch Dominik's eyes briefly, but he averts his gaze. I ignore the pang of disappointment that settles in the pit of my stomach. It's good to know he's equally bummed out about this suggestion as I am.

I shake away the cluster of thoughts overcrowding my brain, knowing the psychoanalyzing never changes anything, nor does it help. But no matter how many times I tell myself that, I can't stop thinking about the tone of Dominik's voice as he said those five words.

We're not going to date.

I glare at my brother, a silent plea to get me out of this with whatever dignity and respect I can scrape up, but he doesn't look at me.

A conversation in private would have been nice. It seems like they have already decided that I should help out, even though the guy involved doesn't even like me. Just as I'm about to leave the room, Tristan suddenly stands up and slowly walks toward me. He brings his palms together, almost like he's signaling a truce between us.

"I'm sorry. I shouldn't have sprung it on you like this. The situation with Dom is a bit time-sensitive. I'd be happy to fill you in, and then you can decide if you want to help or not."

I feel Aaron's eyes on me as I follow Tristan over to the couch.

"I don't need help," Dom utters.

Tristan whips around. "Shut up. You asked for help, and you're going to listen to what I have to say."

Tristan's previous easygoing nature transforms as he dominates the entire room. I half expect Dominik to resist, maybe fight back a little considering how upset he looks, but he takes a few steps back and sinks into his chair.

"He clearly doesn't want anything to do with me. It might be better to ask someone else."

"No, Zoe...that's not what's happening here. He's just embarrassed. You're the right girl for this job," Tristan says, tapping the sofa cushion beside him.

Casting a hesitant glance toward Dom, I notice that his eyes are downcast and his shoulders are slouched, as if he's been defeated. Tristan carefully grasps my elbow and pulls me down on the sofa next to him.

"I'll cut right to the chase. Some recent rumors have come to light regarding Dominik's"—Tristan struggles to find the right words—"night time activities. And considering he's a pro hockey player and in the spotlight, these rumors are really bad for his career. We need to squash them immediately."

"What kinds of things?"

The sensation of several sets of eyes on me makes my skin burn, but I divert my focus to Tristan.

"He's been having a bit too much reckless fun with his dick lately."

"Fuck my life," Dominik groans, dropping his head to his hands.

I bite the inside of my cheek, trying not to laugh.

Tristan loosens his burgundy tie, his knees grazing mine as he shifts a little closer.

"What? She's going to find out the second she goes digging, and she will. She's not stupid."

"Don't go digging." Dom looks up as if just realizing I have access to the internet. He's turning red. Now I'm definitely going to go digging.

"Sure."

He holds my gaze. Tired, gold and blue eyes pull me in, causing a wave of butterflies to take flight in the pit of my stomach.

"Really?"

"No."

Shifting my attention back to Tristan, a smile unconsciously forms on my face as he playfully winks at me, igniting a new kind of excitement within me.

"Try not to believe everything you read. But the threads aren't good. Essentially, we need to find a distraction that proves the rumors are false or that Dom has had a change of heart."

"Change of heart."

"Yeah, we need to make it appear like he's in a committed relationship."

Fat chance of that happening. The man hasn't had a change of heart since he was a teenager. I'm not even sure he believes in dating or knows what the word commitment means.

"And he can't find a real girlfriend?" I ask.

Tristan reaches for his whiskey, sighing. "Not this quickly. He needs to look stable, level-headed, and fully committed. The complete opposite of how he's been behaving. We need to make everyone believe he has fallen in love."

I burst out laughing.

That dreaded word we're all allergic to in this room.

"I know," Tristan utters.

Dominik's cautious gaze is fixed on me. With his elbows pressed into his thighs and his muscular physique straining against his shirt, I find myself becoming distracted and quickly avert my gaze.

I don't understand how Dominik fake-dating me could help.

Clearing my throat, I turn back toward Tristan. "And what does all of this have to do with me?"

"You are the key, Zoe. You work in public relations. You are Aaron's sister, which means we can trust you. You live here now, and the story would match perfectly. Childhood crushes turned into modern-day lovers, together at last. You moved here for work, Dom and Aaron are best friends, and he lives in the same building as your brother. It's perfect. We could coach you both, and once all the drama dies down, you can stage a quiet, fake breakup. Easy and simple."

Easy and simple. Nothing about this sounds easy or simple.

"Are you seriously going to sit there all night and stay quiet? We're family. Fucking say something. Tell him this idea is ridiculous," Dom exclaims to Aaron.

My brother lifts his whiskey glass to his lips, his eyes moving between Dom and me before he swallows and lets out an exasperated breath like we're toddlers and he's sick of our shit.

"I think it's a good idea."

Dominik gasps. "What is wrong with you two? No one would believe it. I've never dated a single woman. I don't even kiss anyone on the lips."

"What?" I blurt out.

Tristan waves his hand. "It's a stupid rule he has."

Dominik grinds his teeth, choking on everything he's not saying as he opens and closes his hands. I wish I could climb inside his head to know what he's thinking, find out exactly which parts of me he hates most. Are they the same parts I hate about myself?

"Did he hurt someone?" I ask Tristan.

"Absolutely not," Dom cuts in.

"No." Tristan shakes his head.

"He's just a broken whore." Aaron snorts.

Not entirely helpful, but I am relieved, knowing I wouldn't be able to play a role in this if he had hurt someone.

"Listen, I don't know what this is all about. Truth be told, I don't do relationships either so I have no idea what you'd expect of me, especially being in public with all of this. But I know for sure it would never work with me. Look at the way he's glaring at me."

Aaron and Tristan both glance at Dominik.

I want to help Dom, I really do. But I think I would make everything worse for him, and he doesn't need that right now.

Tristan leans in. "Let me worry about Dom."

I shake my head. "You shouldn't force anyone into anything. And as much as I want to help him, he needs to want this too, or no one is going to buy it. Look how pissed he is just sitting over there. You're going to sell love with that?"

"He's just having a rough day. He's not always like this, you know that," Aaron says.

"Do I? He's never been fond of me," I whisper under my breath, glancing down at my dry fingers. The winter in New York has a certain harshness to it, although it's not significantly different from Boston.

It's quiet for a long time.

"Zoe…" The sound of my name rolling off Dominik's tongue sends a cold chill down my spine. "I would hate to drag you into my mess. I created it; you shouldn't have to help me clean it up."

Glancing up, my breath hitches as I stare back at Dominik. God, he looks so defeated. How can I not help him?

What if I want to be dragged into your mess?

"I want to help however I can. Even if it's to use my PR experience to help you navigate through the next few weeks."

"Fuck, Zoe, you're the best." Tristan pulls me in for a hug, crushing my lungs against his rock-hard body.

"No…need," I grunt out, and he releases me with a laugh.

"This will never work." Dom slumps back in his chair, his face pointing at the vast ceiling.

Aaron chugs back his whiskey and stands up. "Actually, it is going to work. Tristan is good at dealing with shit like this. I trust

Zoe with my life; I know she won't fuck you over. And Dominik, the same goes for you. I know you won't hurt my sister." Aaron glares at Dominik, and a tense silence fills the air, lingering between them. It almost feels as if they have had this conversation before or are engaging in a silent power struggle.

It's fucking weird.

My brother finally continues. "You're family, Dom. We're all family here. So this plan is going to work for all those reasons. This is your only legitimate shot."

"Can you disown me so I can date your sister?" Tristan breaks the tension with a stupid joke that is about to backfire.

"Watch it, asshole. Not like you're even into women," my brother shoots back, causing Tristan to burst out laughing.

"Do you want proof? Just because I like to be discreet with my affairs does not mean they don't exist."

As he winks at me, a rush of warmth spreads across my cheeks.

"You touch her, and I'll fucking end you," Aaron seethes.

Not this again. Now I'm pissed.

"I'm a grown-ass woman. I can sleep with whoever I want. So back the hell off, Aaron."

"Not under my roof you can't."

Screw this, I'm out of here.

"Good thing I'm into public play anyway."

"Careful, Zo!" Aaron says to my back as I storm off to my room.

Who does he think he is? I love him, but what the hell? He doesn't need to protect me anymore. I'm not some wounded little girl. It's like he's trying to make up for all the times he couldn't protect me from our parents. Too late, Aaron. The damage has been done, and that ship sailed eons ago.

"Where are you going?" Tristan yells.

I wave my hand in the air without turning around, flipping them the bird for a split second before my arm drops.

"But we're not done talking about this!" Tristan pleads.

"We are for tonight. Email me your terms and conditions.

Besides"—I turn at the end of the hallway, facing the three of them —"your friend back there doesn't seem thrilled about this plan. So why don't you focus your efforts on him first and then get back to me."

Just as I turn, I hear Dom's deep voice caress down my back.

"Ball is in your court, Zoe."

CHAPTER 26
ZOE

Two days since the fake girlfriend proposal in Aaron's living room, and I'm still as confused as I was. Not to mention the fact that no one has given me a call or followed up with me. Not even a damn text message.

I had anticipated some sort of communication by now, but nope.

Nothing.

Zilch.

Why are men like this? They say something huge but then go radio silent for days. Meanwhile, I overthink and psychoanalyze everything I do or say. Endlessly torturing myself with the playback loop.

"Ball is in your court, Zoe."

It doesn't feel that way.

Even my brother hasn't bothered to say anything or ask me how I'm feeling about the whole thing. And of course I pretend like it never happened, because I'm not going to be the first one to put effort in. If Dominik needs my help to fix this mess he's found himself in by sticking his dick in every wet hole, then he can follow up or send me a goddamn text.

I spent three hours that night going through Instagram and

TikTok. Looking at photos and videos of Dominik draped over gorgeous women. Models with miles for legs and perfectly golden skin, beautiful, flowing hair, and eyes that even I could get lost in. Of course he pulls women who look like that, why wouldn't he? He's Dominik Lewis. All-star hockey player who looks like he was brought to life at the hands of a world-renowned sculptor.

Before I knew it, two hours passed and I had fallen down a very deep social media hole, drowning in a sea of anger. I couldn't sleep, so I changed into workout clothes and headed to the apartment's state-of-the-art gym. It was close to midnight, so the entire place was deserted, which felt heavenly, especially in a gym like that.

I worked off all my frustrations until I was exhausted and spent, my muscles burning from relentless abuse. I pushed myself until the images of all those women disappeared to a dark corner in my mind.

I'm not jealous. Just a bit surprised, I guess.

I hadn't expected Dominik to be so careless with the way he partakes in sexual activities. Don't men in his position take extra care and maybe settle down with one pussy for a few months at a time? But he's never been a one-woman type of guy, has he? So how the hell am I supposed to sell love when he's never even had a girlfriend?

I, who am average at best, am supposed to make everyone believe that Dominik, with his gorgeous face and body, picked me?

It's impossible. Laughable.

This is such a disastrous idea already.

"Hey, Zoe, can you run across the street and grab me an espresso with extra foam? Here's my card," Tracy, my new boss, says in passing as she drops her Amex on my desk.

"Of course. And good morning," I mutter the last part quietly to myself. Grabbing my phone, I glance over at Via, who is completely in the zone. She's bobbing her head, headphones firmly in place as she drafts an article for a client. She also has a few marketing plans she needs to get through today, so she told me to not bother her unless it's an emergency.

But what kind of friend and colleague would I be if I went to the coffee shop and didn't ask if she wanted anything?

Looking around my desk, I spot a small, orange pumpkin eraser and whip it at her. Why does she even have a seasonal eraser in January? I bite the inside of my cheek to keep from laughing as I watch the small thing bounce across our shared cubicle floor. Via jerks back, pushing aside her earpiece.

"Did you just throw an eraser at my head?"

"I'm running across the street to grab Tracy coffee. Do you want anything?"

"You think you're so funny." I don't realize I'm still laughing until she speaks again.

"Sorry. I meant it with love."

Via narrows her eyes at me, her lips pursed. "Double espresso. And if you interrupt me again when I'm on a roll, I'll cut off your head."

"Noted. Next time, I won't ask if you want coffee."

She points her finger at me. "You *always* get me coffee. Double espresso, four sugars."

Still smiling like an idiot, I shake my head and start to walk away.

Don't get too attached. Via won't be sticking around either.

Sure, thank you for the reminder.

The wait for someone to eventually leave is the hardest part about any relationship. Because good ol' anxiety is right; they do all leave at some point. Nothing lasts forever. Not the good days and not the bad ones either. That's why I've stuck around all this time, knowing the bad days come in waves. I just have to keep my head above water until the worst of it passes.

But then what? Live day to day and look forward to nothing? What have I been waiting for?

I don't want to think about that right now. Sometimes, the intrusive thoughts are so dark, they take me by surprise. I wonder if there are others out there who constantly battle with themselves to stay alive. To find purpose in the every day.

At least I have learned how to detach. Call it self-sabotage or whatever you want, but it's what I like to do, what works for me. It's the only way I get to hold the cards in the palm of my hand and control my expectations in any given situation.

I never get attached.

There is only one time I've regretted walking away first, and that was the night I met Runi. I wish I had said goodbye, thanked him for everything. He was the one person who has ever brought me to life and given me exactly what I had been craving. He was like a shooting star, a captivating and mesmerizing sight. The speed at which he accelerated was so rapid that our time together felt fleeting, over in the blink of an eye.

I'll never forget him.

And I'll never forget the way I slipped out when his shields came down and he drifted off to sleep. I was so tempted to lift his mask, see the mystery man behind the mask ingrained into my brain. But if I had looked, I might not have left. It might have changed everything, and I didn't want to tamper with the perfect night we had created together.

I did the right thing, slipping out in torn clothing with nothing but the memories of that night to cherish. That night will forever be a secret I treasure and the beginning of a lifestyle I knew I couldn't leave behind.

It's been a long time since I've indulged, but now that I'm in New York City, I should be able to find a long-term play partner. I'm going to post on Rabbit Hole once I feel a bit more established, see if I can find a trusting primal player. I cannot waste my time with men like Greg ever again. I'd rather be celibate.

The coffee shop across from the office is always crowded. I settle in for at least a twenty-minute wait close to the door and pull out my phone, searching the BDSM forums on Rabbit Hole.

The coffee shop chatter fades in and out until a name stands out.

"The new girl, Zoe?"

"Yes! They apparently kicked her out of Boston for sleeping with all the men in her office."

"All the men? How? She's not even that pretty."

"I know. I don't get it."

"Wait...I thought she was obsessed with Greg."

"I don't know. All I heard from Julie was that Greg was so scared, he had to get a restraining order and send her here because they were worried she was going to hurt someone! Can you believe we got stuck with the psycho lover?"

Their voices may be just whispers, but it feels as though they are screaming directly into my ear. They are spreading rumors about me, rumors that will only continue to circulate. It's the reason everyone has been so cold toward me. People who don't even know me won't look at me or make conversation in common areas. I wonder what Tracy must think about all of this. Is this why she never greets me in the mornings?

Oh, God.

The knot inside my chest coils tighter, but I try to breathe through it. I pull up Dominik's number and fire off a text before I have a chance to second-guess myself.

"Game on, Lewis. Let's do this."

These bitches are going to regret spreading rumors, and by the time I'm done, Greg is going to wish he never met me.

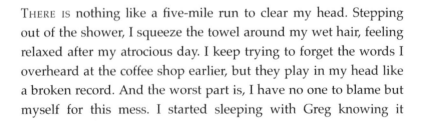

THERE IS nothing like a five-mile run to clear my head. Stepping out of the shower, I squeeze the towel around my wet hair, feeling relaxed after my atrocious day. I keep trying to forget the words I overheard at the coffee shop earlier, but they play in my head like a broken record. And the worst part is, I have no one to blame but myself for this mess. I started sleeping with Greg knowing it would only end badly. I guess I just never anticipated that it would follow me here.

My phone buzzes on my nightstand, the screen lighting up to signify an incoming text message. The fluttering in my stomach has me walking faster toward my phone.

DOM

We'll need to establish some ground rules.

ME

Such as?

DOM

No kissing or physical contact of any sort.

ME

So...you're not going to get anywhere near me even though you've slept with half the city already? How is anyone going to buy this?

Three dots appear then disappear, three...four times before the bubbles reappear. He has no issue touching a plethora of women, but me? Not a chance. Unfathomable. Disgusting. Out of the question.

DOM

I'll initiate the physical contact when necessary. But only when absolutely required for staging purposes.

For staging purposes? Who talks like this? What are we even doing?

ME

Wow, that's romantic. And quit texting like you're talking to a business partner. You've known me forever.

DOM

Believe me, I'm aware of that.

Whatever that means.

ME

I have one condition.

DOM

Let's hear it.

ME

We have to be honest with one another, and if at any point it becomes too much, we walk away. And it doesn't change anything between us. I don't want Aaron to get caught in the middle of all this.

DOM

Deal. But nothing is going to happen.

No, of course not. Heaven forbid he would ever want someone like me.

DOM

You have to come to my games.

I groan, regretting my decision already.

ME

To all of them?

DOM

No. But most. And that might mean a few away games too. I'll cover all the costs.

This might actually work in my favor. I can use Dom's status to shove the Greg rumors in everyone's face.

ME

Deal. And I might need you to show up to a couple of work events, maybe a few social posts or two. I need help squashing some rumors at the office.

DOM

What's going on?

ME

Nothing. Just bullshit from Boston following me here. If they see you, things will definitely quiet down.

DOM

Do you need me to come up so you can tell me what happened?

ME

No. Calm down, it's fine. I'm a big girl. Just...I might need your help.

The dots linger for a long time, and my heart begins to race, wondering if I'm asking for too much. Even a fresh start hasn't been fresh for me. My baggage from back home is too heavy for even me to carry.

DOM

I'll be whatever you need, Zoe.

I'm...speechless.

ME

Thank you, Dominik. I promise to be the best fake girlfriend you've ever had.

DOM

You'll be the only girlfriend I've ever had.

Excuse me? Surely not.

ME

You're joking.

DOM

I'll drop by after work tomorrow to go over my schedule for the next couple of months.

ME

Okay. Night.

He ignores my statement, and I place my phone down on the comforter, still baffled at the fact that Dominik has never had a girlfriend. How is that possible? The guy seems to have it all, except for a couple of loose bolts in his head, but everyone has issues. He could have whomever he wants and he chooses not to date? It must get lonely for someone without abandonment issues.

I get up to hang my towel and my phone buzzes.

DOM

Goodnight. And Zoe...thank you. For all of this.

I smile, imagining him lying in bed, staring down at his phone and typing out the thank you message to me before he falls asleep. I wonder what's going through his head and how much he's hating needing my help right now. If he's never had a girlfriend, this invasion into his personal life must be frustrating as hell. But I would be lying if I said I wasn't slightly excited about it. I'll never tell him that, because deep down, I know he's dreading the next few months he has to spend pretending he actually likes me.

And I'll need a distraction to get through everything going on in my life.

Pulling out my laptop, I open a new browser and type Rabbit Hole into the internet search bar.

CHAPTER 27
DOMINIK

That's the third fucking shot I've missed at practice today. I'm feeling incredibly off my game, and it seems like everyone has noticed. I'm well aware that if I steal a glance at Coach, his face will be as red as a strawberry.

This isn't typical of me. Normally, I don't let external issues affect my performance on the ice. Hockey has been my refuge for as long as I can remember, the only thing that truly helps me escape. But everything is different now.

"Lewis! Get your head out of your ass!" Coach's howl steals my attention. His arms are crossed, his face is beet-red, and he's furiously chewing on gum, likely grinding his molars to dust, all thanks to me.

It's not up my ass, I left it at Aaron's penthouse, apparently.

Do I tell Coach about my new arrangement with Zoe? Tristan said to not tell anyone outside of our circle, and it makes sense. The less people who know, the better. I can't have this getting leaked and everyone finding out I bribed some girl to help make it look like I give a fuck about relationships.

Some girl?

Not just some girl. It's Zoe. *My* Zoe. The only girl I have ever wanted but can never truly have. And now...what am I supposed

235

to do? Just accept this situation? Explore the possibilities of a world where we could actually be together? But the harsh reality will be lurking in the shadows, reminding me that none of it is real. Eventually, it will come to an end, and I'll walk away forever changed again.

How am I supposed to live without her now that I've had a taste? I won't be able to let her go this time. It's not in me to just move on.

There is no moving on from Zoe.

Maybe she'll back out.

She won't. That's not like her.

I skate to the back of the net, juggling my hockey stick nervously between my hands as I catch Liam's sympathetic eyes.

Focus.

Except the more I tell myself to stop thinking about her, the more she occupies my mind. I'm secretly hoping she'll change her mind. Hoping she'll text me after practice and tell me she can't go through with it. That she hates my guts and doesn't want to help me.

I don't know if I can survive her walking away again.

She did it once. Just left me in that cold, dark cabin after the type of night we shared together. I was furious for days, thinking I had done something to hurt her. What if I had traumatized her? Pushed her too far? One minute she was there, and the next, she was gone, as though I had imagined the entire thing.

But if she doesn't back out, I can't either. I need to fix this. This sport means everything to me. It's my life. It's what brings me joy and gives me purpose in this fucked-up game we call life.

My head is straight. I know I'll behave. Play it cool like I used to back in the day until the rumors settle down and we can all slip back into our old lives. Even if it fucking kills me, I won't step out of line. I made a promise to Aaron, and I won't do anything to hurt him. He's my brother.

Smack.

Pain hits the side of my face, and my vision goes black before everything becomes blurry. My body sways as a feeling of weight-lessness takes hold of me right before I slam into the boards, my chest tightening as I try to blink through the veil of darkness covering my eyes.

"Fuck."

"Shit! Dom! Man, I'm so sorry. Are you all right?"

My head and shoulder are pounding as I slide down, leaning my back against the support.

"Get him off the ice." That's Noa's voice.

"I'm fine. Just give me a second."

My vision comes back slowly, and I take in the sight of Noa kneeling in front of me, his arm under my shoulder as he tries to hold me up.

"What the fuck was that, Lewis? Did you suddenly forget how to play? Off the ice. NOW."

"Coach, I'm fine. It was just an accident. I wasn't paying attention." Adjusting the helmet strap on my chin, I squint up at Coach, who doesn't seem the least bit convinced.

First the PR scandal, and now this.

What the fuck is wrong with me?

"No, you haven't been paying attention all practice. Now, let's go. You might have a concussion."

I grit my teeth, knowing talking back right now isn't going to help me. I don't have a concussion, but I know the protocol is not up for debate. Coach watches with his arms crossed while Noa and Liam help me off the ice as I try to breathe through the waves of dizziness.

Okay, maybe a small concussion, but no one needs to know. It'll be gone by tomorrow, and I don't need to get benched because of a tiny, stupid oversight on my end.

We skate toward the rink door as I get escorted off the ice to a distraction-free environment for an evaluation. Whenever a player takes a direct hit to the head or a blow to the body, they have to get properly checked out by a physician. It's a pain in the ass, but a necessary step, and never something we can negotiate on, which is why I don't bother trying. It's saved a lot of the guys from permanent injury.

Dropping my hockey stick and helmet to the side, I steady myself as I begin walking to the trainer's room in the back of the arena.

"You two, back on the ice and resume practice. I'm going to drop him off." A whistle blows, and the sound of skates cutting ice continues in the background. I don't look back but know Coach is following closely behind me.

I almost wish he would berate me, because his disappointed silence cuts deeper than his harsh words would. I've been a massive thorn in everyone's side today. Not just today—I've been making a lot of stupid mistakes recently. My carelessness causing an injury in the middle of practice is just icing on the cake.

I cannot afford to behave like this as captain this close to playoffs.

The blow to the side of my head was avoidable. If I were paying closer attention, it would have never happened. But I've been disgustingly distracted for days.

All because of a girl.

As I grab the door handle, I whip it open and enter the dimly lit room. Leaning against the wall and closing my eyes, I listen as Coach explains what happened to our team physician, Dr. Tamer. Running my hand through my damp hair repeatedly, I eventually push myself off the wall and observe Dr. Tamer making his way toward me, wearing a gentle smile on his face.

"Rough day, Dominik?"

"Something like that."

Dr. Tamer has been our team physician since the beginning and is truly one of the top doctors in his field. Every other physician and physical therapist who works under him is equally exceptional. It also helps that he's got great bedside manners since hockey players can get too blunt at times.

"Let's get you checked out. Follow me into the dark room."

"Keep me posted," Coach says to Dr. Tamer, his hand already

on the door handle. He's got a perma-scowl on his face and refuses to even look at me.

"Will do. I'll walk Dominik back if necessary."

Coach offers him a single nod before he storms out of the room.

My stomach sinks to the floor. I feel like a toddler who just got put in time-out.

"Rough day for him as well."

"All thanks to me."

"It happens to everyone. Don't be so hard on yourself."

I follow Dr. Tamer as he walks to a closed door on the opposite side of the large square office. He opens the door, and I step inside the dark room, feeling his hand on my back as he guides me forward. The door clicks shut behind us, veiling the room in total darkness. The lack of lighting is meant to help ease symptoms relating to concussion or severe head trauma. Tamer clicks on a small flashlight and grips my elbow, helping me onto the examination table. My hockey gear digs into the plastic as I adjust my position.

He sits on a stool in front of me, firing off the usual physical questionnaire.

Headache? Yes.

Pressure? No.

Neck pain? No.

Nausea or vomiting? No.

Dizziness? Yes.

The questions eventually blend into one another. Systematic, since I've heard them a thousand times. Once he's finished, he stands up and begins to examine me in the dark.

"Dominik, you may be experiencing a very mild concussion, but I think you're going to be okay. I recommend you stay in here for twenty minutes and calm your mind if you can. I have a feeling by the time you walk out of this room, your headache will be subsiding."

Thank fuck.

"Thank you, Dr. Tamer."

"No problem. You're done with practice for today and should rest when you get home. Take it easy today. No physical or strenuous activity. If you're not feeling better by tomorrow or your symptoms get worse later in the day, please give me a call."

"Will do, Doc."

"I'll come back to grab you once the twenty minutes are up," he says over his shoulder as the door clicks open, letting in a beam of light right before darkness swallows me whole again.

No more flashlight.

No more distractions.

Just me, myself, and I as I lie here stewing in the thoughts that have been suffocating me for days. The thoughts I was hoping would disappear when I arrived at work today. This is all Tristan's fault. Him and his stupid fake dating proposal.

If Aaron knew how I truly feel about Zoe, he wouldn't hesitate to throw me over his balcony. I'm headed to his apartment after work to meet his sister so we can go over my schedule for the next three months. The same sister I'm going to pretend to be in a serious, committed relationship with. The same girl I chased and fucked in a cabin as though she were my property six years ago. The same one I lied to about my identity. The girl I haven't been able to get out of my mind for years.

The one who haunts my dreams and my future.

The last woman I kissed on the lips, and the reason I don't want to attempt to date anyone else. Because after experiencing a night like we did, with someone I'd desired for so long...nothing else compares. Everything becomes bland and distasteful. No one could ever compare to her.

But I need to forget about all of that. I need to put the past where it belongs and focus on hockey and the playoffs. I want to bring the Cup home.

The truth is that none of this Zoe situation is actually genuine. Can I truly say that I still know her? Time has a way of transforming everyone. People age and alter their perspectives. They become individuals who wouldn't even recognize themselves. That's just how life works. That's why I need to distance myself from this old version of Zoe. I must remain disinterested and concentrate solely on achieving my ultimate goal.

On my career and winning the championship.

But somewhere deep inside, a voice reminds me that no matter what I tell myself, no matter how focused I become or how much control I think I have…there isn't a single version of Zoe Jackson that I wouldn't love.

Not a single one.

CHAPTER 28
ZOE

He's late.

Almost an hour late.

I glance down at my watch for the eighth time, despite knowing time hasn't miraculously sped up since thirty seconds ago. Maybe he's ghosting me.

I doubt he'd go that route, considering he lives in the same building and my brother would rearrange his face. We all know how excessively protective Aaron can be, so it's quite astonishing that he thought this was a good idea in the first place.

Maybe he got hit by a yellow cab and is lying in a ditch somewhere. Or he's fucking some girl behind a back alley.

Will you just stop?

My phone buzzes in my hand, and I expect a message from Dom, but it's a new message from Rabbit Hole.

The twelfth one today.

Ever since I made a post on PrimalConnect, I've been overwhelmed with so many messages, and half of them are bots from different countries. I'm not sure what I expected, but it wasn't this type of response to me wanting to find a personal hunter in New York City. Maybe I was naïve for not thinking that posting in an anonymous, internet black hole would mean getting swarmed with creepy men.

Clicking on the latest message, I cringe instantly.

HEY…YOUR POST SOUNDS RAD. I'D LOVE TO CHASE YOU DOWN AND LICK YOU LIKE A BEAR. HIT ME UP. WE CAN GO FOR DRINKS AND SET UP A SAFE WORD. I'VE ALSO GOT A CONTRACT.

Block and good riddance to you, weirdo.

What the hell is the matter with me?

I should just delete that post. The type of things I want to do should only be done with someone I've known for a while and trust deeply, not some random stranger on a completely anonymous website. I'm just asking for trouble at this point, and not the good kind. I could end up seriously hurt or worse. But it could also be fun. Some nameless chasing with no strings attached. No feelings, and no trace left behind.

Similar to Runi.

I never saw him again, but he likely never searched for me either. Which is fine, because we'd had a mutual agreement: that he would give me a taste of my desires for the night. Nothing more, nothing less.

Skimming through the rest of the bot messages and requests for me to join someone's OnlyFans, I throw my phone on the couch and feel my anxiety creeping up. I shouldn't have had that third cup of coffee today, but I desperately needed it after only getting a few hours of sleep last night.

At four a.m., I'd finally given up and pulled open my laptop, googling fake dating rules and etiquette so I could bring something to the table today. And when Google had proved to be utterly useless, I'd tossed and turned in bed, trying not to think of every scenario in which this could go wrong. I'm going to screw this up somehow. I'm going to end up finding a way to disappoint my brother, and he's the only person I haven't utterly pissed off yet. Aaron is the closest I've had to unconditional love, but when it comes to his best friends, I'm not sure I'd stand a chance.

There is no way I'd put myself in a situation where he would walk away, because I'm not sure I'd survive a loss like that.

That's a little too depressing right now.

Sitting on the couch, I groan in frustration and place my palms against my temples. I try to calm myself by focusing on my breaths, desperately hoping that the intrusive thoughts will eventually fade away. All I want is for my brain to quiet down and give me some peace.

The familiar chime sounds from the foyer, causing my heart to sink deep into the pit of my stomach.

Dominik strides in, clad in a navy pull-over hoodie and black jeans. His curly hair is tousled across his forehead, a few strands grazing over his eyes. He seems a bit nervous, or maybe he just woke up from a nap. He stands on the other end of the kitchen, blinking at me. Both of us are too scared to initiate a conversation.

"You want some coffee?" My voice comes out all wrong.

"I'll never sleep if I do. Have you had dinner?"

Right, it's dinnertime.

I need to figure out a way to soothe my frazzled nerves and take this slowly. No expectations.

"No, I haven't. I was just going to have some coffee with a side of...nothing," I mutter, looking around.

Dominik snickers, placing a white plastic bag on the kitchen counter. He starts pulling out tiny Chinese food take-out containers.

He brought food? That's nice. A peace offering.

"I was hoping you'd say that. Lemon chicken and chow mein still your favorites?"

Not even bothering to hide my silly grin, I spin around and grab plates and utensils from the drawer.

"Of course. Aaron told you?"

"No. I remember from forever ago. You would always add this to our take-out order."

Well, would you look at that? Turns out the guy was paying

attention after all. He begins to place food on the plates, his eyes laser-focused on the task while I stare at him.

I hate how much I like looking at him and the effect it has on my body.

It's almost criminal how he manages to make the simple act of scooping food onto a plate look so incredibly hot. Honestly, I don't blame all those women for yearning after him and feeling upset when he wanted nothing to do with them. They probably thought they were special enough to change his mind after they put out. But men like Dominik don't change their minds.

The delightful aroma of spices and sweet sauce fills the air, instantly making my mouth water. It occurs to me that I skipped lunch and only had a protein shake for breakfast. My anxiety always makes me forget to eat.

"Thank you, Dominik. You didn't have to do all this."

He shrugs. "It's just a meal."

"It's nice."

"It's the least I can do."

His eyes fall to my lips for a quick second before he blinks, refocusing and handing me a plate overflowing with food. Placing it onto the counter, I head to the fridge, collecting two bottles of water and returning to where Dom is seated, already digging into his meal.

I'm suddenly very much aware that it's just the two of us here. Aaron is out late tonight, showing houses to a new client, and he warned me that I'm barely going to be seeing him until his client buys a house. Apparently, a lot of his new clients are celebrities, and they are very picky about the type of real estate they want to purchase here.

It would be nice to eventually spend some time with my brother, but I'm sure the money accumulating in his bank account is keeping his thoughts warm at night.

That was mean.

I just wish he were here so I wouldn't have to be alone with his friend, or alone in general.

No big deal. You've been alone with plenty of men before.

Then why am I so nervous about being alone with this one?

Taking a bite out of the lemon chicken, I groan as the rich flavors burst on my tongue.

"Fuck, that's good."

Dom coughs, choking on a piece of chicken. Maybe he should slow down; his plate is already half empty, and I just took my first bite.

"You okay?" I give him a sideways glance.

He nods, keeping his head lowered. I twist the cap off the bottle of water and pass it to him. He accepts it promptly, tilting his head backward as he swiftly gulps down half of it.

"Thanks. How was your day?" he asks quickly, as if the words feel heavy in his mouth. He chews for a few seconds, but I don't answer. It's then I notice the small bruise under his right eye.

"What happened to your eye?"

He shakes his head. "Nothing. Just a small injury at practice today."

"Did you get it looked at?"

He nods, looking away.

"Shouldn't you be resting?"

He cracks a smile. "I was resting. All day. That's why I was late. Are we going to talk about my unimportant, small injury, or the plan for the next few months? Maybe you'll change your mind after you see my schedule."

"Nope. Unless you've changed *your* mind."

He shakes his head.

"How did you get this?" I reach out without thinking and move a thick curl away from his eye. The last time I was this close to him was the first night I got here when he was black-out drunk. Too drunk to remember our conversation and what he said to me.

Dominik freezes. He stops chewing, and his body goes completely stiff next to mine. As if my touch and being this close to me is physically hurting him.

"Sorry," I murmur.

A long moment stretches between us before he speaks.

"I suppose I should get used to it if we're really going to do this."

"We don't have to. You shouldn't have to do something like this with someone you hate so much."

The words feel like shards of glass as they leave my mouth. And I know it's not going to hurt any less when he confirms every word I just said.

Hearing the distinct clink of a fork, I notice his body shifting in my peripheral vision. He grabs my thighs and quickly maneuvers me to face him, trapping my legs between his own.

I can't focus on anything but Dom's large palms burning a hole through my pants.

"You think I don't want to do this because I hate you?"

His eyes are intense, as if he's trying to understand exactly how I'm feeling by sifting through my thoughts.

"Don't you?" I whisper.

He appears defeated, leaving me unsure of what to believe. Over the years, his actions have consistently given me no reason to think he actually cares about me. I have always felt like an inconvenience, someone he tolerates just to maintain a friendship with my brother.

But right now, I regret even saying the words. His reaction is tearing me up.

"I don't hate you, Zoe. I wish it were that easy, because it would make this..."

The words linger as his eyes rove over my features, making me suddenly self-conscious about every inch exposed to him.

"It would make this what?"

He shakes his head, and I glance away.

Another blocked road.

"I've always felt like I was an inconvenience to you. And it feels like that now, too, like you have to put up with me because I'm the only one you trust to help you with all of this. Your only shitty option."

I don't know why I'm still talking.

His fingers grasp my chin, pulling my attention back and making my skin vibrate with raw energy as he holds me captive under his gaze. Everything is frozen, like I've fallen through a sheet of ice.

"It's not like that at all."

"Then what is it like?" I whisper.

"It doesn't matter. I just don't want you to feel like I'm using you or mistreating you in any way. If you want out of this at any point, promise you'll tell me."

"Why the sudden concern for my feelings, Dom?"

I see the shift in his multicolored eyes the minute the words leave my mouth. I wanted him to let me in, even for a second, but he drops my chin and leans back.

He picks up his fork and resumes eating.

I mimic his movement, pretending like I don't give a shit.

"Aaron trusts me to take care of his little sister, and I don't want you to get caught up in all of this. This is my mess. I need to take responsibility and fix it. That's why I'm concerned."

Of course. It's always going to be about Aaron.

"Don't worry about Aaron. He trusts you more than anyone else in this world."

Dom's jaw clicks as he straightens his back. "I know. He's like a brother to me. I would never do anything to hurt him."

I had a moment of weakness, seeing something that wasn't there, but now it's over. I put on a soft smile and take a bite out of my food.

"Let's see this schedule of yours then."

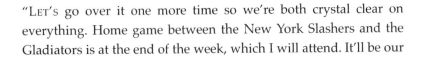

"Let's go over it one more time so we're both crystal clear on everything. Home game between the New York Slashers and the Gladiators is at the end of the week, which I will attend. It'll be our first official public outing. A work event on your end for me, maybe an office drop-by whenever works for you. A few more games, an after-game party, and then we'll reassess in a few weeks?"

After we finished eating, we moved to the living room and turned on the fireplace. I put some cushions down on the ground, and Dominik started taking notes on an empty calendar he'd brought over along with his schedule. He has the messiest hand-writing I have ever seen.

"That's right. I'll get you a VIP pass to the stadium, and you'll sit right behind the bench. That's where family and friends sit to watch the game."

"Okay."

"How's your knowledge of hockey?"

I cringe. "Poor."

Dom looks at me like I'm an alien. "Seriously?"

"Seriously."

He sighs, running his hand through his hair and looking like a GQ model.

"Sorry, I know you just moved here, but you're going to need to start to like hockey a little bit."

"I know."

"Get Aaron to run through some of the basics with you." He scribbles more illegible words on paper.

I chew my lip. "He's busy. I'll ask Tristan."

He pins me with a deathly stare. "Forget it. I'll do it."

I just nod, not bothering to question the angry vein in his neck.

"From this moment on, you are a hockey lover. Because your boyfriend is a professional hockey player."

"Noted. Can I ask you something?"

Dom glances back down at the schedule. "Yes."

I've been battling with this question all night, and my stomach is in knots just thinking about saying the words out loud.

"Have we decided on the rules regarding public displays of affection?"

Dom freezes, pen midmotion, and I hate myself a little more for opening my big, fat mouth.

"Minimal."

"Meaning?" I try not to let the immediate rejection sting as much as it does.

"We'll just be like the normal couples who are comfortable with one another."

"I don't know how to do that."

"We'll figure it out as we go. Just follow my lead, okay? I won't cross any boundaries to make you uncomfortable."

Heaven forbid he use all those muscles and manhandle me a little.

Lord, I seriously need to get laid so I can get some of this pent-up need out of my system.

"Fair enough. Let's announce with a subtle and mysterious social media post. Since everyone is waiting for something from you after all the gossip, your Instagram account is best."

He nods, avoiding eye contact. His expression is twisted, as though he's about to be sick.

Should I offer him one last opportunity to walk away?

But before I have a chance to say anything, he stands up.

"Let's do it now."

"Now?" My voice nearly cracks as I stare up at his giant frame.

"Why not? Let's stop talking about it and get this over with."

He stretches his hand out toward me, and I stare at it for a second before reaching for it. With seemingly little effort, he pulls me up.

"But we're at home. In casual clothes. Not doing anything special."

He releases my hand and starts walking out of the room, disappearing down the dark hallway.

"Where are you going?" Before I know it, I'm chasing the guy as he strolls into my bedroom, no care for privacy. What if my vibrator is sitting on my nightstand?

"Hey! You can't just—" I halt abruptly at my open doorway,

finding him scanning through the stacks of books resting in the corner of my room. I just pulled them all out of boxes the other day.

"What is all this?"

"They're called books. You should pick one up sometime."

Dom glares at me from over his shoulder. "What genres?"

"Mostly horror. Some sci-fi. I recently picked up—"

"You don't have any romance?" he cuts me off.

"Romance?"

"Yes...you know...the stories about love and couples and shit."

"No. I don't read unrealistic books."

He pivots, resting his elbow on his knee and fixing me with a raised eyebrow as he presents *It* by Stephen King.

"And this is realistic?"

Rolling my eyes, I cross my arms and lean against my doorway. "I don't have to explain my reading preferences to you. If you're not planning on borrowing a book, leave my collection alone."

He continues to rummage through my stacks of books for what feels like hours. But then he stands, holding a torn and battered copy of *Wuthering Heights*.

Oh, no.

Not that book. I was certain I had packed it away in my memory box, tucked away safely in the back of my closet.

"I'm pretty sure this is classified as romance." Dominik has a stupid, obnoxious grin on his face as he approaches me. "How many times have you read this? It looks fucking abused, Zoe. My first gift as your fake boyfriend will be to buy you a brand-new copy of this book."

Marching over to him, I try to snatch the book out of his hand, but he raises his arm, glaring down at me and smiling. I get a whiff of his intoxicating, sandalwood cologne.

Fuck, he smells good.

Taking a large step back, I put space between us before extending my open hand to him.

"Please give it back."

He shakes his head. "No. We'll need it as a prop."

"What for?"

"Tell me, Zo… Why this one out of all the romance books?"

I move to turn away from him, but his hand grips my arm.

"I'll need to get to know you a bit, and you'll have to do the same with me for this to work. You can trust me as much as I intend to trust you, and we're going to start with this."

Small shivers cascade down my body at the sound of his soft voice commanding me.

I turn to face him, two seconds away from strangling him.

"No."

Dominik lets go of my arm and opens the book, leafing through the weathered pages of my old copy of *Wuthering Heights* by Emily Brontë.

"Let me guess. Is this because you relate to Catherine's complex and difficult personality? Or maybe to the intense love she and Heathcliff share? But it's so destructive, so tremulous that it makes their love story hard to follow. I personally found her infuriating, but their romance was hauntingly beautiful. Is it because they are both so hard to love, Zoe? And yet, they understand one another so well?"

I don't have words. I am speechless…how…

"What?"

Dom takes a step closer to me.

"No words? That's a shame." He smirks.

"Did you just say tremulous?"

"I think I know you better than you think."

"You've read *Wuthering Heights*? Wait…you read? I have so many questions."

"There is a lot you don't know about me."

Dominik motions to the bed, his mind already elsewhere while I am still processing everything that just happened.

"Lie on the bed, and hold this out in front of your face as if you're reading it. I'm going to take a couple of photos, and we'll use whichever one you think will look best from a PR lens."

Walking to my bed in a haze, I sit down as he hands me the book.

I open it somewhere near the middle, to a random page, and my eyes land on one particular sentence.

"Whatever our souls are made of, his and mine are the same."

Of course it's this quote. I feel the words grab hold of me, reminding me how potent just one sentence can be. This is why I don't read romance anymore. Why I stopped believing in things and emotions that only belong within the world of fiction. They're only as real as ink on paper.

I feel Dominik's hands on my shoulders as he guides me backward onto the bed. He plays with my hair, positioning it as I try to focus on my breathing. Laying the book down on the bed, I close my eyes and remind myself why we're doing this dance right now.

This is all fake. For show.

"Ready?"

I nod, picking up the book and holding it in front of my face.

"Hey, Zo?"

"Yeah?" The room is so incredibly quiet and my heart is beating so fast, I'm worried he can hear it.

"Mind turning the book? It's upside down."

Oh my God.

I turn the book slowly, promising myself to sucker punch him right in the stomach as soon as we're done here. He doesn't give me shit for it though, nor does he laugh, but I do see the shadow of a smile on his face as he snaps some pictures. A minute later, he grabs the book and chucks it onto the bed. Sitting up quickly, I smooth down my hair as he plops down beside me, holding out his phone to me.

I flip through the photos. Not hating a single one.

He's even got an eye for photography.

The dark, gothic lighting is perfect, matching the theme of the book, and every angle covers my face perfectly.

I pause on one in particular. The only one that shows my lips.

The subtle glow from the lamp adds to the allure of it all. My hair is fanned out all around me, a shade darker in the night. There is a small bit of cleavage poking out of my white top, and my all-white bedding provides the perfect backdrop.

"This one. I like the lips poking through." I hand his phone back to him.

"Me too."

Dominik opens Instagram, tapping on the plus button. He pauses for a second, trying to come up with a caption, and I stay quiet, on the edge of my seat wondering what he's going to say.

It doesn't take him long at all.

One word.

"Finally" with a purple butterfly emoji.

A current tugs relentlessly at my heart, making it hard to breathe. Slowly, he tilts his head. His eyes, an electrifying blend of hazel and blue, seize my body. In this moment, I feel myself giving in, a willing captive of his intoxicating stare.

"Last chance, Zo. Are you sure?" he whispers.

I'm too sure.

"Yes. Do it."

CHAPTER 29
ZOE

The post on Dominik's Instagram has generated a lot of buzz already.

I couldn't help myself from scrolling through the comments, reading the reactions of random strangers going wild over the girl who appears to have captured Dominik Lewis's heart. According to the internet, I have managed to do the impossible.

It's crazy how much people care about who these athletes date and how they spend their free time. Why is it anyone's business? Several people are claiming to be scouring the internet, trying to figure out who I am. After all, everyone knows Dominik never dates. He would never willingly make anything official, let alone post about it online. A few anonymous accounts are claiming this is a PR ploy to get the rumors to die down.

Ding. Ding. Ding. We have a winner.

Social media is all fake. Just an illusion to prove, what? That you're better than everyone else?

An online post or photos of smiling family members on a cruise are all just a highlight reel, and people often perceive it as gospel truth. *Look where I am and what I can buy.* Yet there are so many secrets concealed behind closed doors—details no one would ever willingly share. Phony relationships, seemingly joyful family

255

photos masking years of sadness, an overlooked child who never felt a sense of belonging. A beautiful, grand home where the owners are living paycheck to paycheck.

But in cases like this with Dominik, it's the perfect tool.

I haven't heard from Dom since the other night, and I'm a little hesitant to message him. I'm not sure how our dynamic will flow moving forward. I assume we'll only talk when necessary for public viewings and couple duties. For now, I need to focus on getting my life back on track.

Maybe find someone trustworthy to pass the nights with.

Surely I can do that if it all stays anonymous, right?

Speaking of which, since I'm early for work today, I can check the few messages that trickled in while I was asleep. I'm hoping I can start talking to someone and build a foundation of trust before we schedule an initial meetup somewhere vanilla. I haven't done anything like this since the masquerade ball in Boston, but I'm ready for some mind-numbing fun.

Stopping by the coffee shop across the street to grab a cappuccino, I take a seat at an empty booth and open the Rabbit Hole app.

YOURDARKHORSE — 1:23 A.M.

HEY THERE — YOUR POST CAUGHT MY ATTENTION, SO I FIGURED I'D REACH OUT AND SAY HI. I'M SURE YOU'RE GETTING TONS OF MESSAGES, BUT IT'S TOUGH OUT THERE AS A YOUNG WOMAN WITH YOUR PARTIC-ULAR NEEDS. YOU NEED TO MAKE SURE YOU CAN FULLY TRUST WHOEVER YOU LET INTO YOUR WORLD. I'M 30, 6'4" WITH AN ATHLETIC BUILD. I'M MOSTLY INTERESTED IN PRIMAL PLAY, BUT I'D LOVE TO DOMI-NATE YOU HERE AND THERE TOO WITH SOME SENSUAL FUN THROWN INTO THE MIX. IF THAT'S SOMETHING YOU'RE INTERESTED IN, LET ME KNOW. I'D LOVE TO GET TO KNOW YOU BETTER, OUTSIDE ALL THE KINK STUFF TOO.

This just might be the first normal message I've received. The guy seems very casual and friendly. He doesn't give me creeper vibes, which is a plus. I decide to send him a quick reply to say hi and thank him for taking the time to get in touch with me. I ask him what his previous experience is and what he's looking for long term. I hit send and scroll through my other messages, which turn out to be one unsolicited dick pic and two people asking if I have an OnlyFans account.

It's tough out here for kinky women. Especially online. But who wants to venture out alone to a meetup in a new city? Not me. I had a hard time attending the one in Boston and psyched myself out four times before I finally showed up to an event. Maybe I can get Via to go with me eventually, but not right now. We're just getting to know one another, and I already have one shitty rumor nailed to my back; I don't need another one.

I stroll into the office twenty minutes later, enjoying the quiet hum of the elevator and the silent hallways. Tracy's office is dark, and Via's cubicle is messier than yesterday. I'm beginning to wonder if she has naughty elves who like to mess her desk up overnight.

Getting my binders and lists ready for the day, I fire up my laptop and begin skimming through new emails. Plopping in my wireless headphones, I select my favorite Spotify playlist and psych myself up for the email slog. I action items, reply to clients, put in requests for vendors, and schedule phone calls with new clients who came in through our request form.

And then I notice a subject line beside a name I recognize all too well that has me suddenly feeling sick to my stomach.

"WHERE THE FUCK ARE YOU?" From none other than Jenna Joy, an old client from the Boston office.

I know I emailed her before I left, notifying her I was being relocated to the New York office and I would handle her file from here.

Okay, I get it. You have my full attention now. Can you stop ignoring me, please? I'm sorry I messed up, even though I have no clue what I did. My calls aren't going through, and all my emails are going unanswered. I need you, Zoe. I can't deal with that useless twat Greg for another second. If this email bounces, I'm going to personally bring hell to Bloom.

Where are you, and why has your name been removed from the New York Launch Party?! You're the only one who knows exactly what I want, and I'm canceling the entire thing if you don't get back to me. I don't trust anyone else to do this, so you'd better get back to me. Or better yet, give me a call, because I'm beyond pissed.

Lots of love,

Jenna

617-258-3478

I READ the email three more times, because the first two rounds, I'm in a confused haze. What is she talking about? I'm going to the grand opening; I fucking planned it; and it's right in New York City. Tracy already has the file and event date all set up in her calendar. It's my file! Jenna has been my client from day one.

In a panicked state, I scan my events calendar for "Monumental Designs," which is Jenna's baby and the business she's poured her heart and soul into for the last five years. We helped her company flourish in Boston, and now she is launching a storefront in New York City. I helped plan the entire thing with her in Boston. The only reason she stayed with us and didn't hire a PR company in New York was because of me. A lot of the ideas were my own, and it was the first time in my life where someone gave me creative freedom to design an entire space like I had always dreamt of doing. Jenna was thrilled with the final product. Greg, of course, took credit, but I didn't care because I knew they were my designs.

I find the event in our booking system and click on the file, but an error message pops up.

ERROR: Your account has been suspended. Please contact your administrator.

That motherfucker. I'm going to kill him and dance on his grave.

I'm fully aware I shouldn't allow my anger to take over, but at this moment, all I see is red as I grab the phone to dial Jenna's number.

THE DAY IS ALMOST OVER, and I handled the Jenna dilemma with more ease than expected. Jenna had no idea I'd left. It seems they have blocked all outgoing and incoming emails from my inbox. She was beyond furious and said she would handle the situation on her end. Later, she called to say she had fired Greg and demanded I be put back in charge as the lead, and Tracy had no issues with that. She was actually thrilled, since bringing over this type of client full-time means she meets her quota for the next six months.

Greg probably did this with my other clients too. People who wanted to work with me but were told it wouldn't be possible or that I had been let go. He spread a couple of nasty rumors, likely hoping they would organically reach clients and ensure I would never be able to go back to the Boston office. And none of those clients would follow me either. It all makes sense now, and if that was his plan all along, I'm going to make sure my revenge is extra sweet.

I'm hoping he gets an earful from his boss, but I'm trying not to think about it anymore. Easier said than done. Which is why I have my headphones in, counting down the minutes until I can get out of here and maybe down a couple of shots at home.

Today needs to end already.

My desk phone flashes, catching my attention.

"Blooms New York. How can I help you?"

"Zoe, there is someone here requesting to see you."

"Who is it?"

There is a pause. "I don't know. There is a delivery, apparently, but he's only willing to hand it to you."

The receptionist hangs up before I have a chance to ask anything else.

"For fuck's sake."

Via glances over at me, her fingers still clicking away loudly on her keyboard. "What's up?"

"Apparently, there is someone at reception looking to see me?"

"Oh! Maybe you're being served."

Great, now I'm filled with nothing but sheer panic. "What?!"

Via laughs and stops typing, turning her body to face me. "Relax, I'm joking."

Grabbing my phone and work badge, I log out of my computer. "Be right back."

Via springs out of her chair. "No way, I'm coming with."

As we walk toward reception, a few sets of eyes follow us, but I ignore them, wondering what is at the front that requires my attention.

Standing at the reception desk is a bike courier in baggy jeans and a black beanie. He is short and holding on to a rather sizeable box, which only makes him appear smaller. He looks impatiently at every new person who walks by him, likely hoping it's me so he can finally do his job and leave.

Finally, it's our turn.

"Are you Zoe Jackson?" he blurts out, his eyes bouncing between Via and me.

"I am."

He hands me a clipboard, asking me to sign.

"What is it?"

"I don't know, lady. Just sign so I can get on with it."

I rest the box on the counter, asking the girls at reception if they have a box cutter. Two of them ignore me until Via finally reaches over and grabs one tucked underneath the desk.

One of them glares at Via, and she sticks out her tongue, which makes me want to hug her.

"Jerks," she mutters, handing me the small cutter so I can open the box.

"Thanks," I whisper.

Excitedly, I cut open the box, only to discover yet another medium-sized, purple box nestled inside. With Via's help, I remove the first box. The second box is simply stunning, boasting a rich shade of deep-purple and adorned with a lavender, silk ribbon. Curiosity piqued, I tug gently on the ribbon, causing the lid of the box to lift, revealing something unexpected. Suddenly, a multitude of spring-loaded butterflies gracefully take flight, filling the air with their vibrant colors.

"Holy shit."

"Oh my God."

As I peer inside the box, my eyes are immediately drawn to the special edition of *Wuthering Heights*, accompanied by a large VIP pass for the Slashers.

Dominik.

"Oh my God!! Are you the captain's mystery girl?"

It takes me a minute to realize people are chattering around me, talking about what just happened. But all I care to do is run my fingers along the foil-embroidered edge of the book, grounding myself in the moment.

Well played, Lewis. Well played.

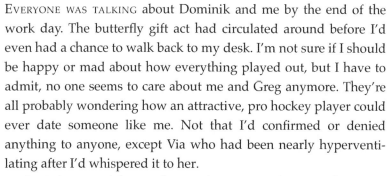

EVERYONE WAS TALKING about Dominik and me by the end of the work day. The butterfly gift act had circulated around before I'd even had a chance to walk back to my desk. I'm not sure if I should be happy or mad about how everything played out, but I have to admit, no one seems to care about me and Greg anymore. They're all probably wondering how an attractive, pro hockey player could ever date someone like me. Not that I'd confirmed or denied anything to anyone, except Via who had been nearly hyperventilating after I'd whispered it to her.

Stepping out of the penthouse elevator, I walk inside the apartment feeling utterly exhausted and realize the place is exactly the same as it was when I left this morning. No new scents, empty sink... Aaron hasn't even been home by the looks of it. It's quiet and dark, the room illuminated by the twinkling city lights outside.

I miss my brother. We haven't even crossed paths in the mornings lately. I'm not even sure if he's been sleeping here. Perhaps he has another apartment closer to his office, considering his intense workload. But wouldn't he tell me that? Maybe he's dating someone and staying at her place? But I can't see Aaron doing that either, or keeping it a secret. We used to share everything.

I'm not going to wallow in the missed opportunities with Aaron tonight. I'm feeling good and have no interest in bringing myself down. Instead, I fire off a quick text to Aaron, telling him I miss him and want to plan a museum date with him soon.

Throughout our relationship, we have always prioritized honesty and maintained open lines of communication. What I appreciate most about Aaron is that he has never tried to change me into someone I'm not. Instead, he loves me in a way that my parents should have but unfortunately didn't. At times, it can feel overwhelming, because I sense that he is trying to make up for their shortcomings. Although his protectiveness might be annoying sometimes, I'm just thankful to have him in my life.

AARON

I miss you too. More than you know. I'm coming to the game with you this week. Already blocked it off at work.

I smile as another text from him comes in.

AARON

Sorry, Zo. I know it's been busy, but I'll make it up to you when I can. I promise. For now, enjoy the place. I'm glad you're there.

Sweet relief wraps around me like a warm hug. Not only will I not be going to Dom's game alone, but I get to finally spend some quality time with my brother. In two nights, I'm going to be showing up to the hockey game as Dominik's new girlfriend. The game where Dom and I will officially go public. In front of his fans and all his teammates. We didn't even talk about the logistics of it the other night, and now with his work surprise, I'm not really sure how we're going to go about it. Do I make a grand entrance? Do I hug him? Do we kiss?

No kissing, he made that perfectly clear. But new couples can't keep their hands off one another, so how exactly are we supposed to make a memorable first impression?

ME

Hey

Bubbles pop up immediately.

DOM

Everything okay?

ME

Yes…I just wanted to ask you a couple of things about the upcoming game. And to thank you for today.

DOM

I hope that shuts down some of the gossip at work. I'll drop by soon.

ME

You don't have to.

DOM

What did you want to ask me?

Deep breaths. No need to be nervous.

ME

Do you need me to do anything in particular at the game?

I keep staring at my phone, counting the times the tiny bubbles appear and disappear before a half-assed response gets delivered.

DOM

Do what feels natural.

ME

My natural may be very different than your natural, Mr. I've Never Had a Girlfriend.

DOM

What do you suggest?

Mulling over his question, I think about the coolest way to say we should probably make out or at least kiss on the cheek one time. There are photos online of him with his lips on some random girl's neck or his hand up someone's skirt; it would be weird if he was keeping a five-foot distance between the two of us at all times. No one would buy it.

Walking into my bathroom, I turn on the mellow under lighting and decide to take a bath. I stare at my phone again, sitting on the edge of the tub as I wait for it to fill up. The guy is utterly useless when it comes to dating, and I'm no better, but at least I'm trying over here.

ME

Make a show of me at some point during the game. Turn toward me, smile...pretend like you're happy I'm there. And afterward, maybe I'll walk over to you, and you can hug me, kiss my forehead...I don't know. We'll need to show affection in some way.

DOM

Kissing isn't a good idea.

ME

Not even on the forehead?

DOM

No

ME

Okay

DOM

Anything else?

Good to know you find me so repulsive.

ME

Nope. Take care.

Pressing down the button on the side of my phone to power it off, I wait for the screen to turn black before throwing the device onto the counter. Stripping out of my clothes, I stare at my reflection in the mirror. I'm a decent-looking woman, and if he doesn't want anything to do with me, that's fine. I'll find someone who will give me the attention I want.

I step inside the scalding-hot water, trying not to let that last comment from Dominik bother me as much as it does. What is it about me he finds so disgusting? Is it because I'm Aaron's sister? A part of me wants to find the answer because maybe it'll be easier to move past it, to finally get some closure and stop the whiplash coming from him at all angles. But the other part of me, the less mature Zoe, wants to never talk to him again.

There is no way in hell he treats other people in his life this way.

I'm overwhelmed with regret for agreeing to this as I draw in a deep breath before plunging my body under the water, hoping it erases the lingering thoughts of Dominik from my mind.

CHAPTER 30

DOMINIK

My eyes are glued to my phone. I've been completely distracted, waiting for her to text me back after our last exchange. It's not like her to ignore me, which means she's likely pissed because I keep shutting down her suggestions to show any form of intimacy. I'm trying to be respectful, and she's acting like a brat.

My palm twitches with the need to punish her for driving me this wild.

Doesn't she understand that there is no other way? I can't kiss her or be too close to her because I don't trust myself around her.

I can't kiss Zoe because she happens to be the last person I kissed. Therefore, whether it's real or not, her lips won't be coming close to mine. Because I'm afraid of what might happen if I taste her again.

Maybe it's better this way.

I want her to hate me. It would make this entire exchange much easier. Which is why I should leave it alone tonight, turn my phone on silent, and go to sleep. What I should not be doing is worrying about her feelings or if she's sitting there stewing or, worse, crying because I hurt her feelings.

It's none of your business. You need to get used to being the mean guy.

Thirty agonizing minutes later and multiple useless attempts at trying to tell myself I don't feel guilty, I finally get out of bed, throw on a pair of gray sweatpants, and decide to go upstairs to check on her.

What if she fell and hit her head? Or something happened to her? What if she got into a fight with Aaron? The last one is unlikely since Aaron hasn't been home much lately.

She could have also fallen asleep. That is the more logical explanation.

Not seeming to give a shit about any of that, I press the button for the penthouse and swipe my access card—an emergency key that I use almost daily, since Aaron's house operates under an open-door policy for Tristan and me.

I'll say a quick hi and make the excuse that I wanted to have the conversation about our boundaries in person. It's better to hash this stuff out face to face rather than over text where tone and meaning can easily be misconstrued. Then I'll say good night and be on my merry way.

My one nipple piercing catches the light in the elevator, the glint stealing my attention to my naked chest.

Should have put on a shirt, dumbass.

The elevator doors glide open, unveiling a brightly illuminated foyer. Despite all the lights being on, the place is too quiet. As I step into the empty foyer, I move cautiously, glancing around to see if anyone is here.

"Aaron? Zo?"

Nothing.

The kitchen and living room are all lit up. Chandeliers, lamps, spotlights...all turned on. Aaron never leaves the lights on when he's not here. He's anal retentive about conserving energy.

I slip my hands into my pockets, making my way toward Zoe's room. The unnerving silence and the blaze of lights increase my concern. Did something happen to her? Perhaps she stepped out momentarily. But where could she have gone at this hour? Another ice cream run?

Her door is slightly ajar, and no lights appear to be on inside her room, a stark contrast to the rest of the house. Poking my head inside, I notice a soft, golden hue coming from the bathroom.

Opening my mouth to call out to her, I freeze dead in my tracks, hearing soft whimpers trickling in from the crack in the door.

Goosebumps break out all over my body, and my cock jerks, hearing the sweet sounds of her soft moans and quick breaths. I fantasize about her noises every time I stroke my cock or whenever I'm with other women. Imagining Zoe and pretending like it's her I'm fucking is the only way I can get off. That's how it's been for the last six long years.

I scan the room, anxiously expecting to find a pair of men's shoes or oversized clothes that don't belong to Zoe, but there's nothing of the sort scattered around here.

She's alone and apparently not angry at all.

Fuck, I shouldn't be here. I'm invading her privacy once again.

"Mmm...yes, that's it," Zoe groans softly, her voice quiet yet urgent in a desperate way.

My cock hardens, and memories of her tied to the bed at the mansion flood me. Her eyes blindfolded and her nipples peaked as my tongue traced down her stomach. I still remember the way she tastes as if it were yesterday.

I should leave, give her this moment to herself. It's not mine to take, but I can't bring myself to turn around. Instead, I step deeper inside the room, trying to give myself enough access to see her while keeping my body hidden in darkness.

I catch a glimpse of Zoe's wet hair draped over the side of the standalone tub. Her eyes are closed and her legs are wide apart, knees resting on each side of the tub. Her head is tilted back, and her lips are slightly parted as she plays, bringing herself closer to the edge of ecstasy.

Fuck, this is so insanely sexy. I grip my angry erection over my sweats, taking in a calculated breath and forcing myself to stand still. All I want to do in this moment is rush over to her, pull her out of the tub, and lean her against the counter as I take my cock out and bury myself inside her. Feel her walls grip me tightly as she presses her soaked breasts against my bare chest. Whimpering for me to move faster, deeper, as her fingers grip my hair tightly.

Fucking Christ, I can't do this right now.

I would do anything to switch spots with her fingers, to feel her soft flesh and taste her on my tongue again.

There is no way either one of us is going to be talking anytime soon. Not with her fucking herself and my raging boner. I need to get the hell out of here before I do something I'll regret.

As I turn, her whimpers turn into moans.

She's close.

Turning to look over my shoulder, I watch as she bites down on her lip, shoulders bunching up slightly as her arm begins to splash quicker in the water, creating a small, foamy current of pleasure.

She's magnificent.

"Oh, fuck...yes...harder, Runi," she calls out right before she falls apart.

One single moment is all it takes to ruin me.

That name on her lips.

The primal need inside me takes over, breaking through every restraint I've held on to over the years, knowing the animal won't stop at anything until I make her mine again.

SHE CONSUMES ME.

It was so hard to slip away, to leave her there like that...hiding in the shadow like a fucking creep. But I couldn't help myself. Every part of me calls out to her, like a beacon of light in the night. Even when I know I don't belong, that I should walk away, keep my distance from her...I can't. Her hold on me is intense, and I need to find a way to sever the tie quickly.

But Jesus Christ.

The way she was touching herself, her lips forming into an O, her face turning toward the ceiling as she came. I wanted to take her right then and there as she called out my name, the name from that night we'd spent together. Wanting to claim her over and over again before wrapping myself around her.

Now I know she thinks about that night too. Despite the passing years and her decision to walk away from me, it brings me comfort to know that it left an indelible impression on her. She left her mark on me like a tattoo, and a part of me has always been plagued by the fear that she didn't share the same sentiments and that's why she had run off before the sun had even come up.

What the hell is wrong with me? I thought I had this all under control, cut her out years ago with a surgical knife, buried those needs in the cabin after I left Boston.

This can't happen, and especially not under Aaron's nose.

Not in his goddamn house.

This obsession with Zoe needs to end.

Stepping onto the cold bathroom tile, I keep the lights off, relishing in the darkness as I close the door and turn the shower knob to cold. My hard-on is still raging from earlier, but I'm not going to give into it. No way I'm jerking off, because the minute I do, thoughts of her and that night will overwhelm me, reminding me of everything I've been missing out on since the masquerade ball.

I should have never been there tonight.

I dip my head under the waterfall shower head as the torrent cascades down from above, rolling past my sore muscles and shocking me in place. I focus on my breaths, trying to ignore the ice-cold pellets hitting my skin. Praying the distraction is enough to get my mind off what I witnessed tonight.

But it's not enough, because all I can think about is how much I want to own her again. To gain control of her body and dig into her mind, to have her willingly give herself over to me. The need to punish her for running off on me that night, for the way she behaves, and for the way she makes me want her.

But I can't because she can never find out who was watching her behind the masks.

My body starts trembling. Adjusting the knob to warm, I inhale deeply, allowing myself to slowly relax. I'll approach this situation like everything else—time will gradually alleviate the need, and I'll adapt to having her around.

This need for her will eventually subside at some point. It has to.

Standing underneath the pulsating stream, I take a deep breath, embracing the warmth as the water washes away the tension coiling deep in my muscles. As soon as I begin to relax, Zoe's bare skin flashes before my eyes. Her in that red dress. The way her hair billowed behind her when she ran through the maze. Her startled face when I took her in my arms. The way her body squirmed underneath me as I edged her for hours.

My dick is so fucking hard.

I have this need to…

To please her over and over again until every single thought in her head disappears. Until she is empty and bare to me. Strip her bare until there is nowhere for her to hide from me. Until she finally allows herself to feel everything she is ashamed to want, to feel and not hate herself for her desires. Until she finally sees just how incredibly exquisite she truly is.

Groaning loudly, I close my eyes, trying to ignore my painful erection. Running my hands through my hair, I turn to face the wall, wishing the tendrils of warm water would cut deep into my soul and purge me of the desire I have for the one woman I can't have.

But all I see is her golden hair swaying down her back and those jade eyes looking up at me. The image of her peaked, pink nipples poking out of the water tonight has me gritting my teeth. And I finally give in, gripping my hard cock. Mewling at the feel of it and hating myself a little more as I begin to stroke myself… imagining Zoe spread out naked in my bed. Her wrists tied up to the bedposts as I take my time feasting on her. Her body squirming, her eyes fixed on me as she anticipates my movements. I never got to see her looking at me at the ball. I imagine her doe eyes pinned on my every move, and when they dare close, I'll command her to keep her gaze only on me. Punishing her with my palm if she closes them.

I'll take my time with her, trailing my fingers torturously up her legs to her thighs, relishing in the feeling of her soft skin. Peppering kisses on her stomach and dragging the tip of my tongue down to her naval. Biting along her inner thighs as I wait for her to start begging me to please her.

To fuck her. To let her come.

I'll wait until she is about to lose her mind with need.

I grip myself harder, tighter, and faster as my mind flips through images of Zoe from all the moments we've shared in the past. Her smile, the sound of her laugh, the smell of her honey hair, the way she looked on Sunday mornings sitting at the kitchen table. Her plump lips wrapped around my hard, swollen cock. And finally, what she looks like as she screams out my name.

"Fuck, Zo…that's it, baby girl."

I lose myself to the movements, drowning in thoughts of her. I let her current take me away as I suffocate in the need to have her. Thinking of all the ways I want to worship her body. How much I want to own every inch of her and ruin her for the rest of her life.

Mine.

Minutes pass, and the steam hovers all around me, fogging up the shower as my legs begin to quiver. My muscles tense up, and my climax begins to rise. The image I've been trying not to think about this whole time, the one that hasn't let me go since that night, begins to resurface. The one fantasy I can't escape and need to scratch again more than anything else…Zoe running in the woods as I chased her down, taking what I wanted from her in that cabin. Fucking her throat as she opened up to me like a good girl. Shoving her face down into the ground with her ass facing the air as I slipped inside her. My balls tighten as the wave of ecstasy rushes through me. My release is like a storm rolling in as ropes of cum begin to shoot onto the shower wall.

Taking in a deep breath, I let go of my dick and press my forehead to the cold tile.

I definitely shouldn't have gone to see her tonight.

That was a big fucking mistake.

I'm losing control.

CHAPTER 31

ZOE

"I still can't believe this is your first hockey game. I could have sworn you went to some of Dom's games in high school," Aaron says, waiting for an aha moment that's not coming because I never attended a single one.

I was never invited.

Aaron holds the car door open, and I refrain from shooting him a scathing glare as I slip inside, gliding across the black leather seats.

"Couldn't we have just walked? The stadium is only a ten-minute walk from here."

Aaron closes the door, leaning back in his seat as he runs a hand down his perfectly pressed pea coat.

"Time is money. And I don't like to waste either one of those things."

I roll my eyes. "You're ridiculous. And no, I never went to any of Dom's games in high school."

"Yes, you did," he says point blank.

I let out an exaggerated sigh. "I think I would remember, Aaron. I was never invited."

"What?" He's somehow shocked by that.

"Not sure if you remember Dominik back then, but he wasn't a fan of me. Actually, I don't think he's ever liked me very much."

"I think you're being a little dramatic, Zoe. Besides, you'll need to forget all those negative assumptions going into this game tonight if you want to actually make everyone believe you two are dating. This is a friends-to-lovers story." Aaron leans in, whispering to ensure the driver can't hear our conversation.

"It could also be an enemies-to-lovers story. That's more believable."

Aaron ignores me.

Only Dom, Aaron, Tristan, and I know the truth behind Operation Fake Relationship Rescue. Dom mentioned he wanted to tell his coach, but we all talked him out of it. The less people who know, the smoother this whole thing will go. And if there are any hiccups, the four of us can handle it quickly rather than getting anyone else involved.

I poke Aaron in the ribs, and his eyes widen at the intrusion. Whatever he was about to say vanishes because I touched him. He's so tightly wound, he needs someone to loosen him up, but his love life is as dry as the Sahara Desert.

Aaron loves to embody the strong, rich, masculine figure all the time. He loves to be in control. But I'm not sure anyone is capable of loosening him up. If anything, he probably gets off on dominating submissive women. If I have kinks, he probably does too. They say it's genetic. But unlike Aaron, no one knows about my kinks. Especially him, who thinks I'm some fragile little bird who needs to be protected. Someone who is one word away from shattering eternally.

But I broke a long time ago and learned how to put the pieces back together.

For some reason, the image of a young Aaron pops into my head. From the time when he used to scoop dirt into a small, plastic bowl, pour water on it to make a paste, and shovel the entire glob into his mouth. Once you witness your sibling doing something like that, you can never unsee it. Not even if they become a billionaire and only wear clothes with hefty price tags.

Tonight, he's wearing casual clothing, by his standards of course. Black dress pants and a signed New York Slashers jersey. The signature of the new team captain marked in black ink in the bottom corner of the jersey. For someone with terrible handwriting, Dom's signature is quite nice.

I'm also wearing a Slashers jersey, given no choice in the matter, with Dom's name and number on the back. I didn't tell him that seventeen is my favorite number.

How else would the universe laugh at me?

"Are you two ready?" Aaron asks.

"Yep. It's all becoming official tonight."

"What is the plan?"

I shrug. "Oh, I don't know. Maybe a cute little dance or something at the end of the game. We'll see. Maybe make out on the ice. Have wild, hot sex in front of all the fans." I glance out the window, watching the tall buildings and crowded streets flash by. A large group is making their way to MSG, a cloud of red-and-black jerseys floating down the sidewalk.

"Very funny. Cut that shit out."

"It's fun pissing you off about this."

"This is serious, Zo. We're all counting on you."

Of course they are. I'm cleaning up a mess I didn't even create.

Taking a deep, slow breath, I try to remain calm as I face my brother. "Maybe he should have thought about his actions before he decided to fuck half the town."

"Zo—"

I put up my hand, stopping him. "No. I said I would help, and I will. Just leave it between Dom and me, okay? I don't need your micromanagement. Just be my brother tonight. Let's have fun."

Aaron stares at me before he finally nods.

"Just don't wing it, okay? That never works for Dom. He needs to wrap his head around shit, and I'm sure he's come up with multiple backup plans for how this is all going to fail."

"Of course he has."

Aaron's mouth twists. "No, it has nothing to do with you and everything to do with him. He is a perfectionist, and this entire fiasco is eating at him."

I know it is. And even if he's not fond of me, I plan on getting him out of this one way or another.

"Everything is going to work out just fine. Trust me. I've been in this industry long enough to know how to magically make things like this disappear. Besides, I made you a promise, didn't I?"

His chin dips. "Yes, but—"

"No buts. I won't let you down. You've opened up your home and life to me; it's the least I can do."

"We're here, sir," the driver announces, halting our conversation.

"Thank you, Robert."

When the car comes to a stop, the driver exits while Aaron stays in his seat until the door opens. There's something about the situation that makes me uneasy, but I choose not to say anything. As a gust of wind rushes in, Aaron leaves the car and extends his hand to assist me out.

"Thanks, Robert!" I say to our driver.

It's only now that I realize we're standing at the back of the arena. It's empty, minus a few delivery trucks and three parked limousines with their drivers still in the vehicles.

"Why are we going through the back, and also, was that really necessary back there?"

"What?"

"Waiting for your driver to open the door for you."

Aaron arches a brow at me. "Yes, it was. Robert has a firm contract in place. I wasn't being rude. And we're with the team, lil' sis. Get used to all this. You're dating a hockey star now." He starts heading for the single, gray back door. "You're about to experience what this life is about. Are you sure you're ready? You've always hated attention."

He winks at me before disappearing inside.

I take a moment to steady my racing nerves as his words settle in. Gazing up at the night sky, I fill my lungs with the chilly air, feeling ill-prepared for what's about to come. But then again, I could use some distraction in my life right now. Smiling, I hurry toward the door, trying to catch up to Aaron.

THE HOCKEY SCENE is not at all what I expected.

I've seen bits and pieces on TV when Dom was over or when my family was watching a game. The first thing that hits me as I walk into the large arena is the smell of freshly cut ice. There is a certain sour tang to it, but the crisp, clean scene and cheerful music is invigorating. The still-cold arena air licks down my spine, eliciting tiny shivers all over my body.

The place is buzzing with excited hockey fans as we make our way down to the team bench. Pop music is blasting throughout the place, but it's nothing compared to the sounds of the growing crowd. I catch a few people staring at me as we walk down the narrow steps, my pulse picking up speed the closer we get to the friends and family section.

As we take our seats, I fixate on the massive, gleaming ice before me. I notice the bustling staff scurrying around, making final preparations before the game starts. It's all so mesmerizing, and that's coming from a non-sports fan.

"Is Dom going to introduce you to the team?"

"I don't know. He mentioned maybe meeting after the game."

"You didn't talk before coming?"

Glancing over at Aaron, he looks at me like he's bored already. Why are we talking about me and Dom again during our first real hangout since I moved to New York?

"Not really. We texted a bit and set some boundaries. That's about it."

Aaron laughs, shaking his head. "This is going to be more entertaining than the game. I'll need some popcorn."

"Can you stop being a prick? You're making me more nervous than I already am about all of this."

He squeezes my shoulder. "It's going to be fine. Dom won't let anything get out of hand. I trust him more than anyone else. He promised he'd take care of you and wouldn't overstep."

"Yes, I know. But I don't need you to protect me all the time. I can handle myself."

"Are you sure?"

I shrug off his hand, annoyed by his inability to cut me some slack. Haven't I proved myself to him after all these years?

"Who do you think took care of me all these years after you left? Who sat with me in the aftermath of a fight? Me. I did. So yes, Aaron, I can handle myself just fine."

I wait for a pained reaction to cross Aaron's face, but he's as still as stone, not revealing his thoughts or emotions. His unnerved mask unwavering.

"I'm sorry I left you behind, but you didn't want to come to New York."

"I wanted to do it on my own, Aaron. I never had their help in the first place, and I needed to learn to be independent. To stop waiting around for them to change. I didn't want to depend on you all the time. If I had come with you, you would have been worried about me and making sacrifices to keep me happy."

"That's not true."

"Yes, it is. I've always been alone, and I'm okay with that."

His brows furrow. "You're never going to be fully alone, Zo. You have me, even if we're apart."

Glancing away, I take a deep breath, not wanting to have this discussion or think about any of this tonight. We're here to have fun, not bring up our shitty childhoods. Reaching for his hand, I squeeze his fingers tight to let him know we're okay. It's always been our secret code when words failed.

We need a subject change before he says something else.

"Do you come to games often?"

"Not anymore. Work has been super busy, and we have some other business ventures that I've been leading, so finding free time has been challenging. But I'm glad we're doing this. I feel like I haven't seen you much since you got here."

"You haven't."

"Sorry...again." Aaron cringes, and I crack a smile.

"It's okay, I get it. I don't expect you to change everything, especially since I showed up out of the blue."

"I'm glad you're here. I've been wanting to get you out of Boston for so long. You're not going anywhere."

Laughing, I lean in and give him a hug. "Thanks for being here for me."

"Always," he whispers.

I struggle to fathom why my parents hold so much hostility toward me. Their disdain and favoritism toward Aaron remain incomprehensible. They've hated me since I could remember. The physical scars faded long ago, but the emotional ones from my childhood will forever linger. I never blamed Aaron for their favoritism, it wasn't his fault. And despite it all, I'm grateful for my brother. He probably doesn't even realize he's the reason I'm still here today.

I shake away the morbid thoughts.

"Who are they playing tonight again?"

"Ottawa Gladiators." Aaron stands and removes his pea coat, laying it carefully across the back of his seat.

"Canadian team?"

"Yeah. Oliver Percy, who is on the Slashers team, is actually from Ottawa, and he used to play for them. It'll be interesting to see the dynamics on ice tonight."

"Is there normally a lot of drama between the players?"

"Sometimes. I'm going to go get a drink. Do you want anything?"

"A beer would be great."

Aaron nods, and I watch as he walks to the end of the aisle, leaving me all alone.

Looking around, I feel my nerves fire up as I notice several sets of curious eyes on me. There is a group of young girls sitting a few rows down.

Withdrawing into myself, I pull out my phone and check my messages. I read a text from Sammy about a new lunch stop near the office and how much she wants to kill Greg. I smile, snapping a photo of the empty ice rink and sending it to her.

There are a couple of text alerts from Dominik, but I purposely don't open them. I've been giving him the cold shoulder since the other night.

I open up the Rabbit Hole app next and notice a red chat alert waiting for me. My stomach flips excitedly, knowing it's likely a new message from my mystery kink guy. We've been chatting for a couple of days, and I've been really enjoying getting to know him.

YOURDARKHORSE — 5:47 P.M.

TELL ME MORE ABOUT THESE NEEDS YOU MENTIONED. I WANT YOU TO BE YOURSELF. ONLY IF YOU'RE COMFORTABLE, OF COURSE. ARE YOU AN ACTIVE PREY? DO YOU ENJOY OTHER ASPECTS OF BDSM? ARE YOU SINGLE? IN A POLY RELATIONSHIP?

I CHECK MY SURROUNDINGS, making sure Aaron isn't walking back before responding to him.

FLUTTERINGAWAY — 7:02 P.M.

I FEEL COMPLETELY FINE OPENING UP TO YOU ABOUT ALL OF THIS. YOU SHOULD KNOW WHAT I'M INTO IF WE'RE EVER GOING TO PLAY IN PERSON, RIGHT? ALSO, BEFORE THIS GOES ANY FURTHER, WE SHOULD EXCHANGE SOME SORT OF MYSTERIOUS PHOTO. I DON'T WANT TO SEE YOUR FACE, OR ALL OF IT, AND I WON'T BE SHOWING YOU MINE. SO LET'S

GET CREATIVE. SPEAKING OF STAYING HIDDEN, I HAVE A HUGE MASK KINK. ARE YOU INTO THAT?

I ENJOY BEING HUNTED DOWN AND TAKEN RAW. THE PERSON I AM IN THIS SPACE AND WOULD BE WITH YOU IN REAL LIFE IS NOT AT ALL THE PERSON I AM IN MY DAY-TO-DAY LIFE, WHICH MIGHT BE WHY THIS LIFE-STYLE INTRIGUES ME. I CAN BE MYSELF, INDULGE IN MY CURIOSITIES, AND GIVE INTO MY DARK SIDE. I HAVE PLAYED BEFORE, DIPPED MY TOES IN BDSM. I LOVE EXHIBITIONISM AND VOYEURISM...ALTHOUGH I HAVEN'T TRIED THE LATTER MUCH. I'D LOVE TO GET INTO IT. I THINK IT WOULD BE SO HOT TO HAVE SOMEONE WATCH WHILE WE FUCK. AND YES, I'M SINGLE.

TELL ME EVERYTHING YOU'RE INTO. AND WHAT ARE YOU LOOKING FOR? SOMETHING LONG-TERM OR A ONE-TIME THING? BECAUSE WITH ALL THIS TRUST BUILDING, IT WOULD BE A SHAME TO DO THIS JUST ONCE.

BITING the inside of my cheek, I press send and squeeze my thighs together. The excitement is already flowing through me at the possibility of finding someone long-term who I trust, who's willing to let me back into the world of BDSM. I have never felt as free as I did that night with Runi, and I need to feel that way again.

Nothing and no one has ever compared to Runi. The way he owned my body, commanded me, dominated me, and the way I just let him. It was so intense, so addicting that I will never get it out of my head.

My phone buzzes, and I glance down to see a new message from Rabbit Hole.

That was so fast.

YOURDARKHORSE — 7:04 P.M.
YOU SAID YOU'VE DIPPED YOUR TOES IN BDSM? TELL ME MORE.

FLUTTERINGAWAY — 7:05 P.M.

IT WAS A LONG TIME AGO, BUT IT WAS INCREDIBLE. A BDSM NIGHT WITH AN EXPERIENCED MAN.

YOURDARKHORSE — 7:06 P.M.
AND DO YOU STILL TALK TO THIS MAN?

FLUTTERINGAWAY — 7:07 P.M.
NO.

YOURDARKHORSE — 7:09 P.M.
FAIR ENOUGH. WELL, I WOULD LOVE TO PUT YOU ON DISPLAY AS I FUCK YOU HARD. MY CUM DRIPPING OUT OF THAT SWEET PUSSY AS I PUSH IT BACK INSIDE YOU, MAKING YOU LICK THE REMAINDER OFF MY FINGERS. I'D TAKE PLEASURE IN CLAIMING YOU. DO YOU WANT OTHERS WITNESSING MY COCK RUINING YOU? I'LL TAKE YOUR BODY, YOUR MIND, AND MAKE IT MINE. IS THAT WHAT YOU WANT, BABY GIRL? BECAUSE I'LL HAPPILY DO ALL OF THAT AND MORE.

I WANT TO RUIN YOU. THAT'S WHAT I'M LOOKING FOR. PREFERABLY LONG-TERM.

TAKING IN A SHARP BREATH, my mind goes numb as I read his words for a second time. Looking around, I try to get my bearings straight and not think about how fucking hot that was. His words were disgusting and possessive, so controlling, they should turn me off, but they seem to have the opposite effect as I feel my core tingle with intense desire.

"Everything okay?"

I nearly jump out of my skin at the sound of Aaron's voice.

"That was fast," I croak.

Aaron hands me a plastic cup filled with beer, his brows twisting as he tries to get a read on me. Quickly tucking my phone under my thigh, I grab the beer and gulp half of it down to wash away the lust oozing out of me.

"It pays to be friends with an all-star player."

Nodding, I scan the arena, taking a few more sips of my beer.

"You look like you just saw a ghost. Everything okay?"

"Yeah...all good. I was just reading something."

Aaron ordered red wine, and he sniffs it before taking a small sip, grimacing and looking down at his cup as if he just tried rat poison.

"I need to start sneaking in my own drinks. This is atrocious."

"Or maybe, just maybe, you should stop being such a bougie douche and drink beer like the rest of us."

"Too many carbs." Taking another sip, his expression twists into an even more pronounced look of disgust as he sets his cup down onto the ground.

"Tell me how this all works. Let's get the boring lesson over with," I say, attempting to distract him and, frankly, myself after that message.

I promised to try to understand the hockey basics for the sake of this agreement with Dom and to make sure I don't look like an ass in front of anyone. The truth is, I don't like hockey. I've never been drawn to the sport. I did try to seriously get into watching sports when I was younger, to appease my parents and try to blend in, but my dad didn't even notice I was there. They got really good at ignoring me over the years. I even skipped school a few times to see what would happen when they called the house, and they just pretended like they forgot to report my absence.

I could have been kidnapped or lying dead in a ditch somewhere and they wouldn't have cared. Those episodes really angered Aaron; he started to become concerned with my whereabouts after that.

The joys of being the unwanted second child. I was an accident, and my parents have never let me forget it. And as the years went on, I stopped trying to prove them wrong. I stopped trying to be somebody and, instead, leaned into all the venom they spat at me.

Proved them right about me being a worthless excuse for a human being and how they should have never had me.

Aaron nudges my shoulder. "Did you hear me?"

I shake my negative thoughts away. "Uh-huh…this is all very cool."

"What did I say?"

Shit…umm…

"Hockey things…skating, hitting with the stick, and getting a little, black blob into the net."

Aaron pinches the bridge of his nose in frustration.

"This is going to be a disaster."

"Stop it. No one is going to quiz me on this shit."

"You asked me to tell you how it all works! Can you try to at least pretend like you care a little bit?"

I laugh. "I don't hate hockey!"

The arena crescendos in volume, vibrating with renewed energy and anticipation. Voices grow louder, and cheers intensify as the seconds tick down to the start of the game. The aroma of popcorn, corn dogs, and cheese pizza wafts by as fans weave through the arena, finding their designated seats. Overhead, the scoreboard hums while bright lights shimmer across the ice. I watch as the last of the arena staff tidy up a few things before hurrying off.

Suddenly, the music amplifies, sending my heart into overdrive as I fixate on the glistening ice rink, waiting for the players to begin trickling out. The yellow overhead lights abruptly switch off, plunging the vast, rounded arena into darkness. Deep-blue and purple lights flicker to life, some remaining static while others dance around the white rink. The scoreboard flashes to life, and madness breaks out all around us as the crowd starts to go wild.

I'm so excited to see Dominik in his element. Some people are born with desire and raw talent burning inside them, and they'll never settle until they do what brings them to life. Hockey has always brought Dom to life.

I've heard about his game play and how he is just a natural on the ice. One of the best hockey players of his time. My dad used to joke that he thinks Dominik flew out of his mom wearing skates on his tiny baby feet.

"Dream On" by Aerosmith booms from the speakers as four referees appear on the ice, skating in perfect harmony as they go around, circling one another. A performance they are all too familiar with, having likely done this dance a thousand times.

There is a lot happening, and even though I'm completely new to this scene, the enthusiasm is contagious.

"The game is about to begin. The Slashers are going to come out first since they are the home team," Aaron explains.

Just then, the crowd starts booing loudly.

"What's going on?"

When Aaron doesn't answer, I look over to see his face in his phone and his fingers moving furiously across the glass screen. Must be work, but I don't dare ask, in case it opens the door to him needing to leave. No way in hell am I sitting through a full hockey game alone.

He glances up for a split second before getting back to his phone. "They always do that. The crowd doesn't like the refs."

"Why?"

"They just don't," Aaron exclaims loudly.

"Thank you for that helpful explanation," I mutter to myself, tempted to grab his phone and throw it over the plexiglass barriers. "Can you put that away? Just for a couple of hours?" I yell, making sure he can hear me this time.

He purses his lips, clearly unhappy, but tucks his phone back in his pocket.

"I'm sorry. It's hard for me to step away from work, but I'm trying."

Or maybe you just don't know how to be less controlling. Not wanting to start another argument or piss him off, I keep quiet and turn back toward the ice.

A strobing, white spotlight appears on my left, highlighting an entrance. Everyone stands, including Aaron. I crane my neck, watching closely, almost at the edge of my seat to see how the team is going to make their entrance.

"Stand up," Aaron says, grabbing my hand.

The arena is full of jovial fans, and the sounds of their cheers grow more intense around us.

I can feel Aaron's eyes on me. He's smiling as he waits to see my reaction, which only has my heart jumping to my throat. The anticipation is starting to drive me a little crazy, but I love the vibrations from the music and the electrifying aura of everyone else here as we collectively wait for the team to make their appearance.

I finally understand the rush of the game and what it means to be part of this crowd—this community of hockey fans. That's saying a lot, considering the game hasn't even started.

And I haven't even seen Dominik yet.

CHAPTER 32
ZOE

Players shoot out one by one like marbles, the sound of skates scratching ice mixing in perfectly with the rest of the commotion in the arena. The crowd goes wild as the players immediately move into some sort of drill, with stretching, mini sprints, and skating around and around. There is a lot going on, and I try to spot Dominik, but I can't find him.

The Slashers are wearing their red-and-black uniforms, with detailing at the edges and bold letters spelling out SLASHERS underneath their hockey mask symbol on the front. Aaron and I are wearing the same jersey, but ours are white. Apparently, they circulate colors based on which team they're playing against so each side is easily distinguishable during the game. See, I did somewhat listen when Aaron was covering the basics earlier.

It's hard to spot anyone at the speed they are skating, especially sitting this close to the ice. The other team also started trickling out, although they didn't get a spotlight like the home team did, and now all the players are skating around, sharing the space as the song comes to an end.

Nervous energy rushes through me, not because I'm sitting here as a complete sham, but because I'm excited to be part of something.

A minute later, three men dressed in suits appear behind the player's bench. One of them is bald, and his head is very shiny, the red lights from above flashing on top of his scalp. Aaron elbows me, stealing my attention back to the ice as my eye catches on a tall player skating close to the wall where we're sitting. The room seems to grow still as my gaze locks onto his gold and blue orbs. Dominik's stare is piercing even from here, with the low lighting and distance between us, even with the crowd spread out all around us.

It all fades away one by one, and amidst the chaos, he gives me the most breathtaking smile that eclipses everything and everyone.

Is he smiling at me?

I glance over my shoulder, intrigued by whoever has earned the unfamiliar smile on Dominik Lewis' face. As I return my gaze, his eyes remain fixed on me, causing a surge of heat to rise to my cheeks. It becomes clear to me why the women who have crossed paths with him are left in awe, knowing they may never experience his presence again. He exudes a captivating aura, and I can't help but feel completely inadequate, even if this is all for show.

Unsure of what my face is doing, I take a second to collect myself as he skates away, flashing across the ice to the other side of the rink.

"Solid start." Aaron's voice snaps me back to reality.

"Huh?"

"You two really made it look like you are smitten with one another. And your face—didn't know you could blush that hard on demand."

Oh, right. The performance.

He's putting on his charm in front of everyone to prove how much he's into you. He would never actually like you. Just look at him and look at you.

As the music dies down, players from both teams line up parallel to one another on their sides of the rink. They all remove their helmets. Some pin them under their arms while others hold them with their free hands.

But I'm watching Dominik. Taking in the way his black hair shines against the red-and-white lights. He is mesmerizing, and that body is completely out of this world, even under all that gear. Actually, I think the gear accentuates his muscular form.

How can someone be so hot in bulky hockey gear? Wait…am I attracted to this?

Day one, and I'm already distracted by his good looks. But it's fine, it'll make playing the smitten girlfriend role that much easier. If I actually want to fuck him, it won't be so hard to pretend. Now I'm thinking about what Dominik is like in bed. Is he the gentle lover, or the hair-pulling type?

It would be a shame if he were vanilla. He could easily throw someone around and roughhouse with his build and height. Not to mention, he gives off big dick energy, and a few people commented about the size of it on the online forums.

What are you doing?

Jesus, what am I doing? This is unproductive, considering we're never going to have any sexual relations.

The Canadian national anthem begins playing, and my eyes trace over the players on the other team as Aaron and I stand. Most of the crowd follows, standing for the duration of both the Canadian and American national anthems. The Gladiators look good. Dressed in all-white hockey jerseys with a gladiator cartoon sketch wearing a hockey helmet on the front.

They're all built to perfection. It's easy to tell, even under all that thick, heavy gear.

How am I just now realizing how hot hockey players are?

Maybe once all this fake dating stuff with Dom and me is over, I can find a hot hockey player willing to keep a secret or two with me.

My eyes travel across the ice to the team lined up across from the Gladiators, our home team.

Taking my time and tuning out the anthems, I study each face and body standing on the ice. A couple of the guys catch my glare, one even nods toward Aaron, and my brother tilts his chin. Do they know I'm his sister? I doubt it. Aaron doesn't talk about me much…at least as far as I know. He's always been extra protective of me, thanks to my neglectful parents.

When I reach Dominik, his eyes are already fixed on me. His gaze penetrates through the plexiglass barrier, so intense that every hair on my body stands on end.

There's something strikingly different about him tonight—the way he captures my attention. It's as if he's seeing me for the first time, allowing himself to truly take me in. Despite the cold air around us, my skin flushes with heat. His presence is magnetic, and although I want to avert my eyes, I'm caged in this intense moment of silent connection between us. It feels like an eternity before he finally breaks our gaze, securing his helmet over his head with a wink directed at me.

The bright, fluorescent lights turn on, flooding the arena as cheerful pop music begins blasting through the speakers.

"You can sit down now."

Shaking away the Dominik haze, I look down at Aaron and take a seat.

"Toxic" by Britney Spears blares, and the crowd starts screaming, mainly the women. Confused, I look around and notice some people are fanning themselves. Others are standing and jumping, clapping as if Henry Cavill has just walked out onto the ice.

The players are all skating around, but I notice some are…wait…

"Oh my God! What are they doing?"

Aaron bursts out laughing. "They're stretching."

That doesn't look like stretching.

"They're humping the ice."

Dominik skates to the other side of the ice, stopping abruptly and causing a spray of shaved ice to dust the air. He gets onto his knees while looking in my general direction. Spreading wide, he starts stretching his quads. He takes his hockey stick, gripping each end, and raises it over his head. A crowd of rambunctious women goes wild behind me.

"LEWIS, DOMINATE ME!"

Laughing, I look back at the flustered women losing themselves watching Dom stretch on the ice. But he's doing it on purpose, trying to get a rise out of them. Sexualizing himself, and they're fucking eating it up right out of the palm of his hand.

"This is hilarious."

"The women love him."

I roll my eyes. "Clearly."

"You don't find him attractive?"

I know when Aaron is trying to set me up. Facing my brother, I raise a brow at him, and he crosses his arms, challenging me. I think if Aaron could have it his way, I'd be asexual. Unfortunately for him, I love sex, and I would have more of it if I could. Sex is completely natural, and people should explore everything that makes them feel good. We like what we like, and there is nothing wrong with that.

But Aaron has always been weird about the topic of sex around me. Although we've never actually talked about it, I know he would rather I never engage in any activity, especially with anyone he might know. Once, he beat up one of my boyfriends in high school because he caught him grabbing my ass.

But that's Aaron's problem, not mine, and if I'm going to stay in New York, under his roof, he's going to realize quickly just how much I enjoy sex. My entire box of toys hidden in my closet can attest to that.

"Depends what you're into."

"Meaning?"

I shrug. "He's not my type." I glance toward Dom, who is watching us. He's on his feet now, doing jump squats on the ice as if he's not wearing skates. I would fall flat on my face and break my teeth if I even attempted anything like that.

"Dom is everyone's type."

Smirking, I look up at my brother. "Is he your type, Aaron?"

"Fuck off."

"Hey...I'm just asking. You're super weird about sex, or the lack of it."

"Not that there is anything wrong with it, but I'm not into guys."

"Tell me more."

"No." His voice is stern, and I know he won't be entertaining this conversation for another second.

Deep down, I know Dom is everyone's type. Anyone with eyes would want to spend a night tangled in the sheets with him. But I'm not interested in a man who's closed off, stubborn, and cold. Plus, the only reason he's giving me any attention right now is to help himself.

"So, you don't find him attractive?" Aaron pushes the subject.

"He's attractive, but I need more than looks. The guy has a mountain guarding him, and he refuses to let anyone in. Also, stubborn, cold men are typically lousy lovers."

Aaron cracks a smile, like he's trying to hide something. "Says who? Actually, don't answer that. You don't have sex."

"You can't be serious."

"Zoe, we're not having this conversation."

"Grow up, Aaron. Your sister likes sex. Get over it."

The song fades out as the referees glide onto the ice. One of them is holding a puck as players take their spots like pieces on a chessboard. The puck drops, and everyone bursts into action. Red and white players soar across the ice with grace and speed, each one expertly moving their bodies in a dance that seems both tousled and perfectly choreographed.

The crowd continues to go wild, energy crackling heavily around us, and I allow myself to get lost in all of it. I really thought I would hate being here. That it would bore me enough to want to read a book on my phone, but to be honest, I'm enjoying myself a lot more than I imagined I would. We're sitting so close to all the action that the smacking of hockey sticks against the boards is louder than the music and crowd combined.

My head ping-pongs back and forth as I try to keep up, but I finally give up and focus on Number Seventeen. I'm enthralled, watching him dominate the game and glide along the ice as if he's part of the rink, sketched from the ice itself. He's a magician, mesmerizing everyone as he weaves in and out with ease, making it look so effortless.

"He's amazing," I sigh, a little surprised to hear the admiration in my own voice.

"I know. He was always meant to be a hockey player. I realized that the first time I watched him play. It's in his blood."

I wonder what it's like to be so utterly passionate about something that your entire body and soul call out to it. That when you're engrossed in the work, it makes you come alive in a way nothing else ever could. The only time I've come close to feeling anything remotely similar to that was when I got the chance to design a building in architecture class in college. I got lost in the process. It didn't even feel like work. But I guess I never wanted it bad enough, because it slipped right through my fingers. That level of true passion can't fade away, because those it captures are bound to it forever. Isn't that what they say about artists too?

I see it in Dom with hockey. With my brother and the empire he's built for himself. Some people have so much passion that they never work a single day in their lives. What would it be like to wake up every day and be excited to go to work because you love what you do? But then again, is it safe to love anything in life? Because what if your dreams don't pan out? What if I pour my heart and soul into something only for it to be shoved aside? I could lose everything, including myself, all over again.

It would be better to never feel it than to have it and lose it. I'm a chaser, working for money and aimlessly walking around looking for pieces of myself in the dark. I'm okay with that, with being a ghost until my time runs out.

Aaron shoots forward in his seat, nudging me with his knee. "Here he goes!"

I zero in on Dominik, who has the puck. He races across the ice, his body moving at a blurring speed as he breaks free, cocking his stick back and sending the puck flying past the goalie right into the net. The New York crowd is on their feet and going wild. His team-mates skate his way, throwing themselves at him and embracing him.

As the excitement dies down, Dom skates close to the bench. His wild eyes find mine. I have the biggest fucking smile on my face, and he's grinning back at me.

CHAPTER 33
ZOE

"I have to head to the office for twenty minutes. Are you sure you don't want to come?"

"To your work on a Saturday night? I'm good, thanks. I'll just see you at home."

Aaron's hand is on my shoulder as we walk down the hallway the players disappeared into after the game.

The Slashers won 4-2 against the Gladiators. The entire arena lost their shit, throwing shirts, hats, and stuffed animals onto the ice. The boys weren't bothered though. They were all in a great mood after a win like that.

Dominik and I planned to meet outside the locker room after the game so he can introduce me to the team. A few other women, presumably girlfriends or wives, already made their way down the hall earlier. I wish Aaron would stay since I don't know anyone here and I'd rather not do this alone, but it would be weird for my brother to hold my hand through this.

"Are you sure?" Aaron asks reassuringly.

"Yes. I have to stay. I need to say hi to Dom, congratulate him… maybe offer him an awkward girlfriend hug."

Aaron's brows furrow. "Do you want me to stay to make sure everything goes well?"

Shaking my head, I nudge him toward the back door. "No, you're fine. I'll see you at home."

Right at that moment, Aaron's phone rings, and he curses under his breath.

"All right. I'll see you later."

Aaron leans in and gives me a quick peck on the cheek.

"This was fun. We'll do more of it soon, okay? And don't just give him a hug in front of his team. Congratulate him, throw your arms around him. Be a proud girlfriend. He did get a hat trick, which is a big deal, by the way. Just follow his lead."

Too bad Dom is as useless as I am when it comes to this physical stuff. Actually, probably worse.

My legs feel shaky all of a sudden. I don't even know what I'm supposed to do. I'm already bad at relationships, and fake ones—where the guy doesn't even want me to touch him—make the entire ordeal so much worse. This isn't good for someone with gut-punching anxiety.

Aaron rests both his hands on my shoulders. "Hey...nothing to be anxious about. It's just business, right?"

"That obvious, huh?" I exhale.

Aaron has deep-gray eyes. They are such a unique color, and he gets compliments everywhere we go. I have the same almond-shaped eyes as him, but the color is nothing special. Our mother has the same shade of gray, and our dad has hazel eyes. Which means, I'm an outcast when it comes to yet another thing in our family.

Maybe I'm the mailman's daughter.

"You're both going to be fine. Love you." He kisses the top of my head and turns, walking down the hallway.

Aaron is different. Older and more mature, but not in a good way. He's not the same Aaron who lived in that small studio apartment when he first moved to New York. Maybe he's hiding too. Don't we all wear masks in some way to hide who we truly are from the rest of the world? Even from people we know and love. I always hoped Aaron and I would never wear any masks around each other. But life doesn't work like that. The fear of judgment and rejection is enough to make me want to hide forever.

I wait until he's out the door before turning to face the shit show that awaits me. There are staff running around, laughing, riding the high from this home game. Hollers and cheers can be heard from adjacent rooms as I make my way to the locker room, sticking close to the concrete wall.

It would be easy to bail right now. I could fake being sick, text Dom and tell him my stomach doesn't feel so great after the arena food. Turning my butterfly ring around and around on my middle finger, I consider chasing after Aaron.

Frustrated and completely uncomfortable in my own skin, I decide to head back down to the glass for a bit to compose myself. The Zamboni is already on the rink, painting on a new sheet of ice, and the place has already cleared out. Fans rushed out early to beat traffic and get back to their lives.

The place is so peaceful, the complete opposite of what it was merely an hour ago.

"It's cool, isn't it?"

A deep sound behind me has me jumping out of my skin.

"Shit, sorry." The mystery man with big, bright-blue eyes cringes, worry written all over his chiseled face.

Are these hockey players living here, sharing bedtime stories with the gym equipment? This guy has impressive shoulders and an athletic build, with muscles that ripple beneath a sun-kissed complexion. A cascade of damp, blond waves sling to the side of his face, intensifying the ice blue of his eyes. Strong jaw, perfectly straight nose, and rosy, kissable lips. He's in a white dress shirt and gray formal pants. My eyes linger on the top few open buttons of his shirt, his muscles peeking through.

I recall Aaron telling me hockey players arrive and leave dressed to impress before and after every game. They are required to wear formal attire, something about the press... I'm drawing a blank because this man is making it impossible to focus on anything else right now.

Say something, you idiot.

"It's okay...I forgive you for trying to give me a heart attack. They have doctors on site here, right?" He smiles brightly at my cheesy response.

"No doc needed. I would have gladly nursed you back to health."

I bite my lip, letting out a peal of laughter at the terrible pickup line. He rubs the back of his neck, grinning wider as his eyes linger on my lips. He was expecting me to be offended, maybe give him a hard time, but I'm nothing special. I'm just here, wearing yet another mask as I pretend to be someone I'm not, helping out a friend...an acquaintance? Can I even call Dominik that?

He extends his hand out. "Hi. I'm Noa... I play for the Slashers. And you are?"

"She's mine." A growl has us both turning.

I barely register what's going on before Dom comes into view, pushing Noa out of the way as his chest presses into me. He wraps his arm around my waist while his other hand finds the small space behind my neck. Fresh tingles burst from the contact and the closeness of our bodies.

"Hi," he whispers, his voice bringing awareness to every place our bodies are touching.

"Hey." I gulp.

The hand around the back of my neck inches up to the front of my neck, his thumb stroking my chin as he lowers his face. His lips are a breath away from my own.

He's hesitant, staring down at me.

"I'm going to kiss you now."

That's the only warning I get before his lips melt into mine. A shock wave of sensation pulses through me, sending my heart into overdrive. The kiss is soft yet demanding, as if he's feeling me out, waiting for me to make the next move and deepen our kiss. I wrap my arms around his neck, running my fingers into his cold, wet hair, tugging to bring him closer. Our bodies fuse into one another, fitting effortlessly as if he were made for me. I get lost in him for a moment, nipping at his bottom lip before parting my lips, inviting him in. Dominik groans as his tongue pushes inside, exploring and leaning into me with a fierce intensity that makes breathing impossible.

I forget my own name as I kiss him back with the same fervor. I have only ever kissed like this once before. The memories of Runi flash through me, sort of like déjà vu, which is impossible since I've never tasted Dom until now. But even in their similarities, this one feels more intense. Making every other kiss before it feel like child's play. His hand weaves into my hair, pulling tightly as I moan into his mouth.

At that sound, Dominik abruptly breaks the kiss, his eyes wild as he looks down at me breathlessly. His nostrils flare, and he appears to be in shock. Our first kiss, which was never meant to happen in the first place.

The man who never kisses just made out with me at his place of work. In front of someone else.

Due to...jealousy?

And he looks pissed about it. The realization of what we just did finally sinks in, and regret takes over. I stand here, feeling nothing but shame and guilt for letting him kiss me like that. For getting lost in the moment. Dropping my gaze, I release him and take a wide step back. Trying to compose myself, I focus on the black, padded flooring we're standing on, taking note of the various-sized cuts inside the foam.

The look of rejection on his face from before burns the back of my eyes, but I can't let it show.

Not here. Not right now.

"I'm sorry, man. I had no idea," Noa says in a soft, apologetic voice.

I watch as a tattooed hand wraps around mine as Dom interlaces our fingers together.

Looking up at Noa, I offer him a knowing smile. He's bright red and cringing at Dom, a little frightened, it seems. Extending my other hand out to Noa, I break the awkward silence lingering between the three of us.

"I'm Zoe, by the way. Nice to meet you."

Noa shakes my hand for a slight second, only to be polite, before he drops it and glances at Dominik to see if he's fine with our interaction.

What the hell? Why is he so skittish? Dominik doesn't own me. Clearly, the guys on the team are afraid of him or Noa wouldn't be this timid right now. Which throws off my future plan to hook up with a random hockey player on the Slashers. It would be hard to get into the sheets with any of these guys if they're so afraid of Dom. Is it because he's captain of the team?

I don't dare look up at Dominik. Not after the way he looked at me after that kiss.

Was it all in my head though? I swear I felt him leaning in, felt his skin burn just as bright as mine. How could anyone fake a kiss like that?

But then again, he specializes in being a fuckboy, so maybe it's all a game to him.

Doesn't matter. I don't want it to ever mean anything.

It's only now that I realize more people have gathered around us. They are all staring at me, some smiling, others with confusion, and some bouncing back and forth between Dom and me as though they are expecting one of us to jump up and say, "Ha! Gotcha! You've been Punk'd."

There is a lot of cleaning up to do here. I need to get close to someone and dig around to see what Dominik is like at work and around his team.

Dom finally introduces me to everyone, firing off names I've already forgotten as I smile and nod, shaking all their hands. It's super awkward and feels a little too forced. My thoughts are all jumbled, and I have this sudden urge to flee. Like I'm being looked at under a microscope.

What will they all say once you're gone?

What they think of me is none of my business.

But it doesn't matter how many times I tell myself that, or any other positive thought, because the negative whispering is always there to feed my anxiety.

"I should go." I look at Dom.

His forehead wrinkles. "Okay, let's go."

"What about the press and the party?" one of the guys pipes up.

Dominik doesn't take his eyes off me. "Not tonight. I'm taking my girl home."

"How did you two meet again?" a female asks. I glance at the group and notice a gorgeous redhead leaning into one of the guys. I think his name is Liam.

How do I answer this question? We didn't cover our back story.

"We met in high school. She's my best friend's sister, and I was stupid enough to let her get away then. Regretted it all these years, but she recently got relocated to New York for work, and I took it as a sign. A second chance I wasn't willing to give up. Not this time," Dominik says, glancing at me with fondness.

Someone needs to pick my jaw up off the floor.

This man is better than I gave him credit for. Dom's cover story is pretty close to reality, and the way he said it, well, even I almost believe it.

If hockey doesn't pan out for him long term, Dom could definitely go into acting.

"That's so romantic! Totally meant to be."

A couple of the guys make a joke, but I don't hear them. My face is scorching hot when I finally look away.

"Have fun, assholes, and don't drink too much."

I hear a few grumbles followed by some laughs. I try to pull my hand away, but Dominik's grip is strong, holding me in place right next to him as we make our way down the hallway.

"I just have to grab my bag," he says, stopping outside the locker room.

"Mm-hmm." I need air and five minutes to myself, or else I'm going to say things that have no business coming out of my mouth.

"You okay?"

"Yeah. I'll wait out here." I try hard not to roll my eyes.

Dominik pauses for a second before he turns, his hand on the door.

"Nice performance, by the way. You deserve an Oscar," I spit out, unable to stop myself.

The mischievous look in his eyes is fucking delicious, and I hate how much I like it.

"Thanks, baby. Worked on it all night."

"Fuck you."

"I know you want to. I'd be lying if I said I haven't thought about it too."

My jaw springs open, and he walks inside the locker room, his laugh echoing inside.

The bastard.

To hell with this.

I storm down the hallway, kicking open the outside door as I step into the cold night.

CHAPTER 34

DOMINIK

I've thought about all the ways I would punish her for storming off on me like that if Zoe were actually my girl. I would bend her over my knee in the elevator and smack her ass so hard, she would be pleading with me to stop, begging me to lick her wounds before my tongue found her wet cunt.

"Would you slow the fuck down?"

"No."

She's such a fucking brat.

"We need to talk," I grit out.

"There is nothing to talk about, Dom. I'll just follow your lead and your rules because, apparently, I have no say in this, right? Even though I'm the one who works at the PR firm and is helping you with a mess *you* caused. But you can decide when it's okay to kiss me because you got jealous."

"I wasn't jealous."

She whips around. "Bullshit."

Looking around the busy street, I grab her arm and lower down so we're eye level.

"Would you calm down and stop shouting?"

Her eyes narrow into small slits. It's incredibly hard not to smile right now, but I know if my lips crack, even slightly, she's going to lose her shit.

"Don't tell me to calm down. You don't get to tell me what to do. I'm not yours."

She tries to shake her arm free, but I pull her into me, trapping her against my body.

"Dominik, let me go," she breathes, her eyes lingering on my mouth.

"And you don't get to talk to me like that," I whisper back, leaning in closer to her and wanting to kiss her again. "Out here, you belong to me."

Fuck, that kiss.

It's all I've been thinking about since our lips touched. It was better than I'd imagined it would be. I didn't even realize how starved for her I truly was until our lips finally met. Until she was pressed close to my body and I could smell her, feel the warmth from her skin...like now, as the animal inside me roars, needing to bind us together once again.

I release her, and she blinks before stepping away quickly.

This is the reason I didn't want to do this with Zoe in the first place. This need I have for her, the way I'm drawn to her, is unlike anything else. The temptation is too great to ignore. And now it's too late to back out. It would make Aaron and Tristan suspicious, not to mention how disappointed Coach would be with me...again.

"Bastard," she mutters under her breath, but it's loud enough for me to catch.

Looking to my left, I notice the small, deserted alleyway tucked in between two buildings. Without a second thought, I grab her arm and drag her with me.

"What the fuck are you doing?"

Walking past an empty dumpster, where I'm certain we won't be seen from the street, I press her up against the brick wall. A look of apprehension and slight terror fills her eyes, but there is something else there too. It's the way her eyelids become a bit hooded and her breaths quicken. She's excited, maybe even a little aroused by the sudden change in my behavior.

"You want to repeat that again? See what I'll do to you for running your mouth like that?" Pressing my leg in between hers, Zoe's knees fall apart as I pin her in place with my body.

She studies me for a second, contemplating her next words. "You wouldn't dare."

"Are you sure about that, Zoe?"

Inching down, I hover close to her cheek, watching her closely as my breath fans across her skin. She squirms, trying to break free, but I'm too strong for her.

"What if everything you think you know about me is wrong? You think you're the only one who likes to wear masks?"

Her shocked expression lights me up, making me want to give into all my needs. To rip her pants off and take her right here, press my palm against her mouth to muffle her sweet moans. But instead, I reach up with my free hand, snaking my fingers around her neck. Zoe shuts her eyes, inhaling a strained breath before reopening them.

"I'm not wrong about you."

I arch a brow at her. "Do you care to find out? Right here, right now?"

As suspected, she shakes her head.

"Don't you ever disobey me like that again or flirt with anyone else."

I'm trying to control her and force her into submission, teach her a lesson for the way she treated me back there. But a part of me wants her to fight back, to stand up for herself and show me that brat. I enjoy thinking of all the ways I could tame her attitude and turn her into a whimpering pet.

And my Zoe never disappoints. She lifts her neck, pressing against my hand as she tries to move me but ends up just bringing her face closer to mine.

Her eyes blaze with an insatiable fire that engulfs me, leaving only a trail of desire in its wake.

"You don't own me, Dominik. You never have, and you never will."

She wraps her fingers around my wrist, digging her nails into my flesh.

My dick hardens instantly, and I tilt my hip so she can't feel my erection, while keeping my fingers resting on her neck.

"That's where you're wrong, butterfly. And if you test me again, you're going to regret it." Our mouths are an inch apart, and it takes everything I have to not fuse us together.

"I'm not fucking scared of you," she bites out, her grip around my wrist tightening. She pulls down my wrist, and I allow her some control as she begins to peel me off of her.

I smirk. "You will be. We're just getting started, baby."

"Don't call me that," she snaps before shoving me hard in the chest.

I stare at her back as she puts more distance between us, gazing up at the sky and praying to whatever god is up there to give me the will to survive the next couple of months.

"LET'S TALK IN MY APARTMENT."

Zoe hasn't looked at me or said two words since the incident in the alley. She's purposely giving me the silent treatment.

"I have nothing to say to you."

"We need to discuss tomorrow and the following game."

"Just text me the details."

I stare at her reflection in the mirror, urging her to look at me, but she's as stubborn as a rock.

"This isn't up for discussion."

Her head whips toward me, her cheeks red with anger. I wish she would take it out on me one of these days. Give me her wrath so I can pin her against the wall and fucking have my way with her.

Only in your dreams, asshole.

"Whatever this new dominance act is you're trying to force on me, drop it right now. I'm not one of your puck bunnies. This is all for show, and I'll behave like the good little girlfriend you need while we're in public, but outside of that, you don't get to tell me what to do. Actually, you don't get to tell me what to do, period."

My heart is pounding with the need to fucking punish her right here inside this elevator and force her to watch. No woman has ever talked to me like this, and there is something about her fierceness that has me going wild. But it's not the time for that right now, because in a minute, I'm going to ruin her entire day, maybe even her week. I need to tell her something, and I can't keep it from her for another minute.

Sighing, I reach for her hand, but she pulls away.

"Don't touch me."

"Zo...your parents are here. They stopped by unannounced after the game and Aaron texted me."

The change in her is instantaneous. Her entire body wilts as she withdraws into herself. She stares off into the distance, as if she's trying to turn off the storm that must be taking shape inside her. Witnessing her in such a state shatters something within me.

"Oh."

Stepping in front of her, I place both hands around her face and urge her to look into my eyes. "You're going to stay with me for as long as you need, and I'm going to make sure you don't see them."

"No, it's fine." She forces a smile.

"You don't need to pretend with me. Not about this."

"I can go to a hotel."

"Over my dead fucking body. I have a spare room, and I'll stay out of your way."

"No. That's not necessary."

"Do you want me to pick you up and take you over my shoulder? Because I fucking will if I have to."

Her eyes bulge, and she shakes her head. "Fine, but just for the night until I figure something out," she finally agrees. "Hey, Dom?"

I glance down at her from the corner of my eye. "Yeah?"

"Is Aaron with them right now?"

"Yeah...he said they're going to stay for a couple of nights, but then he'll find them other arrangements. He's sorry, Zoe."

She nods, looking defeated, likely by the realization that her brother made time for her parents but he didn't do the same when she arrived. I want to tell her it's not personal; it's because he thinks he'll have more time with her. I want to tell her to forget them, that she doesn't need their love and affection. That all she needs is her. She can be the love of her life, and she doesn't need their approval. She never has, because she is amazing in every way.

A smack lands across my chest, startling me enough that my back hits the mirror in the elevator.

"The hell did you just hit me for?"

Zoe smiles, and it takes me a second to sense another shift. She's masking her sadness with something else. I'll happily play along if it'll help her forget about her shitty family.

She shrugs, biting her lip as her smile grows wider. "Are you going to do something about it?"

Fuck, I really want to. I'd love to press her face into the couch in my apartment and empty her mind. Fill her with nothing but pleasure and leave my cum dripping down her legs. My instinct is to reach for her, but I stop myself, dropping my gaze to the floor.

This just got a lot harder.

Fucking hell, she's going to live with me temporarily.

Sweet lord, help me.

CHAPTER 35

ZOE

"**D**id you grab everything you need?" Dominik asks as he props open the door to his apartment. He steps aside and allows me to walk in.

I can't believe my parents dropped in out of nowhere, like a fucking bomb right in the middle of my life. That's their M.O. though; it's like their timing is always intended to spoil any good days I might be having.

Aaron texted Dom to inform him they were going out to dinner. He hasn't called or texted me once, presumably embarrassed or too chicken to say anything to me right now. That's fine, I'm just going to ignore it like I always do when he feels like he's stuck between a rock and a hard place.

Dom and I took the opportunity to run upstairs and pack some bags since I'll be staying with him for a few days. When we were up in Aaron's apartment, I couldn't help but notice the array of gifts and treats on the kitchen island. Bottles of wine, a large bouquet of flowers, little teddy bears as if he's still a five-year-old. It's not like there is an occasion for any of it.

I can't remember the last time we celebrated my birthday as a family. Aaron's birthday is close to Thanksgiving, and my parents always made a big deal out of it. No one was allowed to go anywhere or do anything around Aaron's birthday. There were gifts, parties, a trip to Disney, even. Which is great; I'm happy my brother got so much love. He deserves it. But I'm not going to lie, it fucking stung when, year after year, they forgot about me.

Unfortunately for me, my birthday falls on the week between Christmas and New Year's. Growing up, everyone was always busy during that time and we would either be traveling or getting ready for New Year's Eve celebrations. My parents threw the biggest party around...which meant after Christmas wrapped up, they were busy preparing for that. They would tell me my birthday was part of the celebration, but it wasn't true. Nothing about me was ever included. They just forgot because they never gave a shit about me.

Aaron noticed it as well, and he always made an effort to lift my spirits. His caring demeanor lessened the blow from my parents, but eventually, I stopped celebrating my birthday because it only served as a reminder of how unloved I felt. The holiday season now only brings about bitter memories. And the worst part is how these moments continuously reopen old wounds, making it hard for me to forget and move forward.

"Yeah...I think so." Resting my two suitcases by the door, I slip off my shoes and walk inside.

"It's late. Are you hungry?"

I shake my head and just linger in Dominik's dark foyer.

"Zoe," he calls out to me.

I fear that if I speak, words I shouldn't even entertain will spill from my mouth. They might unlock a floodgate of emotions, causing me to break down in front of a man I hardly know.

"I'm good. I think I'm just going to go to bed."

"Not like this."

"Wha—"

Before I can protest, Dominik takes my hand and guides me toward the back of his apartment.

His place is big and spacious. It's not as big as Aaron's, but it shares a similar layout. Giant, floor-to-ceiling windows that overlook the eastern side of New York, mainly the Hudson River as it shines under the twinkling moonlight. Dominik doesn't have much in the way of furniture. His tastes seem to be more on the minimalist side, which I'm a huge fan of as a designer…or rather, a wannabe designer.

He drags me up a set of floating stairs.

"Where are you taking me?"

But he doesn't answer as we walk down a hallway, driving me insane with his tight grip and freakish strength. I attempt to yank my arm free, but it somehow makes me fall into his back, stumbling right as he opens a door to reveal a stunning, white-and-gray bathroom.

A sleek, glass shower stands beside a spacious bathtub placed prominently in the room's center. Adjacent to the tub rests a small, wooden table displaying a stack of books.

"Wow…"

"This bathroom opens up to that room." He releases my hand, his chin pointing to a closed door to my right. "You can lock this door leading into the hallway if you'd like. Although I don't use this bathroom, so you'll have full privacy."

"Thanks."

He walks over to the tub and turns the faucet. The sound of gushing water echoes through the room, and I watch Dominik stroll over to one of the sinks, opening a cabinet and pulling out a box filled with colorful balls.

Are those…

"Are you drawing me a bath?"

"Maybe."

"That's really not necessary."

Dominik pauses, dropping a ball of pink, sparkly chalk into the tub. His back is to me, but I see the way his muscles flex in irritation.

"Sometimes it's nice to let someone else take care of you."

I bite my lip in frustration. "I don't need you to take care of me."

He turns to face me, his expression unreadable as he stalks toward me.

"Can you just let me do one nice thing for you without making a big deal out of it?" He turns, continuing his task as he pours in bubbles, essential oils, and dried flowers.

Watching Dominik draw me a bath is strange. It all feels out of place, especially after our exchange in the alleyway earlier. He's so hot and cold, I don't know what to make of it when he does something nice for me. I know it's out of pity, which makes me just want to storm off and go to bed. But I can't bring myself to do that.

Maybe he does this type of thing for everyone.

"Do you do this for the other women who spend the night?"

His back is still to me. "No other woman has ever been here. Well, excluding my mother."

I'm too surprised to say anything.

He dips his hand into the water, seeming to test the temperature before he starts putting everything away and heading for the door.

He pauses, turning to face me. "Take a bath. Relax. It's been a long day and a stressful ending to the night. Just…enjoy it. Okay?"

Something pulls in my chest at the sound of his sincerity and the look of utter defeat in his eyes. He feels bad for me.

"Thank you for all of this, but I don't want your pity."

"It's not pity, Zoe. It's me trying to make amends. Now get into the fucking tub."

And he's back.

He leaves quickly, and I hear his footsteps retreating down the stairs before I shut the door and turn my gaze on the mirror. I stare at my own reflection, stripping off my clothes quickly before sinking into the warm tub.

God, this feels nice. I can't even pretend like his bath game isn't strong, because it's everything I didn't know I needed.

It seems like my entire life is falling apart one piece after the next. First with Greg and my job in Boston. Then moving to New

York and living with my brother. Dominik and his playboy act. My disastrous career. And now my parents showing up unannounced.

Groaning, I take a deep breath and sink to the bottom of the tub.

DOMINIK HAS the best bath towels.

They're double the size of normal bath towels and the softest things I've ever wrapped around myself. Screw clothes, I want to live in this. Whoever said money can't buy happiness never experienced these comforts.

Actually, I might have to sleep wrapped up in this tonight since I forgot to bring my bags up.

Securing the towel around my chest, I open the door leading to my room, and the first thing I notice are my bags propped up next to the bed.

Rushing over, I open my tote and pull out some leggings and a sports bra. Towel-drying my hair, I try to make out any noises coming from outside my room, but it's dead silent.

Grabbing my phone, I notice it's almost midnight.

He's probably asleep by now.

It's aggravating remembering that my parents are upstairs, peacefully asleep, completely unaware that I'm here. I wonder if Aaron told them I'm staying with him. Probably not, considering how effortlessly he sidelined me, shoving me off for his best friend to handle. At the same time, it's not fair of me to be angry with Aaron. He's in a difficult situation too and wants to shield me from the confrontation with our parents. Our reunions are never pleasant, and the last one ended in a huge argument.

The scent of lavender clings to my skin as I tiptoe through the unfamiliar apartment. Moonlight filters through the big, open windows, casting shadows along the clean, hardwood floor. These late-night cravings for ice cream are starting to get annoying. I need to start hitting the gym regularly and give up the sugar, but tonight...I'm going to take all the comfort I can get. I'm praying Dom has something in his freezer, because there is no way in hell I'm venturing outside after that bath.

I hesitate for a second, glancing behind my shoulder as I stand in the middle of his kitchen. I feel so out of place, intruding on yet another person's life. The difference between Dominik and Aaron is that Dom doesn't want me here; he's only putting up with me because he loves my brother.

Aaron is everyone's favorite.

He's the favorite child. The better looking one. The most successful. The one with the faithful friends who always show up for him. It seems like Aaron was just handed the luck card from birth, and I was...I don't even know.

Too lost in thought, I prop open the freezer and stand there, staring in utter shock.

I'm not sure I believe what I'm seeing.

He didn't.

There is an assortment of ice cream pints spread across every shelf. Every single shelf is just ice cream after ice cream, in every flavor imaginable. Neatly lined up beside one another, as if I've just walked into a shop and am trying to decide what I'd like to order.

There are classic choices like vanilla and chocolate, but also exotic ones like salted caramel drizzle, raspberry ripple, rocky road extreme (whatever that is), mint chocolate chip, mango supreme... the list goes on and on.

My lips curl into a smile. "You've got to be shitting me."

I don't even know which one to reach for.

Reaching for rocky road extreme, I close the freezer door and turn, nearly jumping out of my skin.

Dominik is sitting at the island, mostly naked with his tattoos on full display. He looks pleased with himself as he watches me, like he's enjoying a funny sitcom special on TV. His unruly, black hair is damp and curled, adding to his effortless charm. His eyes hold a mixture of surprise and amusement, one brow tilted up and a stupidly large grin on his face. He is loving the fact that he just caught me red-handed, knowing I'm dying a little on the inside.

I'm trying really fucking hard not to stare at his bare chest, but the tattoos draw me in. He's got a massive lighthouse in the center of his chest, with scribbles along the side of his arms. A text I can't read from here on his rib cage. And what appears to be edges of black wings curling around the top of his right shoulder.

And is that a nipple ring?

Lord, have mercy.

"I'm happy you found the ice cream already."

"I'm sorry," I offer, biting my lip and turning to put the container back into the freezer.

"Don't you fucking dare. Grab two spoons and get over here."

His tone sends a shiver down my spine that has nothing to do with the frozen treat I'm gripping tightly in my hand. I turn, opening a couple of drawers before finding the one containing utensils. Dom doesn't offer any assistance, and I know he's enjoying watching me struggle to find my place in his kitchen.

"I thought you were asleep," I say, walking gingerly to the island and placing a spoon in front of him. I open the carton, and my mouth waters instantly. Normally, I would dig right in, grab a heaping spoonful and stuff my face, but I'm too shy to be the first to dig in.

"I was craving something sweet," he says with a playful grin, his unwavering gaze fixed on me as he grabs the spoon.

Lifting the spoon filled with delicious ice cream, he takes his time licking it, his tongue swerving around the metal. Half his features are hidden by the dark while his eyes remain locked on mine, as if he's making love to the cream. I have this sudden need to cross my legs.

My heart flutters in my chest, pounding so quickly, I fear he can hear it across the island.

Something about this entire thing feels wrong. Dominik is

eating ice cream, and all I can think about is how his tongue would feel all over my body.

My number-one priority right now is getting some ice cream in my belly and going to bed.

That's it. Nothing more, nothing less.

"Didn't know you were such a huge ice cream fan. You bought the entire store."

Scooping the spoon into the pint, I pick up a small dollop and raise it to my lips. Rich, chocolaty flavors burst in my mouth, with hints of hazelnut, walnut, caramel, fudge...and can't forget the signature marshmallow chunks.

"God, that's good," I groan, going in for a bigger spoonful immediately.

Dom shifts in his chair. "I'm not big into sugary treats."

I stare up at him in confusion. "What are you talking about? You have an entire storefront in your freezer."

Dominik shrugs, reaching in for more ice cream, his eyes cast down. "Thought you might need some comfort tonight, and I know how much you like late-night frozen treats."

My cheeks could light up an entire fireplace with how red they are.

"You got all this for me?"

He shrugs. "I didn't know which flavor you liked, so I got them all."

I...I don't know what to do with that.

"Don't do that. Don't say things like that, then turn around and do the opposite, because then I'm not sure which version of you to believe."

"Which version of me do you need, Zoe?" Dominik leans in and steals all the oxygen from the room.

Shaking my head, I place the spoon down on the counter.

"I don't need anything from you, Dominik."

I watch for the flinch, the anger, the pain...for something, but it doesn't come. He's in control of his emotions and everything around him. He even controls the fucking room we're standing in.

"You don't mean that. I know you don't. You're only saying that because you're in my kitchen right now, while the rest of your family is upstairs...together, pretending like you don't exist."

His words feel like a raw display of my innermost thoughts, like he's uncovered and laid bare everything I detest about myself. Is he intentionally trying to hurt me? Frankly, I'm at the point where I'd welcome the pain, embrace it with open arms. Sometimes, drowning in the dark feels better than not feeling at all.

"You're right. I'm worthless. Unlovable. Discarded trash. Is that what you want to hear? You want me to be weak so you can tear me down too? Guess what, Dom? You can't break something that's already broken."

He swings forward, his hand snatching out before I can take in a breath as his fingers grip the back of my neck. Dominik brings me close, pressing our foreheads together, and everything stills.

Everything...the ticking clock in the other room, the quiet buzzing of the fridge, our shared breaths.

They all stop.

"I don't want to break you, Zoe. I want to put you back together. I want to hurt them for hurting you. I want you to be yourself around me. You don't need to hide, not from me."

I'm not doing this with him. Not now. Not ever.

I pull away, feeling the familiar burn stinging behind my eyes.

"Don't do that. Don't pretend like you care about me. Not after all these years. Don't forget that this is just a business arrangement, an acquaintance relationship at best that you're putting up with because you have no other option. Stick to the plan, and keep your words to yourself because they mean nothing."

Turning away, I bolt and run up the stairs. I feel the tears falling down my face as I step inside my room and close the door. Sliding down to the floor, I pull my knees to my chest, dropping my face and releasing the tears I was clutching on to so tightly. I open the door to the pain and force myself to feel it all. I like the torment because it means I'm still capable of feeling.

Until it fades away and a quiet numbness takes over.

CHAPTER 36
ZOE

I t's been a couple of days since the ice cream incident, and I've barely seen Dominik aside from the game tonight, which consisted of a forced wave and an air kiss after intermission.

No text.

No notes around the apartment.

We've either missed one another with our schedules or he's avoiding me. I have been staying later at the office and hiding out in my room whenever I'm home, but I figured a run-in would have happened by now.

Was I too harsh the other night? Yeah…maybe a little, especially after he bought every flavor of ice cream for me, drew me a bath, and let me crash at his place without hesitating for a second. And then I flipped out on him because he was showing me an ounce of kindness?

It's because he said things that made me feel something I don't want to feel.

"I want to put you back together. I want to hurt them for hurting you."

We seem to be doing this weird dance of hate and affection, where he feels like he needs to control me but then he softens up to me. It's giving me whiplash, and I'm starting to think it might be a good idea to leave. Going into credit card debt would be worth it if it means I'm not mooching off people anymore.

Aaron came to see me yesterday, trying hard not to give me details about my neglectful parents. He's been busy with work and unable to spend a lot of time with them, but by the sounds of it, he's already tired of them being in his space. Which felt good to hear. A part of me is thrilled that Aaron is not having the time of his life with good ol' Mom and Dad.

Everything with Aaron, my parents, and Dominik has amped up my anxiety.

I need a distraction.

I need to get out of this house and out of my head for a little while.

I need to empty my mind.

Sitting cross-legged on my bed, I open up the Rabbit Hole app and start typing a message to my mysterious friend.

FLUTTERINGAWAY — 9:43 P.M.

ARE YOU UP FOR A LITTLE GAME OF HIDE-AND-SEEK TONIGHT? LET'S MEET AT A PUBLIC BAR BEFOREHAND. I'D LIKE TO MAKE SURE OUR CHEMISTRY IS MATCHED IN PERSON, AND MAYBE AFTER I DOWN A COUPLE OF SHOTS (THAT YOU WON'T JUDGE ME FOR), WE CAN HEAD OUT TO THE FOREST. WHAT DO YOU SAY?

MY SKIN TINGLES with nervous energy as I watch the message deliver into our open chat box. I want this. I want him. We've been talking for days, and he's just the type of person I would like to get to know. He actually reminds me of Runi in ways I'd like to forget. His banter, the way he speaks…it all takes me back to that night.

It's time to take this to the next level.

YOURDARKHORSE — 9:45 P.M.

I THOUGHT YOU'D NEVER ASK. NAME THE TIME AND PLACE.

GIVING myself one last once-over in the full-length mirror hanging from Dominik's front hallway, I smooth out my curls and fan out my lashes.

It's just a drink, and if anything feels off, I can say thank you and call an Uber. There is no reason to feel this nervous. Although, I recall feeling the exact same unsettling energy choking me right before I left for the BDSM masquerade ball in Boston.

The sound of a lock opening draws my attention as the apartment door swings open. Dominik steps inside, dressed in a sharp, black suit that's tightly clinging to his taut body. His hair is slicked back, jaw tight as though he's been clenching it for hours, and his eyes are cold. This is not the demeanor of a happy man, which is a confusing sight since they won their game earlier today.

Even angry Dominik is fucking hot. It's so unfair. Why couldn't he be slightly unattractive? Just enough so I have something to work with.

"Hey," I mutter, stepping aside to give him some extra space.

"Good. You're ready. We're heading out."

His muscles catch my attention as he unbuttons and removes his coat.

"We?" I barely manage to get out, casting my eyes up to his.

"Yep. We… There is a party tonight, and I have to go. You're coming as my plus-one."

Well that's unfortunate, because I'm busy.

"I can't. I have plans."

"Cancel them." His eyes are locked on mine as he continues to undress right in front of me. He unbuttons his shirt, and I let my eyes trace over his tattoos. Watching as they wrap around his muscles. Indulging in every curve and dip of his body, wondering what each tattoo means to him. Where was he when he got them done? What would his skin feel like under my touch? The feel of his nipple ring, and what he would taste—

Stop.

A shiver runs down my spine, making me very aware of my body's reaction to Dominik and the way it's making my core tingle.

"What are you doing?" my voice cracks.

"Changing." He drops his shirt beside my feet.

Oh, fuck me sideways.

"Don't you have a bedroom for that?"

Dominik takes a step closer, and I take an involuntary step back, hitting the wall.

"It's my place, Zoe. I can strip wherever I want. Surely, you've seen your fair share of skin."

His hands drop to his belt. I hear the clang of the buckle snap open and the pull of the zipper as goose bumps erupt along my arms. Not daring to look anywhere but in his eyes, Dominik bends, his face inches from mine as he takes off his pants.

Sweet Jesus on a fucking cracker.

Can someone suffocate from holding their breath for too long? Because it feels like I might right now.

He's overcrowding me without even intending to. I can feel him everywhere, see his skin and all the ink scattered on him from my peripheral vision. All I want to do right now is let my eyes wander, but this is a power game for Dominik, and I fully intend to win.

He wants me to submit, but I know just how to make him sweat.

This is great practice for later, actually.

Slowly releasing the breath I've been holding, I let myself fully take in Dom's beautifully sculpted body. Reaching out, my fingers meet his warm skin as I begin tracing the spider on his torso.

He grabs my wrist. "What are you doing?"

Smiling, I glance up to find him all shades of surprised and annoyed.

"Admiring the beautiful artwork on your body."

"This isn't funny."

My brows furrow. "Did it sound like I was joking? You're the one who started to strip down in front of me."

His jaw ticks, but he releases my hand and bends down to pick up his clothes. "We're leaving in five minutes."

Biting my cheek, I force the smile away, watching him strut out of the room in tight, black boxers.

Stop staring at his ass.

Averting my gaze, I allow my grin to spread, knowing I won this round.

I can't believe I'll be meeting my mystery man from the internet for the first time. This might turn out to be the dumbest thing I've ever done. I might have to drop my location to Aaron or Dominik right before I leave.

Aaron would be suspicious and come looking for me, but Dom would likely leave me be if I asked him not to get involved. To only come looking for me if I were to go missing.

Shouldn't be too much of a problem.

Before I know it, he's back and sporting dark, fitted jeans. The denim clings to his thighs, highlighting the sheer strength of a hockey player. He's put on a black, form-fitting shirt that seems to accentuate every contour of his broad shoulders, taut chest, and nipple ring.

I fought hard not to stare before, when he was almost naked standing a foot away from me, but now I don't even bother fighting my eyes as they take him in completely.

If he wants to play this game, I'll fucking play. He's the one who started it.

Good lord, I'm so fucked.

Look away.

I can't, and honestly, I'm not sure I want to anymore. He's staring back at me, those dual-colored eyes holding on to so many secrets as they remain locked on mine. His presence is too magnetic, drawing me in with an irresistible force. I can't have this attraction toward Dominik. Not only is it a waste of energy, but it's futile and completely disastrous for both of us.

I'm in a daze when I hear the door open.

"After you," he whispers, making me shudder.

There's something about tonight that's making my stomach churn. I can't quite pinpoint if it's because of this party or the fact that I'll be doing something afterward with a complete stranger. Then again, it could be this intense, newfound energy between Dominik and me that I'm struggling to resist.

CHAPTER 37

DOMINIK

The skyline is a sea of stars tonight as the elevator doors of the luxurious high-rise building slide open onto the vast, penthouse floor.

"Good lord…people actually live here? It looks like a museum." Zoe gasps.

A pair of grand, double doors swing open, revealing a modern-art-inspired space bathed in ambient lighting. The penthouse offers panoramic views through floor-to-ceiling windows that stretch along one massive wall. It is very similar to Aaron's place, but even bigger. I bet he would love the opportunity to sell a place like this.

"It's crazy, isn't it? Some Upper East Side fan. The girls are always eager to host parties after games, and if they've been around long enough, we happily accept."

"This is straight out of an episode of Gossip Girl."

Casting a sideways glance down at Zoe, I smile as she takes in her surroundings. She's taken aback by it all, and I remember feeling the same way when I was first introduced to the scene. It was just strange to see how wildly different some people live compared to the rest of the world. Almost didn't feel like it was the same planet, the same world…and now that I've been in it for this long, I know it's not. It takes a lot of determination and self-aware-ness to stay true to yourself.

Coming to this party was a last-minute decision, and one I regret making. But seeing Zoe standing by my door earlier, all dressed up and ready to go meet some random guy, had my blood boiling. She'd taken off before the final whistle had blown at the game tonight, still determined to avoid me at all costs.

I've been trying to keep my distance, but it's fucking hard, with her currently living under my roof, making every effort to avoid me while leaving her enticing fragrance on all my belongings. It serves as a constant reminder of how effortlessly I could possess her and fulfill her deepest desires. The ones I know she craves the most.

I know she wants it too, based on the conversations she's been having on Rabbit Hole.

Am I a sick fuck for keeping tabs on her? Yes, but I've been doing it for a long time, and I wasn't about to stop now that she's living in the same city. I know it's wrong, but some part of me can't be bothered enough to care. It's clearly for her own good. I don't feel guilty at all after seeing the type of post she made on that sketchy site.

I've been able to track her online whereabouts by hopping onto Aaron's wifi, a neat trick I learned years ago when I decided I was going to go full stalker on her. My curiosity peaked when I realized she created an account on Rabbit Hole, but when she posted on a BDSM thread, it made me furious. Enough to want to storm upstairs and confront her about being so fucking reckless. Doesn't she realize how dangerous it is to talk to random strangers online? She could end up dead in a ditch or kidnapped to be sold off, or kept in some sick fuck's basement. Why would she take the risk?

But after I had some time to cool down, I decided it would be more fun to play along, and cue: yourdarkhorse.

For some reason, I thought she had gotten all those urges out of her system in Boston. That maybe she'd wanted to dip her toes into the BDSM world and be done with it. But that wasn't the case at all, since she seems to be chasing the high like a drug addict.

I don't even want to think about it. What is this need and obsession I have with this woman? I should just let her be and not meddle in her business, but I'm an addict too. She was my first high, and I've been chasing her from the very first hit.

If I can't have her, no one can.

Zoe belongs to me, and I don't care how twisted that sounds.

As we approach the double doors, her fingers wrap around my elbow.

"Before we go in, can I talk to you about something real quick?"

Turning to face her, I glare down, watching her throat bob as she swallows nervously.

"What's up?"

"Can you not look at me like that?"

"How am I looking at you, Zo?"

"Like you want to eat me alive."

Leaning down, I inch my face close to hers, smiling. "I do, Zoe. I want to fucking devour you."

"You're such a weirdo."

I shrug, nudging my head and urging her to go on. She rolls her eyes, the act so brat-like, I'm dying to correct it. To give her something else that will force her eyes to roll back into her skull.

Tame the beast.

"I need a favor, and considering I'm doing all this for you," she says, pointing behind her in the direction of the party, "you owe me."

"Wow, must be something important." Giving her a sly grin, I cross my arms and wait for her to finally spit it out.

Her eyes narrow, and her cheeks turn a beautiful shade of pink. "I need you to just call my brother in case I don't make it back to the apartment tonight."

"Why wouldn't you make it back to the apartment tonight?"

"I have plans after this."

"Do you now?" I grit out.

"Just keep an eye out for me. You know, maybe don't wait four days to see I'm not around."

"Where are you going?"

She takes a deep breath and glances behind her shoulder. "You know what? Forget it."

I step in front of her, blocking her from trying to leave.

"Are you getting into trouble? Are you meeting a man?"

Her cheeks burn bright red now as she glances up at me, worrying her bottom lip between her teeth.

"No. Absolutely not."

"You've always been such a terrible liar."

"I'm not lying. And besides, it's none of your business. As long as I'm discreet, I can do whatever I want in the dark."

"Is that so? I thought I was very clear the other night."

"You don't own me. This isn't a real relationship," she whisper-yells, her eyes glowing with rage.

Crowding her space, my lips graze her cheeks. "Real or not, you belong to me. So behave, or there will be consequences."

Zoe has always been stubborn, and she won't back down from a fight, especially if she knows she's in the right. Which I respect the hell out of, but she also won't win this fight with me. She will obey, one way or another. Even if what she's saying is valid. We never agreed that she's not allowed to be with other men, but I don't give a shit about that. No one else is allowed to touch her.

"Whatever, Lewis. I'm not afraid of you or your small words," she says before storming off toward the party.

I should have arranged for her to stay at Tristan's house while her parents were in town. But there was no chance in hell I was going to allow Zoe to stay anywhere but with me. I wanted to be there for her, to protect her in case her walls came down one night and she needed someone. In case she needed me. But that still hasn't happened, and my grasp on control continues to slip away.

I'm going to have to talk to Aaron about these living arrangements because I'm not sure how much longer I can pretend to be the good guy. Although, I don't trust myself around Aaron right now either, worried that the first time we come face-to-face, I might say something I'll regret. The way he treated Zoe when his parents showed up out of the blue was just uncalled for and downright unacceptable. He should have offered to pay for them to stay in a hotel. Instead, he got rid of Zoe without a thought, as if she was a dirty secret he needed to sweep under the rug.

I push through the doors and walk inside the modern apartment. A black marble bar dominates one corner of the room, overcrowded with people, as two servers prepare and serve cocktails to guests.

It's packed in here. Way more than our normal crowd.

I spot the guys, all gathered around the sofa in the back corner of the apartment. Noa glances up at me as I get closer, a strained smile tugging at his lips as the girl beside him leans in to whisper into his ear.

I look around, trying to spot Zoe, but don't see her anywhere. She couldn't have gotten far. If I find out she fucking took off after our spat, I'm going to riot. She wants to meet a primal who will chase her through the woods? She doesn't have to look hard. I'm amped up and ready to go.

"Hey, Lewis, you made it. Are you here alone?"

I curse myself internally before turning to face Noa.

"No. Zoe is here, but I don't know where she ran off to."

"How are you two doing? I'm surprised you're still together, even though it's only been two seconds. Figured you'd be on to the next already."

"Hilarious, Noa."

"Ah, come on, man. You don't do relationships. You've said it yourself."

I narrow my gaze at him. "This one is different."

"Seriously though...how's it going?"

The guys haven't asked much about Zoe since I introduced her after our game earlier this week, but I knew, sooner or later, they would start poking around. They're trying to gauge my sudden change of heart and how quickly Zoe popped up after my personal life started trending online. The guys aren't dumb, and they probably know this is all a front, but I'm not about to come clean. There are only three people in this world I trust with my life, and there is no need to expand that number. People have an easy time disappointing you once you let them in.

I'm not sure what to say, but I know it's always best to stick as close to the truth as possible.

"It's going well, but we're treading slowly since both of us are new to all this."

Noa quirks a brow at me. "Her too?"

"Oh, yeah, she's worse than me."

He's taken aback. "Seriously? She's a smoke-show. Figured she could pull any man she wants."

"She can, but she likes to bail. It's her thing. Her way of protecting her heart."

Understanding fills Noa's face. "Ah...one of those. Get out before they get in."

Zoe's always the first one to leave, and that has everything to do with the way her entire family abandoned her. Everyone she has known and loved always leaves. So she gets out before they have a chance to. Before anyone finds a way to infiltrate her heart and make a home.

I get it.

Why would anyone ever choose to end up like my mother? Lost and lonely, always waiting for someone who will never come. Haunted by the memories of a life you once cherished. When does it all fall apart? Because if each of us knew the exact moment of impact, would we willingly pursue? Would we still choose to fall for someone knowing, one day, it was all going to fade away?

Noa's eyes catch on something behind me, and the look of sheer shock is what has me turning around.

There stands Zoe, charm fixed on her gorgeous face, as she leans against the wall, staring up at some guy who appears to be fixated on her.

That little shit.

If we weren't in a room full of witnesses, I'd fucking ring his neck in front of her before throwing her down on top of his body and fucking her ass.

She's trying to prove her point, send me a message in a room full of people. If that's what she wants, then game-fucking-on. I'm going to unleash on her.

He reaches out and touches her arm. She smiles up at him, the sight stabbing me square in the chest.

My fists clench at my sides, and I imagine all the ways I could punish her right now, not giving a shit about where we are or who's watching.

She's being such a dirty brat, and punishing a brat like her gets me so hard.

I can hear Noa calling after me, but his voice sounds distant as I stride across the room. It's as if the crowd effortlessly splits apart, creating a clear path for me to break up this little get-together by shoving myself in between them.

Giving my back to the asshole, I tower over Zoe. "We need to talk."

She watches me carefully, her smile fading away. "Can it wait?"

My palms burn with the need to spank her. Bend her over my knee right here in front of everyone and teach her an important lesson.

"No, it can't," I hiss right before grabbing her arm and walking us into a room three feet away.

Shoving her inside, I lock the door and lean up against it, trying to calm the monster raging inside me.

"What is it you're trying to accomplish here? You want to piss me off? Get a rise out of me because I told you not to do something?"

"I don't want anything from you," she yells.

Zoe marches over to me, getting right up in my face with no care or hesitation whatsoever. She's so fierce, I want to pull her into a bruising kiss, fill her so deep that by the time she leaves this room, she's wobbling with no thought left in her mind but the way my cock feels buried deep inside her.

"That's not true. Stop hiding from me."

"Stay away from me."

"I can't," I finally say.

Zoe closes her eyes. "Stop talking. Stop...just stop. Let me go, Dom."

"When are you going to realize I'm not going anywhere?"

"I don't care."

Grabbing her waist, I switch our positions in seconds. Hearing her back thud against the door, I pin my body against hers.

"Say that again. I fucking dare you."

This is a battle for control, internally with ourselves and with one another.

"I don't care about you or your opinions or what you think we are. You don't own me." Zoe leans in, our noses touching as she grits out every single word as if I'm slow to understand.

Wrapping my hand around her throat, I firmly hold her jaw in place and lift up her chin. Her breath hitches, but her gaze does not falter as we remain locked in a storm of forbidden longing—a battle between restraint and surrender, hate and love. I find myself unwilling to loosen the hold, even though I should.

"That's where you're wrong, Zo. While you're with me, coming to my games, whispering my name...real or not, you belong to me. Every inch of your skin, your mind, and your heart is mine. Mine to hold. Mine to touch. Mine to mold as I please. You touch another man again, there will be consequences."

I expect her to fight, to push away from me, claw at my wrist, but she doesn't. Zoe remains still, her body fitting perfectly against mine.

Then a vicious smirk breaks across her face.

"Are you threatening me, Dominik? Didn't I tell you the other day? I'm not scared of you."

The primal beast within me, the one I have been fighting so hard to cage when I'm around Zoe, stirs to life with a hungry growl. A twisted mix of desire and anger swells in my chest, threatening to rage and take her with me.

I have to maintain control, but she's making it incredibly fucking difficult.

"You think you're not scared of me. Until I decide to hunt you down and take what's mine. I play dirty when provoked. And you're fucking provoking me."

Her small fingers wrap around my wrist as she digs her nails into my skin. Closing my eyes, I welcome the pain. If only she knew it turns me on more, making me want to throw her onto the bed, shred her clothes, and fuck her into oblivion.

"You're all talk, Dom. All talk and no play."

The scent of her defiance, the spark of rebellion in her eyes is all it takes to push me over the edge. To tilt her chin and dive for her lips. To kiss her as if I'm trying to brand her. She fights against me, but it's no use. My grip around her neck tightens a little, and a small whimper escapes right before she gives into the kiss.

The sound of her submission is all I need.

Sucking on her bottom lip, I bite down until I taste copper. Letting go of Zoe completely, I pull away, a dangerous smile on my face as I look at her swollen, red lip.

"What the fuck! Did you just bite me?" She swipes her thumb across her lip and looks down.

I take her hand and suck the blood from the pad of her thumb, keeping my eyes pinned on hers.

"You're insane," she hisses.

My eyes fall to her lip and the blood that is starting to reappear. Gripping her hair tightly, I lean down and lick the remaining blood. Zoe lets out a soft moan, which makes me want to lose myself in her again, but I fight the temptation.

I barely have enough time to shove her aside and yank the door open, booking it out of there before I change my mind and go back for more.

I am incapable of controlling my emotions or the way my need takes over when I'm around Zoe. Constantly wanting to claim her, own her, make her submit. Make her see that there is only her and me, that nothing else could ever be.

But that's a fantasy I've made up in my head. It's not reality, and it will never be our life. We are from two different worlds with unfortunate lines drawn in the sand.

Perhaps, in another life, we'll get to have our chance.

Or maybe she's destined to haunt me for the rest of this one.

I can't do this with her anymore. I need to talk to Aaron and call off the fake girlfriend agreement. I'll take the heat and deal with the repercussions of my actions head-on.

I've reached my limit.

I cannot be trusted around her anymore.

CHAPTER 38
ZOE

My lip is throbbing, pulsating with its own beat, all thanks to that asshole who attacked me out of nowhere. I still can't figure out what the hell happened back there. And even worse, I can't comprehend why I responded the way I did. Jesus, I haven't been that turned on in a long time; I don't even recognize myself.

I need this meeting tonight to go well so I can release all this sick, pent-up need and forget about Dominik. And so I can breathe freely around him again.

As I make my way through the massive penthouse, I lick my dry lips and pass by the recently opened champagne bottles. Laughter fills the air, but amidst the chaos, I can't seem to locate Dominik anywhere.

Screw it, I'm leaving.

I QUICKLY MESSAGED my potential playmate, urging him to meet me at Central Park by the bridge before I could reconsider. I stormed out of the party, too furious with Dominik to bother seeking him out for a farewell. Now, here I am, wandering through the dark, eerie park in the dead of night. Normally bustling with life, tonight it's deserted. Perhaps it's the lateness of the hour, the chill of mid-January, or simply a quiet Saturday night.

This has to be one of the top five worst ideas I've ever had. Might even make it to the top three by the end of the night, only time will tell.

The air is silent, the opposite of my anxious heart. I clutch my coat tighter as a chill runs through me. My hurried footsteps are muted by the soft blanket of fresh snow, and the city's distant hum reminds me that I'm not too far from safety. But far enough. Central Park has transformed into a haunting bubble as the outside world continues to slip further away from me.

As I lay my eyes upon the bridge, my heart starts doing somer-saults. I scan the surroundings, hoping to catch a glimpse of any signs of life, perhaps a figure or a man waiting patiently. However, all that greets my gaze are mere shadows. Doubt creeps in—am I losing my sanity? Should I reconsider and head back home?

What home?

I don't have a home.

Aaron's? Occupied by my neglectful parents.

Dom's? I bet he's changed his locks by now and has my things outside his door. Even though he said some possessive shit earlier, I'm going to chalk that up to him wanting to look like he's in charge in front of his buddies.

Tough shit, Lewis. I'm not scared of you. Life has thrown way worse at me, so give me your best shot.

Walking up and down the bridge for what feels like an eternity, I halt, leaning my back against the cold stone and gazing up at the night sky.

Everything is so still. So incredibly quiet. Just me and the vast nothingness.

Sometimes, I wonder what it would feel like to float up above. To find another universe with an alternate life. I always think about what it would be like to be someone else. To slip into another body and write a different ending. Would I be happier if I could start over? To be someone else for a day? Or will my past always weigh me down, reminding me who I really am? That I am unwanted and unlovable.

I don't think I'll ever stop grieving over the person I could have been. The woman I would have turned out to be had I been given a different start. Most just learn to live with it, but I'm not sure I've really done that either. I've just avoided it and tried to do things to forget. But my past continues to pull me back like a magnet. Unescapable. Unavoidable.

The buzzing of my phone in my pocket pulls me back to the present.

"Fucking Christ," I mutter, seeing Dom's name written across the screen.

> DOM
>
> Where are you?

Leaving you on read, that's where I am.

Tucking my phone away, I do another sweep to see if anyone has arrived. He's almost an hour late.

I'm definitely being stood up.

My phone buzzes again. It's Dom, and he's calling me this time. I hit decline, not remotely in the mood to talk to him. Instead, I tap the Rabbit Hole app and begin typing.

FLUTTERINGAWAY — *11:03 P.M.*

Guess you're not coming. You could have told me you were bailing an hour ago. Your loss.

A new message from Dom pops up instantly.

337

DOM

I'm not playing games here, Zoe. Answer your
fucking phone before I come get you.

ME

I'm on my way back. Calm your tits.

DOM

You're in so much fucking trouble.

Pfft, bring it, pretty boy. He thinks he can tame me with one
bite? Who does he think he is? I'll chew him up and spit him out
without a second thought. Thankfully for me, Dominik Lewis has
no hold on me, and he has no clue how much of a brat I can be. If
we were sexual partners, I'd wear him out.

Too bad that's never going to happen. It would be fun to see
what he's made of, what kinks lie beneath all that fake big boy
energy. Because no matter how many times we go back and forth,
how many times he leers down at me or I defy him, we always fall
back into our old roles.

Where he treats me as if I'm only Aaron's little sister, and I treat
him like he doesn't matter.

Fighting against the rising sense of disappointment curdling in
my gut, I wrap my coat tighter around myself and begin my walk
back to the apartment. I've officially hit a new low: being stood up
by an anonymous person from the depths of the internet. He was
probably some old, fat guy living in his parents' basement.

It's for the best.

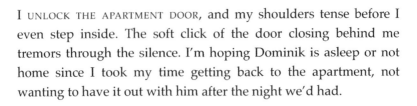

I UNLOCK THE APARTMENT DOOR, and my shoulders tense before I
even step inside. The soft click of the door closing behind me
tremors through the silence. I'm hoping Dominik is asleep or not
home since I took my time getting back to the apartment, not
wanting to have it out with him after the night we'd had.

All I want to do right now is strip out of my cold, damp clothes and stand under a hot shower for twenty minutes before crawling into bed and forgetting the last twenty-four hours. An unwelcome sense of unease prickles at my skin, a gut feeling like something's off as I enter the dimly lit living room. It feels like someone is watching me.

As I turn around, I'm startled, almost jumping out of my skin, as I catch sight of a figure shrouded in darkness, sitting perfectly still. Once my eyes adjust, I recognize Dominik, perched on the chair in the corner, bathed in the gentle radiance of the moonlight seeping through the curtains. His disheveled hair falls freely, accentuating the intensity of his gaze. Those eyes possess an undeniable spark, as if they could ignite the entire room, especially when directed at me.

I'm ablaze under his gaze.

"Zoe." His anger is palpable, radiating off of him and filling the entire room with unmistakable tension.

A part of me is screaming for me to turn and run.

"Oh, you're still up," I say coolly.

Where is his shirt? Does he always lounge around in only sweatpants?

Focus.

"Did you have fun? I hope whoever you were with was worth bailing on me," he says, taking a slow sip of his drink.

"I wasn't with anyone."

"Is that so? I thought you were meeting up with someone in Central Park."

I never told him that.

"How did you know that?"

"I know everything." He gives me a dark smile.

"Whatever." Getting tired of his mind games, I drop my bag and kick off my boots, determined to head upstairs because I'm done with this conversation.

"We're not done here," he commands, and I whip around to face him.

"Why? So you can yell at me for 'disobeying you?' Scold me some more? No, thank you. I'm not in the mood for your shit tonight. I'm tired and cold."

Dom is no longer in the chair across the room. He's stalking toward me, pinning me with an icy glare I've never seen before.

"You're such a fucking brat."

"And you're a fucking psychopath."

"Says the woman meeting a strange man at the park in the middle of the night."

I blink at him. "What?"

"Do you think I don't keep tabs on you? Track your movements? Have my car follow you around? Do you think I don't know who you're talking to?" He tips his drink back and sets the glass down.

"Are you kidding me? Invading my privacy? What the fuck is wrong with you?"

"Everything is wrong with me when it comes to you."

Dom's stare is fixed on me, digging through the layers inside my soul, as if he's set on unraveling the hidden parts of me. Those twin whirlpools of blue and gold seem capable of stirring up every emotion, surfacing memories and desires long buried. They threaten to drag me into a chaos of feelings we left unspoken, fears I've held on to tightly over time.

"What do you want from me?" I finally whisper.

"I need you to not be such a reckless woman. I want you to take care of yourself and stop chasing death as if you aren't scared of anything."

"I'm not scared of anything," I bite back.

Dominik takes a step toward me, closing the gap between us.

"Stop lying to me, Zo. I know you. I see past all the lies you tell everyone, including yourself. I see past the masks you wear. So cut the crap and be real with me." His words are laced with frustration and a type of hunger I can't quite make out.

"Thank you so much for that insightful information, but I can take care of myself. You need to butt out of my business. We're acquaintances. Not even that. We just put up with one another because we love Aaron, so stop pretending like you give a shit about me all of a sudden. It's maddening."

Dom's jaw tightens, and a sudden surge of electricity fills the air.

"No, what's maddening is that I have been pretending. Pretending to hate you so I can keep my distance to keep you safe and try to keep my promise to my best friend. What's maddening is how you're suffocating me. Everything about you is suffocating, and I can't fucking breathe. I'm drowning."

His words are like a dagger plunging into my chest. You'd assume it would hurt less over time, each experience dulling the next, but it never does.

"I'm sorry. I'll get out of here so you can finally breathe."

"That's not what I meant at all. You're not hearing me."

Turning to storm out of the apartment, I barely take a step when he grabs my arm again and whips me around.

"Stop walking away from me."

"Let me go," I grit out, my face inches away from his as I peer up at him angrily.

"I'm suffocating with need. Tired of wanting you all the time. Tired of the way you have a hold on me. I'm sick of pretending like I haven't thought about you every single day since I first laid eyes on you. Some days, I wish I had never met you, Zoe. This is absolute torture, wanting you and knowing I can't have you. I want to punish you for this craving."

I'm not certain if I heard him correctly. Were those words aimed at me?

"What?" My voice quivers.

"I can't turn it off, Zo. I've tried so hard. I can't do it anymore."

Absently, I take a few steps back, but my surroundings are a blur, and I couldn't care less. I'm attempting to make sense of what he just said, questioning if he was speaking a different language.

That, or I'm having a stroke.

His inked arm reaches out. The warmth of his hand presses

into my cheek. Dom's touch is tender as he grips the back of my neck, pulling me tighter into his body. My hands press against his bare chest, feeling the rapid beat of his heart mimicking my own.

"You're not making sense," I say.

"I'm done fighting this."

In an instant, I go from standing to being forcefully pushed back, abruptly landing on his couch. He swiftly descends, positioning himself above me, hovering like a hungry eagle.

"You want someone to take from you? To hunt you down and do as they please? You want to empty your mind? Give up control? Forget your own name? I'll take everything from you until there is nothing left. Own every inch of your body until every sound coming out of that sweet mouth of yours belongs to me."

Time stands still, and everything I thought I knew ceases to exist. Dominik closes the small space between us, pressing his lips to mine. The kiss is fiery and intense. I open up to him without thought. Drinking in the feel of his body against mine, the taste of his lips, the way his tongue explores my mouth. It all feels so familiar. My lips mold against his as if they have muscle memory, even though we've never kissed like this before. He engulfs me entirely, and I eagerly melt into him.

This feels good. Like everything I've been needing for so long.

And suddenly, the realization that this is wrong hits me like a wave, causing me to instinctively pound against his chest. However, my actions only seem to strengthen his grip on me as he wraps his arm around my waist and firmly pins me down with his body.

"Dominik," I breathe out, meaning to put an end to this feud between us, but the way his name comes out sounds way more seductive than I meant it to.

The terrifying truth is that I'm enjoying getting lost in him. There is no audience around, no one but us. Which means this isn't an act anymore, or maybe he's doing it to prove he holds the cards. That he can control me, make me bend. Own me.

I bite his bottom lip, causing him to growl as he pulls away. His lip is still grasped between my teeth as he stares down at me.

Tasting copper, I finally release him.

"I'm going to fucking ruin you."

"You wish you had that type of power," I push.

He smiles, watching me intensely as his tongue darts out, lapping up the blood.

"You're going to wish you never said that."

"You don't have what it takes," I snicker.

Before my brain has a chance to catch up to his words, Dominik flips me onto my stomach. His nails dig into my back as he grips my jeans and tugs them down in one harsh motion.

I yelp. My ass is in the air, bare and exposed to him.

"Tell me to stop, Zoe. Right this second, tell me to stop, and I will. But if you choose to stay silent, I won't be able to control myself."

I should tell him to stop. I need to, but I can't say the words. Because we both know that's the opposite of what I want right now. I want to see what happens. I'm tingling with the need to find out.

My skin breaks out into goosebumps the second I feel his fingers brushing down my behind.

"Last chance," he whispers.

I feel an instant wave of shame as I become aware of how my body is responding to him. It's unsettling to experience this intense reaction to his touch, to the forceful display he's subjecting me to. However, what disturbs me even more is the undeniable craving I have for this kind of play, for his touch.

The sharp sound of his palm on my ass fills the apartment. Dropping my face into the couch cushion, I let out a shriek, trying to hide the way my voice curls into a moan at the end.

"You like being punished? Do you like driving me mad with need?"

Another slap, and an undeniable moan this time.

"Fuck...you," I breathe out.

"I warned you that I play dirty. I enjoy it, actually. You want someone to chase you? Imagine yourself lying in the mud, your face covered, your needy pussy ready for cock? Is that the game you want to play, Zoe?"

"I don't want to play with you," I grit out, but it only causes Dominik to laugh.

"Then tell me to stop."

I stay quiet, my core tightening as I feel my wetness in between my thighs.

"You want this enough to meet up with a stranger and allow them to touch you. Touch what belongs to me. You're mine, and I'm going to make sure you don't forget it."

Smack.

Smack.

His palm lands on the same spot, sending a shot of pleasure straight to my clit.

My ass is already throbbing, but the pain feels so good.

"You were going to let someone touch you here." Dom's breath falls on my back while his finger brushes along my pussy.

"No."

"Filthy, lying brat."

Smack.

He lands a slap on my swollen clit, and this time, I can't stop the moan that erupts from me. My pussy pulses, and I feel the evidence of my arousal begin to slide down my thighs.

His palm moves, gripping my other ass cheek. I arch my back, pressing up against his crotch as Dominik lets out a deep grunt.

He circles the pad of his finger at my entrance before thrusting it inside as a jolt of lightning bursts through my body. Curling his finger, Dominik plays with my G-spot, forcing my eyes to roll to the back of my head.

"Oh, fuck," I breathe out.

"You're drenched, Zoe. Such a beautiful liar. You know what I like to do to pretty brats? Punish them." His lips brush the back of my neck, driving me crazy with need.

Dom inserts a second finger inside, stretching me as he pumps in and out. His teeth graze the skin near my collarbone, and he bites down, instantly erasing any coherent thoughts as pleasure and pain intertwine. Simultaneously, his other hand wraps around my throat, drawing me closer to him while his fingers continue their thrusting motion.

"Do you still want me to stop?" he whispers against my ear.

But I don't answer him because I don't have words. I'm trying really hard not to come all over his fingers right now. My disgusting body has been starving for this type of abuse.

His hand moves from my neck and into the back of my hair as he fists a handful of my locks, gripping tightly. I whimper, feeling myself become embarrassingly aroused. His fingers slide in and out of me with ease as he groans into my neck right before he bites me again. His tongue brushes against the marked skin before kissing the bruised flesh.

"Answer me."

"No. Don't stop," I blurt out too quickly.

"Good," he says along my jaw, watching me lose myself to the feel of his fingers inside me, pushing me closer and closer to my climax. His thumb presses into my clit, circling that sensitive spot that's going to make me lose control.

"You're so fucking beautiful," he utters, pressing harder and deeper. Our bodies moving in rhythm to his fingers.

"Oh my God," I moan, grabbing the back of his neck. I pull on his hair, pressing him closer against me as the buildup starts to take hold of me. I'm falling deeper and deeper into the abyss, and I pray it never ends.

"That's it. Come all over my fingers. I want to feel your juices dripping down my hand."

And then I'm screaming, calling out his name as my body is consumed by a storm of undeniable pleasure, sending me into the darkness. When I come to, still trying to catch my breath, he's no longer behind me. My back is glued to the couch, my body a trembling mess as I finally clear the fog from my head and look up at his towering body above me. Dominik lifts his soaked fingers up to his mouth, and they disappear between his lips. He takes his time, sucking on his fingers before pulling them out and lifting his hand. He dips his head, licking up the evidence of the remainder of my orgasm trickling down his arm.

Jesus fucking Christ.

I try to sit up, but the second I move, he turns and walks away without a single word, leaving me bare and exposed on his couch, covered in post-orgasm sweat as I try to make sense of everything.

Make sense of what Dominik and I just did.

Everything I believed to be true before now has just shattered into irretrievable fragments, leaving me in uncertainty.

CHAPTER 39
ZOE

Opening my eyes, I scan the white walls and remember I'm in Dominik's apartment. My brain finally catches up with reality as everything from last night comes crashing down on me.

That all happened, didn't it? I didn't imagine it?

Him coming on to me like that. Me enjoying it. Us not talking about it afterward as he walked off like it meant nothing at all.

Like it was all a mistake.

Is he yourdarkhorse? Had I been talking to him the entire time and just hadn't realized it? How long has he been tapping into my messages? Keeping track of me? How far has he taken all of this?

If that's the case, then I've been telling him exactly what turns me on, what I'm looking for. What I crave in the dark.

Shit. Shit. Shit.

I told Dominik about all my fucking fantasies. That's why he came on to me like that last night. A bit of CNC like a seasoned dominant, he wrapped his hand around my throat and fingered me until I fucking detonated.

This is all kinds of wrong.

If Aaron finds out, he'll cut off both our heads and have them preserved so he can put them up as decorations inside his fancy apartment. A reminder for anyone else who dares defy him.

Before I fully panic, I need to get a hold of Dom so we can talk about what happened. I need to figure out where we go from here.

Part of me wants to just pretend like it never happened.

Sleep was nearly impossible last night. With everything floating around in my head, even a warm bath couldn't ease my nerves. My body was still buzzing from the aftermath of that orgasm. I wanted more. I felt ashamed for it. I never imagined he'd have that type of animal inside him, and I suspect that was just a taste. My desires might be twisted and dark for most people, but for me, they provide a momentary reprieve from everything in my life.

An escape.

Rolling over, I reach for my phone on the nightstand.

Almost ten thirty in the morning. Fantastic. He's probably long gone by now, although it is Sunday. Even if he's not working, I'm sure he's hiding somewhere far away from here.

I'm not surprised to find he hasn't texted me.

If he thinks he can drop all of this on me and not even stick around to have an adult conversation, he doesn't know me as well as he thinks he does. I don't take shit like this lightly.

I begin typing out a message to him.

ME

We need to talk about last night.

My eyes are glued to the text box, waiting for the moving bubbles to pop up, but they never materialize. It's a struggle to look away and put my phone down.

There is no reason to be this nervous. It's not like anything even happened. Not like we had sex. It's not too late to pretend it was all a dream and get on with our lives. No one has to know, especially Aaron.

Striding toward the bathroom, I flick on the lights, only to be startled by the reflection staring back at me. My hair looks like it got into a fight with a blow dryer and lost. My bottom lip is purple, swollen, and tender to the touch. A nice little unwanted gift from Dom. And my neck is also bruised with teeth marks in two spots.

He fucking marked me like an animal.

Tracing the bite marks with my fingers, I clench my thighs as memories from last night start trickling in until they're a tsunami. Wave after wave, the desire got stronger and we became entangled in one another. I lost myself in him. I want to tell myself I hated it, that I wish it never happened, but that couldn't be further from the truth. Last night was a taste of everything I've been missing. After Runi, I never thought I'd feel that way again.

I shudder as I recall the feel of his fingers inside me, stretching me, exploring as he brought me to orgasm. The way his eyes stayed on me the entire time, as if he were memorizing each reaction and sound coming from me. He drank me in with such intensity, I almost believed he wanted me.

But I know Dominik, and last night was all an act of control. He wanted to claim his territory and teach me a lesson for the way I'd behaved. I'd been out of line, and he wanted to prove a point. He's so used to getting his way and having all the attention, he can't stand the fact that I don't bend the same way as everyone else. That my legs don't part on command whenever he walks into a room.

I brush my teeth quickly and comb through my tangled mane before stepping out of my bedroom.

"Dom?" I call out, peeking my head downstairs, but I don't hear anyone moving around.

Glancing down the empty hallway, my eyes fall to his closed bedroom door.

"Dominik…are you here?"

Only silence answers back as I pad toward his room.

I linger in front of his door, contemplating my options before deciding to go for it.

If he's going to ignore me and pretend like we don't need to talk, then I might as well go digging in his room to try to find out more about him.

What if he's inside, sleeping?

Then I guess he's going to wake up.

Before anxiety and paranoia have a chance to make me change my mind, I open the door and step inside Dominik's bedroom.

He's not here.

The black, silk sheets and comforter on his bed are twisted, as though he struggled with restlessness throughout the night too. The walls of his room are painted in a deep, forest-green hue. Sparse yet striking, a handful of large, abstract art pieces adorn the walls, complementing the apartment's minimalist aesthetic. In one corner sits a simple, white dresser, accompanied by a solitary, brown, leather chair.

It feels wrong being here, invading his privacy like this, but I just can't seem to find it in me to care enough to turn around and leave. Especially not after he admitted to invading my privacy for days, weeks? Who the fuck even knows?

The closet door is slightly open, and I notice that the light inside is turned on. Curiosity tugs at me, compelling me to approach it as if there is something beckoning me from within.

His walk-in closet is spacious, with everything neatly arranged. The closet is filled with a spectrum of attire from various formal wear such as suits, dress shirts, and pants in a multitude of colors. On a dedicated rack, there is a meticulously organized assortment of shoes. A glass case proudly showcases an array of watches. On the other side, the casual section is meticulously lined up, indicating that someone has taken the time to curate this space specifically for him.

A collection of sweaters and gray pants catches my eye. The sight brings a smile to my face; it's obvious he prefers comfort over business. My fingers brush over the soft fabric, and the room envelops me in his scent.

A black box catches my attention as it sits on the top shelf. Standing out amidst a multitude of white and beige craft boxes, it piques my curiosity. Two delicate, silvery butterflies adorn each side of the box, their translucent beauty adding to its allure. I can't help but wonder what lies inside. Perhaps it holds something dear to Dominik's heart, or maybe it's just an expensive man purse.

Either way, I'm snooping, and I feel no shame about that.

Running back to the closet door, I poke my head outside to make sure the coast is clear one last time. Hoisting myself onto one of the shelves, I reach up and snatch the box before falling back to the ground. I place it down on the floor and sit cross-legged in front of it.

This is so wrong. What if he walks in?

There is a strange compulsion pulling me to this box, something I can't shake, and I know I won't be able to leave until I look inside.

Taking in a deep breath and feeling my pulse skyrocket, I quickly pull open the thick lid.

Holding my breath, I stare down at the contents within the box.

Polaroid photos filled to the top. Photos of…me, when I was in high school. And then in college. To recent photos just in New York City.

What the fuck…

Candid photos of me walking down the school hallway. Laughing with a friend. Talking to Aaron in the family room. Reading. I reach down and grab a photo of me sitting on my bed. It's taken from right outside my bedroom, the door must have been ajar. I'm hugging my knees, my chin resting on them as tears stream down my face.

Oh my God.

These are extremely private moments.

Suddenly, it's impossible to catch my breath as I flip through the photos, taking them out of the box… There are tens, maybe hundreds of Polaroids here. From so many different occasions and timelines.

My fingers hit something soft. Beneath all the photos, there are articles of clothing. My favorite Nirvana T-shirt that I believed I had lost forever. Alongside it, a pair of sleep shorts. And, oh my God, my fucking butterfly necklace. The one Aaron gave me on my sixteenth birthday.

What the hell is all this doing here, in Dom's closet?

My heart is racing as I dump out what remains in the box.

I wish I could turn back time. I wish I hadn't stepped foot inside his room.

I blink several times, wishing this could all disappear.

My vision is blurred by tears as I gaze down at the two items that were left at the bottom of the box. One is a mask that I recognize, with two Xs instead of eyes and a sinister, stitched-up smile. Even though it appears lifeless, I have a feeling that if I were to turn on the mask, it would emit a red glow. Right next to it lies another mask, distinct in its matte black color. It covers half of the face on one side and dips below the eye on the other side.

These are the same masks Runi wore at the masquerade ball.

These are Runi's masks from that night in Boston.

It can't be.

It must be some sort of coincidence.

Dominik wouldn't do that to me or to Aaron. He wouldn't lie to me like that, use me, uncover the deepest parts of me while hiding his true identity. He wouldn't betray me and Aaron like that.

But then a detail from that night pops into my head.

Runi's eyes appeared strangely artificial, as if he was wearing contact lenses. I remember thinking about it later and how adamant he was about keeping his face concealed from me the entire time. He never once removed his mask, and he made it explicitly clear from the start that I wouldn't see his face. At the time, I didn't think much of it.

But now…it all makes sense.

The masks stare back at me, mocking me as they reveal the most vile secret from the best night of my life. Unveiling the truth like a bucket of ice-cold water.

This entire time?

The image of Runi in my head turns black before it disintegrates.

My hands tremble as I grip one mask per hand. Tears stream down my face, and the familiar numbness grabs hold of me, blurring all the lines.

Past and present. Truth and lie. Then and now.

Everything I believed I'd gained from that night fades to dust. I thought I had taken back control, empowered myself by owning my sexual desires.

It all feels tainted now.

As I turn my head, I catch a glimpse of Dominik standing near the closet door. My vision is blurred from the tears, so I can't make out any specific details. Even breathing feels so hard right now.

My palms tighten around the masks, digging into them firmly.

"How could you?" I croak.

I will never forgive him for this.

Never.

TO BE CONTINUED...

ACKNOWLEDGMENTS

There are so many people to thank for this book but first and foremost, I have to thank myself. I'm proud of you, Tina for surviving this and everything else life threw at you during this book. You did it, despite the odds, you fucking did it.

Publishing books is a challenge unlike anything else but it has also led me to meeting so many wonderful people. People that have become like family to me. Book lovers who I'm lucky to call friends and sisters today. Your love and support means everything to me.

I'm sorry about the cliffhanger. It was a necessary evil or this book would have been ridiculously long. Dominik and Zoe were always a difficult duo, and that is why they demanded a second book, which has been challenging to write at best. I wrote that ending after several revisions and I hope you enjoyed it all the same, it will forever be one of my favorite continuations.

To my beautiful family: thank you for being my number one fan and believing in me. For always being so understanding and supportive. Thank you for allowing me to chase my dreams.

Amy and Heidi: thank you for accepting me and loving me without borders. We may be separated by distance, but both of you are like sisters to me. Amy, I still can't wrap my head around the fact that you purchased a Kindle just to read Wonderlight in advance, which ultimately brought us together and formed the most incredible friendship I could ever dream of. I know it will endure for a lifetime. And then you introduced me to Heidi, so we could fawn over Cass endlessly. The rest, as they say, is history. You both have become my own version of a found family trope, and I love you both so much.

Danielle and Jenny: thank you for loving and supporting my books from day one. Thank you for the late night chats and all the laughs. And for being an amazing beta team. You ladies are the best and I love you. The Slashers men belong to you.

To my amazing author friends (Allie, Ann, E, J): this journey led me to meeting you beautiful women. I love you all so much and I am so grateful for you. We will always be a hype team and I'm blessed to have such a supportive community of strong women to call friends. To my soul sisters, thank you for ALL of it, especially the non-book stuff.

To the book community, my ARC team and the Hopeless Romantics reader group: THANK YOU. You bunch make all of this so enjoyable. If it weren't for your love and support, none of us authors would be here, pulling all nighters and losing sleep to share our stories with you. Thank you for everything and for continuously supporting us Indies. Please keep dropping into my DMs, I love hearing from you.

A huge thanks to my editors Erica and Rachel: this book wouldn't be what it is without your help. I appreciate you both immensely. And Rachel, you're amazing. I'm so sorry for the cliffhanger. I live for your commentary and VMs. Never change. I love you and you're stuck with me.

Writing is such a solitary job, but it takes an entire village and support group to get your book out there, and I wouldn't be able to do any of this without my amazing village. I am so fucking grateful to all of you. I will never get over the fact that I'm actually doing this, writing books, and chasing my dreams. Thank you for being a part of my journey. I love you all.

ALSO BY TINA SPENCER

SHATTERED HEARTS

Read book two now! The second and final installment of this duet. (bit.ly/shatteredhearts1)

WONDERLIGHT

Subscribe to my newsletter (tinaspencerbooks.com/links) and stay informed on what's coming next! Maybe a little pre-Shattered Obsession novella including Dominik, Aaron, and Tristan? That would be fun. And more news coming soon on Aaron and Tristan's books. I'm so excited to share all this with you!

Find me on IG for all book related news and content.

For more, visit www.tinaspencerbooks.com

ABOUT THE AUTHOR

Tina Spencer has held a lifelong passion for spinning tales since early childhood. When Tina's not spending her free time writing and agonizing over her fictional characters, she's working through her endless TBR, spending time with her family, traveling, and attempting to get *some* sleep. She enjoys writing about flawed characters and their meaningful journeys through life and love. If you're looking for emotional and inspirational books with spice, then you've come to the right place.

Join Tina Spencer's Facebook Reader Group, Hopeless Romantics, for exclusive sneak peaks and info on upcoming books.

facebook.com/authortinaspencer
instagram.com/tinaspencerauthor
goodreads.com/authortinaspencer